P9-CDV-208

GENIUS SQUAD

GEN
SQ

HARCOURT, INC.

ORLANDO AUSTIN NEW YORK SAN DIEGO LONDON

CATHERINE JINKS

IUS

JAD

Acknowledgments
The author would like to thank Richard Buckland, Jamie Grant, Jill Grinberg, Margaret Connolly, and Peter Dockrill for their assistance.

www.HarcourtBooks.com

First published in 2008 by Allen & Unwin, Australia
First U.S. edition 2008

Library of Congress Cataloging-in-Publication Data
Jinks, Catherine.
Genius squad/Catherine Jinks.
p. cm.
Sequel to: Evil genius.
Summary: After the Axis Institute is blown up, fifteen-year-old Cadel Piggot is unhappily stuck in foster care with constant police surveillance to protect him from the evil Prosper English until he gets an offer to join a mysterious group called Genius Squad.
[1. Genius—Fiction. 2. Identity—Fiction. 3. Crime—Fiction. 4. Good and evil—Fiction. 5. Australia—Fiction. 6. Science fiction.] I. Title.
PZ7.J5754Gen 2008
[Fic]—dc22 2007030373
ISBN 978-0-15-205985-9

Text set in Ehrhardt MT
Designed by April Ward

First U.S. edition
A C E G H F D B

Printed in the United States of America

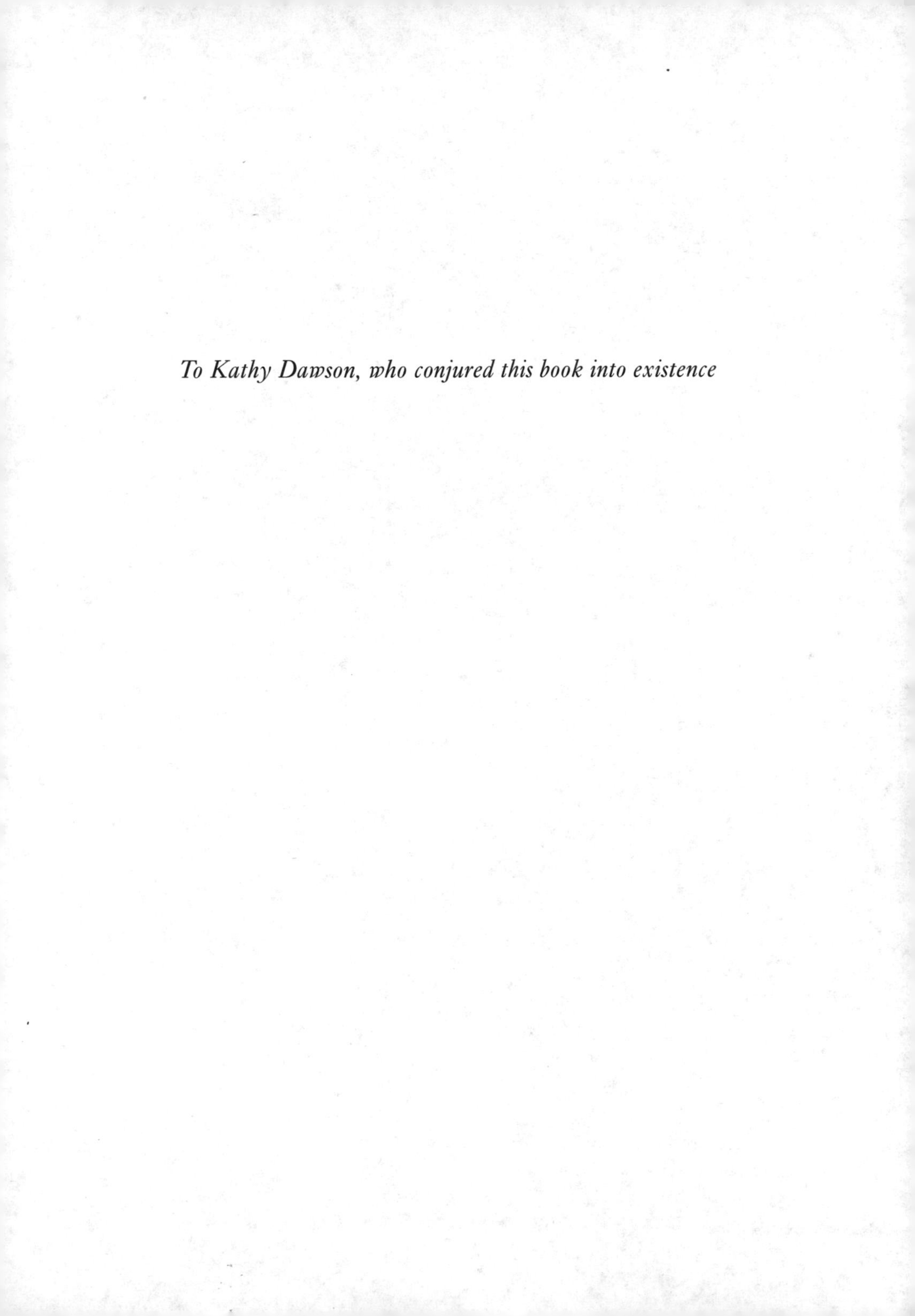

To Kathy Dawson, who conjured this book into existence

PART ONE

ONE

Cadel was in a very sour mood when he first met Detective Inspector Saul Greeniaus.

The day had started badly. To begin with, Cadel had been woken up at 3:00 A.M. by the sound of piercing screams coming from Janan's bedroom. Though only six years old, Janan had the lung capacity of a whale. He also suffered from night terrors, and the combination was deadly. Cadel usually felt sorry for Janan, who had been living in foster homes for most of his life. But it was hard to sympathize with *anyone* at three o'clock in the morning, let alone a kid who could scream like a hysterical gibbon.

As a result of his interrupted sleep, Cadel was late for breakfast. Not that it mattered. He didn't have to go to school, so Mr. and Mrs. Donkin never insisted that he be awake at a specific time. But Mace and Janan did attend school, and were finishing their eggs just as Cadel arrived in the kitchen. Had Cadel been feeling more alert, he would never have sat down to eat just then. He would have waited until Mace was out of the house and running to catch the bus, his gray shirt untucked and his thick legs pumping.

Had Cadel used his brain, he would have sensed trouble in the air, and tried to head it off.

The whole problem was that he couldn't protect his own bedroom. There was a house rule about always knocking first, and another rule about respecting privacy. These rules were written in beautiful script on a piece of handmade paper that was pinned to the door of the pantry cupboard. (Hazel had done an evening course in calligraphy.) But both rules were quite easy to break, because Hazel had banned locks and keys from the Donkin premises.

Cadel could understand her point of view. One of her previous foster sons had locked himself in his bedroom before trying to set it alight. Leslie, her husband, had then been forced to smash through the door with a hammer. So although Hazel continuously said nice things about sharing, and everyone "always being welcome everywhere," Cadel felt sure that her open-door policy was rooted in fear. She was afraid of what might happen if, during an emergency, she couldn't reach any of the kids in her charge.

This was certainly Fiona's opinion. Fiona Currey was Cadel's social worker. She had told Cadel about the locked-bedroom incident, after Cadel had finally complained to her about Mace, who liked to mess around with other people's possessions. It was pointless complaining to Hazel, as Cadel had discovered. Her answer to every problem was what she called a "family conference."

"I'm sorry, Cadel," Fiona had said. "I know it must be hard, but it won't be forever. Just hang in there. Mace isn't nearly as bright as you are; surely you can handle him for a little while? Until things are sorted out?"

Most people seemed to jump to the same conclusion about Mace, whose real name was Thomas Logge. They thought that he was stupid. They looked at his lumbering form, his vacant grin, and his clumsy movements, and they made allowances. They heard his slow, awkward speech patterns and dismissed him as a big dumb kid. Whenever he smashed something, they called it an accident; cracked windows and broken doorknobs were explained away. Mace, they said, had badly underdeveloped fine motor skills for a fourteen-year-old. He didn't know his own strength. He might have poor impulse control, but he wasn't malicious. He wasn't clever enough to be malicious.

Only Cadel had doubts about this interpretation of Mace's conduct. In Cadel's opinion, Mace was a lot smarter than he let on. Not brilliant, of course, but cunning. Had he been as stupid as everyone made out, Mace wouldn't have been so quick to take advantage of the few minutes granted to him while Cadel was eating breakfast.

How many minutes had it been? Six? Seven? Long enough for Cadel to gobble down an English muffin. Long enough for Mace to empty his bladder into Cadel's bed.

When Cadel returned to his room, he found his mattress wet and stinking.

"Mace did it," he told Hazel.

"No, I didn't!" That was another thing about Mace; he had perfected the art of sounding completely clueless. "I did not! He's blaming me because he wet his bed!"

"Did you really wet your bed, Cadel?" asked Janan, who wet his own bed all the time. He sounded pleased—even excited—to discover that someone else shared his problem. Especially someone who had recently turned fifteen.

"There's nothing wrong with wetting the bed," Hazel assured them all, in soothing tones. "I have plastic covers on the mattresses, and I can easily wash the sheets. You don't ever have to feel bad about wetting the bed."

"I don't feel bad," said Cadel, through his teeth. "Because I didn't wet it. Mace did."

"I did not!"

"Then why are my pajamas bone dry?" asked Cadel, holding them up for inspection. Mace blinked, and Hazel looked concerned. She never frowned; her wide, plump face wasn't built for frowning. In situations where other people might have worn grim or angry expressions, Hazel merely looked concerned, dismayed, or disconcerted.

"Oh dear," she said.

"He probably didn't even *wear* his pajamas," Mace remarked cheerily, demonstrating once again—in Cadel's opinion—that he wasn't as thick as everyone assumed.

"Those pajamas were clean last night," Cadel pointed out, trying to stay calm. "Hazel, you gave them to me, remember? Do they smell as if I've worn them?"

Hazel took the pajamas. She put them to her small, round nose. Cadel knew that when it came to laundry, Hazel had the nose of a bloodhound. After bringing up four children and twelve foster children, she was thoroughly trained in the art of distinguishing dirty garments from clean ones.

A single sniff was all that it took. She turned to Mace, looking disappointed.

"Now, Thomas," she said, "have you been lying to me?"

Mace shook his head.

"Because you know what I've said about this, Thomas. Sometimes we feel angry and frustrated, and do things we're ashamed of. Then we lie about them afterward, to protect ourselves. But most of the time, there's no need to lie. Because it's the lie that people find hard to forgive, not the offense . . ."

Cadel took a deep breath, willing himself to be patient. Hazel, he knew, was a really, really nice person. He admired her selflessness. He was grateful to her for cooking his meals, washing his clothes, and letting him use her computer.

But she was also driving him mad. Sometimes he could understand why Janan threw such terrible tantrums. Cadel was often tempted to throw one himself, after sitting through yet another gentle, stumbling lecture on why it was important not to kick a football at somebody's face. He had to make allowances; he realized that. No doubt Hazel was used to dealing with kids who *didn't* grasp how wrong it was to throw large, heavy objects at people. Or spit in their food. Or piss in their beds.

All the same, he found it hard not to lose his temper. Because Mace, he knew, needed no reminding about the proper way to behave. That dumb act was all a front.

"Okay, okay," Mace finally conceded. It seemed that he, too, could only stand so much of Hazel's well-meaning counsel. "I did it. I was joking. Can't you take a joke?"

"But it's not a very nice joke, is it, Thomas? Cadel doesn't see it that way. Would you like it if he went to the toilet on *your* bed?"

Mace shrugged. He was still smiling a big, goofy smile.

"My brother used to *crap* on my pillow," he said. "Everyone used to laugh."

"I know." Hazel was very earnest. Very sympathetic. "It must have hurt when your brothers laughed at you. Still, that's no reason to make other people feel bad, is it?"

Hazel proceeded to explain why she was going to ask Mace to strip and remake Cadel's bed. But Cadel didn't want Mace in his room again. Enough was enough.

"It's all right," he interjected. "I'll do it myself. Or Mace will miss the bus." (And if Mace missed the bus, there was every chance that he wouldn't end up going to school at all.) "I don't mind," said Cadel. "Really. There's not much else for me to do, anyway."

Everyone stared at him in utter disbelief. So he pursed his lips and opened his big, blue eyes very wide—and it worked, as usual. Nobody looking at his angelic face would ever have suspected that he was planning to dump the soiled sheets on top of Mace's prized football boots.

"Well, that's nice of you, dear," said Hazel, somewhat at a loss. "I hope you're going to apologize to Cadel, Thomas?"

"Oh, yeah," Mace replied, with an obvious lack of enthusiasm. He opened his mouth. He took a deep breath. Then suddenly he yelled something about hearing the bus, and bolted into the garden.

Every footfall shook the house. His schoolbag knocked a calendar from the wall. The screen door slammed behind him with an almighty *crash*.

Cadel peered through the kitchen window at his retreating form, as it moved across a large patch of mangy grass toward the front gate. Beyond this gate lay a wide, almost treeless street. Cadel could see a pair of sneakers, their laces tied together, dangling from a suspended power line. He could see a small plastic bag skipping along the footpath in a fitful breeze. He could see a sparrow pecking at something edible in the gutter.

But the school bus was nowhere in sight.

"I'll make him apologize properly when he gets home," Hazel promised, before hustling Janan into her car. For about twenty blessed minutes, while Janan was being delivered to school, Cadel had the house to himself. But then Hazel returned home, and settled in front of her computer (she had a part-time data entry job), and Cadel, once again, found himself with nothing to do.

Nobody seemed to want him anymore.

None of the universities wanted him. Even though he had completed high school more than a year before, at the age of thirteen—even though he had scored perfect marks in all his exams, and knew almost everything there was to know about computers—Fiona could not find a single faculty anywhere that would admit him. This was because he had no official status in Australia. He was an illegal alien. No one knew exactly when he had arrived, or exactly where he had come from. It was thought that he had been smuggled into the country at the age of two. It was also thought that he might have been born in the USA. Australia, therefore, didn't want him. But the United States didn't want him, either. Since no record of his birth existed, there was no proof that he could legitimately claim U.S. citizenship.

Most importantly, no one could be sure who his father and mother were. The woman who may have been his mother had died mysteriously, in the States, when he was still an infant; officially, her murder had never been solved. And the man who had once claimed to be his father (off the record) now refused to admit it in public.

Even his own *father* didn't want him.

Cadel was therefore living in a kind of limbo, with nothing whatsoever to do. He didn't even have access to his own computer. At one point he had owned two computers, but both had been confiscated by the police as evidence. They were part of an ongoing investigation into the activities of Prosper English (alias Thaddeus Roth), who may or may not have been Cadel's father. Prosper was in jail now, awaiting trial on charges ranging from fraud to homicide. His network of employees had disintegrated. His assets were frozen. His various properties were being treated as crime scenes.

It was all a huge mess, and Cadel was sitting right in the middle of it. Nobody knew what to do with him. He had no money. No family. No country of origin. He didn't even appear to have a name. Originally, he had been called Cadel Piggott. Then his surname had been changed to Darkkon, when Dr. Phineas Darkkon—the criminal mastermind and genetic engineer—had suddenly appeared in his life, claiming to be his father. But Phineas was dead now, killed by cancer, and very probably hadn't been his father after all. Prosper English, Darkkon's former second-in-command, was a far more likely candidate. Only Prosper wouldn't admit to anything.

So what was Cadel supposed to call himself? Cadel English? Cadel Doe?

Fiona called him Cadel Piggott, because Piggott had been the assumed name of his adoptive parents. Not that they had *really* been Piggotts. And their adoption of Cadel had never been officially recognized. They'd never even been married. Dr. Darkkon had simply employed them to raise Cadel as a screwed-up little weirdo.

Cadel didn't know where they were now. Nor did he know what had happened to the house in which he'd lived between the ages of two and fourteen. His whole former life had been torn up and thrown away, like so much scrap paper.

All he had left was one friend. Sonja Pirovic. She was the only person who had never lied to him. So Cadel decided to visit her, on the day he first met Saul Greeniaus.

He hoped that visiting Sonja might cheer him up.

TWO

Unfortunately, Sonja lived a long, long way from the Donkins' house.

To reach her, Cadel had to spend an hour and a half on public transport. He had to catch a bus, then a train, and then another train. That was why he sometimes booked taxis. And why, as a consequence, he was always broke—despite the fact that he received a small allowance from the government.

It was all quite maddening, because the police could easily have given him a lift. On the morning of the urine incident, Cadel wandered into Versailles Street at about half past nine and saw that two plainclothes policemen were sitting in an unmarked car, as usual, some distance from the Donkins' driveway. One of the policemen looked familiar. The other did not. Cadel wasn't sure exactly which agency they belonged to—whether they worked for the Australian Federal Police, the Australian Security and Intelligence Office, or even the U.S. Federal Bureau of Investigation. All he knew was that the Donkins' house was constantly being watched and that whenever he left it, he would always be followed.

At first this had pleased him. He had felt safer knowing that Prosper English couldn't get at him without alerting the authorities. Once or twice he had even asked his bodyguards for a lift. Their response, however, had been disappointing. He had been told that the officers assigned to tail him were not his personal chauffeurs. They were there to do a job. Cadel's job was to pretend that they didn't exist and to go about his normal business without acknowledging that they were dogging his footsteps.

"But I'm catching a bus," Cadel had protested, during his first conversation with the surveillance team.

"Then one of us will catch it with you," was the reply.

"But wouldn't it be easier just to drive me to Sonja's house?"

"No."

"Why not?"

"Because it's not in the job description."

And that was that. No matter whose shift it happened to be, not one of Cadel's watchdogs would help him. Instead, as he trudged along the street to the bus stop, they would drive past him, park up the road a little, and wait until he had left them behind, before driving on again. Even when it was raining, they refused to pick him up.

Cadel resented this attitude so much that he had begun to toy with various notions that he should never have entertained: notions of shaking them off, just to annoy them. He could have done it quite easily. He had dodged pursuers before, on numerous occasions; Prosper English had always tried to keep him closely monitored. But behavior like that belonged to his past life—a life of subterfuge, manipulation, and despair. It was not a life that he remembered fondly. He was *ashamed* of the person he had been back then. Through the agency of the Piggotts, Prosper English had raised him as a scheming, friendless, emotionally stunted freak. Cadel had left that freak behind and did not intend to welcome him back by indulging in the sort of nasty intrigues that had once kept him fully occupied.

Still, it was annoying. More than annoying. It was, in fact, *unfair* that on such a damp, miserable, overcast morning, the men in the unmarked car wouldn't give him a lift to the station, at least.

Was it any wonder that Cadel should have been in such a foul mood?

Nothing about his surroundings cheered him up, either. The Donkins lived in a flat, dreary suburb on Sydney's western outskirts. There weren't many trees or parks or Internet cafés in the area. People either lived in mean little houses on rambling, untidy blocks of land, or in brand-new mansions squeezed so tightly between boundary fences that they barely had any gardens at all. The local library was hard for Cadel to reach. The local walks—along culverts or across sun-baked football fields—were deeply depressing. The buses always arrived late at the nearest bus stop, and sometimes didn't arrive at all. The bus stop itself was in a bleak and windswept location; Cadel could foresee that it would be a very cold place to stand on winter mornings.

Fortunately, however, winter was still a few months off. So at least Cadel didn't have to wait in the freezing cold for twenty minutes, while the two policemen sat watching him from their warm car. Still, he was glad when the bus arrived. Not only did it mean that he could sit down, at long last, it also meant that one of his bodyguards was forced to abandon half a cup of take-out coffee. Cadel was feeling so resentful, it pleased him to see someone deprived of a hot drink.

The coffee-deprived policeman followed Cadel onto the bus, and took care to sit some distance away. He was short and stocky, with close-cropped hair and a glum expression. Perhaps he was glum because he didn't like playing nursemaid. Or perhaps he disapproved of the trip itself. Cadel was well aware that the police would have preferred that he didn't visit Sonja. Such visits, he realized, were a bit risky. Prosper English knew about Sonja. He knew how much Sonja meant to Cadel. Though Cadel's whereabouts were currently a well-kept secret, it was much harder to hide Sonja. There weren't many places where a girl with her special needs could safely live.

If Prosper's agents wanted to trace Cadel, they only had to find Sonja first.

Cadel had therefore been advised that he ought to consider rationing his visits to Sonja's house. Such trips required two surveillance teams instead of one, and left him very exposed to a possible assault. Cadel had been reminded that he was chief witness for the prosecution—that Prosper might want to stop him from testifying. Prosper, after all, was a ruthless and intelligent man. Did Cadel really want to risk putting himself in harm's way?

"Prosper won't try to kill me," Cadel had declared. "I know he won't. He tried before, and he couldn't. He just couldn't bring himself to do it." Seeing the skeptical looks that had greeted this statement, Cadel had tried even harder to explain. "You don't understand," he'd said. "I'm scared of Prosper, but not like that. He doesn't want to kill me. He wants me to be on his side, that's all."

The police disagreed, however. So when Cadel finally reached Sonja's house, he found two unmarked police cars stationed nearby: one around the back of the house, the second near the front.

After months of being followed, he could spot them quite easily. To begin with, they were sparkling clean. All were recent-model sedans. Each was normally occupied by two passengers, both of whom sat in the front. And when Cadel waved at them, or poked out his tongue, or did anything else designed specifically to irritate the people inside, he received no response at all.

Cadel passed through Sonja's front gate without bothering to glance back. He knew that the policeman from the bus was behind him somewhere, having accompanied Cadel on both train trips as well. No doubt there had been some kind of surreptitious radio contact. No doubt one of his bodyguards had already checked the license plate of every car parked on Sonja's street.

When Cadel rang the doorbell, Rosalie answered it.

"Hello, Cadel," she said.

"Hello, Rosalie. Is Sonja feeling all right today?"

"Yes, come in. Sonja will be very pleased to see you, for sure."

Once upon a time, Sonja had lived in a large institution called Weatherwood House. Then it had closed, and its occupants had been moved to smaller houses, containing fewer people. Cadel didn't think that this change had been for the best. Sonja's new quarters were rather shabby. She was now living in an old brick building, full of narrow hallways and awkward corners, which hadn't been designed for people with special needs. Despite all the new ramps and doors and handrails, there was an air of discomfort about the place. Most of the floors were covered in cheap vinyl. Most of the windows were hard to open. Sonja had to share a cramped bathroom with three other people, and her own room was also quite small. Because her bed, desk, and wheelchair took up so much of the available space, there wasn't even a stool or a beanbag for her visitors to sit on. Cadel always had to use the bed. He felt awkward about that, because he couldn't help rucking up the quilted bedcover when he sat on it. And then someone like Rosalie, the caregiver, would have to straighten it out.

Rosalie was a nice woman. She would hustle Cadel through the front door with a big, beaming grin, and make him tea, and feed him biscuits. "Your beautiful boyfriend is here!" she would crow. "Look, everyone! Sonja's beautiful boyfriend has come!" It was embarrassing, but well meant. Rosalie seemed genuinely fond of Sonja. Nevertheless, Sonja missed Kay-Lee, the nurse who had looked after her so well at Weatherwood House. Kay-Lee had gone overseas to work, and although she e-mailed Sonja every week, things just weren't the same.

They weren't as good.

"Hi, Sonja," Cadel said shyly, upon reaching her bedroom. "How's it going?"

He was conscious of Rosalie, hovering at his shoulder. There was no doubt in his mind that Rosalie would have liked him to greet Sonja with a smacking kiss, or some other extravagant gesture. He felt uncomfortable when the caregiver was around, and couldn't really relax until she had gone to make tea.

Then he closed the door carefully behind her.

"New poster," he observed, his gaze fastening on an unfamiliar eye-puzzle pinned to the wall. Sonja's bedroom was plastered with posters and printouts, most of them relating to mathematics. The parchment shade of her bedside lamp was decorated with numeric equations, written in a flowing copperplate hand. Birthday-cake candles, each molded into the shape of a different digit, were ranged across her desk. Even the geometric pattern on Sonja's shirt was complex enough to suggest mathematical formulas.

This shirt was worn over stiff corduroy pants and fluffy slippers. Cadel recognized the slippers. He had given them to Sonja for her birthday, because no one seemed to bother much about her feet, and it worried him. Sonja's involuntary muscular spasms sometimes knocked her feet about quite badly; he'd decided that they needed more padding and protection.

The spasms were always more violent when she was feeling stressed or excited. Looking now at the taut angle of her neck, Cadel could tell that she was distressed about something. And because he knew that she communicated more easily when she was calmer, he sat down and started to talk about mathematics.

"I saw something really interesting on the Net yesterday," he said. "It was on that website—SIGGRAPH, you know? The mathematics of programming? They were talking about diffusion-limited aggregations in the digitally simulated growth process."

As he rambled on, Sonja watched him, her brown eyes straining to keep him in focus as her neck tried to twist in the opposite direction. Finally her juddering hand found her DynaVox machine, which was propped on a mounting arm in front of her. One rigid finger jabbed at the screen, jerked away again, then returned to the screen once more.

Slowly, the DynaVox began to talk in a flat, robotic voice.

"*I-saw-SIGGRAPH,*" it said, speaking for Sonja. "*Your-friends-came-too?*"

"Today? Oh, yes." Cadel nodded. "They're outside now. Four of them."

"*Would-they-like-tea?*"

Cadel grinned. "That would be funny," he said. "Or we could ask them if they want to use the toilet. I'm always wondering what they do about going to the toilet. Maybe that's why they're so crabby. Because they're busting to go."

Sonja abruptly changed the subject. It occurred to Cadel that going to the toilet wasn't easy for her, either; he could have kicked himself.

"*Any-news-from-Mel?*" she asked, and he sighed. Mel Hofmeier, his lawyer, did unpaid work for the National Children's Law Center. News from Mel usually reached Cadel through Fiona Currey.

"Nothing much," he replied. "I'm still on a temporary protection visa. The immigration minister is still my guardian, and the Department of Community Services is still my custodian."

"No-orphan-pension-yet?"

"God, no." Fiona had been exploring the possibility of an orphan pension for Cadel, to augment his special benefit. But since his parents were still unidentified, it couldn't be proven that they were dead. "If Phineas Darkkon was my father, then I might have a chance," he explained. "If Prosper's my father—well, he's not dead yet, is he?" Cadel suddenly remembered something. "Oh!" he added. "And it turns out that Darkkon was definitely cremated. So unless they can find some preserved tissue somewhere, they can't do a paternity test on *him*."

"But if-he-had-cancer—"

"Yeah, I know. They took out a tumor. And maybe some healthy tissue, as well." (This, too, had been considered.) "Why should anyone have kept it, though? Yuck."

"What-about—," the DynaVox began, then stopped. Sonja's arm lurched sideways, skittering off the glassy surface of the screen. It wasn't a voluntary action.

Cadel's own fingers closed gently around her clawlike hand. He returned it to the DynaVox and held it there for a moment.

He knew why she was agitated. Any mention of Prosper tended to trouble them both. And she didn't want to upset him.

"You mean—what about Prosper?" he asked. She nodded (a single jerk of the head), and her tongue rolled around behind her teeth.

"No word from Prosper," he said. "Things are looking pretty good for him, so why should he admit to anything?" For perhaps the hundredth time, Cadel pondered the State's case against Prosper English. It still looked shaky. The police were determined to prove that Prosper had been Phineas Darkkon's right-hand man, largely responsible for running the Darkkon criminal empire. They were searching for proof that the

Axis Institute (one of Prosper's many responsibilities) had been a University of Evil, designed to train criminals rather than help bright young people in need of emotional support—as Prosper claimed.

But much of the Axis Institute had been blown up. Its records had been hastily destroyed. If its staff hadn't died or disappeared, they had lost their minds, or escaped from custody. Moreover, hardly any of the students had been identified, since most had been enrolled under assumed names. And the ones who hadn't been killed were now lying low.

Except for Cadel, of course.

"I'm still the only student who's come forward to testify about the Axis Institute," Cadel admitted, with a dismal little laugh. "I'm all the police have right now—they can't find any corroborating evidence. No wonder Prosper won't open his mouth. The *last* thing he'd do is admit that I'm his son. Because if I'm telling the truth about that, then I might be telling the truth about the rest, as well."

Sonja already knew all this. Impatiently, her hand worked free of Cadel's clasp, sliding across the DynaVox screen until it arrived at a key.

Cadel waited.

"Paternity-test?" the DynaVox squawked at last.

"Nope." Cadel shook his head. "He's still refusing. He claims that the police can't do a paternity test on him, because my paternity isn't directly related to the crimes with which he's been charged."

"Poor-Cadel."

"Not really. In a weird sort of way, I don't even want him to have a paternity test." Cadel explained that he had recently received some very bad news from Fiona Currey. If Prosper English turned out to be his father, then Cadel would be placed with Prosper's closest relative—a cousin who lived in Scotland. "And I don't want to go to Scotland," he said. "I don't want to leave you."

There was a long pause as Cadel mulled over his circumstances. They were pretty grim. Ironic, too. "It's funny," he continued. "The police want to prove that I'm Prosper's son, because it corroborates some of what I've said. And they want me to stay in Australia or I won't be able to testify against him. But if I turn out to be Prosper's son, then I *can't* stay in Australia. So what are they going to do?"

Sonja didn't have an answer to that question. Neither did Cadel. So they abandoned the subject and talked about Sonja's problems instead. Sonja wasn't happy in her new "shared support" accommodation; in fact, she had already applied for a transfer, though she wasn't likely to get one. (There weren't many places around with facilities for people like her.) Although the care that she currently received was adequate, she didn't get out much. Resources were stretched, and staff were overworked. While her caseworker was nice, he didn't visit her often. And when he did, he sometimes left her feeling very depressed.

"He-thinks-I-don't-understand," she told Cadel.

"Understand what?" he asked.

"Anything. Much."

Cadel bit his lip. A lot of people underestimated Sonja's intelligence. After taking one look at her twisted posture, her writhing tongue, and her distorted limbs, they assumed that she was mentally handicapped.

"Hasn't he been told?" Cadel demanded. "About what you've done?"

"Yes, but-he-doesn't-believe-it," Sonja replied. *"Not-deep-down."*

Cadel was suddenly furious. He felt like punching the nearest wall.

"I wish I could hire someone," he said angrily. "Someone really clever. A postgraduate student to take you places, and help you with things. Just you."

"Talking-of-students," Sonja interjected, through the medium of her DynaVox, *"what-news-on-universities?"*

"No change." Cadel scowled. "No one wants me. You know, I've been thinking—there are probably some things that I could do to earn money. Like that old Internet dating scheme I set up—"

"No."

"But—"

"No."

Cadel studied Sonja's face. Though her mouth was almost never still, and her thin face was often cruelly contorted, her eyes always remained rock steady. They were fixed on him now, and he saw the reproof in them.

"There was nothing *illegal* about it." He faltered. "It was just a bit of a scam. And it did make money."

"We-had-an-agreement," was Sonja's firm reply. After a moment's flurry, during which she tried to control one flailing arm, she added, *"You-hurt-a-lot-of-people-with-that-dating-service."*

"Yeah," Cadel muttered, "but it wasn't a total rip-off. If I hadn't set it up, we would never have met."

"You-lied-to-people," the DynaVox replied, without expression. *"That-was-wrong."*

"Yeah . . ."

"Don't-even-think-about-it, Cadel."

Cadel grimaced. Then he sighed. Then he nodded.

"Okay. I won't," he said.

And they started to talk about differential equations.

THREE

Cadel stayed so long with Sonja that he missed his usual train. This meant that he missed his usual bus as well. And missing his usual bus meant that he had to wait for thirty fruitless minutes at a noisy roadside bus stop, when he *could* have been working away on Hazel's computer.

It was infuriating.

Everyone living at the Donkin house had to abide by a carefully planned computer schedule. On weekday mornings, Hazel used the machine for her data-entry job. After school, for about three hours, Janan and Mace divided the computer between them. (Occasionally they did their homework on it, but mostly they just played mindless war games.) During dinner, no one was allowed near the computer. And afterward, Leslie Donkin would usually spend a quiet evening writing e-mails, or pursuing his genealogy research over the Net.

As a result, Cadel only had access to the computer for three hours a day, between twelve thirty and three thirty in the afternoon. On weekends he sometimes managed four or five hours, if he woke up early. And he also spent as much time as he could on the library computers. Nevertheless, he felt deprived. Almost disabled. It was like walking around on crutches, or trying to peer through misty glass. Without a computer, he couldn't function properly.

That was why he had decided to build his own. It was also why his thirty wasted minutes at the bus stop were so frustrating. He couldn't bear the thought of missing a second on Hazel's computer. Even more exasperating was the knowledge that the police could easily have given him a lift home. There was no real *need* for him to stand around breathing in gas fumes. Why should he have to suffer like this, just because his surveillance team was determined to be uncooperative?

Then, when he finally reached the bus stop near the Donkins' house, it started to rain. Though the drops were still light and scattered, a brooding mass of cloud to the south suggested that a storm was heading in his direction. Cadel wondered how far away it was. The walk home usually took about ten minutes; would he beat the downpour if he ran? Pulling up his collar, he set off at a rapid pace—but before he had even rounded the first street corner, something caught his eye.

It was a computer monitor, sitting by the side of the road.

Cadel had been vaguely aware of the forthcoming municipal council cleanup. He had noticed the piles of junk that had begun to accumulate on the curb: broken cane furniture, rusty paint tins, stained foam mattresses, split curtain rods. But he had never expected to see discarded computer equipment. *Certainly* not discarded computer equipment that appeared to be no more than four or five years old.

He dashed over to the monitor, hoping that it might be accompanied by a keyboard, or even a hard drive. Instead he found that it was sitting beside a length of cracked concrete pipe, a roll of dirty carpet, and a three-legged coffee table.

"Damn," he said, looking around. An unmarked police car (silver, this time) was lurking some distance away. The raindrops were pattering down more heavily. Quickly Cadel slipped off his denim jacket and draped it over the monitor. With a grunt and a heave, he lifted the unwieldy machine and began to stagger along, clutching it against his stomach. It was a deadweight.

"Excuse me," he gasped, when he reached the silver car. "*Excuse me!*"

The driver's window slowly descended. A gray-haired man with a seamed, pouchy face was sitting behind it.

"Keep moving, son," he said.

"Yes, I will," Cadel panted. "But could you take this monitor for me? Please? So I won't have to carry it home?"

"No can do. Sorry."

"Oh, *please!*" Cadel exclaimed, adjusting his grip on the heavy piece of equipment. "You wouldn't be giving *me* a lift, just the monitor!"

The man's gaze ran over Cadel's damp curls, flushed cheeks, and pleading expression. He seemed to hesitate for a moment. But his younger colleague beside him said, "Get away from the car, kid. You know the rules."

Cadel lowered his chin. He narrowed his eyes. Something in them must have unnerved the older man, because he frowned and adjusted his sunglasses.

"You start glaring at people like that, my friend, and you're going to get in trouble one of these days," he declared. "Now step away from the car. Go on."

Cadel swallowed. He wanted to throw his monitor through the car's windshield—and might have done so, had it been possible to lift the heavy component higher than his breastbone. Instead he turned away, fuming. Then he trudged home through the rain, concentrating on geometric multigrid algorithms in a fierce attempt to disassociate himself from what he was actually doing.

It was a technique that he'd often used when helping Sonja to get dressed. By gabbling on about something she might be interested in—like Laplace equations, for instance—he was able to distance himself from the whole embarrassing and undignified procedure.

By the time he reached the Donkins' house, he was wet, sore, and utterly exhausted. It was ten past two. Cadel knew that he only had one hour and twenty minutes of online exploring left. After kicking off his soggy sneakers, he deposited the rescued monitor in his bedroom and threw himself in front of Hazel's keyboard, conscious that he hadn't yet eaten lunch. It didn't matter, though. There were more important things than lunch to worry about.

Heaving a sigh of relief, he prepared to plunge into the virtual world, where he felt truly at home.

And then the doorbell rang.

Cadel caught his breath. Surely that couldn't be a visitor? *Please,* he thought, *let that be someone trying to sell cosmetics or charity chocolates. Please don't let them come in here and start yak-yak-yakking away while I'm trying to concentrate.*

He clenched his teeth as Hazel waddled past him to answer the front door. A murmur of voices soon reached his ears, followed by the sound of approaching footsteps.

Three sets of footsteps.

He looked up to see Hazel emerging from the hallway with two people behind her: a man and a woman. The woman was small and slim, with extraordinarily thick, reddish, flyaway hair escaping from various combs and pins and loops of elastic. The man was neat and wiry, with dark hair going gray, and somber brown eyes.

Cadel knew the woman. She was Fiona Currey, his social worker. But he had never seen the man before.

"Hi, Cadel," said Fiona, with an apologetic smile. "I hope we're not disturbing you."

Cadel wasn't about to lie, so he remained silent. It was Hazel who spoke for him, assuring the newcomers that they were very welcome, and offering them a cup of tea—or perhaps coffee?

"No thanks, Hazel, that's okay," said Fiona. "To be honest, I hope we won't have to stay long. We just need a few words with Cadel. In his room, perhaps? I realize it's a bore."

There was a hint of exasperation in Fiona's voice. Cadel knew her well enough by now to realize that she was annoyed with someone. For a moment he studied her curiously, noting the flush on her chalky, freckled skin. Then his gaze traveled to the man beside her, who was staring at Cadel in obvious surprise.

"This is Detective Inspector Greeniaus," Fiona explained. "He wants to talk to you, Cadel; I'm sorry."

Her tone confirmed that she wasn't pleased. The detective put out his hand, which Cadel took reluctantly.

"I'm very happy to meet you," said Mr. Greeniaus, whose accent branded him as North American. "You can call me Saul, if you want."

"It's your computer time now, isn't it?" Fiona sounded genuinely worried as she addressed Cadel. When he nodded, she winced. "I'm so sorry. I had a feeling it might be."

"Then I'll be quick as I can," Mr. Greeniaus remarked. Though the detective's manner was very mild, it was somehow clear that he would brook no argument. So with an aggrieved sigh, Cadel rose from his seat in front of the computer and led the way to his bedroom.

Here there were only two places to sit: on a battered old typist's chair or on the bed. Cadel chose the typist's chair. He felt ill at ease in his room, which still bore traces of its previous occupants: a name ("Carlie") scratched into the baseboard; half a dozen hooks screwed into the ceiling; a unicorn transfer peeling off the windowpane. Nothing in the room had been chosen by Cadel, apart from the clothes in the wardrobe, the books under the bed, and the monitor sitting on the floor.

"Oh!" Fiona exclaimed, when she saw this piece of technology. "Have you bought a computer, Cadel?"

"No," Cadel replied. "I'm going to make one. Out of spare parts." He caught sight of the detective's raised eyebrow, and growled, "I didn't *steal* it, you know! Someone left it in the street!"

He knew that there were policemen who still distrusted him, and he assumed that Mr. Greeniaus was one of them. But the detective shook his head.

"I'm not accusing you of anything," he murmured. "I just can't get over it, is all. You look so young to be building your own computer."

"I'm fifteen."

"Yes. I realize that."

"Cadel's seen a lot of police over the past few months," Fiona observed, dropping onto the bed. "You'll have to excuse him if he's a little sick of it."

Cadel suppressed a smile. He knew quite well that Fiona was the one who objected most strongly to all the police interviews that he had endured. For one thing, she thought them unnecessary. For another, she was usually required to be with Cadel when they were conducted, since he had no family members to look after his interests.

Fiona was a busy woman—too busy to be constantly running off to the Donkins' for yet another police interview.

"Yes," said Mr. Greeniaus, fixing her with a serious look. "We realize it's been difficult."

"Especially since there doesn't seem to be much communication *between* all you people," Fiona went on. "I mean, he keeps getting different guys from different units asking him the same questions."

"I understand." The detective nodded. "That's why we've taken your complaints on board. I've been officially appointed as Cadel's liaison officer. I'll be asking all the questions from now on. Even if the FBI or the NSA want to know something."

"Aren't you *from* the FBI?" said Cadel, and Mr. Greeniaus shook his head.

"No."

"But you're American, aren't you?"

"I'm Canadian." The detective spoke quietly and patiently. "I was with the Royal Canadian Mounted Police until I came to Australia. Then I joined the police force here."

"You mean you were a *Mountie*?" Cadel exclaimed, in astonishment. He tried to imagine Mr. Greeniaus wearing a red jacket and funny pants, sitting up on a horse. It was difficult.

"I don't ride, if that's what you're thinking." The detective didn't smile, but there was a glint in his eye as he looked at Cadel. "The RCMP is a regular police force, driving regular cars and wearing regular uniforms. Except on parade."

"Why did you come here?" Fiona inquired, with real interest.

"I married an Australian," was the calm response. Because Mr. Greeniaus was now positioned on the bed beside Fiona, Cadel—who sat facing them—saw the way her curious gaze dropped to the detective's unadorned left hand. No wedding ring was visible. "It didn't work out," Saul Greeniaus declared, and the subject was closed.

At that instant, someone knocked on the bedroom door. It creaked open a few inches.

"Excuse me," said Hazel, without attempting to cross the threshold. "I'm sorry to interrupt."

"Come in, Hazel. It's your house," Fiona urged. But Hazel shook her head.

"No, no, that's all right. I just wanted to say—I have to go and pick up Janan from school. So if there's anything you want before I leave . . ."

"No, we're fine," said Fiona. "Don't worry."

"Because I've put fresh Anzac biscuits on the kitchen table, if you'd like some. Just help yourself."

"Hazel, the *last* thing I want is for you to fret about us," Fiona replied. "You go and do what you have to do."

"Okay. Well, I'll be back soon."

"Thanks, Hazel."

The door closed gently. Cadel said to Fiona, "If you want some biscuits, you'd better get them now. Before Mace comes home and scarfs the lot."

Fiona glanced at her watch, sighing. "How long before he gets here?" she asked. "About an hour?"

"A bit less."

"Oh lord." Fiona turned to Mr. Greeniaus. "Once the other kids come home, we won't have a second's peace," she pointed out, as the detective plucked a small cassette recorder from inside his gray jacket.

Moved by a sudden mischievous impulse, Cadel said, "By the way, Mace pissed on my bed this morning." With some satisfaction he then watched the two adults jump to their feet. "It's all right, though," he assured them. "I changed the sheets, and he missed the bedspread."

Fiona clicked her tongue. "Oh, Cadel," she said, gingerly settling back onto the bed. "I am sorry. Did you tell Hazel?"

"Course."

"What did she say?"

Cadel shrugged. "The usual," he rejoined. "Mace reckoned it was a joke."

Fiona muttered under her breath. Cadel had always liked Fiona, because she tended to say what she thought instead of hiding behind a sweet and gentle facade. Though she tried to stay pleasant, she couldn't always keep her temper in check.

Mr. Greeniaus, on the other hand, didn't look like a person who lost his cool easily. He was still on his feet, regarding Cadel with a speculative expression in his dark eyes.

"I notice you don't have a lock on this door," he said.

"No."

"So this kid—Mace—he can get in here whenever he wants?"

"Yes."

"Must be annoying. To have someone poking around in your stuff."

Cadel was about to nod when something about Saul's tone caught his attention. Peering up into the detective's face, he flushed suddenly.

Saul was having a dig at him.

"Hacking a system doesn't mean that you have to trash it," he spluttered. "*I* never did. Not even when I was seven years old."

"And I hope you're not here to make accusations!" Fiona cried, as she realized what was going on. "Because if you are, I'll have to call a halt and contact Cadel's lawyer!"

Mr. Greeniaus took a step back, raising one hand. "I'm not accusing anyone of anything," he said softly. "I'm just here to ask questions."

"Then ask them!" snapped Fiona. "We haven't got all day."

"You're right," said the detective. And he turned on his cassette recorder.

FOUR

For his eleventh birthday, Cadel had received a very special cell phone from Dr. Darkkon. It had been a fully functioning computer, with wireless capacity, photo function, hard drive, and DNA wiring (courtesy of Dr. Darkkon's secret nanotechnology lab). The phone had worked well for a number of years, but had abruptly stopped functioning after it was confiscated by the police.

Cadel had never expected to see it again. One day, however, he had found himself sitting across a table from two representatives of the U.S. National Security Agency, who had bombarded him with questions about his computer phone. Apparently something had gone wrong with the biological portion of its wiring. Some kind of short circuit had fused most of the DNA substrate. But the NSA was determined to replicate the original design, because DNA wiring would mean an end to many of the heat problems associated with electrical high-speed processing. "This is breakthrough technology," Cadel was assured. "We want to know where it came from and how it can be imitated."

So Cadel had tried to help. Though his understanding of the technology was incomplete, he had answered all the questions put to him.

For that reason, perhaps, the NSA had kept asking them.

"Here's another list of queries from the NSA," Mr. Greeniaus said, removing a folded sheet of paper from his pocket and placing it on Cadel's desk. "If you could write down some answers, Cadel, I'll convey them to the interested parties."

"All right," Cadel agreed. He didn't mind answering questions about computers.

"Now . . ." The detective seated himself on the bed again, carefully positioning his cassette recorder so that it was pointed directly at Cadel. "I want you to cast your mind back to your appointments with Prosper English—or Thaddeus Roth, as he called himself. Because originally he was supposed to be your therapist, is that right?"

"Yes."

"And you would go to his office and have counseling sessions."

"Except that they weren't really counseling sessions," Cadel admitted. "Sometimes we'd talk about how to lie, or how not to get caught sabotaging systems. But mostly we would make broadcasts to Dr. Darkkon."

"Who was in a California prison at that time."

"Yes." Cadel nodded. "They had a special transmitter."

"And you would talk about your future—perhaps about some of the projects that you were involved in?"

"Cadel's already covered this," Fiona interrupted sharply. "He's told you what he did, and it was all with that man's encouragement. If you're going to touch on it again, I'll have to call a lawyer!"

"As a matter of fact, I'm more interested in Prosper's other clients," said Mr. Greeniaus. Cadel met his searching gaze with a look of surprise. "Any kids you might have seen coming or going, when you were at the office. He was supposed to specialize in troubled children, wasn't he?"

"I-I think so." This was a new area of inquiry for Cadel. He had never given it much thought. "I did see other kids, once or twice," he confessed. "But I thought—well, wasn't it all a front? I mean, he wasn't *actually* working as a psychologist, was he?"

"That we don't know yet."

"I guess I assumed that those other kids were just . . . well, some of his people." Cadel shifted uncomfortably. "He had a lot of people working for him."

"Can you describe them to me, Cadel? The kids you saw?"

Cadel tried. He cast his mind back to the dark old terrace house where Prosper had received him; to Wilfreda, the strange receptionist with black teeth; to the morose-looking teenagers who had sometimes passed Cadel in the hallway, or on the stairs. He didn't like thinking about the old days in Prosper's office.

Just the memory of Prosper's sardonic, penetrating stare gave him a chill.

"There was a girl called Bella," he recalled. "I saw her twice. She was quite tall and—you know—big. With greasy hair. She was wearing a school uniform."

"What did it look like?"

"Maroon blazer. A kind of checked, pleated skirt . . ."

Cadel continued haltingly, racking his brain for relevant details. When he couldn't think of anything else to say, the detective moved to his next area of inquiry.

"With regard to the Axis Institute, which you attended for several months last year," he said, "you've told us that Prosper English called himself the chancellor of this institution, is that right?"

"Yes."

"And you've given us full details of the teaching staff who conducted courses in forgery, embezzlement, computer hacking, assassination, and so forth. Most of whom are either dead or missing."

Cadel waited.

"There were even some support staff—kitchen workers, I believe," the detective went on. "You've described them to us already."

"Yes." Cadel sighed. "I never knew their names."

"Do you recall any other support staff? Gardeners? Secretarial? Administrators? Anyone at all?"

Now, *that,* Cadel decided, was a *good* question. It was the question of someone who was seriously searching for corroborative evidence.

"There were gardeners," he said slowly. "I remember them. The grounds were so well kept. And there *had* to have been people who fixed things, because of all the explosions and break-ins and spontaneous combustion that happened." Cadel forced his reluctant mind down paths he would rather have avoided. "I think—I think there was a guy who used to collect stray dogs and cats for lab experiments," he added. "In a white van."

"Can you tell me anything more about him? Did you ever see him?"

"No. I was told about him."

"And the gardeners? What about them?"

Cadel was still struggling to recollect something—*anything*—about the gardeners at the Axis Institute when Janan arrived home. His pounding footsteps and loud, high-pitched voice distracted Cadel for only a moment. There were more important things to concentrate on.

"I've been wondering if some of the people I met later might have been working as support staff at the institute," he mused. "Like that old guy Nikolai, who used to follow me around. And Vadi. The man with the gills. Surely he didn't spend his whole life cleaning Prosper's house?"

Suddenly a piercing scream made them all jump. It was followed by a huge *crash,* then by more wild yelling. The floor shook as if from repeated blows.

Fiona and Saul sat up straight, clearly alarmed.

"It's only Janan," said Cadel, in a resigned voice. "He probably lost his chocolate-bar wrapper." Seeing the two adults exchange a questioning glance, he felt obliged to elaborate. "Janan collects these chocolate-bar wrappers," he explained. "When you've got twenty-five, you can send them in and win a mountain bike, or something. He's completely obsessed. Hazel gives him a chocolate bar for lunch every day at school, and when he gets home, he puts the wrapper away in a special box." Cadel cocked his ear, listening to the tattoo of fists bouncing off walls. "My guess is that he lost today's wrapper."

Fiona grimaced. "Maybe I should go and help," she proposed. But Cadel discouraged her.

"There's nothing anyone can do," he said, "except give him another chocolate bar." As abruptly as it had begun, the clamor unexpectedly stopped. Cadel listened for a moment. So did his companions. After a brief pause, they heard a faint murmur of voices. "There," said Cadel, with some satisfaction. "I told you. Chocolate-bar wrappers. She must have found a replacement."

Fiona shook her head glumly. Mr. Greeniaus was frowning. He darted another quick look at Fiona—but when he spoke, he addressed Cadel.

"Let me get this straight," he said. "Nikolai was one of the men in the car that picked you up when you escaped from police custody, is that correct?"

"Yes. He followed me on a train once, too. I recognized him."

"And you think he might have worked at the institute?"

Cadel bit his lip. "I don't know. There *was* an old guy who shuffled around with a toolbox. I remember seeing him from the back. He was fat and gray-haired."

"But you didn't see his face? Just his back?"

"That's right. So I don't know if it was Nikolai or not."

"And Vadi? Did you ever see *him* at the institute?"

"No. But I mean, why would Prosper use a human fish just to clean his house?"

"And you don't remember seeing anyone else? Or hearing any other names?"

"Sorry," said Cadel. Whereupon Mr. Greeniaus grunted.

"There's no need to be sorry," he assured Cadel. "You've done very well." Almost to himself, the detective then remarked, "Not that it matters about Vadi or Nikolai. They've gone underground." He folded his arms. "Or underwater, perhaps."

Cadel managed a faint half smile. Then he said, "Mr. Greeniaus?" And paused for a moment.

The detective watched him. So did Fiona.

"Do you—I mean, have you ever met Prosper English?" was the question that Cadel finally put to Saul, who hesitated before replying.

"Yes, I have."

Cadel didn't know how to phrase his next query. But he didn't have to; Saul apparently read his mind.

"We don't talk about you," the detective revealed. "Prosper is always very careful not to display much interest in you, Cadel. I suppose if he did, it might support your claim that he's your father."

Cadel nodded. He cleared his throat, painfully conscious of Fiona's troubled scrutiny. Then Hazel knocked on his door again.

Her voice sounded higher than usual.

"Uh—excuse me?" she trilled. "Can I interrupt?" Without waiting for an answer, she poked her head into the room. Her tight gray curls were uncharacteristically ruffled. Her small green eyes looked anxious. "There are police here," she blurted out. "They're asking after Cadel."

Mr. Greeniaus instantly rose, clicking off his cassette recorder. Fiona gaped.

"I *told* them that the police were here already," a flustered Hazel continued. "I didn't know *what* to say."

"Don't worry." The detective's manner was all at once very businesslike. "I'll take care of this."

He brushed past Hazel on his way out of the room. As he stuffed his recording equipment back into the lining of his jacket, he revealed that he was wearing a shoulder holster—with a pistol protruding from it.

Fiona gasped when she saw the pistol.

"For god's sake!" she hissed fiercely. "How can he? There are *children* in here!"

An image flashed into Cadel's head: an image of the loaded gun that had once been placed against his temple. It was his most frightening memory, and it still haunted his dreams at night. Of course, Prosper hadn't pulled the trigger. Something had prevented him from doing so. But that hadn't made his actions any less frightening, in retrospect.

To block out what he had no wish to recall, Cadel hurried after Saul Greeniaus—and encountered Janan heading the opposite way. Wide-eyed with fear, the six-year-old shot past and dived under Cadel's bed.

"What the—?"

Cadel stared after the silly kid, in consternation, before looking around for their foster mother. But Hazel was already in the kitchen with the police.

Only Fiona Currey had remained behind.

"Oh dear," said Fiona.

"What's Janan doing?" Cadel wanted to know.

"Hiding."

"But—"

"He's had a hard life. There was a police raid on his mother's house once." Fiona returned to Cadel's bed and crouched down beside it. "Janan?" she crooned. "What's the matter, sweetie? No one's going to hurt you."

Cadel decided that Fiona was better off without him and went to find out what was going on in the kitchen. He fully expected to see Saul and Hazel conversing with a pair of familiar men in wrinkled suits and sunglasses. To his surprise, however, his surveillance team was nowhere in sight. Instead, two uniformed police officers—one male and one female—were standing by the fridge.

". . . complaint from a neighbor," the policewoman was saying. "About a car following a child down the street." She nodded at Cadel. "*That* child, I would say. From the description."

"Yes. I see." Saul retrieved his identification from her. "You should have been informed. This child is a witness. For his own protection, he's being monitored at all times."

"Well, *we* haven't heard about it," said the policewoman.

"No. I'm sorry. That was a serious oversight."

"We're going to have to make a report."

"Yeah. Look—what would you say if I talked to your duty sergeant . . ."

All of a sudden, Cadel was distracted by the distant sound of approaching footsteps. He recognized the *slap-slap-slap* of large, rubber-soled feet galloping down the side path. Mace, he knew, was heading for the kitchen, kicking over flowerpots on his way.

". . . has to come through official channels . . . ," the uniformed policeman was saying. Cadel tensed as he heard Mace thudding up the outside stairs. Even Saul Greeniaus had noticed the racket by this time.

Hazel shuffled toward the back door, but Mace reached it first. He flung it open, exploded into the room, then stopped abruptly when he saw the uniformed police.

His face reddened. Cadel was by now familiar with that dull rush of color, which was always a bad sign. When Mace was really, really angry, he always turned red. Then he would sit somewhere out of the way, swearing under his breath for perhaps ten minutes, before his rage erupted in a series of destructive acts.

Cadel found himself edging closer to Saul Greeniaus.

"Oh. Hello." The policewoman addressed Mace in a friendly voice. "It's Thomas Logge, isn't it? How are you, Thomas?"

There was no reply—just a glower.

"I've heard good reports about you," the policewoman continued. She was small and stocky, with a hard-edged drawl and stiff blond hair cut short. "I've heard that you seem to have settled in here pretty well. Been going to school. Good on ya."

In response, Mace slammed out of the kitchen, heading for his bedroom. He must have hurled his bag at the wall as he went, because there was a huge *thud,* followed by a rather nasty crunching noise. Then a door banged at the other end of the house.

The policewoman sniffed.

"You've got your work cut out for you there," she said to Hazel. "I've had dealings with his family."

"Oh, Thomas is responding very well," Hazel rejoined, sounding almost defensive. "You don't have to worry about *him.*"

"Good," said the police officer. But she didn't seem wholly convinced.

There followed a brief burst of activity, which was kicked off by Fiona—who suddenly appeared and dragged Hazel out of the room for a talk with Janan. Saul Greeniaus then accompanied the uniformed officers to their car, while Cadel, left alone in the kitchen, wondered what he should do about Mace.

Mace was already in a foul mood; he would probably explode when he saw that his football boots were sitting under the pile of dirty sheets that Cadel had dumped on them. To prevent Mace from trashing all his belongings, Cadel would have to keep an eye on the bigger boy. But that in turn would require staying within easy reach of Mace's fists.

Cadel considered his next move. The smartest tactic, he decided, would be to shut himself in his own bedroom for the rest of the day (with something shoved against the door, perhaps). Even if Mace set fire to the house, Cadel could always crawl out the window. Not that he really expected Mace to commit arson. But there was bound to be trouble of some kind, and Cadel was determined to stay well away from it.

As he made for the kitchen door, however, he found Fiona blocking his escape route.

"Oh, Cadel," she said. "Where's Mr. Greeniaus?"

"He went with those coppers, back to their car," Cadel replied.

"You mean he left?"

"I don't know."

"He could have said something," Fiona remarked crossly. "A simple 'thank you' would suffice!"

"Is Janan okay?" Cadel asked, suddenly remembering that the six-year-old, when last seen, had been disappearing under a bed. "Did you get him out of my room?"

"Oh yes. Don't worry. He's in his own room now, with Hazel. Poor little kid, he's so traumatized." Fiona's gaze shifted, and Cadel turned to see what had caught her interest.

It was Saul Greeniaus, quietly reentering the kitchen.

"Sorry about that," said the detective. "That shouldn't have happened. Some kind of glitch."

"Hazel's the one you should apologize to," was Fiona's tart response. "It's her house, after all."

"Yes." Saul nodded in agreement. "Where is she?"

"In there," said Fiona, jerking a thumb. "Counseling her foster kids. Are you finished with Cadel now?"

"I think so. I don't think there's much point trying to continue, in these circumstances."

"Then don't feel you have to hang around," Fiona declared—quite rudely, in Cadel's opinion. The detective must have shared this view, because he fixed Fiona with such an intent, questioning look that she was compelled to elaborate. "Those poor kids in there have had some very bad experiences involving the police," she explained. "They don't respond well to any kind of police presence."

"No," Mr. Greeniaus said thoughtfully. "I've just been told about Thomas Logge's experiences with the police." He reached into his jacket and turned to Cadel. "Listen," he said. "I want you to call me if you're worried about anything. Do you have a cell phone?"

"No," Cadel answered.

"Well—take this, anyway." Saul crossed the room, holding out a small white card inscribed with his name, rank, and contact numbers. He pressed it into Cadel's palm. "Night or day, you call me. Understand?"

But Fiona was bristling.

"He's not supposed to talk to the police unless I'm present!" she protested. "You *know* that!"

"Ms. Currey, this is only a precaution," the detective replied. "In case there's a problem like the one we just saw. Or something similar."

"He wouldn't have *had* a problem if there weren't so many police hanging about all the time!"

"That's nonnegotiable." Saul spoke flatly. "We can't afford to leave him alone. You should understand that by now." He extended his hand, which Cadel shook for the second time. Though Fiona received only a nod, there was a gleam in Saul's quiet gaze as he said good-bye to her. "I don't want to outstay my welcome," he remarked, deadpan. "So I guess I'd better be leaving."

Then he walked out the door.

"Well!" said Fiona, heaving a sigh. "I'm glad *he's* gone, at last!"

But Cadel wasn't. For some reason, the detective's withdrawal had left him feeling vulnerable and exposed. Perhaps it had something to do with Mace and his toxic temper.

Cadel was very uneasy about his foster brother's state of mind.

FIVE

When he finally returned to his bedroom after saying good-bye to Fiona, Cadel discovered that he was too late. Mace had already been there. With Janan and Hazel finally out of the way, Mace had scanned the room, seen Cadel's rescued computer monitor, and emptied half a can of lemonade into its air vents.

"He can't call *that* a joke!" Cadel cried, upon reporting this crime to Hazel. "It's deliberate sabotage! How am I supposed to use it now, when its guts are full of sugar?"

"I'm sorry, dear, I'll have a word with him." Hazel was apologetic but distracted. Though the police were long gone, Janan remained curled up under his bedclothes, in a state of shock. Hazel didn't know what to do. She had left a message with his caseworker. "Mace isn't *really* angry with you," she said. "He's upset about the police coming here."

"Well, that's not *my* fault!"

"I know." Hazel patted Cadel's shoulder. "You have to understand, Thomas is very mixed up. He's hitting back because that's all he's been taught to do. You're such a clever boy, Cadel, I know you'll be able to fix your computer. I know you'll cope. You've so much sense. Just put yourself in Thomas's shoes for a moment, that's all. When he looks at you, he can't help feeling clumsy and stupid in comparison, so he lashes out."

"And what am I supposed to do in the meantime?"

"Just be patient, dear. I'll talk to Thomas. I'll have a word with him."

Cadel set his jaw. "When you do," he said, through his teeth, "you can tell him that if he comes in my room again, he'll get himself electrocuted."

Hazel blinked.

"Oh, now, Cadel," she began, looking worried.

"I mean it! He's twice as big as me! I have to defend myself somehow!"

"There's no question—you mustn't—I'm going to talk to Miss Currey," Hazel stammered, much to Cadel's surprise. He had been expecting another placid reminder that consensus was the best way of handling disputes. Hazel's fearful expression was something he'd never seen before.

It took him a moment to realize that she must have heard certain stories about him. From Fiona, perhaps? Fiona was familiar with some of his background. She may have warned Hazel Donkin that her new foster son could be very, very dangerous if sufficiently provoked. And Hazel had believed her.

The police were the same. They didn't trust Cadel. They were afraid of his high IQ. (Not to mention his warped upbringing.) And the last thing Cadel wanted now was to ring any more alarm bells. Finally, after months of being as good as gold, he had begun to sense that Fiona, for one, no longer regarded him as a kind of human time bomb. He honestly believed that she liked him. And he didn't want Hazel calling her with the news that he had threatened to electrocute his foster brother.

If that happened, he would find himself back at square one.

"I'm sorry," he muttered, swallowing his rage. "I wouldn't really electrocute Thomas." And he put on his most innocent face, which seemed to reassure Hazel somewhat. She looked relieved. She even managed a smile. When she spoke, however, her voice was still shaky.

"I'll be reporting this to Thomas's social worker," she said. "It's a problem he's going to have to work through. A problem we'll *all* have to work through."

Lying in bed that night, Cadel wondered why *he* should have to work through Mace's problems. He didn't want anything to do with Mace's problems—or Mace himself, for that matter—and was still seething at what had been done to his defenseless equipment. A brief inspection had told him that the damage would be almost impossible to rectify. What *right* did that hulking great moron have to bully him like this?

In the old days, he could have dealt with Mace quite easily. Mace was no different from a lot of mean-spirited kids who had paid for their bad treatment of Cadel over the years. Not that they'd ever understood that they were being punished. Oh, no. Back in high school, when various bullies had received their just deserts, no one had understood that Cadel was ultimately responsible. He had disguised his involvement far too well. He had planned his many acts of revenge so carefully that there was never any obvious link between himself and each peculiar sequence of events that resulted in the downfall of yet another foe.

Of course, Cadel had long ago rejected his murky past. Such petty, vindictive schemes were nothing to be proud of. All the same, he couldn't help pondering the possible alternatives, should he ever decide to teach Mace a lesson. Plotting variables was so much easier when your target lived in the same house, followed the same schedule, and used the same bathroom. . . .

By the time he fell asleep, Cadel had devised a neat little scenario, which, though it would hurt Mace cruelly, could not possibly be blamed on Cadel. A perfect crime, in other words. But when he woke up in the morning, he felt ashamed. He told himself that such thoughts were unworthy of Sonja—that they were part of Prosper's poisonous legacy. And he got out of bed resolved to be more tolerant of his foster brother's quirks.

Unfortunately, his good intentions came to nothing. After he'd been sneezed over, tripped up, and trodden on, Cadel lost patience. None of these incidents had been "accidental," despite what Mace said. As far as Cadel was concerned, they had been hostile acts.

So he set about robbing Mace of his most prized possessions.

These happened to be a set of dirt-bike magazines sent to Mace by his elder brother, who was in prison. Cadel had been forbidden to touch them, of course. He knew, however, that Mace kept them near his bedroom window. He also knew that their covers were very sticky, because Mace would often read them while he was eating sweets. And he knew that Mace's room had once been invaded by ants when a glass of soft drink had been left on the windowsill.

Knowing all this, Cadel could make some fairly detailed calculations, using a series of complicated probability algorithms that he had developed himself. Though his method was by no means perfect, it had served him well enough in the past. And this time, too, it was successful.

All he had to do was swap Mace's packed lunch with Janan's. Then, after his two foster brothers had left for school, he laid a trail of sugar particles from Mace's bedroom windowsill to his treasured magazines. Once these two steps were accomplished, Cadel had no further *active* role to play in the process. He could simply sit back and watch events unfold, from a discreet vantage point.

He had a while to wait. Hazel never collected any discarded clothes from the bedrooms until she had finished her data-entry work, at about midday. So Cadel entertained himself by answering the NSA's list of questions. He could have gone out, but it was threatening to rain—and besides, he wanted to be on hand. It was very, very important that the timing be right. Any variations would have to be dealt with at short notice. (By delaying Hazel with a brief talk, for instance.)

Cadel found it hard to concentrate. He was restless and couldn't settle, making many trips to the kitchen and bathroom during the course of the morning. On one of these trips, he noticed something that made him do a double take. Frowning, he approached Hazel's computer—and crouched in front of it.

Had he imagined that flash? Were his eyes playing tricks on him?

Hazel had taken a phone break. He could hear her chatting to her sister in the kitchen. Her computer, meanwhile, had lapsed into "sleep" mode.

Yet he could have sworn he'd seen the little light blink on her hard drive.

For a while he squatted motionless, waiting for another hint. Another clue. It came just as Hazel appeared in the kitchen doorway: The light blinked again.

"What is it, dear?" Hazel asked.

"Oh—nothing." Cadel sprang to his feet. "I thought I saw a spider."

In fact, he'd seen a different kind of bug. An invader. Something running on the system that shouldn't have been there. But he couldn't do much about it—not while Hazel was working. So he wandered back to his room, where he occupied himself with mental arithmetic until the moment of truth arrived. Lying on his bed, he heard Hazel enter Mace's room. She must have seen at once that the dirt-bike magazines were crawling with ants; there was a shriek, followed by a slapping noise that may have been the sound of Hazel hitting the magazines with a dirty sock or a pair of underpants. As Cadel had predicted, she then rushed back out to the laundry, where she grabbed a can of fly spray. The hiss of it was audible in Cadel's bedroom as Hazel covered most of Mace's belongings with a fine layer of insecticide.

After that, she picked up the magazines and took them out of Mace's room, heading for the garden. Here she was probably planning to shake and swat the infested journals until every ant clinging to them had dropped into an empty flower bed. But she was halfway to the door when the phone rang—at which point she set her burden down on the hall table, so that she could pick up a nearby telephone receiver.

Cadel, who was watching from behind his bedroom door, heaved a sigh of relief. His calculations so far seemed to be panning out.

As expected, the caller was from Janan's school. Apparently Janan was throwing a tantrum because Hazel had not packed his chocolate bar. "But I did!" Hazel protested, all in vain. A nougat bar had been substituted for the chocolate one. Hazel would therefore have to replace the unwanted nougat variety with Janan's regular chocolate treat.

It had happened once before, when Hazel herself had mixed up the packed lunches. This time, though not to blame, she was nevertheless forced to fix the problem. She had to rush off to Janan's school with a new chocolate bar before Janan hurt himself—or someone else. And in all the commotion, she forgot about the pile of magazines left on the hall table.

Cadel had been counting on this memory lapse.

Owing to the placement of the telephone, lamp, and address book, Mace's magazines had been dumped directly above a black plastic bin full of old paper and cardboard, destined for recycling. Cadel checked the relative positions of these two bundles with a measuring tape. He was satisfied with what he saw. Then he positioned himself in front of Hazel's computer, from which vantage point he could look down the hallway if he leaned sideways a little and turned his head.

He was waiting for Leslie to return home from his early shift. Unless this happened while Hazel was out, the whole plan would be ruined. Nervously Cadel glanced at his watch. Absentmindedly he logged on to Hazel's e-mail address, one ear cocked for the noise of Leslie's car engine. For the moment, he had forgotten about the mysterious activity on his foster mother's hard drive. He was far too concerned about the success of his scheme.

Cadel always made a habit of cleaning out the Donkins' electronic mailbox. He had been shocked—even appalled—to discover how much garbage had accumulated there before his arrival. For months, spam had been piling up among the meager trickle of personal messages, because neither Hazel nor Leslie knew how to filter or erase unwanted mail. It had been like walking into a house and finding that the entire building was piled high with rotten food and old newspapers. Cadel had never seen anything like it before.

His offer to clean out the trash had been met with heartfelt gratitude. Hazel had even given him her password—apparently without a second thought. This, too, had appalled Cadel. No one knew any of his passwords, and nobody ever would. Not even Sonja.

Running his eye down the short column of spam that had recently slipped through Hazel's filters, Cadel couldn't help noticing one new message whose tagline promised: "Win a computer!" He hesitated. The sender had a fairly innocuous address, and was probably harmless, but

Cadel remembered the blinking light on the hard drive. Would it be wise to proceed cautiously? Perhaps. Perhaps not. He found it hard to believe that there was any connection, but all the same . . .

Something wasn't right. He could feel it, instinctively. A submerged drag on the system.

As if it was ever so slightly preoccupied.

Cadel didn't trust this particular computer. Like Mace and Janan, it had been badly treated early on—exposed to all sorts of nasty, marauding behaviors—and the results were hard to fix. Cadel had done his best. He'd shaken out a lot of infections and updated a lot of programs. He'd changed passwords and plugged holes. But still he felt uneasy, wandering around behind a wall that had been breached so many times. He couldn't help feeling that he might have missed something; that something might still lurk in the shadows, waiting to pounce.

That was why he so badly needed a new computer. That was why Mace deserved to be punished for ruining Cadel's precious monitor with lemonade.

Fortunately, Leslie arrived home right on time. Cadel had just decided that the contents of a spam file were nothing that he couldn't handle; he was in the process of opening the new one when his foster father shuffled through the front door, tired and slightly damp. Leslie was a short man, but he had plenty of bulk. Though mild-mannered, softspoken, and middle-aged, he still carried enough muscle to intimidate a boy like Mace. None of Mace's "accidents" ever seemed to happen when Leslie was around.

The trouble was that Leslie worked such long shifts. And was always so tired at the end of them.

Cadel sat rigid, watching his foster father's every move. There was a *thump* as Leslie set down his plastic case. A *clunk* as his keys hit polished wood.

"Cadel?" he said. "What are these magazines doing here?"

"I dunno," Cadel replied.

"Are they supposed to go out for recycling?"

"I dunno."

Leslie paused. He seemed to be thinking. Cadel knew how slow the man's thought processes could be after a nine-hour shift, and tried not to show his impatience. Instead he focused on the screen in front of him, surprised to see that the sales pitch he'd downloaded was for an unfamiliar, online puzzle site. An endless slab of text pleaded with him to sample its wares: *Challenging riddles or secret symbols, wordgames or runes—don't shilly-shally about calling round! Our site tops incompetent competitor sites . . .*

The strange thing was that it didn't include a single website address.

Suddenly Leslie picked up the pile of dirt-bike magazines, dumped them in the recycling bin, and lifted the bin from the floor. Then he lurched back outside with it, leaving Cadel almost light-headed with relief. So far, so good.

Cadel scrolled down the rambling advertisement, trying to calm himself. *Focus,* he thought. *Just focus. Why does this text feel so wrong?*

. . . Every customer account receives discount specials . . .

Moments later, Leslie returned. "Woof!" he said. "That rain's about to come down really hard." And he wiped his balding scalp with a handkerchief. "Where's Hazel? Her car's not here."

"She's gone to school," Cadel replied, his attention suddenly snagged by the words on the screen.

Hang on a minute, he thought. And he reached for a pen.

. . . So sample our offering today and download it . . .

"Which school?" Leslie wanted to know.

"Uh—Janan's."

Leslie sighed. "Okay," he said. "Well, I'll be in bed if she wants me."

Cadel nodded, without really listening. He was scribbling down the first letter of every word in what was, he felt certain, a simple acrostic.

Sure enough, he'd soon uncovered the secret message. It read: *Crosswords, acrostics, diagnostics, enigmas, labyrinths, letter-locks, e-cards, tangrams, sotadics, ciphers, anagrams, target, codes, Hackenbush, unending puzzles. Click on mindbenders.com.*

And there, at last, was the address of the site. Cadel wondered what a "sotadic" might be. He was almost tempted to find out. But it would be most unwise to go poking around an unknown website before he had investigated the possibility of a new virus in Hazel's system. Such a virus would mean that her antivirus programs were malfunctioning—or too antiquated. And since Cadel was responsible for writing some of these programs, he found the idea of a breach very alarming indeed. Only an exceedingly nasty little germ could have slipped past *his* scans.

Unless the virus had been lying low, disguised as something else?

Cadel clicked his tongue and shook his head. As he closed the "Mindbenders" file, his glance strayed to the message he'd scrawled on one of Hazel's Post-it notes. *Crosswords, acrostics, diagnostics, electronic labyrinths . . .*

C-a-d-e-l.

There it was. A double acrostic. Another message hidden in the first. It leaped out at him quite suddenly, as if the letters themselves were glowing.

Cadel-lets-catch-up-com.

SIX

The shock was immense.

For a while Cadel sat motionless, hardly able to breathe. He couldn't believe his eyes. *Cadelletscatchupcom.* Was that a Web address? A dot-com site dedicated to catching up with *him*? Or was it—was it—?

Feverishly, Cadel entered the message as an address, with a "www." in front of "Cadel" and a full stop inserted between the "up" and the "com." But there was no connection. The address didn't exist.

Cadel-lets-catch-up-com. Cadel had once known a person named Com. He had been a student at the Axis Institute—a computer hacker. Could he have tracked Cadel down? Was that how the message should read: *Cadel, let's catch up. Com.*?

Cadel gnawed at his fingernails, thinking hard. Com had been a very, very peculiar guy. Pudgy and pale, with shiny black hair cut in a straight line all around his head, Com had been more like a machine than a man. In fact, he'd barely been able to communicate with human beings at all, preferring the company of computers. On reflection, Cadel couldn't recall having heard him utter a single, recognizable word in any language—just grunts, squeaks, and hisses. And hardly any of these noises had been directed at Cadel, who was only a distant acquaintance.

So why would Com want to catch up now?

It was possible that the answer could be found at www.mindbenders.com. But Cadel wasn't sure that waltzing unprotected into Com's territory would be a very good idea. What if Com had laid an ambush of some kind? It would be much safer if Cadel found a back way in.

He knew that his most promising lead was the e-mail itself. This probably would have been issued from a false address. Com might have attempted to disguise its origins. However, by working through the encoded route description hidden in front of the message, Cadel would be able to identify any invalid legs in its back trail.

He was still engaged in this fiddly job when Hazel returned, bringing Janan with her. Cadel glanced at his watch.

"We decided to come home early," said Hazel. "Didn't we, dear?" And she patted Janan's head.

The six-year-old—whose dark eyes were bloodshot and whose sallow, skinny face was covered in scratches—wandered over to where Cadel was sitting.

"Can I play, too?" he asked.

"This isn't a game," Cadel replied shortly.

"Can we play Colossus?"

"No."

Janan stuck out his bottom lip. Next thing, Cadel felt a hand on his shoulder.

"Do you think you could swap your computer time with Janan today?" Hazel inquired. "His social worker's coming over at three, so you could get back on then."

"But—"

"Just for today. I'm sorry." She lowered her voice. "I think it might calm him down. Things have been a bit tough."

Cadel toyed with the notion of revealing that her computer had been tampered with. After a moment's thought, however, he decided not to. If word got out that there was something wrong with Hazel's computer, he himself might wear the blame.

So he grudgingly surrendered his seat, stomped back into his bedroom, and slammed the door. He was sick of being the one who always had to make allowances, just because he wasn't totally screwed-up or abysmally stupid. No one seemed to realize how much he *needed* a computer. To other people, computers were simply useful tools, or sources of entertainment. But to him, computer access was a human right. Especially now that someone was out there looking for him.

He wondered if he should tell the police. It was possible that the encoded message actually came from Prosper English, who could be using Com's name to lure Cadel into a secret conversation. On the other hand, if the message *was* from Com, then Cadel was in luck. Because Com would be able to provide testimony about the Axis Institute.

Cadel decided that, before calling the police, he would see if he could finish his trace. That would be a start, at least. He might be able to work out whether his old classmate had really sent the message, by identifying its ultimate source.

At three o'clock, Janan's social worker arrived, shaking rain off her umbrella. She had some difficulty dragging Janan away from his game of Colossus, but finally she and Hazel coaxed the six-year-old into his bedroom with a chocolate bar, shutting the door behind them. Clearly, an important meeting had been scheduled.

Leslie was still asleep. Mace had not returned home. After checking that Hazel hadn't brought the dirt-bike magazines back inside (she hadn't), Cadel settled down in front of her computer. He was just about to strike a key when something caught his eye.

The hard drive had blinked its little light again.

Damn, he thought. *Damn, damn, damn.*

He knew that he had to be sensible. To start a trace before disinfecting the computer would expose him to all kinds of threat. No matter how keen he was to locate the source of Com's message, his first task was to ferret out any overlooked virus signatures, or other evidence of infiltration. He didn't want someone eavesdropping on his trace. Nor did he want to infect the computer that he might eventually track down.

So Cadel started to run sweep checks. And when *they* turned up nothing, he began to pick through Hazel's programs byte by painstaking byte, searching for clues. At last he found what he was looking for. Someone had been rather ingenious, taking advantage of Hazel's online naïveté. As far as Cadel could make out, a really exceptional programmer had disguised an information probe as an overlarge and slightly deformed cookie from a homewares website. Hazel herself had invited it into her system by obediently carrying out the instructions that were given to her, stamping it "approved." And every time she uploaded her data-entry work, the cookie disgorged its latest cache of encrypted information (gleaned from the bowels of her hard drive) into a waiting chat-room drop box.

Cadel frowned. It wasn't going to be easy, pinning down the user of this drop box. Even if he could take over the chat-room server, there was every chance that past messages received there hadn't been logged. And the user himself would no doubt have sought anonymity by employing many different computers, in different time zones. That, at least, would have been Cadel's tactic.

He was just pondering his next move when Mace arrived home and kicked open the front door. Cadel heard him pounding down the hallway, yelling at the top of his voice.

"Who did it?" Mace bawled. *"Who did this to my magazines?!"*

Cadel jumped up. His foster brother was home earlier than usual. Leslie was still sleeping. Hazel was shut up in Janan's bedroom.

So Cadel was in a very vulnerable position.

With lightning speed, he calculated his chances. If he took cover in his bedroom, there would be no escape route. If he ran out the back door, he would find himself in the pouring rain. Unless, perhaps, he hid under the house?

But it was too late. Before he could exit the living room, Mace caught up with him.

"You did it!" he shrieked, grabbing a handful of Cadel's hair. *"I'm going to kill you!"*

"Ow, ow, stop—"

"Thomas!" Suddenly Hazel was beside them. "Let go! *Let go!*"

Cadel's eyes were awash with tears of pain. Nevertheless, he could see that he was lucky. Both of Mace's hands were occupied—one with his dripping magazines and one with a hank of hair. So he didn't have a free fist to punch with.

"He ruined my magazines!" Mace cried. *"Look what he did!"*

"I didn't—ow—"

"He didn't! Thomas!"

And then, all at once, Leslie's booming voice thundered in their ears.

"WHAT THE HELL IS GOING ON?"

Mace froze. His grip relaxed slightly, allowing Cadel to break free. As he regained his balance, Cadel saw that his foster brother was crying. Tears were mingling with the raindrops on Mace's puffy cheeks.

"Look—look what happened!" Mace sobbed. "My magazines . . . they're all stuck together . . ."

He clutched the soggy bundle to his chest, sniffing and wiping his nose. Across the room, Leslie seemed to deflate.

"But they were put out for recycling," he protested. "Hazel? Weren't they put out for recycling?"

"Oh no!" Hazel breathed. Her hands went up to her face. "Oh no, I-I forgot! Oh Thomas, I'm *so* sorry!"

"You mean they *weren't* for the recycling?" asked Leslie.

"I left them there by accident! They were covered in ants! I was going to shake them out in the garden, but then the school rang . . ." Hazel looked as if she was about to cry. "Oh Thomas, it was all my fault!"

"And mine," said her husband heavily.

"What can we do, dear? Can we dry them out with a hair dryer?"

Cadel eyed the magazines, some of which were already turning to pulp. He knew that no hair dryer would ever revive them; his plan had worked. Nobody, moreover, would ever learn of his part in the affair. His sugar trail had been carried away by ants. The Donkins had accepted full responsibility for leaving Mace's precious magazines out in the rain. Cadel had well and truly covered his tracks.

All the same, he didn't feel good about it. Hazel was very upset. Leslie was furious with himself. Even Mace cut a pitiful figure, as he pathetically tried to separate the sodden pages, his eyes brimming and his nose running. He mumbled about his brother while Hazel patted his back, and Leslie offered him a handkerchief, and Janan suggested that a chocolate bar might help him feel better. Even Janan's social worker hovered sympathetically in the background, assuring Mace that his brother would never blame him for what had happened to the magazines.

Everyone ignored Cadel. Everyone seemed to have forgotten that Mace had threatened to kill him.

Standing alone and isolated in one corner, Cadel realized that what he had just done would have made Sonja cringe, and Prosper smile. In other words, the old Cadel had reared his ugly head. By punishing Mace, Cadel had been dragged down almost to his foster brother's level.

Later, sitting in his room, Cadel vowed not to make the same mistake ever again. If only he weren't so *bored.* He remembered an old saying: The Devil makes work for idle hands. That was his problem, without a doubt. He didn't have enough to do.

Talking with Sonja might have helped, but Sonja always found telephones difficult. And the computer, at present, was out of bounds. Even though Mace wasn't actually using it, he was entitled to. Even though it was just sitting there, going to waste, Cadel knew quite well what would happen if he went anywhere near it. Mace would immediately claim that it was *his* turn and throw a fit.

The only solution would be to log on that night, while everyone else was asleep.

Not that this would allow him to chat with Sonja, since she, too, would be sleeping. He would, however, be able to leave her an e-mail message. And he would also be able to finish his trace. The only challenge would be staying awake for long enough—because Cadel couldn't set an alarm clock. An alarm clock would disturb everyone else. But if he fell asleep *without* setting an alarm clock, there was no guarantee that he would wake up before morning.

To solve the problem, Cadel tucked a flashlight and a hairbrush into his bed that evening before he climbed under the covers. Then he lay on the hairbrush and occupied himself with a very complicated mathematical structure. Every so often he would stop to check his watch in the glow of the flashlight; every so often his binary associative operations would get a little fuzzy and he would have to pinch himself. Eventually, however, the hallway floor stopped creaking. The toilet stopped flushing. The light showing under his bedroom door was suddenly extinguished. It was twenty past eleven.

After waiting another fifteen minutes, Cadel slipped out of bed. He padded across the room on bare feet, and winced at the noise that his doorknob made. The living room was dimly lit by the glow of a streetlamp filtering through the venetian blinds. The only sound was the hum of the Donkins' fridge, the ticking of their clock on the sideboard, and the distant chirping of crickets.

The beige shag carpet muffled his tread.

When he sat down in front of Hazel's computer, her typist's chair creaked alarmingly. The snap of the ON switch sounded like a whip crack in the silence. The grinding of the processor seemed extraordinarily loud. Even the click of the mouse made him hold his breath.

Trying not to shift his weight in the creaky old chair, Cadel set about reconfiguring the information probe concealed on Hazel's hard drive. Instead of dismantling it, he planned to use it. The next time it dumped its load, the information deposited in the chat room would be tagged with something vaguely like a homing signal. Cadel might therefore be able to follow its subsequent route and locate the person collecting it.

"Cadel!"

He jumped, then turned. Hazel was standing in the doorway, wearing flannelette pajamas.

"What are you doing?" she whispered. "Go back to bed!"

"I was just—"

"This is *sleep* time, Cadel. This isn't computer time!"

"I know, but there's something I have to do."

"Not at midnight, you don't."

"It's not midnight. Yet."

"Now, Cadel." Stepping forward, Hazel cocked her head, folded her hands across her ample tummy, and addressed him in a calm but reproachful tone. "I have to set some limits, you must understand that. If I don't, what's to stop you from spending all night on the computer? It's not healthy, dear. It's bad for you."

"But—"

"A boy your age needs his sleep. If you really, really want more computer time, I'll drop you at the library tomorrow when I take Janan to school."

"But those library computers are always booked up!" Cadel hissed. "And anyway, I'm doing this for *you*. I'm trying to stop a hacker! Someone's been hacking into your machine!"

"Well, I'm sure we can sort it out," Hazel replied soothingly. "Not right now, though. Right now I want you back in bed."

Cadel stared at her in amazement. Had she no idea what it meant to have a hacker in your system? Obviously not. Her expression was tranquil as she turned off the machine. Tranquil but firm.

"I won't take any of the power cables with me," she said, "because I trust you. You're an honest boy, and a clever boy. You're smart enough to know that this isn't going to do you any good at all."

Cadel slumped. How could he possibly argue with a person who didn't understand the full implications of a hack-attack? It was impossible. He would be banging his head against a brick wall.

So he went back to bed without further protest.

SEVEN

The next morning, before Mace left for school, he and Cadel were sent outside to collect the empty trash bins. These bins had to be moved from the front gate to the backyard, once the garbage trucks had done their job.

Normally, it was a chore that took them all of three minutes. But when Mace reached the path that ran between the garage and the side of the house, he began to mutter.

Oh no, thought Cadel, quickening his step. He had picked up the black recycling bin (as usual), because the green wheelie bin was bigger and more unwieldy. Mace was in charge of the wheelie bin. He would drag it behind him—*bumpety-bump*—along the path. He even liked the din that it made. And he had enough muscle to maneuver it into its customary spot, by the old laundry shed.

But as large as it was, the wheelie bin didn't slow Mace down very much. After Cadel had dropped his black bin near the laundry, he turned to find a flushed Mace looming over him.

"You did it," said Mace, with infinite menace. "I *know* you did it."

"Did what?" Cadel was playing for time. "What are you talking about?"

"I don't know how you did it, but you did it." Mace took a step forward. "And I'm going to kill you for that."

Cadel ducked sideways and might have escaped if he had judged his route more expertly. As it was, he almost ran up against the hot-water system when he rounded a corner on his way to the back door. And that split-second delay was all Mace needed. Closing the gap between them, he grabbed Cadel's T-shirt and jerked him backward.

Suddenly Cadel was on the ground, crushed beneath a heavy weight. He could hardly breathe.

"*You better admit it,*" Mace growled, shoving his contorted face into Cadel's, "*or you're going to die.*"

"Can't . . . ," Cadel wheezed. One big, beefy forearm lay across his throat, pressing down hard. *Leaning* on it. Mace was choking him.

"Get off!" Cadel gasped. "Yeowch!"

"I told my brother about you," Mace went on. "He said I should teach you a lesson, and that's exactly what I'm gunna do now, you little *dickhead*!"

Cadel was growing dizzy. He couldn't expand his lungs. His vision was darkening at the edges.

And then, all at once, the pressure was gone. He could breathe again. Move again.

He rolled over, coughing. It was a moment before he could look up. When he did, he saw that Mace was being held in a professional-looking armlock by none other than Saul Greeniaus.

Cadel gaped in astonishment.

"All right," said Saul, calmly addressing Mace. "Are you listening to me?"

The reply that Saul received was just a torrent of profanity. So he waited, keeping a firm grip on Mace as he nodded at Cadel.

"Okay. You finished now?" the detective said at last, when Mace had run out of insults. "Because I want you to listen. What I saw then was a clear case of assault. You can end up in juvenile court for something like that. And you will if it happens again." Saul applied a slight pressure to his armlock, causing Mace to wince. "Okay—I'm gonna set you free," the detective promised. "And you're not gonna do anything stupid, like attack a police officer. Because you're *not* stupid. Are you?"

Mace shook his head, whereupon Saul released him. The two of them stood for a moment, surveying each other: Saul with his hands on his hips; Mace rubbing his elbow.

"Now, I want you guys to get along," the detective commanded. "No fighting. No sabotage. No pissing on beds."

"He ruined my magazines!" Mace squawked. But Saul held up one hand.

"I don't want to hear it," he replied flatly. "I'm not interested. From now on, you guys are gonna be polite to each other. And if I find out that you've laid a hand on this kid again," he concluded, fixing Mace with his dark and somber stare, "you'll be in a lot of trouble. Is that clear?"

Mace grimaced. His eyes were wet and his face was red. He looked as if he could hardly contain his protests.

But he managed a nod.

"Good," said Saul. "I knew you were a smart kid. Now, off you go; I don't want you late for school."

"You hurt my arm." Mace narrowed his eyes. "How can I do any work if my arm hurts?"

"It won't last."

"It might."

The detective regarded Mace thoughtfully, as Cadel's foster brother raised his chin. They were almost the same height.

But while Mace was heavier, Saul seemed more formidable.

"Well, sure," the detective eventually remarked. "You can lay a complaint if you want. With your record, though, there are bound to be questions." He shrugged. "It's up to you," he said. "Personally, I wouldn't want to be drawing attention to myself."

Mace seemed to concur. As Cadel scrambled to his feet, his foster brother slouched away, disappearing around the side of the house. Only when Mace was out of sight did Saul turn his attention to Cadel.

"Are you all right?" the detective asked.

"Uh—yeah." Cadel cleared his throat experimentally.

"Has he done this before?"

"Done what?"

"Tried to strangle you."

"Oh." For some reason, Cadel felt slightly sheepish. "Well, not exactly."

"He's had a hard life," Saul acknowledged, squinting toward the house. "But I want you to stay out of his way."

"That's what I've been *trying* to do."

"No. I mean it." The detective's clear, brown gaze fastened on Cadel. *"Stay out of his way."*

"And how am I supposed to do that?" Cadel demanded. "When he won't leave me alone? Do you think it's easy?"

In response, Saul cocked his head.

"What's all this about magazines?" was his measured rejoinder. And Cadel swallowed.

He tried not to look as guilty as he felt.

"Nothing," he said. "Mace's magazines got wet."

Saul Greeniaus absorbed this in silence. Then he began to fish around in the lining of his jacket.

"I'm familiar with your record, too," he announced dryly. "I know what you're capable of." At last he found what he had been searching for, and produced it like a conjurer producing a white rabbit. "Here," he said. "I've brought you a cell phone. You can use it to call me if you're worried about anything."

Cadel blinked. Wordlessly he accepted the neat little mobile phone.

"It's not yours to keep," the detective warned. "I'm just lending it to you. And if you start running up big bills, you'll be paying them yourself. Unless the calls were made to me or Ms. Currey."

He fell silent, as if waiting for an answer. So Cadel obliged.

"Thanks," he said.

"You're welcome." Saul glanced at his watch. "Well—I'd better go. I only dropped in to give you that." He nodded at the phone. "Ms. Currey will have my hide if I talk to you for too long without her."

"Uh—Mr. Greeniaus?"

Cadel was almost surprised to hear his own voice. He hadn't given much thought to what he was going to say.

Saul didn't speak. He just waited, motionless.

"I—um—I've had a message from Com," Cadel continued. "Remember him? The guy from my infiltration class, at the Axis Institute?"

"Go on."

"It was a coded message. On e-mail. It said 'Cadel, let's catch up. Com.' That's all." Conscious of Saul's intent regard, Cadel added, "I haven't finished tracing it, yet, so I don't know if . . . I mean, it might *not* be Com. It might be . . ." He trailed off, unnerved by the detective's grim expression. "It was sent to Hazel's address," he finished. "Disguised as spam."

"Did you reply?" Saul queried.

"No. I didn't want to. There's been a hacker poking around in the system, you see, so—"

"You haven't been talking to anyone else? Online? You haven't mentioned your name, or where you live?"

"No, but—"

"Damn it to hell." Saul uttered these words so slowly and carefully that they hardly sounded like a curse. "How would anyone know you were here?"

"Well, the police know," Cadel pointed out. "Fiona knows. My lawyer knows. The address is bound to be on a computer file somewhere. It wouldn't be hard to find."

Saul frowned. He seemed to be thinking. After a while he said, "What was that about a hacker?"

"Someone planted an information probe in Hazel's system," Cadel explained. "It's been gathering data."

"For whom?"

"I don't know. I was going to finish the trace today, before I went and tracked down that e-mail." Cadel was suddenly struck by a dazzling idea. He straightened, and his whole face lit up. "Do you want to see?" he eagerly inquired, anxious to commandeer the computer. "I can show you—"

"No."

"But—"

"Listen." Saul put a hand on Cadel's shoulder. "Don't you *touch* that machine. It's out of bounds. Understand?"

Cadel caught his breath.

"What—what do you mean?" He gasped.

"If what you say is true, then we can't risk having you go anywhere near the computer. Just in case."

"But that's ridiculous." Cadel was shell-shocked. "There's no risk. I'm going to reconfigure the cookie so that nothing will go out unless it's tagged. And the tags will be like route markers."

"No."

"But you can't!" Cadel cried. The horrible truth was finally beginning to sink in. "You can't stop me using the *computer*!"

"I have to." Saul moved his hand to the top of Cadel's head, bending down until they were eye to eye. "My first priority is to keep you safe," he said firmly. "That's my job. We don't know who we're dealing with right now, so we can't be too careful. There's no saying what might happen if I let you wander about online unprotected."

"But I can protect *myself* online! Way better than anyone else could!" Cadel found it hard to believe that Saul was unable to grasp this fact. "Don't you understand? It's what I do!"

"Listen to me." Saul's grip tightened on Cadel's scalp. "There are people I can bring in here to conduct an online investigation. They can turn that machine inside out in a couple of hours. They're experts."

"So am I!"

"Yes, I know. But you're also the target." Saul's tone was grave. "Your safety is paramount. *Paramount.* I don't want Prosper English messing with your head."

Cadel tried to speak, but he couldn't. There was a lump in his throat. Something of the anguish that he felt must have shown in his face, because Saul's own expression changed slightly. Before the detective could say anything, however, Hazel addressed him from beside the hot-water system.

"Mr. Greeniaus?" she said, and he swung around.

"Good morning, Mrs. Donkin."

"Thomas *told* me you were here, but . . ."

"It's a little early, I know."

"Isn't Miss Currey with you?"

"No. I'm afraid we have a problem." Saul's tone was very formal. Very official-sounding. "I'm afraid we're gonna have to confiscate your computer for a short time."

Hazel's mouth formed a perfect O.

"We may not have to remove it from this site, but it will be out of bounds to all the occupants of your home," Saul went on. "Until such a time as we're satisfied that it's safe to use."

"But—but why?" Hazel asked. Her glance shifted toward Cadel, who stiffened.

"This isn't Cadel's fault," the detective quickly assured her. "On the contrary. He's the one who uncovered the problem."

"But—"

"Let's go inside, shall we? I need to make some calls."

So they went inside, where Saul immediately took over the whole house. He dispatched a sullen Mace to the bus stop. He sent Hazel off to school with Janan and left a message on Fiona's voice mail. He put through a request for some kind of forensic information technology team. Then he made a full report to his superior, using his own cell phone.

When he'd finished, he settled in front of the computer and addressed Cadel—who was slumped on the living-room couch, fiddling with the TV remote.

"Am I correct in thinking that Mr. Donkin has already left for work?" the detective asked.

"He leaves early," Cadel replied, without glancing in Saul's direction. "He works a morning shift."

"Then I'm out of order." Saul clicked his tongue. "I shouldn't have sent Mrs. Donkin away until Ms. Currey arrived." After a moment he added, "I'm sorry, Cadel, I really am."

Cadel said nothing. He stared straight ahead, glum and embittered, wondering why he had ever opened his big, fat, stupid mouth. It was all so *insulting.* First they'd taken away his computer. Now they were going to take over his trace. And what was he supposed to do in the meantime? Sit in front of the TV?

Slowly he became aware of the lengthening silence and turned his head. Had Saul left the room? No—he was still perched on the typist's chair, his clasped hands hanging between his knees, quietly watching Cadel.

After a moment, Cadel discovered that he could no longer contain himself.

"I've got to e-mail Sonja," he insisted. "I've *got* to. And I can't use the phone, because she can't talk on the phone! I need a computer!"

They studied each other for perhaps half a minute. Then Saul said, "After I've finished here, I'll take you to the library. You can e-mail Sonja from there."

"Are you kidding?" Cadel scoffed. "All the library computers will be booked out! They're always booked out!"

"Not if *I* ask for one," the detective retorted, with unassailable confidence. "Anyhow, it'll only be one e-mail. You can tell Sonja that you're coming to visit her this afternoon. If you pay her a visit, you can talk to your heart's content." Hearing Cadel sniff, he added, "I'll even ask Mick and Ray to give you a lift. As a special favor. The only thing is . . ." He hesitated. "The only thing is, you have to promise not to use her computer, or I can't let you go."

Cadel took a deep breath. His hands were crawling around in his lap. But his voice, when he spoke, was fairly steady.

"You don't understand," he said. "You just don't understand . . ."

"What don't I understand?"

"I've *got* to have a computer." Cadel was trying not to sound melodramatic. Or hysterical. Or downright mad. Nevertheless, he felt compelled to explain. "I'm not like other people," he said. "I might as well die if I don't have one."

Saul's brows snapped together.

"Come on now," he objected. "It can't be that bad."

"Stuck out here? With nothing to do?" Cadel scowled. "Sometimes I almost wish Prosper *would* contact me. Just so I could talk to someone who understands!"

Saul stood up—so abruptly that Cadel flinched. But the detective didn't seem cross. He was as calm as ever.

"If Prosper English gave a good goddamn about you," he said flatly, "then he'd acknowledge that you were his son. He hasn't, so he doesn't. As for this computer ban, it won't last long. Can you survive off-line for a day or two?"

It wasn't a question. It was an order. Cadel knew that any further resistance would be futile.

"I guess so," he muttered, into his chest.

"Good." The doorbell rang, but Saul didn't let it interrupt him. Instead he kept talking, his arms folded, his eyes on Cadel. "In that case," he said, "I'll make *you* a promise. I promise I'll do all I can to get you the hell out of here."

Cadel's head jerked up. He stared at the detective in surprise.

"You don't belong in this place," Saul declared, as if stating the blindingly obvious. "You think I haven't worked *that* out? I'm a detective. I can see what's under my nose."

Then he turned, and went to admit his forensic computer team into the Donkins' house.

EIGHT

As it turned out, Cadel didn't need a lift to the library after all. Because when Saul's cybercrime experts arrived, they were carrying a couple of laptops. Cadel used one of these laptops to send Sonja a message, announcing that he would visit her around lunchtime.

His mood had changed for the better since the appearance of Sid and Steve. In many ways they were *his* kind of people. Even though they wore jackets and ties, the jackets were too big for them, and the ties were covered in pictures of cartoon characters. Steve sported a goatee, and Sid had several holes in his right earlobe. Both tackled the Donkins' computer with a breathless concentration that reminded Cadel of his old infiltration classes at the Axis Institute. Though not brilliant, Sid and Steve were confident and capable. Cadel enjoyed their company.

He almost forgot his many problems, as he and the two police techheads pored over Hazel's infected programs. At first, Sid and Steve adopted a jauntily patronizing tone when they addressed Cadel. This soon changed, however. By the time Fiona arrived, at about ten o'clock, they were positively *deferring* to Cadel—who couldn't help preening himself a bit under their astonished regard.

"Is everything all right?" Fiona demanded breathlessly, pushing past Saul into the living room. "Hazel, what's going on here?"

"I don't really know," Hazel replied. She was sitting meekly on the beige velour couch, nursing a cup of tea. "Apparently there's something wrong with my computer."

"It's been infiltrated," Saul quickly explained, springing to Cadel's defense before the obvious question could even be asked. "By an unknown person."

"And what's Cadel doing?" said Fiona.

"I'm helping," Cadel interjected, knowing full well that she wouldn't be happy to hear it. "You don't have to worry. I'm only answering technical questions." Struck by a sudden thought, he turned to Saul Greeniaus. "By the way," he added, "I've finished that questionnaire from the NSA. It's on my desk."

Saul nodded, then retreated into Cadel's bedroom. Fiona gazed around in a bewildered fashion. Her hair looked even more disarranged than usual; she was carrying an enormous, overstuffed handbag and wearing another of her curiously retro outfits, which comprised a pink tweed suit and chunky little shoes.

"So what do you want me to do, exactly?" she asked. "Cadel?"

"I don't know." Already Cadel's attention was being drawn back to the Donkins' computer. "There," he said to Steve, pointing. "You see?"

Steve grunted. "You say you've been encrypting your e-mails?" he queried.

"Of course," Cadel replied.

"Well, I hate to tell you this, but someone's been capturing your keystrokes *before* they're encrypted."

"A key logger?" Cadel shook his head. "Nuh. I took that off ages ago. There was a whole lot of crap spyware installed on this thing, and I got rid of it all."

"What do you call this, then?"

"*Excuse* me." Fiona had raised her voice. "I don't want to interrupt, but can someone please explain why Cadel is being asked to help the police without having a lawyer present?"

Cadel tried to point out that he didn't need a lawyer, but Fiona refused to listen. She took him into the kitchen and told him quite forcefully that she had to look after his interests.

"For all I know, you might be incriminating yourself just by talking about things that you've been doing on the computer," she said.

"But that's crazy." He was genuinely baffled. "How could I? All I've been doing is telling them about the hacker—"

"Cadel, *you* were a hacker once. How do you know they won't use this information against you?"

"Because they couldn't."

"Don't be too sure of that. I'm sorry, but I can't let you talk to them if I don't know what you're talking *about.* I'll have to check with Mel Hofmeier first."

Cadel looked at her hopelessly. It was clear that she did not—*could* not—comprehend.

"But I know what I'm doing," he assured her. "I don't need a lawyer's advice. Why don't you trust me? *I know what I'm doing.*"

"Of course you do." (She sounded unconvinced, however.) "All the same, I have to follow the correct protocol. It's been put in place to protect you."

"But—"

"You're not an adult, Cadel. Legally, you can't make these decisions. Would you like me to ring Mel?"

"There's no need," Saul interrupted. He was hovering in the doorway. "If you're uneasy, we shan't require Cadel's input."

"But you *will*!" Cadel didn't want to be sidelined. "Sid will never trace that hacker without me! I'm *better* than he is!"

"Nevertheless, he'll manage," Saul replied. "If Ms. Currey has reservations, of course we'll proceed without your help."

"Then you won't find the hacker," Cadel warned.

"Maybe not."

"And what happens if you don't? Will Hazel get her computer back? Will I be able to use it?"

"We'll decide that in due course."

"Cadel, it's for your own good," Fiona interposed. "I realize you're a computer whiz, but you don't know much about legal procedure."

"Well, that's not *my* fault!"

"I'm not saying it is. I'm just saying you have to be very, very careful."

"Not around me, he doesn't." For the first time, there was an edge to Saul's voice. "My job is to protect him, Ms. Currey. I'm not trying to get him in trouble."

"Mr. Greeniaus, I'm not questioning your motives. But I represent the Department of Community Services. Which means that *I'm* the one who has to protect Cadel."

"Is that so?" Saul narrowed his eyes and leaned forward. "In that case," he murmured, "why don't you get him the hell out of this place?"

Fiona's head snapped back, as if she'd been punched.

"What—what do you mean?" she said.

"Well, do *you* think he belongs here?"

Fiona took a deep breath, glancing over the detective's shoulder to make sure that Hazel wasn't listening.

"Obviously, it's not ideal—"

"Obviously," Saul growled.

"But it's only a temporary measure!"

"And meanwhile he has to get beaten up by that thug with the crew cut?"

Fiona gasped and turned pale. "Is that true?" she asked Cadel. "Did Thomas attack you?"

Cadel shifted uneasily. "Yeah," he mumbled. "I guess . . ."

"You're looking at an eyewitness here." Saul tapped his own chest with one finger. "I had to haul that juvie off him. So don't talk to me about protecting Cadel. He'd be a lot safer somewhere else."

"I know."

"Somewhere he can use his brain."

"I *know*." Fiona spoke too loudly. She covered her mouth, then continued at a lower volume, her cheeks flushed. "Do you think I don't realize?" she hissed. "Do you have any idea how *hard* it is? I'm doing my best, Mr. Greeniaus! I'm doing my very best for Cadel!"

"Good," Saul remarked levelly. "And so am I. I'd be grateful if you could remember that."

Cadel glanced up at Fiona. He was hoping that she might have been persuaded to reconsider her views. But he was doomed to disappointment. Though she looked troubled, she wouldn't budge. No matter how good Saul's intentions were, she said, they could easily be undermined. Suppose Cadel advised Sid and Steve on how they might penetrate this hacker's system? Suppose they were eventually asked to testify in court? Could they *deny* that Cadel had demonstrated a clear knowledge of hacking techniques? No, they could not.

"I'm sorry," she said, "but if you want to pursue this, Mr. Greeniaus, I'm going to have to call Cadel's lawyer."

So she did. Unfortunately, Mel could not be reached at that precise moment—and Fiona herself soon ran out of time. She had other clients who needed her. Other appointments to keep. She couldn't stay, though she wanted to.

"Could I drop you off at the library?" she suggested, and Cadel shook his head.

"I want to stay here," he replied. Sid and Steve had hit a dead end; as Cadel had anticipated, the hacker was making use of different time zones to ensure his anonymity. Even when everyone *did* wake up in Prague, it would be tricky wresting an Internet protocol number out of a Czech-speaking service provider.

Cadel could have offered several solutions to this problem, if he'd only been allowed to speak up.

"I'd rather you didn't stay here," a harassed-looking Fiona pleaded, hovering near the couch on which he was sprawled. "Not without a supporting adult in attendance."

"Last time I looked, Hazel was an adult," Saul remarked coolly, from one corner. Though he hadn't been saying much, very little had escaped him.

Fiona flashed him an impatient look.

"Hazel's been imposed on enough!" she snapped. "In fact, you're lucky she hasn't called her *own* lawyer! How long have you been here now—two hours? This isn't a crime scene!"

"As a matter of fact, it is," Saul replied. "Cybercrime isn't a virtual offense, Ms. Currey."

"Oh, you *know* what I mean!" Fiona said tartly. "Anyway, my point is—"

"That you want Cadel out of here," Saul finished. "Well, for your information, he's due at Sonja Pirovic's house in an hour or so. I was going to arrange a lift for him—unless you've a problem with that?"

Fiona hesitated. Clearly, she would have liked Cadel to make his own way to Sonja's house. When she saw his mutinous look, however, she raised her hands in submission.

"All right," she said. "I won't argue. I haven't the time."

"There's no need to worry," Saul maintained, as he accompanied her to the front door. "Mick and Ray aren't talkative types."

"I hope not."

"If you want, they can always take Mrs. Donkin along with them."

Fiona's withering glare was met by a shrug. Cadel (who had followed them both) somehow sensed that Saul was teasing Fiona, though the detective remained absolutely poker-faced. It was curious to watch the two of them standing side by side, because Fiona was always so restless, and Saul was always so still. They could almost have belonged to different species.

"Bye, Hazel!" Fiona yelled. *"I'll call you this afternoon!"* Then she squeezed Cadel's arm. "Have a nice time with Sonja," she said. "Give her my regards."

Cadel nodded. As Fiona clattered down the front steps, he waited for Saul to retreat inside. But the detective seemed interested in her progress. He stood watching while she headed for her car.

"You're fortunate to have Ms. Currey as your caseworker," he declared, once she had roared off down the street. Cadel saw with surprise that he was in earnest. "She's very serious about her job."

"Yeah," Cadel conceded. "I guess she is."

"My advice is that you get Mrs. Donkin to pack you some lunch,"

Saul continued, nudging Cadel back into the house. "Then you can take it with you to Sonja's and stay until dinner. What time would you be expected home?"

"Oh, about five, I guess." Cadel looked up, pursing his lips and widening his enormous eyes. "Can I get a lift back, as well?" he asked.

For a moment they stared at each other. Saul's face revealed nothing. When he spoke, however, his tone was wry. "Yeah, okay," he said. "But don't push your luck, my friend. I can be just as stubborn as Ms. Currey."

Cadel soon realized the truth of this remark. For Saul wouldn't allow him to go anywhere near Sid or Steve. The detective insisted that Cadel remain in the kitchen, helping his foster mother assemble a casserole, until half past eleven. Then Saul escorted him all the way to the spotless silver sedan in which Mick and Ray were sitting, consuming a matching pair of chicken-salad wraps.

The surveillance team welcomed Cadel into their vehicle with a noticeable lack of enthusiasm.

"Don't get too comfortable in there," Saul warned him. "And don't drop any of your sandwich crumbs onto the backseat."

"I won't," Cadel sighed.

"Mr. Mattilos is doing me a favor out of the goodness of his heart, so don't give him any trouble," Saul added, before addressing the driver. "Thanks for this, Mick."

The driver inclined his head. Saul slapped the roof of the car and stepped back. As the engine turned over, Cadel leaned toward the window.

"Mr. Greeniaus?"

"What?"

"If something happens—if Sid gets lucky—can you please ring me up? I just want to know what's going on."

"I'll see what I can do," Saul replied.

But whether this constituted a promise, Cadel couldn't be sure. He watched the detective's wiry figure diminish in size as Mick drove away from the Donkins' house, and wondered which of the cars now left in the street belonged to Saul. No doubt Mick or Ray could have told him, if only Cadel had had the courage to ask.

Eyeing the backs of their heads, however, he decided not to. The stiffness of their necks was somehow intimidating.

He therefore remained silent during the entire length of the trip. His companions didn't say much, either. The traffic was quite heavy, and Cadel couldn't help feeling nostalgic as he studied the complicated matrix of one particularly busy intersection. He had once brought Sydney traffic to a halt by diverting a road crew to this very convergence of arterials. But that, of course, had been in the old days, when Prosper was still pulling his strings. He no longer messed with traffic flows or railway timetables. Not since he had learned to consider the consequences of a delayed ambulance or an overcrowded train.

Sonja had taught him to think about people, as well as systems.

They reached her house shortly after twelve, and parked near the front gate. Cadel was then forced to sit in the car for seven minutes while Mick and Ray waited for what they called their backup. With the engine turned off, it seemed very quiet. Cadel worried that the men in the front seat would hear his stomach rumbling, because he hadn't dared eat his lunch. Not after Saul's comment about the upholstery.

At last, to cover the noise of his growling gut, he said, "What happens when you want to go to the toilet?"

There was a creaking, squeaking sound as Mick craned around to study him. Mick was wearing sunglasses, and his mouth looked as if it had been hacked into his face with an axe.

"What?" said Mick.

"I was just wondering—what happens when you need to go to the toilet?"

Mick's expression remained stony. His eyes were hidden by his reflective lenses. Finally he said, "None of your business."

Then Ray's walkie-talkie spluttered to life, and after a brief three-way conversation among Ray, Mick, and the "backup," Cadel was informed that he could get out now. So he did. On his way to Sonja's front door, he realized that it was in fact a very nice day—sunny, but with a slight chill in the air—and he decided that he might offer to take Sonja out for a walk after lunch. Provided, of course, that she felt up to it. Sometimes her muscular spasms could leave her exhausted by midafternoon.

"Cadel!" said Rosalie, when she answered the doorbell. "Hello, come in!"

"Hello, Rosalie. How's Sonja?"

"Good! Good! She has many visitors today."

Cadel stopped in his tracks.

"Many visitors?" he repeated. "You mean—her social worker?"

"No, no." Rosalie bustled along the dingy hallway ahead of him, without pausing. "Visitors from Clearview Center, you see."

"From *where*?" Cadel hurried to catch up. "Wait! Rosalie—"

Rosalie, however, had already reached Sonja's room. She rapped on the door, announcing, "Your boyfriend is here!" And then she pushed it open.

Stumbling to a halt beside her, Cadel saw that Sonja's little room was occupied by three people. Sonja sat in her wheelchair. Perched on her bed was a fat, middle-aged woman with long, frizzy gray hair, who wore funky red-rimmed glasses and layers of flowing skirts, most of them either Indian or tie-dyed. And standing near the window was a bronzed, wide-shouldered, slim-waisted man with perfectly styled brown hair, dazzling white teeth, and startling green eyes. He was dressed in casual, elegant clothes that looked expensive.

He smiled at Cadel.

"You want some tea?" Rosalie asked, before Cadel could say anything.

"Uh—no," he replied. "Thanks, I'm—I've brought my lunch."

"Oh! Okay." Rosalie nodded. "Lunch in half an hour, Sonja. Is that okay?"

"Yes-thanks," the DynaVox squawked.

"You okay, now? Not too many people?"

"No."

"Okay. Well—half an hour. I'll be back."

And with that, Rosalie departed, leaving Cadel alone on the threshold. There was a moment's silence, as he looked to Sonja for an introduction.

But she was in such a highly nervous state that she couldn't control her limbs.

"Hi," said the handsome man, pushing himself off the wall. "My name's Trader. And this is Judith."

"Um . . . hi." Cadel glanced from one to the other. "You're not—? Am I—?"

"You must be Cadel Piggott. Or should I say English? Or maybe Darkon?" Trader's gleaming smile widened. "I suppose it's hard to decide, at this point."

Cadel's jaw dropped.

"It's all right," Trader continued. "Prosper didn't send us. On the contrary. We're here with a proposition . . . for you *and* Sonja."

Cadel stared at Sonja, who was still struggling with her own wayward limbs.

"But perhaps," Trader added, still smiling, "you had better shut the door first."

NINE

"It's-all-right-Cadel." As Cadel stood slack-mouthed, Sonja finally forced her errant right hand to obey her. *"Just-listen. This-is-interesting."*

Cadel blinked. Confused and disoriented, he found himself unable to reply. So Trader picked up where Sonja had left off.

"I think you'll be glad to hear us out, Cadel," he said, in cheerful tones. "Trouble is, we can't really discuss it unless we have a bit of privacy . . ." And he nodded at the bedroom door, which still stood ajar.

Mindlessly, like an automaton, Cadel shut it.

"There," said Judith. "That's better." She had a loud, rough-edged bark that perfectly matched her hefty frame and vibrant outfit. "Sorry about all the cloak-and-dagger stuff. This must be a bit of a shock for you."

"Or maybe it isn't." Trader's gleaming grin flashed over Cadel. "God knows, you must be used to cloak-and-dagger stuff, after the Axis Institute."

"Who *are* you?" Cadel said hoarsely. "What do you want?"

Trader and Judith exchanged glances. Then Trader took a deep breath. "To be honest, Cadel, we want you. You and Sonja. We need your help," he rejoined, whereupon Judith slapped at the rumpled bedspread.

"Maybe you'd better sit down," she recommended. "This is going to take a while."

Cadel, however, was reluctant to leave the immediate vicinity of the door. Flattening himself against it, he appealed to Sonja for enlightenment. "What's this all about?" he demanded, knowing that Sonja would tell him the truth.

But Sonja was having difficulties. Though Trader and Judith seemed happy to let her answer Cadel's question, her hands wouldn't stay on the DynaVox screen. They kept sliding off.

With a sinking heart, Cadel realized that she was too excited to communicate properly.

"It's not much of a solution, is it?" Judith observed, after a short wait. She was scowling at the DynaVox. "Surely we can do better than that old thing? For Chris'sake, this *is* the twenty-first century."

"We'll look into it," Trader promised. Then he addressed Cadel. "I'll come straight to the point, because I don't know how long it'll be before the police realize that we're here—"

"How did you get in?" Cadel interrupted—and Trader's smile, which had dimmed slightly, flashed out again at double the wattage.

"We're meant to be social workers," he explained, with a twinkle in his eye. "But I'll talk about that in a minute. First we have to discuss GenoME."

Cadel sucked in his breath. GenoME was one of Phineas Darkkon's creations: a company that, unbeknownst to the general public, had once been part of Dr. Darkkon's criminal empire. GenoME offered a very expensive gene-mapping service, designed to "maximize the genetic potential" of its clients. According to Earl Toffany, GenoME's chief executive officer, gene mapping was the only scientific way of identifying where a person's strengths and weaknesses might lie. Without a gene map, he had often said, life was one big shot in the dark. GenoME's motto was Messages in Matter Are Messages That Matter.

But GenoME was secretive about its methods. It wouldn't reveal the formula used in its gene-map analysis. Some people had therefore claimed that the entire company was founded on a lie—that it was impossible to understand a person using DNA, and that GenoME was defrauding its gullible clients.

Knowing Phineas Darkkon's history, Cadel had always been inclined to believe these accusations.

"Are you from GenoME?" he gasped, and Judith winced.

"Of course not!" she yelped. "Give us some credit!"

Clearly, she was appalled at the very idea. Trader, in contrast, seemed tickled. He gestured at his own immaculate person.

"Do I *look* as if I need to maximize my genetic potential?" he queried. "Go on—you can tell me." He lifted one foot, and joked, "Maybe the shoes could be improved. I was a bit worried about these shoes when I bought them."

"GenoME is a corrupt and dangerous organization," Judith interjected, "and we're part of a group that's been given the job of bringing it down."

"Which isn't going to be easy," Trader said. Suddenly his smile vanished, and its disappearance transformed his face. All at once he looked less like an advertisement for expensive aftershave, and more like someone with a formidable intellect. "Legally speaking, GenoME is ironclad," he added. "There's no obvious link to the Darkkon Empire—not one that you could take to court. If there had been, GenoME would have been torn inside out when Prosper English got arrested." Suddenly his dazzling smile was switched on again, warming the whole room. "But I probably don't need to tell *you* that," he breezily allowed. "You must be pretty familiar with the whole GenoME setup."

"Not really. No," Cadel answered. He was still pressed against the door, wary and watchful and poised for flight.

Trader raised a perfectly arched eyebrow.

"Oh, come on," he coaxed. "With your background, you can't be completely in the dark about GenoME, I'm sure."

Cadel swallowed. He felt an almost imperceptible chill.

"What do *you* know about my background?" he asked, trying not to sound as worried as he felt.

Trader didn't answer immediately. He seemed to enjoy dangling his secret in front of Cadel—the way a child might enjoy dangling a piece of wool in front of a kitten. At last, however, he teasingly remarked, "Heard from any old friends lately?"

Sonja's squawk made everyone else jump. When Cadel turned, he saw that she was writhing in the grip of a severe muscular spasm, brought on by her desperate need to communicate. But though she poked repeatedly at the DynaVox, she always missed her mark.

Cadel lunged for her hand and caught it just before it knocked against the arm of her wheelchair.

"It's all right," he assured her. "Don't worry, calm down." Then he swung back to confront Trader. "Com!" he said accusingly. "You've talked to Com!"

But Trader shook his head.

"No," he admitted. "Unfortunately not. We only used his name to attract your attention. It was his sister who first told us about you."

"His *sister*?" Cadel was astonished; he'd been unaware that Com had any family at all. But Trader wasn't about to expand on the subject of Com's sister. There were other, more important things to discuss.

"His sister, yes. Of course she didn't know much, but what she did know was very interesting. And when we tracked you down through the police and welfare networks, we found out a lot more." Trader jerked his chin at Sonja. "About the pair of you, actually. We've been monitoring Sonja's e-mail—which is how we knew you were coming here today."

"So *you* were the one inside Hazel's machine?" Cadel was following his own train of thought, back to the mysterious cookie. It all made sense now. "*You* designed that program?"

"Not personally, no," Trader replied. "A kid called Hamish did it. You'll like him—he's in our group."

Cadel, however, wasn't interested in Hamish. Hamish hadn't been enrolled at the Axis Institute. "Com's sister," he said sharply. "Can I talk to her?"

Trader shrugged. "Maybe," he replied. "She's part of our group."

"Does she know where Com is?"

"I wish." Trader heaved a regretful sigh. "We none of us know where to find Com. If we did, we'd have him on board as well. I gather he's a bit of a whiz."

"Com studied at the Axis Institute." Cadel was thinking aloud, more for Sonja's benefit than for any other reason. He squeezed her crooked fingers. "Com would be able to corroborate my story. He could talk to Detective Greeniaus!"

"Ah. Yes. Now here's the thing, Cadel." Trader once again took charge of the conversation. "We know you're being pestered by the police. It's why we've had to approach you in such a roundabout way," he said. "Judging by all the activity on Hazel's system, I'm assuming you must have mentioned our encoded message to the authorities?"

"Yes." Cadel's tone was defensive. So was his body language. He released Sonja's hand and folded his arms. "Why? Is that a problem?" he asked, with a sarcastic edge to his voice.

"Oh, no," Trader assured him. "We expected you to do something of the sort. In fact we were *hoping* you would, because we wanted the police to get really nervous about leaving you at the Donkins' house." He assumed a very earnest mien. "But from now on, Cadel, we'd prefer it if you stopped shooting your mouth off like that. There's no point, since we don't mean you any harm."

"Prove it," said Cadel. He was growing alarmed at all this talk about covert operations. "Who are you exactly? You're not the police, I can see that—"

"Can you? Thank god!" Trader wiped his brow with comical emphasis. "So my shoes can't be *that* awful!"

"I told you who we are," Judith weighed in. "We're part of a private group of network infiltration specialists. Our job is to investigate GenoME. We have to find out how it's been breaking the law, and bring it to justice."

"Judith is our forensic accountant," Trader explained, his white teeth gleaming. "She's in charge of following money trails and disentangling company structures. We're hoping that she might uncover a few questionable activities in GenoME's financial records."

"But we can't do that unless we get into its computer system," Judith finished.

Both she and Trader stared at Cadel: Trader with a seductive smile; Judith with a serious expression on her face.

Cadel glanced from one to the other.

"And that's where I come in, is it?" he said flatly. Whereupon Trader gave a brisk nod. His casual pose was slightly undermined by his keen gaze and set jaw.

"We need your computer skills," he confirmed. "You'd be working with our network infiltration team. And Sonja would be useful in our forensic accounting team, because of her mathematical abilities."

Cadel's eyes found Sonja's. She was watching him just as closely as the two adults were. Nothing in her eager attitude suggested that she doubted the truth of Trader's claim.

But then again, she hadn't been brought up by Prosper English. She hadn't been raised to question everything she'd ever heard.

"GenoME is based in the U.S.," Cadel objected, turning back to Trader. "I can't go to the States, and neither can she."

"Hell, no!" Judith exclaimed, as if she could imagine nothing more abhorrent than a trip to the United States. Her tone seemed to amuse her colleague, whose smile widened into a grin.

"GenoME's security in America is impenetrable," Trader informed Cadel. "We haven't been able to infiltrate the company on any level—not over there. But when we found out that GenoMe was planning to open a new branch in Australia, we saw our chance." Trader must have realized that his words had struck a chord with Cadel, because he continued in a more jaunty and confident manner. "Security is always shaky in a new operation—as you probably know," he said. "That's why we're concentrating on the Australian subsidiary. That's why we've set up a special investigative team Down Under."

"*And-they-don't-mind-having-kids-like-us-on-the-team,*" Sonja finally interjected, through the agency of her DynaVox.

The fact that she'd managed to communicate at all was something of a relief to Cadel; it meant that she was calming down. Before he could comment on this, however, Judith reached over and patted her arm.

"Of course we don't mind," said Judith, robustly. And Trader jumped in with his own contribution.

"What we've discovered is that some of the people we need for this job are under eighteen," he pointed out. "I don't know why; maybe you just have to grow up with computers to really understand them." He winked at Cadel. "But it makes things rather difficult for us, because we're trying to keep a low profile. This is an unofficial investigation, you see. On the one hand, we don't trust the police to keep their mouths shut, and on the other hand . . ." He spread his hands, in a roguish sort of way. "Well, let's just say that certain surveillance activities aren't legal unless you have a warrant. And how can you get the evidence you need for a warrant, unless you go poking around a bit first?"

"So—"

"So," Trader went on, finishing Cadel's sentence for him, "if we have to use spyware, or illegal hacking techniques, or anything of that nature, we don't want to be worrying about police interference. That's why we need to keep our operations private."

But this was more easily said than done. According to Trader, employing "a bunch of kids" for top secret activities had caused any number of problems. It had soon become apparent that a house full of teenagers would attract the attention of neighbors and social workers. Questions would be asked. Objections would be raised.

"So we came up with a clever idea," Trader revealed. "We thought that if we disguised our headquarters as a youth refuge called Clearview House, and our adult team as social workers, no one would start wondering what we were up to."

"And it's worked," Judith interposed.

"And it's worked." A satisfied nod from Trader. "Our kids can live at Clearview House. They can spend all the time they want in the basement—which is where we keep our technology. We call it the War

Room." He leaned forward, and his smile became positively alluring as he rubbed his hands together. "You won't believe what we can do, Cadel. We've got the biggest collection of gigabytes you've ever seen."

Cadel swallowed. His mouth was almost watering at the prospect of all that computer hardware; he longed to see it. Yet he was determined not to be sweet-talked into anything dangerous. *Certainly* not if it involved Sonja.

He searched Trader's finely modeled features for any hint of deceit. The good-humored smile and friendly crow's-feet were reassuring enough, but what about that supremely confident intelligence lurking behind the brilliant green eyes? Could that be trusted?

"The police follow me, you know," Cadel finally announced. "They sit outside Hazel's house in unmarked cars."

"I realize that." Trader remained serene. "Like I told you before, we've been trawling through their network."

"And that wouldn't be a problem? Having the police around all the time?"

"It's been factored into our arrangements."

"Why?" Cadel's scrutiny shifted to Judith. He surveyed her with a frankly skeptical look. "Why put up with that kind of risk, just for my sake?"

Taken by surprise, Judith blinked, and glanced at her colleague. Then she uttered a shaky little laugh, and said, "I guess you're worth the trouble."

"Because of what I can do? Or because of who I am?" Cadel rounded on Trader. "I've told you, I hardly know anything about GenoME. And I wouldn't dream of asking Prosper English about it, because he and I don't communicate."

"Cadel—," Trader began. But Cadel hadn't finished.

"Or is there something else you were hoping to use me for? Bait, perhaps?" Cadel decided to lay his cards on the table. He was sick of being pushed around. Of being underestimated. "Because I think you're probably right," he went on. "I think GenoME *is* dangerous. I think the world would be better off without it. But not at my expense. Not with me as bait."

Trader shook his head. "We don't want to put you at risk," he insisted. And Cadel gave a snort.

"Oh, please. Do you think I'm a fool?" Glimpsing Sonja's restless movements from the corner of his eye, he gripped her fluttering hand again. "Don't try and tell me that you haven't wondered what would happen if the head of GenoME ever found out where I was."

As Trader pondered this remark, Judith butted in with a question of her own. She sounded genuinely curious.

"What do *you* think he would do?" she asked.

"He wouldn't want to kill me, if that's what you're wondering," said Cadel. "I know nothing about his business. And I don't have any claim to it, since I'm not Dr. Darkkon's legal heir. So I'm no threat to Earl Toffany at all. There's no reason on earth why he should break the law just to get rid of me."

"Then there's no need to worry about our motives. Is there?" Trader blithely queried. Whereupon Cadel fixed him with a somber look.

"Yes, there is. Because Prosper English *is* a threat to Earl." Cadel couldn't help assuming that Trader, at least, must have worked this out already. So his tone was impatient. Grudging. "Prosper knows all about GenoME. If he hadn't been arrested, he would have taken over the company after Dr. Darkkon died. And if he ever gets out, he'll try to do just that. Which probably isn't something that Earl Toffany wants to happen. Why should he?" Cadel felt the vibration of Sonja's involuntary muscular spasms through his fingers, and tightened his grip. "On the other hand, if Prosper *doesn't* get out, he might try to cut a deal with the authorities by telling them everything he knows about GenoME. Either way, Earl Toffany would be in trouble. So he'd be looking for ways to threaten Prosper."

"Ah." Trader inclined his head, as if the penny had dropped. "So what you're saying is—"

"What I'm saying is that maybe you *want* Earl to kidnap me! Because if you catch him breaking the law, it'll help you to bring down GenoME!"

"Ingenious idea," Trader had to confess, with a kind of rueful admiration. But Judith colored. Her brows snapped together.

"For Chris'sake, what do you think we are?" she protested. "As if we'd ever consider something like that!"

"You might. Why not? I don't know you. You could be anyone." Before she had a chance to defend herself, Cadel turned to glare at Trader. "You could be working for Prosper English. You could have made everything up, just to get me into your car!"

For some reason, Trader was hugely diverted by this proposal. He began to laugh, much to Judith's annoyance.

"It's not funny," she growled.

"Yes, it is. What a mind!" Trader leaned across and slapped Cadel on the back, still chortling irrepressibly. "If I was working for Prosper English, kid, I wouldn't be driving a car," Trader quipped. "I'd be driving a Humvee. Or maybe a secondhand Batmobile."

"We don't work for Prosper English." Judith broke into Trader's fanciful repartee with obvious impatience. "We work for Rex Austin."

"Who?" said Cadel, mystified.

And then his cell phone rang.

TEN

As Cadel reached into his jacket, Trader delivered himself of a rapid and fervently argued appeal.

"That might be the police," Trader said. "If it is, could you stall them? Just until we're finished. Then you can decide what to do." He took a step backward and plucked a large yellow envelope from Sonja's desk. "How can you draw a valid conclusion if you haven't got all the data?" he queried, waving the envelope temptingly under Cadel's nose.

Cadel hesitated. His gaze traveled from the envelope to Trader's smooth, vivid face and back again. Then he looked at Sonja, whose tongue was churning anxiously behind her teeth.

Then, after a moment's quiet reflection, he answered the call.

"Hello?" he said.

"Cadel?" It was Saul. *"Are you all right?"*

"Yeah. I'm fine."

"Who's there with you?"

"How did you know—"

"WHO IS IT, CADEL?"

Conscious of Trader's bright-eyed regard, Cadel said slowly, "Just a couple of social workers." And he saw Trader bite back a grin.

"I'll be there in a few minutes," Saul declared. *"Don't move. Don't go anywhere. Just stay put."* He broke the connection.

Startled, Cadel pulled the phone away from his ear and stared at it.

"We don't have much time," Trader announced. He thrust the yellow envelope at Cadel, who couldn't examine its contents until he had released Sonja and pocketed his mobile. The envelope was stuffed with newspaper clippings, all of them about the mysterious Rex Austin. Apparently, Rex was an American oil and shipping magnate, worth billions of dollars. His grown-up son, Jimmy, had died in mysterious circumstances after becoming involved with the GenoME organization. Rex blamed GenoME for Jimmy's death.

In Rex's opinion, his son had been killed because, after investing millions in GenoME, Jimmy had grown disillusioned and had wanted to pull out. So far, however, Rex had been unable to prove that GenoME was responsible for killing Jimmy. The newspaper clippings reported that Rex had spent hundreds of thousands of dollars pursuing GenoME through the American courts, to no avail. But Rex had also vowed that he would never give up until the organization was brought to justice. And after studying his photograph, Cadel believed him.

Rex Austin was a lean, leathery, sun-whipped old man with the coldest eyes and hardest mouth that Cadel had ever seen.

"Our boss," Trader informed Cadel, flicking the photograph with one manicured fingernail. "He's unusually generous, for a wealthy man. If you join our team, Cadel, you'll receive a lump sum of fifty thousand dollars."

Cadel nearly dropped his envelope.

"Fifty thousand dollars?" he squawked.

"With an extra five thousand dollars a month if the job extends for more than three months," Judith hastened to add, in a manner that Trader seemed to find amusing. He grinned at her fondly.

"Judith deals with our pay packets," he said. "You'll have to discuss the tax implications with her—if you've got a week to spare."

His chuckle indicated that he was poking fun at Judith, who rolled her eyes. She didn't seem offended, though. "The tax system in this country is obscene," she informed Sonja, "but there are ways of avoiding it if you have to. I mean, why fund the programs of a morally bankrupt government?"

"Don't worry," said Trader, still grinning. "Judith has *never* been charged with tax evasion. She's too damn smart."

Cadel was growing tired of all this banter. It was clouding the issue. What he wanted was a straight answer to a straight question.

"You still haven't proved that you're on the level," he said. Whereupon Trader shrugged, philosophically.

"I'm telling the truth, Cadel," he declared. "This has nothing to do with Prosper English. Our job is simply to find out how GenoME might have been breaking the law, either by murdering people or by committing fraud or whatever. We did hope that you might be able to shed some light on the Darkkon Empire, but it's your hacking talents that really interest us. So if you want to join our team, we'd be grateful."

"And if you don't," Judith advised, "we'll pay you to keep your mouth shut. Five thousand dollars, paid over a three-month period."

As Cadel absorbed this startling information, Sonja began to spell out a question, laboriously, on her DynaVox.

"*Is-Clearview-House-convincing?*" she asked, and didn't need to elaborate. Trader seemed to understand exactly what she meant.

"Totally convincing," he assured her. "You can't fault the setup—it's been inspected half a dozen times."

"Shabby but not too shabby," Judith agreed. "That's the trick."

"Whatever you decide to do, you can call me on this number," Trader concluded, as if conscious of an imminent deadline (or an approaching policeman, perhaps). Reaching into the breast pocket of his stylish linen shirt, he pulled out a business card, which he surrendered to Cadel. "All you have to do is tell me if you're interested in moving to Clearview House. Or you can get your social worker to do it, if you'd prefer."

"I can understand how you feel," Judith assured Cadel, "but don't shoot yourself in the foot. I mean, you're surrounded by coppers. What *can* happen? Christ, we had a hard enough time getting a message through to you."

"Give it some thought, anyway." Trader didn't seem the least bit put out. On the contrary, he was smiling again as his gaze traveled from Cadel to Sonja. Gently he plucked the yellow envelope and its contents from

Cadel's hand. "I like the way you approach things," he said. "Every angle covered. It's a rare gift. We could do with more of it in Genius Squad."

"Genius Squad?"

"Our nickname," Trader divulged, with a laugh. Even Judith was smirking now. Smirking and shaking her head.

"Hamish thought it up," she said. "What a character."

"You'll have a lot of fun at Clearview House," Trader confirmed, lowering his voice as the distant *slap-slap-slap* of footsteps on linoleum reached their ears. "And you'll be doing the whole world a favor in the process. It's a win-win situation, I guarantee."

"But what about the police?" Cadel asked. "They're trying to trace that message you sent. What if they manage to do it?"

Trader's smile didn't flicker.

"Like I said, Cadel—we're Genius Squad," he replied, in a voice so low that it was barely a murmur. "The police haven't a hope in hell of tracking us down."

Suddenly the door sprang open, revealing Saul Greeniaus on the threshold. Behind him stood Mick Mattilos, the plainclothes officer. Both were slightly rumpled and breathing heavily.

Saul scanned the room at lightning speed.

"Sorry to interrupt," the detective remarked, his gaze snagging on Trader. "But I'm afraid this is an unauthorized meeting."

Trader blinked, and his smile vanished. It was replaced by a wounded look.

"I beg your pardon?" he said, as Judith rose. Then Saul caught sight of the card in Cadel's hand and twitched it away.

"I gather you're a social worker, Mr. . . . Lynch," the detective observed, reading out Trader's surname. "The staff here have informed me that you run some kind of kids' home?"

"Clearview House," Trader agreed. "We specialize in out-of-home care and shared-support accommodation. We've been contracted by the Department of Community Services to look after children like Sonja."

He nodded in her direction. "Our objective is to facilitate the emotional development and social integration of bright kids with dislocated backgrounds."

"I see," was Saul's rather flat response.

"And who might you be?" Judith demanded, folding her arms. Cadel decided that her mulish demeanor and eccentric clothes made her a far more convincing social worker than Trader, who was too well dressed. Saul certainly seemed to think so, at any rate. His manner became notably less hostile as he answered Judith's question.

"I'm Detective Inspector Saul Greeniaus," he said. "I'm here because Cadel is under twenty-four-hour surveillance. Can I please have *your* name, ma'am?"

"Not until I see some identification," Judith retorted huffily. "And don't call me ma'am. I'm not the queen."

Even Sonja snorted at that one. Trader smothered a smile. Saul studied both their faces, in an appraising fashion, while he produced his identification for Judith. Then he addressed Sonja.

"You must be Sonja Pirovic," he said. "I'm very pleased to meet you." He reached for her hand, his fingers closing over hers with such delicacy that he might have been trying to capture a butterfly. "Sorry to bust in like this. But I guess you must understand the situation."

"*I* certainly don't," Trader complained. "We're totally aboveboard, Detective. Clearview House is regulated by the New South Wales Children's Guardian Office. We've been approved by the Association of Children's Welfare Agencies. You can check with them both—we've every right to be here."

"No, you don't," Saul bluntly replied. "You need an AFP clearance to approach Cadel, and it has to come through DoCS via his caseworker—"

"But we weren't approaching Cadel!" Judith pointed out. "We came here to visit Sonja!" She went on to explain that Sonja had requested a transfer to more suitable accommodations, and that Clearview House was a possible alternative to Sonja's present address. "We've got everything she might need in the way of special facilities," Judith said, counting these features off on one hand. "Ramps. Handrails. Renovated bathroom. It's ideal for her."

"And for Cadel," Trader hazarded, replacing his injured expression with something far more genial and benign. "I don't know if you're aware of this, Detective, but several submissions have been made to DoCS on Cadel's behalf," he said. "Apparently there's a wide-ranging belief that his current circumstances aren't exactly ideal."

"I know." Saul's tone gave nothing away. "I made one of those submissions myself."

"Oh, did you?" Trader's high-voltage smile had a visible effect on the detective, who drew back, startled. Wearing such a smile, Trader resembled a soap-opera star on the cover of a glossy magazine. "Well, isn't that extraordinary? First Cadel turns up, and now you," Trader said. "If his caseworker were with us, we could make our arrangements right here!"

"But only if Cadel is interested in moving to Clearview House," Judith amended.

"Well, yes. That goes without saying." Trader beamed at Cadel before fixing his attention once more on Saul Greeniaus. The effect, Cadel thought, was rather like being caught in a spotlight; when Trader flashed his shiny white teeth at you, it was hard not to shade your eyes. "Though I gather there's some sense of urgency attached to this particular submission?" Trader inquired. "I seem to recall it was red-flagged—"

"Cadel has some very special requirements," the detective interrupted. "Whether your facility can satisfy them or not will be a matter for his caseworker to decide—once various other factors have been given due consideration."

"Yes, of course," said Trader.

"It shouldn't take long," Saul allowed. He cut a quick glance at Cadel. "There have been certain developments . . . certain breaches of security . . ." Saul hesitated. Cadel knew exactly what he was referring to. Clearly, Saul had been greatly alarmed by the message from Com. "If we could expedite matters, that would be helpful," the detective concluded, "but not to the point where Cadel's safety is compromised. What I suggest, Mr. Lynch, is that you proceed with your application, *through the correct channels,* while I have a word with Cadel's caseworker. Perhaps we can find a solution that will meet with everyone's approval."

"I certainly hope we do," said Trader, as if nothing in the world would please him more. Almost immediately, however, he attached a proviso that was practically a veiled threat. "We would very much appreciate a speedy response, however," he added, "because there's such a high demand for the kind of services we provide. And I'd hate for Cadel to miss out."

"*So-would-I,*" Sonja volunteered, unexpectedly. Everyone stared at her. Even Cadel was taken aback.

Don't tell me she's made up her mind, he thought.

"Well . . . I'll do what I can," was the detective's promise, offered up after a long pause. Then he turned back to Trader, reaching into his jacket as he did so. "In the meantime—and I hope you don't take this the wrong way, Mr. Lynch—but I would appreciate it if you'd notify me personally before you or any of the other Clearview House staff come here again." He produced one of his cards, which Trader accepted with every manifestation of sunny goodwill. "Cadel often visits Sonja, and I wouldn't want there to be any unfortunate misunderstandings."

Judith pulled a face. "Talk about Big Brother," she grumbled. But Saul didn't appear to take offense. Instead he observed quietly, "I don't believe you mentioned your name, ma'am."

So Judith was forced to introduce herself, while Trader examined Saul's card with a glint in his eye. That giveaway glint was the only crack that Cadel had so far witnessed in Trader's otherwise flawless facade; in every other respect, Trader came across as a gregarious, jovial, backslapping enthusiast.

His movie-star smile was flashing again when he thrust his right hand at the detective—who, though taken by surprise, recovered quickly. Their palms met in a civil enough farewell, even if Saul did seem a trifle bemused by Trader's energetic pumping action.

"We don't want to create problems for you, Detective," Trader declared, "so we'll take our leave now, as a demonstration of our desire to cooperate. Nevertheless, I'm sure we'll meet again very soon—and in more favorable conditions, I hope."

Saul grunted.

"I'm quite convinced you'll find Clearview House a satisfactory option for Cadel," Trader continued. "Our policy is to have one adult supervisor per child at all times, except on night shift. And we try to encourage a lot of staff/resident interaction, so that the children have constant access to carefully screened role models."

"We're just like one big family," Judith interposed, as if she meant it. Saul didn't look impressed. But Trader did; he bestowed a lustrous smile on his colleague, very briefly, before focusing his attention on the only other female in the room.

"Good-bye, Sonja. It's been a real pleasure. Good-bye, Cadel. Have a think about what I said." Moving toward the door, Trader clapped Cadel on the shoulder as he passed. "Come on, Judith. I get the feeling that we'd better clear out, don't you? No point treading on official toes."

Judith sniffed, but complied. Saul stepped aside to let her leave. Before she had crossed the threshold, however, he said, "I'll have Detective Constable Mattilos show you both out."

The last thing Cadel heard from Sonja's visitors was the sound of Judith's scornful muttering, as she and Trader and their plainclothes escort trudged away down the corridor.

"I have to apologize," Saul remarked, almost formally, upon turning to Sonja. "They should never have got in here. There was a procedural glitch—we weren't notified when they first arrived, because they had official visitor clearance from DoCS. It was Mick who picked up on what was happening."

"There's-no-need-to-apologize," Sonja insisted, using her DynaVox with unexpected agility. And Cadel said, "We were glad to hear about Clearview House. It sounds like it might be a good idea."

"You think so, do you?" The detective's grave regard aroused uneasy feelings in Cadel, who made his eyes very big, and his mouth very small, as he presented his defiant rebuttal.

"Well, I'd rather live with Sonja than with Mace," he said. "Anyway, don't you *want* me to move? That guy—Mr. Lynch—he was talking about how you've been trying to get me out of the Donkins'." Seeing Saul hesitate, Cadel took advantage of the detective's obvious unease to shift the subject slightly. "I mean, *someone* sure knows I'm living there, or I wouldn't have got that message. Have you worked out who sent it yet?"

"No," Saul had to admit. But he wouldn't be distracted. "So you'd prefer to live at this youth-refuge place?" he queried. "Is that what you're telling me?"

"I don't know," Cadel replied. And he didn't. There hadn't been time to make a decision.

He hadn't yet analyzed all the available data.

"Maybe you two need to talk about it," Saul suggested, looking from Cadel to Sonja and back again. "I'm gonna have to discuss it with Ms. Currey, that's for sure. It strikes me as a peculiar kind of setup." His voice didn't change as he adroitly switched directions. "By the way," he said, "what was in that yellow envelope? Did he show you?"

"No," Cadel answered, without a second's thought. Only later, when Saul was driving him back to the Donkins', did it occur to Cadel that the detective might have been setting a trap. What if Saul should seek out Trader and ask him the same question? What if Trader's response proved to be different from Cadel's?

What if the detective started to smell something fishy as a consequence?

It will only matter, Cadel concluded, *if I decide to join Genius Squad. If I don't, I'll just tell the truth.*

And he stared out the car window, fretting away with feverish concentration behind a perfectly tranquil, sweetly disarming countenance.

PART TWO

ELEVEN

Cadel sat in Fiona's car, heading for Clearview House.

He was still worried about visiting the place. Though he and Sonja had spent hours discussing Trader's proposition, he couldn't help feeling that they had made the wrong choice—simply because it was the obvious one to make. Why *not* choose Clearview House? It was full of like-minded people and cutting-edge technology. It was frequented by Com's sister, who might have some idea of her brother's whereabouts. Best of all, it came with a salary. Fifty thousand dollars for three months' work! And five thousand a month after that! How could anyone with even half a brain turn down such an offer?

Cadel viewed the money as a kind of insurance. Even if Clearview House closed its doors, he and Sonja would have enough put by for Sonja's care, at least. That was the important thing. Cadel's own future was so hazy that there wasn't much point fretting about it; for all he knew, he might be in another country by the end of the year, and out of Sonja's reach. So he was determined that, if she did end up in a nasty little house full of people who didn't understand her, she would have the funds to pay for a full-time attendant with a cheerful personality and an interest in mathematics.

He had said as much to Sonja, though he hadn't mentioned going away. She found the subject too upsetting. They had agreed that the money was a big plus. They had also agreed that living in the same house would be a definite advantage. (Sonja had called it "a dream come true.")

They had discussed all the possible drawbacks of the scheme—unknown housemates, questionable practices, lying to the authorities.

"I-don't-like-breaking-laws," Sonja had said. *"But-tapping-phones-and-intercepting-mail-isn't-too-bad. Especially-if-it-stops-more-people-getting-killed."*

"And we can make sure things don't get *too* illegal," Cadel had remarked, trying to salve his own unsettled conscience. "We can go to the police if we're concerned."

"Because-the-police-will-always-be-around." Fighting a wearisome battle against her own capricious and wilful body, Sonja had finally tapped out an exhausted *"We-won't-be-in-danger-if-the-police-are-tailing-you."*

Sonja's heart had been working against her head; Cadel understood this only too well. She was so desperate to share a house with him, and to spend time with mathematically inclined people, that she was willing to overlook all her niggling little doubts. Cadel was the same. Apart from anything else, he couldn't bear to see her disappointed again—because disappointment had so far been her lot in life. Having been born with cerebral palsy, abandoned by her parents, and stuck in a series of state-run institutions like an unwanted package, she was overdue for a bit of good luck.

So Cadel had decided in favor of Clearview House. Nevertheless, something about it disturbed him. He felt that the people running it might have a secret agenda. He couldn't quite believe everything that he'd been told; all his instincts were prompting him to be cautious. But were those instincts reliable? Or had they been warped by his childhood training?

If only I could calculate the probabilities, Cadel thought, as he sat in Fiona's car. Alas, however, his algorithms were useless, simply because he didn't have enough data about Clearview House and its occupants. There were too many variables.

"Here we are," Fiona announced. With a grinding of gears, she pulled up in front of a big iron gate in a high brick wall. Treetops were visible above the wall; through the gate, Cadel could see a gravel drive leading to something that looked like an Edwardian mansion. "This must be Clearview House," Fiona said. "I wonder how we're supposed to get in?"

"There's an intercom," Cadel pointed out. He was on the verge of suggesting that he should look for a button when the gates began to open automatically, swinging slowly apart on well-oiled hinges.

"Goodness," said Fiona, with a frown. "This is all very elaborate."

Cadel wondered where the security camera had been installed.

As they drove into the grounds, Cadel realized that the gates had been slightly misleading. Though Clearview House was big, it had definitely seen better days. Its gutters were rusty and its paint was peeling. Something fuzzy and green was growing on one of its chimneys. Apart from a few straggly, overgrown flower beds, its garden was all unkempt grass and disintegrating asphalt.

Shabby but not too shabby. Cadel remembered Judith's comment. Peering at what looked like a bedsheet hanging in one of the bay windows, he couldn't help thinking that Trader and his friends had overdone the shabbiness.

But Fiona seemed to find this rundown aspect reassuring. More reassuring, at least, than the silently welcoming gates.

"Well," she said, with a cheerfulness that was only a little bit forced, "it's certainly not cramped." And she stopped near the front steps.

Cadel unbuckled his seat belt. They both climbed out of the car and approached the house, which was three stories high, with all kinds of gables and verandas and bits of fretwork trimming. Two other vehicles were parked near the entrance: a battered blue van and a rather sleek four-wheel drive.

Cadel made a mental note of their license plate numbers. He also scanned the facade of the house for signs of electronic surveillance—and was pleased to discover an almost invisible wire running along one pediment. If there were any cameras, however, they were well disguised. Extremely well disguised.

A bicycle and a canvas hammock were cluttering up the front porch.

Fiona's knock was answered immediately. The door swung open to reveal Trader, looking lean and tanned and remarkably well groomed. Fiona's jaw dropped. Though she quickly tried to conceal her amazement, his chiseled features and Hollywood smile had a very obvious effect on her. She lost every trace of self-confidence, groping for her handbag and stammering out a feeble explanation.

"It's Cadel. And me. I'm Fiona. Currey."

"Yes, of course. We've been expecting you. I'm Trader Lynch. How do you do, Ms. Currey?"

"We're here to see if we like the look of this place."

"I know. Come in."

As he ushered her inside, Trader directed a surreptitious wink at Cadel. Then he swept them both into a large and lofty room, which occupied most of the front part of the house. Although this room had ornate ceilings and enormous windows, it was very shabby, with scuffed floors and scarred woodwork. It contained three battered couches, a beanbag chair, a television set, a DVD player, a bookshelf, and a coffee table heaped with old magazines, dirty cups, compact disks, and tangles of earphones.

It also contained two people. One, a teenaged boy, was slumped in the beanbag chair, reading a computer magazine. His feet were dirty, and a black woolen beanie was pulled down low on his head, concealing his hair color. He wore olive green cargo pants and a drab zippered sweatshirt, both so baggy that it was hard to judge his build. But whether thin or fat, he was certainly very pale. And he had terrible acne.

Opposite him, on the couch, sat a heavy teenaged girl with a pierced lip and eyebrow. She was dressed all in black. Even her hair was black. Though she had the same small dark eyes and plump cheeks as her companion, her skin was much better than his.

The impression that she conveyed was a restless one, because she was simultaneously chewing gum, painting her toenails, and humming through her nose.

The humming stopped when she saw the new arrivals.

"This is Lexi," Trader announced, gesturing at her. "And this is her twin brother, Devin. Lexi, this is Cadel Piggott. I told you about him."

There was a moment's silence. Devin didn't even look up. Lexi stared, her face a mask of astonishment. Then she burst into delighted giggles.

"Oh, man!" she exclaimed. "He's so *cute*!"

"And this is Cadel's caseworker, Ms. Currey."

"Hello," said Fiona.

But Lexi was interested only in Cadel.

"He's such a little doll!" she yelped, ignoring Fiona. "Can I keep him? Please? I won't break him, I promise!"

"Behave yourself, Lexi." Addressing her brother, Trader added, "Aren't you going to say hello?"

Devin grunted, still not looking up. Lexi, however, jumped to her feet—with such energy and enthusiasm that the floor shook.

"Are you showing them around?" she asked. "Can I come, too?"

Trader glanced at Cadel, wearing an apologetic half smile. Cadel hesitated. Though he found Lexi intimidating, he didn't want to admit it.

"Sure," he mumbled. "She can come if she wants."

"So this is the lounge room?" Fiona interrupted—rather stupidly, Cadel thought. But perhaps she was trying to distract Lexi, who was still devouring him with her eyes.

"Yes, this is the lounge room," Trader confirmed, retracing his steps into the hallway. "And down here, behind it, we've got Sonja's bedroom—with attached bathroom—and beyond that is the kitchen . . ."

Heading toward the back of the house, he pointed out various newly installed ramps and handrails, while Fiona stumbled along beside him and Cadel brought up the rear. They passed a sweeping staircase, then turned right. Lexi kept nudging against Cadel as they walked.

"I can't believe you're fifteen," she said. "You look about ten. Have you really finished school already?"

"We've widened the door here, and all the switches and controls are on one remote circuit," Trader continued, advancing into Sonja's room. It was very big and furnished with a brand-new desk, bed, chair, and built-in wardrobe. "We turned this parlor next door into a bathroom, so it's nice and big," Trader went on, proudly indicating an enviable array of fixtures, fittings, taps, and tiles. (Cadel couldn't wait to tell Sonja about them.) "And she'll be right next to the kitchen," Trader finished, "so everything will be within easy reach . . ."

"Is she a friend of yours? This spastic girl?" Lexi asked Cadel, in a low voice. "Judith says she's supersmart."

"She is," Cadel said shortly. They were now back in the hallway and moving toward the kitchen, which lay at the rear of the house. Cadel could smell food cooking. He wasn't surprised when, upon entering a spacious room full of pine cupboards, they found a man stooped over a six-burner stove. This man was wrapped in an apron and stirring the contents of a massive steel pot.

"Meet Zac Stillman, one of our trained youth counselors. He's on lunch duty." Trader surveyed the unoccupied chairs and deserted sink. "Where's Hamish?" he asked the cook. "Isn't he rostered on today?"

Zac turned, wiping his hands on his apron. Tall and thin and bearded, he wore his blond hair tied back in a ponytail. Everything on him appeared to be tie-dyed, except his sandals. Cadel judged him to be somewhere in his thirties.

"Hamish is upstairs." Zac's voice was as gentle as his placid face and washed-out blue eyes. "I've asked him twice, and he keeps saying he just has to finish one more thing."

"Don't ask him again," Lexi pleaded, loudly and plaintively. "We'll all die of food poisoning." Leaning toward Cadel, she screwed up her little pug nose. "Do you know what he did last time? He tried to cook chicken schnitzels in the toaster."

"I seem to recall *you* once tried to feed us hot-dog soup, Lexi," Zac remarked, and extended a damp, red hand. "You must be Cadel," he said. "Welcome to Clearview."

Suddenly the doorbell rang. Everyone seemed surprised—even Trader. When Fiona assured him that she hadn't invited anyone else along, he pursed his lips and told her to stay put for a moment. "I'll just go and see who it is," he said, training his radiant smile on her. But Cadel saw him shoot a quick glance at Zac, who gave an almost imperceptible nod.

Clearly, life at Clearview House wasn't as casual as it might appear.

"I want to find out what you think of your room," Lexi informed Cadel, as they listened to the sound of Trader's receding footsteps. "Because I helped Judith fix it up."

"Oh. Thanks," said Cadel.

"You're right on the top floor. Next to Hamish," Lexi added, in tones of commiseration. "He snores, but he doesn't smell. Much."

Cadel didn't know what to say to this, so he said nothing. During the silence that followed, he could hear a faint rumble of voices. One belonged to Trader; the other was flat and deep, with a distinctive Canadian accent.

Cadel recognized it instantly.

"That's Saul!" Fiona exclaimed, before he could open his mouth. "What's *he* doing here?"

She hurried from the room, her heels rapping out an urgent rhythm. Cadel was about to pursue her when Lexi grabbed his arm, detaining him.

"Who's Saul?" Lexi demanded.

"He's a detective," said Cadel, trying to pull away. Zac winced.

"Oh, no! The fuzz!" Lexi cried. She struck a theatrical pose of exaggerated alarm, throwing up her hands and allowing Cadel to break free. He hurried into the hallway, aware that Lexi was right behind him. Saul, he could see, was at the foot of the staircase, conversing with Trader. The detective looked terribly neat and formal in his dark suit. He stood stiffly, his face very serious, while Trader lounged against the balusters, smiling and joking and waving his hands about.

When Cadel appeared, Saul inclined his head.

"Hello, Cadel," he murmured, interrupting Trader's description of the Clearview schedule. "I hope you don't mind, but I came to check this place out myself."

Cadel shrugged, pretending to be unconcerned. "I don't mind," he said. "Why should I?"

"Ms. Currey mentioned you were coming," Saul continued. "I

thought I'd better make sure that you were going to be safe on this little tour."

"Oh, you don't have to worry about his *safety,* Detective," Trader joked. "We keep all our velociraptors under lock and key in this establishment. House rules." Struck by a sudden thought, he laid a friendly hand on Saul's shoulder. "Speaking of house rules, would you like a copy of our mission statement? I gave one to Ms. Currey, but I'd be happy for you to see it."

"I've seen it," Saul replied, shaking off Trader's clasp. At that moment, Devin appeared at the door of the front room. After briefly contemplating the boy's bare feet and sullen slouch, Saul locked gazes with him—until Devin yielded, glancing away.

Lexi said, in strident tones, "It's the fuzz, Dev, you'd better hide your spliffs!" And she manufactured a vicious sneer as Saul studied her.

"You must be Alexis Wieneke," he said, to Lexi's obvious surprise. Fiona frowned, and Trader's smile became slightly starched looking.

"I see you've been doing some research," he commented. "I suppose it's understandable."

"There isn't much on file." Saul's manner was calm but authoritative. "That's why I came. To see for myself."

"And is there anywhere you'd like to start?" Trader inquired, with just the faintest edge to his voice. "What can I do to set your mind at rest, Mr. Greeniaus?"

"Not a lot," Saul admitted. "I'm not paid to be satisfied." He laid a hand on Cadel's shoulder, in a pointed fashion. As if he were marking out his territory. "Maybe we should start with Cadel's room."

"Very well. Cadel's room it is," said Trader. And he began to climb the stairs.

TWELVE

Though Trader's ultimate destination was the top floor, he didn't head straight for Cadel's room. On the contrary, he made a slight detour when he reached the first landing. "Just wait one moment," he requested, "while I have a word with Hamish." And he strode toward the front of the house, where the old master bedroom had been stocked with computers, dartboards, stereo equipment, and a half-sized pool table.

None of this equipment was new, but it seemed to be in working order.

"Hamish!" said Trader, upon reaching the door of the games room. Peering past him, Cadel could see someone seated in front of a glowing monitor, tapping away at a keyboard. Galvanized by Trader's greeting, this bowed figure straightened and spun around on the pivot of an armless office chair.

Cadel felt a twinge of dismay when he saw Hamish. While the twins looked convincingly like juvenile delinquents, Hamish did not. He was a juvenile, all right; Cadel judged him to be about fifteen. But despite his studded leather jacket, grubby bandana, and enormous biker's boots, Hamish didn't make a credible delinquent. He had the glasses, the braces, the bleached skin, and the springy, unmanageable hair of a stereotypical computer geek.

His knobbly hands seemed far too big for the rest of him.

"Hamish," said Trader, "aren't you supposed to be helping out in the kitchen?"

"Uh . . . yeah." Hamish pushed his glasses up his long, straight nose.

His nails were bitten down to the quick. His wobbly voice occasionally tripped up on a stammer. "I just have to d-do this first."

"Get down there, Hamish," Trader said sternly. "I won't tell you again."

"And don't boil eggs in the electric jug this time!" Lexi warned, from behind Cadel's shoulder. Glancing in her direction, Hamish narrowed his smoky gray eyes. He had spotted Cadel.

"Are you the new kid?" he asked.

"Yes," said Cadel.

"This is Cadel Piggott," said Trader, "and this is Ms. Currey, his case-worker, and Detective Inspector Greeniaus."

Hamish goggled at Saul, while Cadel scrutinized the computer screen. Even from a distance, Cadel could recognize a fully operational PIN scan when he saw one.

Saul, however, obviously couldn't.

"What are you doing here?" Hamish demanded of Saul, blankly incredulous. "Are you the bodyguard?"

"In a manner of speaking," Saul replied.

"You mean you're going to *stay*?" Hamish sounded so appalled that Cadel couldn't help cringing. Fortunately, the detective didn't notice Cadel's reaction. He was staring at Hamish, one eyebrow raised.

Then Trader intervened.

"Go on, Hamish. Off you go," he said encouragingly. "Zac's waiting for you."

"Yeah, yeah. I'm going." Hamish began to rise, engineering a quick withdrawal from his Nmap program as he did so. Cadel decided not to ask him about intrusion-detection systems—not yet, anyway. Not until Saul Greeniaus had left.

Then Lexi nudged Cadel in the ribs.

"Do you want to see my room?" she queried.

"Uh—"

"Come on. It's right next door."

Tugging at his sleeve, she dragged him past the first-floor bathroom into what she called her boudoir, which had purple walls and a black ceiling studded with glow-in-the-dark constellations. It wasn't very tidy (there were great heaps of clothing, magazines, and CD covers everywhere) but Cadel immediately spotted some interesting books on her bookshelf, including *Computers and Intractability: A Guide to the Theory of NP Completeness.* These books looked very well thumbed. In fact one of them was practically falling apart. And they aroused within him a new respect for Lexi.

"That's a good book, isn't it? *Computers and Intractability*?" he said.

"Oh, yeah." She darted forward. "But I tell you what's even better. It's this new thing I picked up, about asymmetric ciphers . . . You wouldn't believe how good it is . . . Where the hell's it gone?"

As Lexi began to rifle through her bookshelf, pulling out volumes and casting them aside, Cadel glanced back to see Saul and Fiona hovering on the threshold. Saul's calm gaze moved swiftly and efficiently from one side of the room to the other, taking in the crucifix, the heart-shaped cushion, the black sateen duvet, the knitted unicorn.

Suddenly, a piercing shriek almost deafened Cadel. It was Lexi, screaming at her brother.

"DEVIN!" she yelled. *"WHERE'S MY NEW BOOK?"*

Even Saul flinched, shocked out of his professionally detached air. Lexi bolted past him into the room next door, which was labeled DEVIN ONLY—KEEP OUT. She began to throw her brother's things around, making a great deal of noise in her search for the missing book.

"Come on." Saul beckoned to Cadel. "Let's go upstairs."

Cadel hurriedly complied. He escaped just ahead of Trader, who was shaking his head ruefully; together they followed Saul and Fiona to the top-floor landing, where they almost collided with a middle-aged man dressed in a neatly pressed white shirt and gray trousers. The gurgle of plumbing announced that this man had just emerged from the upstairs bathroom.

"Ah! Tony!" said Trader. "Everyone, this is Tony Cheung. Tony, this is Cadel Piggott, and his caseworker, Ms. Currey. And this is Detective Inspector Greeniaus."

Tony smiled politely. With his slicked-back hair and gold-framed spectacles, he looked like a lawyer or an accountant. There was a silver pen tucked into his breast pocket, and a fancy watch strapped to his wrist. When he shook Cadel's hand—apparently oblivious to the banging and screeching just below them—he did it in a brisk, businesslike way, his palm warm and dry.

"Tony has a diploma in nursing as well as social work," Trader revealed. "Though he'll mainly be caring for Sonja, he's good with more wayward kids, too."

As if in response, a terrific clamor arose from downstairs. Cadel realized that the twins were battling over Lexi's missing book. Either Lexi had gone to confront Devin, or Devin had answered Lexi's summons; they were now locked in mortal combat. It was hard to distinguish one from the other, because they were both yelling like football hooligans.

"Excuse me," said Tony Cheung, in his light, pleasant, well-modulated voice. "I think perhaps I should intervene."

"Thanks, Tone." Trader spoke gratefully. "And make sure Hamish is in the kitchen, will you? I sent him down, but you know what he's like."

"Of course," said Tony, inclining his head. "Pleased to meet you, Cadel. Ms. Currey." Then he scooted off without a backward glance, his pace steady, his footsteps practically inaudible. Trader heaved a long-suffering sigh.

"Those two . . ." He groaned and gestured at a nearby door. "That will be your room, Cadel, right next to the office. We've put a couple of beds in the office for staff on shift work, but you'll find it's very peaceful up here. Even Hamish doesn't make much noise—not like those Wienekes." The words were hardly out of his mouth when the twins' racket abruptly stopped, as if someone had flipped a switch. Cadel could only assume that Tony Cheung had reached them. "If there's anything you don't like, just tell me," Trader added, leading the way into Cadel's bedroom. "I'm afraid Lexi had a bit of a hand in this, but we were very firm. We vetoed her offer to decorate the walls with famous graffiti tags."

Having seen Lexi's taste in interior decorating, Cadel was almost expecting to see bloodred paint or fluorescent curtains. To his relief, however, he found himself standing in a perfectly ordinary space, lit by one large window. Though the color scheme was uninspired, it wasn't offensive. And all the furnishings—including the built-in wardrobe, desk, chair, bed, and bookshelf—were brand-new.

"Goodness," said Fiona. "Aren't these lovely!"

"Aren't they?" Trader stroked the desktop like a furniture salesman. "Ash veneer. Lexi chose the lamp."

"It's nice," Cadel said, astonished that Lexi should have picked such an elegant, streamlined piece of equipment. He noted with approval the number of outlets (all newly wired, he felt certain) and the lock on the door. No one would be getting into *this* room without his permission.

"So what do you think?" Trader inquired. And Cadel turned to Fiona.

"When can I move in?" he said.

Trader laughed. Even Fiona smiled. But Saul remained impassive.

"You can move in anytime," said Trader. "Tonight, if you want."

"Perhaps we ought to discuss things first," Fiona suggested, and Trader agreed.

"Take your time," he told Cadel. "Get a feel for the place. I just have to duck down and see that everything's in order." He offered everyone his toothpaste-advertisement grin. "Give me a yell when you're done," was his advice. "I'll probably be in the kitchen, showing Hamish how to crack eggs."

And he made for the door, still smiling. Before he could cross the threshold, however, Saul Greeniaus detained him with a question.

"I checked with DoCS," he said, "and they gave me a list of names. One of those names was Hamish Primrose. Is that the Hamish we just saw?"

"Yes," said Trader, as Cadel caught his breath in disbelief.

"Would he be the same Hamish Primrose who hacked into the Digital

Image Department of the Roads and Traffic Authority?" asked Saul. Whereupon Trader's smile became a little lopsided.

"You remember that, do you?" He shrugged. "It was a long time ago."

It *had* been a long time ago: two years, to be exact. Cadel recalled the incident vividly. Details of the attack had been all over the Internet: Hamish had been tampering with speed-camera photographs, altering the MD5 hash of each shot. There had even been newspaper coverage. But the name of the offender had been withheld.

"I thought Hamish Primrose came from a privileged background." Saul pressed on, remorselessly. "What's he doing in a place like this, if he's got wealthy parents?"

Trader opened his mouth to reply. It was Fiona, however, who answered for him. Her cheeks were flushed and her tone was sharp.

"I don't see how that's any of your business," she scolded, addressing Saul. "These kids aren't under suspicion of any crimes, are they?"

"No," Saul was forced to concede, "but—"

"Then, if you have a question, you should go through the proper channels," Fiona concluded. "Even children have a right to their privacy, Mr. Greeniaus!"

This unexpected broadside had a visible effect on Saul. He stood for a moment, pondering, while Trader glanced from his face to Fiona's and back again. Trader seemed impressed. There was a twinkle in his eyes.

Cadel felt bad. He couldn't have said why, exactly, but he didn't like to see Fiona and Saul arguing. Especially when the subject of the argument was Clearview House.

At last Saul requested a private word with Fiona—and Trader took the hint. He politely departed, leaving his guests to talk among themselves. Cadel heard his footsteps on the stairs, loud in the sudden silence.

It was an awkward moment.

"I need to have a talk with Ms. Currey," Saul finally remarked. "We can do it in the office, if you want to stay here, Cadel."

Cadel shook his head.

"It's okay," he replied. "I'll go and check out the office."

"Are you sure?" Fiona sounded worried. "Don't you want to have a better look at this room?"

"No," said Cadel, and withdrew, shutting the door behind him. But he didn't head for the office. He was far more interested in what his two advisors were going to talk about.

So he pressed his ear against the closed door, listening hard. And he caught the low rumble of Saul's voice.

"Look." The detective was trying to be patient. "It's inevitable that we should have different objectives, but the one thing that's paramount for both of us is Cadel's safety. And how can I ensure his safety if I don't know exactly who's living with him?"

"Mr. Greeniaus," said Fiona, "this place has been approved and accredited."

"I know. I realize that."

"And I honestly can't see why you're being so negative," Fiona went on. "This seems like a perfectly good stopgap solution. The staff are well qualified. The facilities are excellent—"

"Yes," Saul interrupted. "The facilities *are* excellent. That's what worries me. The security is too good. That gate, for example. And the alarm system. And there's a camera by the front door."

Cadel frowned. He was angry with himself for missing the camera. He was also filled with a new respect for Saul Greeniaus.

"But that means nothing," said Fiona. She wasn't about to admit defeat. "What makes you think all those things were installed by Mr. Lynch? They were probably put in by the previous tenants."

"Well . . . maybe."

"I just can't see what you're getting at. If this isn't a legitimate operation, then what is it?"

"I'm not sure." During the pause that followed, Cadel tensed. Without their dialogue to guide him, he didn't know where Saul and Fiona actually were. He couldn't tell whether they were leaving the room or not. "You have no idea what Phineas Darkkon's network was like," Saul continued at last—much to Cadel's relief. Clearly, the detective hadn't moved a muscle. "It was gigantic. We still don't know what it was capable of." Saul's tone became uncharacteristically strained, though he was still speaking quietly. "Cadel isn't an ordinary kid. We can't be too careful—it's an exceptional case."

"Then why don't the *police* pay for his out-of-home care?" Fiona demanded. "If you're so worried about Cadel?"

"We can't. The funds haven't been allocated. We don't have the jurisdiction."

"Well, what do you expect me to do, then? You didn't like Mace, and now you don't like Clearview House. What are the alternatives?"

A sigh. Cadel suspected that it might have been Saul's.

"You said it was an urgent priority, to move Cadel," Fiona went on. "You said he was at risk in the Donkins' home, because of that computer message."

"All I want," Saul said patiently, "is to make sure that Cadel is all right."

"Oh, and you think I *don't* want that? You think I don't care—that I'd prefer to off-load him?" Realizing, perhaps, that she was talking too loudly, Fiona adjusted her volume. "You don't understand what this is like for me," she hissed. "I'm not supposed to play favorites—I have an enormous caseload—if I could look after him myself, I would, but I can't! I just can't!"

Cadel swallowed. Then he heard a noise and swung around.

A woman was emerging from the office: a small, dumpy woman with oily black hair tied up in a knot. She wore a striped blouse, a navy blue skirt, and flesh-colored stockings.

When she spotted Cadel staring at her, she put a finger to her lips.

"What—?" he began, at which point something clicked in his head. The shiny black hair. The double chin. The heavy eyebrows. They were all familiar. "Hey!" he said, then remembered where he was, and began to whisper. "Hey! Wait! Please!"

He wanted to ask if she was Com's sister, but she wouldn't stop. Nor would she reply. She just kept walking past him, toward the stairs. She walked at a rapid, steady pace, like a machine. Her high heels clicked rhythmically.

Before he could run after her, the door behind him swung open.

"Cadel?" said Fiona. "Are you all right?"

"Yes, I—yes." Cadel was embarrassed. He wondered if Saul would guess that he had been eavesdropping.

Saul, however, seemed more interested in the woman on the stairs. "Who was that?" he asked.

"I don't know," Cadel replied.

"She didn't tell you her name?"

"No," said Cadel.

"Well, she didn't *look* very dangerous," Fiona remarked, and put her hand on Cadel's shoulder. "Listen, sweetie. Mr. Greeniaus has agreed that you can stay here, at least for a short period. And I can't see any problem. So when do you want to move in?"

Cadel felt weak with relief. He had to clutch at a banister. "Can I move in now?" he said. Then he saw Fiona's expression and corrected himself. "I mean—this afternoon?"

Fiona hesitated. Saul glanced at his watch.

"What about four o'clock?" the detective proposed. "I can meet you at the Donkins' place. After my next appointment."

Fiona blinked.

"Oh, but—"

"I'll help with the heavy stuff," Saul declared, to Fiona's evident consternation. Her forehead puckered.

"That's not necessary," she pointed out. "We'll have Leslie to help us at that end, and all the Clearview staff at this end. You don't have to bother."

"I'll help with the heavy stuff," Saul repeated flatly, and Cadel saw at once that the detective was determined to have his way.

Fiona must have realized this, too. Because she started downstairs without uttering another word.

THIRTEEN

One of Cadel's most treasured possessions was a mug that Sonja had given him for his fifteenth birthday. It was covered in mathematical equations and bore the legend YOU'RE NUMBER ONE!

Mace managed to drop this mug while he was transporting it to Saul's car. When Cadel arrived on the scene, he found the driveway scattered with delicate shards of porcelain. Mace was insisting that he had broken the mug by accident—that it had simply fallen out of the box he was carrying.

Cadel knew better.

"Who said you could touch my things?" he demanded, white with rage. "Who said you could set *foot* in my room?"

"I did," panted Hazel, who had also appeared. She was lugging a bin liner full of Cadel's clothes. "I told Thomas he could take some books. Thomas, why did you put that mug in there?"

"I was trying to help!" Mace whined. But Cadel wasn't fooled. He knew that Mace was determined to exact a fitting revenge for the lost bike magazines, before Cadel disappeared altogether.

"I don't want your help," Cadel said through his teeth. "Just put that box down and leave my stuff alone."

Mace scowled. Then he let go of the box in his arms, which hit the concrete driveway with a huge *thump.* Hazel squeaked. Cadel gasped.

From his car, Saul yelled, "What's going on?"

"Oh, *Thomas*!" For once, Hazel had no illusions. "How *could* you?"

"He told me not to touch his stuff," Mace replied, hands on hips. He was in a dangerous mood. While probably glad to see his foster brother leave, he must have resented the fact that Cadel seemed so happy about going. "It's only books, anyway."

"Thomas, I know you must be upset about saying good-bye."

"He's not upset. He's jealous," Cadel snapped, so angry that he didn't care how deep a wound he inflicted. "He's jealous because somebody actually *wants* me. And nobody wants him."

Mace grabbed Cadel just as Saul cried, "Hey!" Though Mace ignored this rebuke, he couldn't get a proper grip on Cadel before the two of them were being wrenched apart. Cadel then ducked behind Saul, already regretting his flash of temper.

Mace backed off. He wasn't stupid enough to start fighting with a policeman.

"What happened here?" asked Saul, gazing down at the shattered mug.

"It wasn't my fault," Mace began, just as Cadel exclaimed, "He did it on purpose!" Saul held up his hand, silencing them both.

He turned to Hazel.

"Too many cooks spoil the broth," he said. "We don't need another body—perhaps Thomas can go and do something else."

This wasn't a suggestion; it was an instruction. And Mace didn't argue with it. Instead he stomped back into the house, passing Fiona on his way.

She was lugging a sports bag heavily weighted with shoes.

"What's wrong?" she said, as Hazel surrendered her own plastic bag to Saul. He took it over to the trunk of his car, while Hazel made a hurried report to Fiona.

Cadel followed Saul. He stood watching the detective, who looked much thinner than usual in jeans and a shabby old shirt. Saul was trying to insert the overstuffed trash bag between boxes of books and compact discs.

"Sorry about the commotion," said Cadel. "It's just that he smashed Sonja's birthday present. Deliberately. And I had to say *something,* even if it did get him mad."

Saul slammed the trunk shut. He stood for a moment, contemplating his car's gleaming exterior.

"I don't like Clearview House," he replied. "But I can understand why you want to go there." And he glanced toward Hazel's front door, his expression bleak. "Anything's worth getting out from under that poisonous little prick."

Cadel couldn't have been more surprised. It was the first time he had ever heard Saul use such strong language. All at once Cadel realized that Saul disliked Mace just as much as he did.

This thought was very comforting and helped Cadel to endure the good-byes that took place after the packing was done. Hazel shed a few tears. Janan's bottom lip trembled (though he brightened up when Cadel promised to send him some chocolate-bar wrappers). Even Leslie looked sad. Cadel thanked the Donkins sincerely and gratefully for their kindness; he knew that he was in their debt, and wished that he could have been an easier charge. The fact that Hazel cried at their parting, however, encouraged him. It meant that he hadn't been too much of a burden.

Happily, there were no more encounters with Mace—who stayed holed up in his room until after Cadel had left. But Cadel did glimpse his tormentor through the rear window of Fiona's hatchback. As the car pulled out of the Donkins' driveway, Cadel turned to wave at his foster parents and saw Mace behind them, hovering at the window of Cadel's old bedroom.

No doubt Mace was setting up some kind of booby trap for the room's next occupant.

"Now, sweetie," said Fiona, who had insisted that Cadel ride with her, rather than with Saul, "if there *is* anything that worries you about Clearview House, then give me a ring. Not that I'm expecting any problems. Mr. Greeniaus is paid to be suspicious, and I don't want him getting you all paranoid. Because I'm sure there's no need to be."

"Oh, I'm not," said Cadel.

"You've got to understand that policemen have a very one-sided view of the world. It's not their fault. You just have to remember they can be a bit overcautious."

"Mr. Greeniaus is all right, though, don't you think?" Cadel was moved by a vague desire to defend Saul. "I mean, he's pretty smart."

Fiona blushed. Cadel saw this and wondered why her cheeks had grown pink. But all she said was, "Well, you should know about being smart, I guess."

The drive to Clearview House was a long one, ending in a quiet suburban area full of tree-lined streets and high, ivy-clad fences. When Fiona and Cadel finally arrived at their destination, they found Saul already unloading his car in the fading light. Cadel rushed to help him. Though Saul refused to let Cadel lift any heavy boxes, both Fiona and Cadel were allowed to carry clothes. Fiona picked up some jeans and jackets. Cadel shouldered a pillowcase full of socks, pajamas, and underwear.

He could sense that he was being watched from various upstairs windows. No one came out to greet him, however, until he had almost reached the front door—which was suddenly flung open by a man whose face he didn't recognize. This man was short and stocky, with a gray crew cut, a broken nose, and a gruff voice. Everything about him was square: his jaw, his build, his hands, his outfit.

"Ah," he said. "You must be Cadel. I'm Cliff Wylie. How are you?" He stuck out his hand, which Cadel politely shook. "I comanage Clearview House with Trader Lynch," Cliff explained. "My background is . . . Well, let's just say it's in logistics," he said, rather obliquely. "Trader looks after the staff, and I look after the premises. Repairs. Maintenance. Supplies. That sort of thing." Then he introduced himself to Fiona, who had followed Cadel to the door.

Saul was still heaving boxes around nearby.

"That looks like a job for two lazy young punks I happen to know," Cliff rumbled, peering at the detective. Turning to Cadel, he said, "Can you find your own bedroom?" And upon receiving an affirmative reply, Cliff excused himself. "I need to find Hamish and Devin," he explained. "That pair always manage to disappear when there's hard work to be done."

He promptly plunged back inside, leaving Cadel and Fiona to make their own way upstairs. It wasn't quite the greeting that Cadel had expected. But no sooner had he ventured over the threshold—with Fiona in close pursuit—than Lexi appeared at one of the doorways that opened off the entrance hall.

And her enthusiasm more than made up for Cliff's abruptness.

"There he is!" she cried. "He's back! Hurray!" She zoomed up to Cadel. "Is this your stuff? Can I carry it?"

"Uh . . . no," he muttered. "I'm fine."

"Trader's in the office," Lexi continued. "Is this all you've got? It's not much, is it?"

"There's more," he said, glancing over his shoulder. Sure enough, Saul Greeniaus had finally joined them. He was toting a heavy box of books and made very slow progress up the stairs, behind Fiona—who could hardly see over the pile of clothes in her arms.

Lexi surged ahead, two steps at a time, jabbering on about meal rosters and allergies and downloading television programs. As he passed her bedroom door, Cadel noticed that the knob was missing and that there were new scratches in the paintwork. He decided that the twins must have been fighting since his last visit.

Trader was waiting for them on the top-floor landing.

"Hello!" he said, with a breathtaking smile. "I thought I heard a car." He squinted at Saul's box. "Is anything else down there?"

"Yes," Saul grunted.

"Then I'll go and get it."

Moving to the left so that Trader could squeeze by, Cadel wondered if Com's sister was around. He even glanced into the office on his way past, but it was empty. No one was occupying his bedroom, either—not until Lexi burst into it, just ahead of him.

"Did you bring any posters?" she demanded. "Or stickers, or anything? You'll need to brighten up these walls." Then she caught sight of the garments that Fiona was dumping onto Cadel's bed and gave a little shriek. "Oh my god! Are these your clothes? Let me see, let me see!"

Saul staggered into the room just in time to witness Lexi pouncing on Cadel's collection of anoraks like a cheetah on an antelope. The detective deposited his load very carefully beside the bed, while Lexi began tossing aside jacket after jacket, sweatshirt after sweatshirt.

"Oh, *gross*!" she exclaimed, screwing up her nose at the sight of an old school blazer. "No *way* can you wear that; it's got to go. And this! What's this? You don't seriously want to be seen in this?" She clicked her tongue over a pair of brown corduroy pants. "Uh-uh. Not possible. You need a totally new look."

Cadel was speechless. Even Fiona was at a loss.

Only Saul seemed utterly unfazed.

"Hey," he rasped, "this is Cadel's room, not yours. Why don't you give the guy some privacy here?"

"Why don't *you*?" Lexi retorted. "You're not his dad!"

"It's all right, Mr. Greeniaus," Cadel said quickly. He didn't want Saul changing his mind about Clearview House, just because Lexi had lost her temper. "I don't care, really I don't."

The detective fixed him with a level, speculative gaze as the *clomp-clomp-clomp* of heavy footsteps became audible. Cadel remembered a certain pair of enormous biker's boots, and identified the newcomer before Hamish had even lurched through the door.

Hamish was red-faced and sweating. His glasses had steamed up, and his bandana was slipping over one eye. He was carrying another box of books.

"*Woof!*" he grunted. "Where do I put this?"

Saul pointed silently at a spot on the floor, then went to fetch more luggage from the car. Fiona left, too. But Cadel stayed, because he wanted to ask an important question.

When he was sure that Saul and Fiona were out of earshot, he said, "Is Com's sister here?"

"Com's sister?" Hamish was sprawled on the bed, recovering from his climb. "You mean Dot?"

"Dot?" Cadel echoed. "Is that her name?"

"She's not here now," said Lexi, who was dividing Cadel's clothes into little heaps. "Do you like what I did with Hamish? That whole outfit was my idea. So was the buzz cut. What he *really* needs is a couple of tats, but he won't have them."

"No, I won't!" Hamish whined. "Tattoos hurt!"

"But you're such a geek, Hamish—you won't convince anyone, without tats." Lexi sighed before turning to Cadel. "It doesn't totally work with him," she conceded, "but it'll work with you. You'll look so hard when I'm done."

"That is such crap." Devin had suddenly appeared, bearing Cadel's sports bag. He dropped this bag as if it were on fire, then squatted down to examine the box of books. "How are you gunna make *him* look hard? He looks like a fluffy bunny."

"A fluffy bunny with a bomb in it," said Hamish, and sat up to address Cadel. "Did you really wipe out the Axis Institute? Dot says you did. She says you killed half the faculty."

Stunned, Cadel stared at Hamish. There was a long silence.

"I never killed anyone," Cadel croaked at last. Then, to change the subject, he added, "Why do I have to look hard, anyway? I mean, what for?"

"Because this is a youth refuge," Lexi explained. "Because we're all supposed to be *difficult*. Problem kids. You know." With obvious relish, she described the type of kid she meant. "The sort you'd be scared to sit next to on a bus. The sort that never pays for anything."

"But aren't we trying to infiltrate GenoME?" Cadel couldn't believe how stupid Lexi was sounding. It worried him. "If that's our goal, we have to look harmless. We have to blend in. I was always taught that the worst thing you can do is draw attention to yourself, especially if you're up to no good." Realizing that it was Prosper English who had told him this, he had to clear his throat before continuing. "There was a teacher at the Axis Institute who got clean away. His name was Alias, and he managed to escape because he never stood out in a crowd. Unless he wanted to. But *we* don't want to. Do we?"

Hamish goggled. Lexi frowned. Devin rolled his eyes.

"Jeez," he said. "Another Cliff Wylie. Cliff's always going on and on about keeping a low profile. He never shuts up about it."

"That's because it's his *job*, knobhead," Hamish pointed out. "That's because he spends all his time spying on people."

"Does he?" Cadel pressed, eager for information, and Devin sighed before answering.

"Yeah. Lucky sod. I wish *I* could do some of that gumshoe stuff, but he won't let me. He won't even let me sit in a surveillance car, let alone follow people around."

"Well, I'm not surprised, the way your feet stink," Lexi retorted. "You can smell 'em a mile away."

At that moment a bell clanged somewhere below them. Hamish and the twins immediately ran for the door, though Lexi was kind enough to fling the word "Dinner!" at Cadel, over her shoulder. Cadel didn't know what to do. He wasn't sure if there would be a place at the table for him. So he hesitated, and only followed the others when they were well out of sight. The thunder of their feet announced that they were already a couple of floors down, heading for the kitchen.

Upon reaching the top of the stairs, he found himself face-to-face with Saul. The detective carried two well-packed trash bags under his arms and looked slightly disheveled—as if he had just emerged from a scrum of famished teenagers. He asked if he could have a quick word with Cadel in private. And Cadel nodded.

They returned to the bedroom, where Saul dropped his load.

"That's the last of it," he declared. "Are you going to be all right here?"

"Oh yes," Cadel replied.

"Because if you're worried about anything, you should call me. Day or night."

"Fiona told me to call her," Cadel objected, and Saul frowned.

"Ms. Currey is a good person to have on your side," the detective allowed. "But she doesn't carry a licensed firearm." Seeing Cadel blink,

Saul dismissed the subject with a wave of his hand. "You're not stupid. You'll know the right person to call, when the time comes. And remember there'll always be a team watching this house."

"Yes. I know."

"Don't let your guard down. Not yet. You can't afford to." Saul inclined his head, listening hard. "I think that's Ms. Currey now," he concluded.

It was. She had come upstairs to join them, though not because she was carrying more of Cadel's belongings. Instead, she had brought news of dinner.

"You're to go and join everyone," she said, a little breathless from her climb. "If you want, I can start unpacking while you eat. Would you like that?"

"No, thanks," said Cadel. He didn't want Fiona wandering around by herself upstairs, in case she stumbled on any suspiciously expensive bits of technology. "I'll do it myself."

"All right, then. I'll leave you to settle in. But I'll pop by soon, just to see how you are." Stepping forward, she gave Cadel a quick hug. "I hope it works out for you, sweetie. I'm sure it will."

"So am I," he muttered, his cheeks burning. Fiona had never hugged him before. He couldn't remember the last time anyone had hugged him; he stood awkwardly, at a loss. He almost resented her goodwill, because it implied that she trusted him, and he was currently in the process of betraying that trust. It was a huge relief when she and Saul finally agreed to make their way downstairs.

Cadel accompanied them as far as the front hallway, where Trader had stationed himself, all shining teeth and sparkling eyes. Trader thanked his two visitors for helping with the move.

"And of course you're welcome to visit anytime," he insisted, as he ushered Fiona out into the dusk. (Cadel noticed that Saul followed her with obvious reluctance.) Trader stood smiling and waving cheerily until both Saul and Fiona were safely in their cars. Only when the cars themselves were rolling down the driveway, headlights on, did Trader relinquish his post.

He stepped back inside and shut the door firmly, engaging several locks.

"I thought they'd never go," he said. Then he turned to Cadel, sporting a mischievous grin. "So. Cadel. I think it's about time you met everybody for real, don't you?"

FOURTEEN

When Cadel entered the kitchen, he saw that it was very crowded. Hamish was sitting with the twins at an enormous table, which was covered in a plastic cloth. With them was Cliff Wylie, who looked more like a gardener than a spy because of his squared-off, nuggetty build and weather-beaten skin. Or perhaps it was Tony Cheung's close proximity that made Cliff appear so rough-hewn. In his crisp white shirt and gold-rimmed spectacles, Tony could have belonged to a different species. He had the sort of mild, pouchy face that is the product of years spent in air-conditioned comfort, beneath artificial lights.

Judith was also present, a dominating figure in many swirling layers of orange paisley print. She was ladling risotto out of a cooking pot into several empty pasta plates. Zac had been given the task of distributing full plates to the hungry diners; he shuffled around in floppy sandals, still wearing his apron. Cadel wondered if he had set foot outside the kitchen since lunchtime.

A ragged cheer went up as Cadel made his appearance.

"Here he is at last," said Trader, who had come in behind Cadel. "Now, where's he going to sit?"

"Next to me!" cried Lexi, patting the empty chair to her right. But Judith overruled her.

"He can sit wherever he wants," Judith said, loudly and assertively. "Don't let that girl bully you, Cadel—I've told her to ease off. Do you like risotto?"

"Yes," Cadel replied.

"Not allergic to anything?"

"No."

"Hamish is allergic to seafood, dairy, and nuts." Judith sighed. "As if we didn't have enough to worry about."

"Come and sit beside me, kid." It was Cliff who spoke. "And we'll tell you what's going on."

Somewhat relieved, Cadel slid into the proffered chair. He was feeling horribly out of place. Although he'd become used to living a dislocated existence, full of strange houses and unknown people, the uprooting process was never easy. It always involved a brand-new set of names and rules and faces to learn. It always required a careful search for safe havens and potential risks.

Scanning his surroundings, he realized that—despite its many attractions—Clearview House would be a hard place to settle into. Unlike Hazel's residence, or even the series of safe houses that he'd previously occupied, his new address was crowded, busy, and riddled with complications. Not that this troubled him too much. Complex systems were his specialty, after all. But it was one thing to study a complex system from the comfort of a stable platform. It was another thing entirely to be floating around in a maze or flux, trying to navigate one's position.

At this point, Cadel knew, he had only two constant factors in his life: Sonja Pirovic and Prosper English. The move to Clearview House meant that, once again, he was confronted with the difficult task of surveying, analyzing, appraising, and defining a totally foreign environment.

So he took a deep breath, picked up his fork, and got to work—just as a heaped plate of risotto was placed in front of him.

"Can you please start with what I'm supposed to be doing?" he requested. "Can you tell me where I fit into your plan?"

It was Trader who obliged. In fact, Cadel very quickly deduced that Trader was top dog at that table, with Cliff running a close second; everyone else deferred to them somewhat (though Judith clearly did so with some reservations). From his seat across the table, Trader began to reel off various facts about Genius Squad, while the others held their tongues.

According to Trader, there were three teams on the squad: the network infiltration team, the forensic accounting team, and the recon team. Cadel would be part of the network infiltration team, which also included Hamish, Dot, and the twins.

Cadel pricked up his ears upon hearing this.

"Dot?" he said. "You mean Com's sister?"

"She's downstairs," Hamish mumbled, spraying rice across the tablecloth. And Trader laughed at Cadel's bewilderment.

"Have you forgotten about the War Room?" said Trader. "We still have to show you that."

"All in good time," growled Cliff, who then proceeded to explain that when Sonja finally arrived, on Tuesday morning, she would become part of Judith's forensic accounting team—along with Tony Cheung. "Al Capone was a murderer, but he was finally jailed for tax evasion," Cliff remarked, in his gravelly voice. "Maybe we can bring GenoME down by finding out where its profits come from, and where they go." As for the recon team, its membership was confined to adults only: It was made up of Cliff, Zac, and Trader. "You need experience when you're dealing with the real world," Cliff announced, with a repressive glance at Devin. "Virtual reality is for cutting your teeth on."

Then Trader took over again. He explained that Cliff was a highly experienced private detective, while he himself had been trained in covert operations, specializing in spyware and the breaching of physical security (like alarm systems, for instance). Zac, on the other hand, had been chosen for his background in genetic research. His chief contribution would be made when they finally *did* manage to acquire GenoME's secret gene-plotting formula: It would be Zac's job to work out whether the infamous formula was really a big fraud.

Meanwhile, he would run errands, help around the house, and collect information by posing as a new GenoME client.

"He'll be our Node-in-Residence," Hamish snorted, much to Cadel's confusion. Whereupon Trader stepped in to interpret.

"GenoME calls its clients nodes," he said chirpily, "because each individual is at the intersecting point of a lot of genetic lines. Every client's gene map, or genome, is called a node-code. And its counselors are called potentializers."

"GenoME likes to keep its language obscure," Judith interjected. "So its clients won't understand much."

"I'm sending Zac in there as a client tomorrow," Cliff went on.

Cadel was taken aback.

"You mean the Australian branch is already up and running?" he said.

Around the table, everyone nodded. Some even grunted through mouths full of risotto.

"Unfortunately, they took us by surprise," Trader confessed, his fork poised above his plate. "If we'd managed to enter their building before they set up, we could have installed a few bugs. But they moved very fast."

"And now that place is like a fortress," Cliff complained. When Cadel asked why, there was a general groan. Judith slapped down her ladle and went over to an outlet that was fixed to the wall above the sink.

Then she flipped the switch and addressed the socket.

"Dot?" she said. "Could you bring up your plan for number eleven, please? Thanks."

As she settled into her own chair, Cliff began to describe Australia's new GenoME branch at number 11, Karajan Close, Burwood. According to Cliff, it was a freestanding structure with a drainage channel on one side, a gas station on the other, and a big cement car park at the rear. As a result, there was no way of burrowing into any of its walls from an adjacent building. In fact there was no way of approaching the branch at *all* without being seen. However, Cliff had managed to secure a plan of its layout from the local municipal council, because GenoME had submitted a development application before installing a laboratory on the first floor of its premises.

"The lab processes DNA samples." Cliff paused for a moment, to swallow a mouthful of food. And Trader took up where Cliff had left off.

"There are two lab technicians," Trader said, "who input Australian DNA profiles. The details are then sent to the U.S. for 'interpretation,' and the results come back pretty quickly. Over in America, GenoME has a huge databank full of node codes."

"So the system here and the system there must be linked," Lexi announced. "It's our access point to the U.S. network."

"Except that it's so well defended," her brother said gloomily. Cadel decided that Devin wasn't a particularly happy sort of person. While Lexi bounced, Devin slouched. It seemed odd that they should be twins.

"Apart from the two lab technicians, there are five potentializers, one marketing manager, one receptionist, and two information technology people," Trader proceeded, listing the complete roster of GenoME staff. "And there's the branch director, of course. Carolina Whitehead."

"She's our number-one target," Judith remarked, from the other end of the table. "If we can get something on her, it'll be a good start."

"Why?" asked Cadel. At that moment, however—before anyone could respond—there was a disturbance in the pantry. Peering through the door of this little room, Cadel saw one stack of shelves disappear sideways into a wall cavity, along with their lavish stock of tinned fruit and condiment bottles.

Amazed, he realized that the shelves were actually a heavily disguised sliding door and that the door itself belonged to an elevator. Stepping out of the elevator was Dot, who carried a laptop under her arm.

"Ah. There she is," said Trader. "Can you call up that map for us, Dot? We need to show Cadel." Then, with a sudden smirk, he remembered his manners. "By the way, I don't know if you've been formally introduced. This is Cadel, your new colleague. Cadel, this is Dot."

Dot made a clicking noise—which may or may not have meant "hello"—and deposited her laptop on the table near Cliff. She barely glanced at Cadel, preferring to focus her attention on her search for the required data.

Cadel, who had just placed a wad of sticky risotto on his tongue, munched away desperately; he was keen to ask her about Com, and couldn't do so until he had swallowed what was in his mouth. But he wasn't given the opportunity to speak. He still hadn't finished chewing when Dot cleared her throat, stepping back from the computer screen as if to announce that her job was done.

Cliff pushed the laptop toward him, indicating a portion of the displayed blueprint.

"As you can see, the GenoME branch is three stories high, with a big warehouse area stuck on the back," Cliff said. Crisply he proceeded to label all the rooms shown in the building plan, including the reception area, the conference room, the kitchenette, the lab, the bathrooms, and all the numerous offices. He even knew which offices belonged to which staff members.

Cadel wondered how.

"And then there's the warehouse," Cliff said, tapping the screen with a blunt, squared-off finger. "What's interesting about it is that GenoME's put a demountable shed in there. We know they did because the building is leased, and GenoME had to get permission from the owner to install a shed. We also know that the shed is being used for secret meetings."

Cadel blinked. "How?" he demanded. "I mean, how do you know about the meetings if they're secret? And how did you find out about the owner's permission?"

Trader and Cliff exchanged glances. Wide grins blossomed all around the table. Finally Trader reached across and gave Cliff a playful jab on the shoulder. "We can thank Cliff for his work in the real estate agency," Trader said. "He's good at getting hold of confidential files."

"And we can thank Trader's spyware for everything else," Cliff rejoined. "Laser eavesdropping is a marvelous thing."

Seeing Cadel's amazement, Trader expanded on the subject. "We trained our lasers on some of GenoME's windows when people were talking inside. And we measured the vibrations of their voices on the glass." He wiped his mouth on a paper napkin. "Believe me, it's not foolproof. I would have preferred an old-fashioned bug. Trouble is, GenoME's security is so tight that I didn't want to risk arousing their suspicions."

Trader described how his eavesdropping device had been set up in a series of different cars, and the cars parked in various locations near the GenoME building. From information collected during these "probes," it had been established that Carolina never seemed to discuss anything even mildly controversial with her staff in any of the offices. Occasionally, however, she would ask her second-in-command, information technology manager Jerry Reinhard, to "step out the back for a quick word."

Jerry and Carolina were the only Americans working in the branch.

"The potentializers all trained in the U.S. for years, but they were born in Australia and New Zealand," Cliff said. He was about to elaborate when Zac spoke up for the first time. Pushing aside his empty plate, Zac remarked in his gentle, breathy voice, "From what I've heard, they're true believers."

All eyes swiveled in his direction. Conscious of this, Zac presented his argument slowly and carefully.

"You've read the transcripts, haven't you?" he said. "I think everyone here would have to agree that most of the staff in that place are being conned. They all sound as if they're buying into the GenoME propaganda."

But Cliff shook his head.

"Doesn't mean a thing," he countered gruffly. "You know how security conscious they are. For all we know, there's a policy about keeping their talk squeaky clean in any room with windows." Bridling at Lexi's derisive snort, he added, "Hey—it's possible. There's a policy about everything in GenoME."

"So what?" said Lexi, and Judith patted Zac's arm.

"I'm with Zac," said Judith. "I reckon Jerry and Carolina are the only ones in that place who really know what's going on. Because they're the only ones who have secret confabs in the shed."

"Boy, I wish we could get into that shed," mumbled Devin. And Trader said, "We have to get into the building first."

There was a brief pause. Most of the diners had finished eating, though Dot hadn't even started. She was standing behind Cliff, attentive but expressionless, her hands clasped in front of her. It occurred to Cadel that she possessed the same slightly robotic air as her brother. Certainly she was no more talkative than Com had been. And her face didn't move much. Tony Cheung, who had also been very quiet, didn't seem nearly as detached as Dot, because he kept responding to what was being said, frowning or nodding or pursing his lips.

"Any questions?" Cliff inquired. All movement ceased as Cadel found himself the object of general scrutiny. Even Judith had stopped eating.

He gazed around, suddenly aware that he was the smallest person in sight.

"I—uh—yes," he said, and turned to Trader. "Can I check out that laser eavesdropping machine?"

Trader laughed. He pushed back his chair and jumped to his feet. Then he slapped Cadel's shoulder.

"I think it's time you checked out *everything* in the War Room," he said. "I mean, who needs dessert when you can sink your teeth into the stuff we've got downstairs?"

Then he conducted Cadel to the elevator, ignoring Lexi's protests about washing-up duty.

FIFTEEN

The War Room contained no windows. It was a large, air-conditioned concrete bunker, lined with desks and packed with technology. Cadel had never in his life seen so much cabling or hard-drive capacity stored in one place.

"Disguising our power consumption is quite a chore," Trader admitted, stepping out of the lift ahead of Cadel. "But there are ways of spreading the load a bit. Hydroponic cannabis growers do it all the time." He stopped beside one of the pale gray desks—which perfectly matched the gray concrete floor and walls. "Here's your workstation, Cadel. And this is your laptop." He lightly touched a wedge of black steel and plastic. "As you can see," he said, "it's been custom built for our requirements."

Cadel's breath caught in his throat. The laptop was like nothing he'd ever seen before; its size and weight hinted at the beefed-up capacities lurking within. Reverently he popped open the screen and ran his fingers over the keyboard.

"Not cxactly portable," said Trader. "Not for someone your size."

"It's *beautiful,*" Cadel breathed.

"You think so?" Trader seemed amused. "I think it's ugly as hell, myself. Personally I prefer my technology sleek and slimline—otherwise you can't hide it." He spread his hands. "However, since you won't be getting out much, I don't suppose it matters how big this thing is."

Cadel looked up, momentarily distracted from his loving contemplation of the computer.

"What do you mean, I won't be getting out much?" he asked.

"Well . . . it's recon that does most of the legwork around here," Trader replied. "And we wouldn't want you going anywhere near the new branch, in case you're recognized. Don't forget that Dr. Darkkon founded GenoME. It's possible that most of the senior staff there know who you are."

"Oh," said Cadel. He could see what Trader was getting at. It made sense to keep a low profile, though Cadel was anxious to inspect the GenoME building in person.

Under cover of darkness, perhaps?

"Anyway, you won't need to stake out that place," Trader continued, as if reading Cadel's thoughts. "Your job is to penetrate their computer network, and we've got everything you need for that right here." Flinging out his arms in a theatrical gesture, Trader indicated exactly what they did have. "What do you think? Pretty impressive, eh?"

"It's wonderful." Cadel couldn't have been more earnest in his praise. After enduring such a long technological drought, he felt as if he had wandered through the gates of paradise. "Is this why everyone agreed to join Genius Squad? Because of all the equipment?" he said.

Trader laughed. He informed Cadel that the motivations of their fellow squad members were many and varied. For someone like Tony Cheung, the motivation was money, pure and simple. Judith's rationale was more complex. She hated big corporations (having previously worked for one) and believed that they were responsible for most of the world's miseries. As a result, she believed that toppling a large and sinister organization like GenoME was the right thing to do. In fact, she was quite happy getting paid for doing what she normally did as a hobby.

"Judith doesn't believe in paying personal income tax when most big corporations are tax dodgers," Trader revealed. "She likes ferreting out their dirty secrets in her spare time, and leaking the details to various government authorities." His green eyes crinkled at the corners. "Just don't get her started on the subject of tax havens," he warned, "or she'll never shut up."

According to Trader, Zac's dislike of GenoME was more specific. In Zac's opinion, if GenoME really did have a gene-plotting formula, then this knowledge should be shared with the world. And if the formula was a fake, then GenoME was undermining the whole science of genetics and ought to be stopped.

Cliff, on the other hand, was not nearly as selfless.

"Cliff's been underemployed," said Trader, sounding genuinely sympathetic as he spoke of his colleague's plight. "There's not a lot of work about for someone with his expertise. Besides, he and Rex Austin go back a bit. He's done jobs for Rex before."

Then there was Hamish. Hamish had jumped at the chance to join Genius Squad. He was a born hacker who wanted to pursue his interests free of the well-meaning interference of concerned parents, prying counselors, and suspicious teachers. Ever since his run-in with the Roads and Traffic Authority, Hamish's activities had been closely monitored. His access to the Net had been circumscribed. So he had been only too pleased to start throwing temper tantrums, running away from home, and pretending that he was on drugs.

In the end, his parents had allowed him to live at Clearview House because they were at their wits' end. They didn't know what else to do with him.

"Of course, he's a perfectly reasonable sort of bloke, really," Trader insisted. "All he wants to do is flex his electronic muscles a bit—and who can blame him? No one with a gift like his should be forced to rein it in. Not when it can be used against a criminal setup like GenoME."

The twins, he went on, were neither as stable nor as disciplined as Hamish. Devin seemed to like destroying things: databanks, protocols, networks, infrastructures. And Lexi was a commonplace girl with a curious quirk. While for the most part she was "painfully uninteresting," she had the occasional flashes of brilliance in one very specialized field.

"Cryptanalysis," Trader said. "It's her fascination with codes and ciphers that makes her so valuable. Devin's been putting it to good use. They're a pretty formidable team."

"Why?" said Cadel. "What have they done?"

Trader was taken aback. Clearly he found it odd that Cadel didn't know about the twins. But he answered Cadel's question civilly enough.

"They've been launching attacks on the Advanced Encryption Standard, for a start," he related. "Lexi's obsessed with the AES. She won't leave it alone." He dimpled, and shook his head indulgently. "That's how I met them both. We had a mutual acquaintance who organized a timing attack on the AES through a very large bank."

Cadel's eyes widened. Sonja, he knew, was quite attached to the AES—a system that allowed financial data to be encoded and exchanged throughout the world. She had told Cadel that she admired the Rijndael algorithm on which the AES was based because it was such an "elegant" mathematical equation.

Somehow Cadel didn't think that she would appreciate having Lexi messing about with it.

"Anyway, I figured that if I could get the twins focused on something a bit more constructive than trashing the global banking system, it would be better for everyone," Trader observed. "Especially since they were running wild. They've had a pretty rough home life, you see. No father. Mum's a drug addict, so their grandmother's been looking after 'em. But she's getting too old to crack the whip." He gave a soft chuckle. "Cliff and I—we know how to handle the twins. In some ways, it's just a matter of keeping them busy."

Cadel's attention was divided. He had been booting up his laptop during Trader's long lecture, and some of its default settings were far more provocative than Trader's theories about managing the twins. But when Trader fell silent, Cadel looked up again.

"What about Dot?" Cadel asked. "Why did Dot join the squad?"

"She's searching for her brother. Or so she says." Trader shrugged, and lowered his voice. "To be honest, I'm not a hundred percent sure about Dot. She's a hard person to read. But Hamish vouched for her." According to Hamish, Dot had been making contact with as many "hacker types" as she could, in the hope that they might be associating with

Com—who had disappeared after the destruction of the Axis Institute. No doubt Com was simply keeping quiet to avoid police interference. Nevertheless, Dot claimed that she was worried about him. "Dot thought that you might know where he is," Trader said. "When she told us about you, and we decided to bring you on board, she agreed to join us."

"But I was going to ask *her* about Com!" Cadel cried in dismay. "I've no idea where he's got to!"

"Yes, you made that pretty clear the other day." Trader seemed unconcerned. "So I suggested that maybe you two could put your heads together. Trace him over the Net, or something. And she didn't have a problem with that."

Cadel sighed. He had been searching the Net for months, desperately trying to find anyone else who might have been enrolled at the Axis Institute. There had been a handful of infiltration students who (if they had survived) would surely have popped up online somewhere. But if they *were* around, they'd changed their names. And they'd also managed to disguise their signature-programming styles.

Cadel wondered if Com had changed his name.

Maybe Dot would know.

"And you?" Cadel asked, emboldened enough to challenge Trader. "What brought you here?"

Trader adopted a relaxed pose. He folded his arms and cocked his head.

"Oh, well," he said. "I suppose I just figured it would be a lot of fun." Then he smiled again, as if at a private joke. "I have to admit, I get bored very easily."

He was showing Cadel the laser eavesdropping machine when the lift door opened and several people spilled out: Judith, Devin, Hamish, Cliff, and Dot. Suddenly Cadel was in the middle of a small scrum, as Devin and Hamish and Cliff clustered around him. Even Dot displayed a certain amount of interest, hovering in the background.

Before Cadel could ask her anything, he himself was bombarded with questions.

"What are you going to be working on?" Hamish demanded. "Are you on firewalls with Lexi, or exploits with me, or what are you d-doing?"

"Has Trader shown you the schedules yet?" Judith wanted to know. "Lunches, dinners, dishwasher, and bathrooms. You all take turns."

"Have you seen the background files?" Cliff queried. "Before you do anything else, you should have a look at them. They're under *GenoME/data*. You won't understand what's going on if you don't check them out."

Cadel shrank from the noisy barrage; he didn't know what to say. Trader must have seen this, because he started to wave his arms as if flapping away a cloud of insects.

"Guys, guys!" he protested. "Give the poor kid some space; don't swamp him! If you carry on like this, he'll take off!"

"He should go and unpack first," Dot declared. Though her voice was weak and rusty, everyone stopped to listen—perhaps because she so rarely spoke up. "Before he gets too tired."

There was a buzz of agreement. Next thing Cadel knew, he was being escorted up to his bedroom by Trader, who insisted on carrying the heavy laptop. On their way upstairs, they passed Lexi and Zac in the kitchen; Zac was wiping down surfaces as Lexi sullenly stacked the dishwasher, making far more noise than was absolutely necessary.

Tony Cheung had taken out the garbage.

"Where do *you* sleep?" Cadel asked, and Trader explained that he didn't live at Clearview House. None of the adults did, though they all spent a lot of time on the premises and sometimes used the office beds. In fact, a shift roster had been instituted.

"One more thing," Trader added, when he reached Cadel's room. "The doorbell is attached to an alarm system that covers the entire house. If you hear the alarm, and you're down in the War Room, *don't leave.* Stay where you are. Because anyone who presses the doorbell is an intruder, and the War Room is our little secret. We wouldn't want the wrong sort of people to find out about it."

"Like Mr. Greeniaus, you mean?" said Cadel, studying Trader's beautifully proportioned face.

"Like anyone who doesn't belong to Genius Squad," Trader replied. Then he advised Cadel to unpack, told him that bedtime was optional, and left.

Cadel immediately locked the door. It was hard to resist taking advantage of that gleaming new lock, or the privacy it afforded him after so many lockless months. With a deep sense of satisfaction, he then proceeded to inspect his personal domain, opening every drawer and examining every outlet. As far as he could tell, there were no miniature cameras or listening devices secreted anywhere in the room. But he wasn't an expert; not like Trader Lynch. Cadel sensed that, when it came to spyware, Trader was way ahead of him.

Nevertheless, Cadel felt reasonably secure. Certainly more secure than he had felt at the Donkins' house.

He didn't bother unpacking. Instead, when he had finished familiarizing himself with the contents of his room, he opened up his new computer. And the first thing he did with it was to check out the *GenoME/data* file, as Cliff had recommended.

It was quite a hefty file, stuffed with information. Some of this information concerned the now-defunct Darkkon Empire. There was a structural tree incorporating many of Dr. Darkkon's pet projects, such as his fake gene patent company, his faulty vending machine franchise, and—of course—GenoME. Another featured subsidiary was something called NanTex Laboratories Inc., which Cadel recognized as Phineas Darkkon's old nanotechnology lab. NanTex had been responsible for Dr. Darkkon's various genetic experiments—or so everyone seemed to think. It was generally assumed that most of the money made by Dr. Darkkon over the years had actually been channeled back into NanTex, to fund his crazy genetic mutation schemes.

Unfortunately, there was no way of proving this in court. Cadel remembered having a long talk with an FBI agent, who had told him that the notorious laboratory was not yielding any useful evidence. Its exact whereabouts had been discovered only after Prosper's arrest, and by the time it was raided, the lab was just an empty shell. Most of its equipment and all of its staff had vanished.

That was why no one had ever arrested Chester Cramp, the man thought to have been its former chief executive officer.

Cadel saw with interest that, according to the Genius Squad files, Chester was now in charge of a company called Fountain Pharmaceuticals. Even more interesting was the fact that the former head of NanTex was actually married to Carolina Whitehead, the head of GenoME's new Australian branch. Studying the photographs provided, Cadel saw that Chester Cramp was a pale, slight, balding man wearing very thick spectacles. In contrast, his wife was as tall and glamorous as her husband was small and insignificant. In fact, Carolina Whitehead reminded Cadel a bit of Tracey Lane, one of the Axis Institute teachers—except that Tracey had always looked rather vacant. Carolina didn't look vacant. On the contrary, she wore a cool, shrewd expression in every one of the three photographs that Cliff had obtained. Somehow it was obvious that a very sharp mind lay behind all her shiny lip gloss and lacquered blond hair.

Cadel wondered why on earth she had married a shrimp like Chester.

There was a photograph of Prosper English, as well. One look at that beaky nose, enigmatic smile, and dark, piercing gaze was enough for Cadel. He scrolled past the familiar face quickly, trying to ignore the sudden chill that ran down his spine. He didn't want to think about Prosper English. Memories of Prosper would spoil his mood.

So he began to focus on the GenoME data, which had been divided into several subsections. One of them concerned the new Australian branch. Cadel was surprised at the amount of material that had already been collected; somehow Cliff had acquired photographs of every staff member. There were snapshots of people caught climbing out of taxis, or eating in cafés, as well as more formal shots from passports or driver's licenses. Upon reading the reports attached to every picture, Cadel realized that Cliff had been following the staff home from work, recording their car registration numbers, and eavesdropping on restaurant chats.

Internet checks had been run, and mail had been intercepted. Cadel wondered uneasily what Saul Greeniaus would say if he ever found out about these activities.

With any luck, however, Saul never *would* find out.

According to Cliff's notes, Carolina and her second-in-command, Jerry Reinhard, occupied separate apartments in the same high-security block of flats, while the five potentializers lived in a single house, like students. These potentializers seemed to do almost everything together: eating, shopping, commuting—even going to the movies. *It's like they belong to some kind of religious cult,* Cliff had remarked, at the conclusion of his report.

The rest of the staff lived pretty normal lives, judging from Cliff's observations. In fact, Cadel was reading all about the marketing manager's boring credit history when his eyelids became heavy. Next thing he knew, he was standing in Prosper's old office, on the top floor of the gloomy terrace house near Sydney Harbor. Cadel recognized the maroon couches, and the array of bogus certificates on the wall. A familiar computer was sitting on Prosper's desk. Everything was unchanged, except for the photograph of Cadel. That was new. It lay on top of a very thick file, which Cadel was afraid to open. Somehow he understood that this file contained his whole life, carefully labeled and analyzed.

He rushed to the door, but it was locked. So were the French windows. He couldn't get out. And Prosper was coming; he was climbing the stairs. Cadel could hear approaching footsteps. He could see the doorknob jiggling.

And then the door opened.

Like a fox caught in the glare of headlights, Cadel watched as Prosper approached him. Though wearing a set of orange overalls, Prosper was otherwise unchanged; he studied Cadel with a kind of quizzical intensity, his hooded eyes unreadable.

"So. Cadel." It was the same old voice—gentle and precise—with the same old undercurrent of barbed amusement. "I see you've been rather active." And Prosper paused beside the desk to flick at Cadel's bulging file with one long, bony finger.

Cadel couldn't respond. He had lost the ability.

"I'm not angry, dear boy. Just disappointed," Prosper went on. "How many times have we discussed this? You're being stifled. Reined in. You're not being allowed to spread your wings and reach your full potential."

Still Cadel couldn't talk. But he shook his head frantically, signifying his disagreement.

"You think that you're at liberty, but you're not," Prosper insisted. "Believe me—I know. I know what you've been up to." He bared his teeth in a slow, vulpine smile. "It seems to me that you've forgotten what I always used to say. Trust nobody. Doubt everyone." Leaning forward, he reached for Cadel's shoulder. "*Watch your back*, my dear, or you'll find yourself in a lot of trouble."

Cadel retreated from the advancing hand—and woke abruptly. He was slumped at his new desk, his head pillowed in his arms. The overhead light was still blazing. Beside him, the laptop screen announced that it was 1:05 A.M.

He had been asleep for three hours.

Cadel sat up. His mouth was dry. His neck was stiff. His heart was still pounding like a jackhammer, from the shock of his dream. On the whole, however, he felt surprisingly alert.

So he rubbed his eyes, adjusted the position of his computer, and plunged back into *GenoME/data*. After all, no one was going to stop him.

As Trader had said, bedtime was optional at Clearview House.

SIXTEEN

Cadel wasn't the first down to breakfast. When he arrived in the kitchen, at about half past six, he discovered Hamish eating burnt fruit toast at one end of the table, and Dot drinking coffee at the other. Both were studying their laptop screens, utterly absorbed.

"Hi," said Cadel. But only Hamish glanced up.

"Oh. It's you," he said. Then he focused on his computer again.

Feeling slightly snubbed, Cadel wandered over to the nearest cupboard. Upon opening it, however, he saw that it contained pots and pans. So he moved on, checking drawers and shelves and canisters until Hamish finally asked, "What are you looking for?"

"Coffee," Cadel replied. Though coffee wasn't something he normally drank, he wanted to demonstrate that he was a mature kind of person—the kind who had coffee and toast for breakfast, instead of milk and sugary cereal.

"I'll get it," said Hamish, and surged to his feet. Startled, Cadel watched him retrieve a plastic container from a high cupboard. It seemed odd that Hamish should have decided to be so helpful all of a sudden. It didn't make sense. And why keep the coffee up there? In such an inaccessible spot?

Cadel accepted the container hesitantly, bemused by Hamish's big, metallic grin. Sure enough, as the receptacle changed hands, Dot remarked, "That's not coffee. That's ground cinnamon."

Whereupon Hamish made a wet, explosive noise.

"Oh, *jeez!*" he cried, stomping back to his seat in a huff. "You're no fun, Dot!"

"The coffee's in the fridge," Dot continued, fixing her blank gaze on Cadel. "It's instant, though. The espresso machine is downstairs."

"That's okay." Cadel quietly placed the cinnamon on a nearby countertop, wondering if he had made a mistake.

Would Clearview House prove to be full of idiots and bullies after all?

"Don't mind Hamish," Dot continued dryly. "He has a puerile sense of humor, but he's quite acceptable in other ways."

"At least I *have* a sense of humor," Hamish retorted, and Dot set down her cup.

"There's nothing wrong with my sense of humor," she said coolly. "For instance, I find your outfit very amusing."

Cadel had to suppress a smile. Hamish did look rather odd in his oversized Hell's Angels T-shirt and his studded leather wristband. Like a woolly lamb in body armor.

But despite his feeble appearance, he still had enough courage to launch an attack on Dot.

"Well, what are *you* d-dressed as?" he demanded scornfully. "A 1950s librarian?"

Dot stared at him for a moment, expressionless, before turning back to her computer. Cadel toyed with the idea of asking her about Com. He was trying to think of a good opening line when she abruptly sprang to her feet, snapping her laptop shut. Even Hamish seemed taken aback by this unexpected burst of energy.

"I'll be down in the War Room," she declared, and made for the lift. She moved so quickly that Cadel had to blurt out the very first thing that came into his head.

It was: "When did you last see your brother?"

Dot paused on the pantry threshold. Her eyes ran over him in a curiously detached way, as if she were swiping a laser beam across a bar code. At last she said, "I'll send you a report."

Then she disappeared into the pantry.

"That's what she always says," Hamish remarked, after a brief silence. "*I'll send you a report.* She prefers e-mails to conversations." Sprawled in his chair, he pushed his glasses up his nose and peered at Cadel through their thick, distorting lenses. "So have you worked out what you want to do yet?"

"How do you mean?" asked Cadel.

"Well—have you had any good ideas? Or d-do you want to help someone else?" As Cadel considered this question, Hamish continued impatiently, "We're trying to get into the GenoME system. You know *that,* don't you?"

"Yes, of course."

"We can't prove that GenoME's been doing anything illegal unless we get into its system," Hamish declared, going on to relate that the squad was hoping to bring down GenoME by doing one of three things: either by proving that the company was responsible for killing Rex Austin's son, or by establishing that its genetic analysis technique was a scam, or by determining that there was a financial connection between GenoME and Fountain Pharmaceuticals. "Because if Fountain Pharmaceuticals is really the new NanTex, and GenoME is sending it money, then GenoME is b-breaking the law by funding an illegal corporation," said Hamish. Whereupon Cadel thought back to the files he'd been reading the previous night.

So far, there didn't seem to be much data on Fountain Pharmaceuticals. Except for the fact that Chester Cramp was its chief executive officer.

"So what do you want to do? We've already done all the obvious stuff," Hamish continued, counting off various options on his knobbly fingers. "They've been really careful with their off-the-shelf defaults—they've changed every one of them. They've got RootKit Revealer. They run tests on the firewall *continuously*—"

"How do you know?" Cadel interrupted.

"Huh?"

"How do you know all this, if you haven't got in yet?"

"They discuss it," Hamish replied. He informed Cadel that Trader had picked up conversations between Jerry and his assistant using the laser eavesdropping technology. Trader tended to concentrate on Jerry's office, because Jerry was "the tech guy," and occasionally talked about subjects other than traffic, football, and clearance sales. "The good thing is, they've got a webpage," Hamish revealed. "So I figure that's how we'll get in. Unless this thing works with Zac, of course."

Cadel frowned. "What thing?" he said.

"The honeytoken." When Cadel blinked, Hamish added, "Didn't you hear about the honeytoken?"

"No."

"Really?" For some reason, Hamish looked delighted. "Well, Zac's got an appointment with one of the potentializers at nine thirty. He's pretending to be a client. And we know he'll have to fill in a form, b-because that's how GenoME manipulates people. By getting hold of their information."

"Oh, right." Cadel nodded. He had seen a scan of the GenoME application form in the electronic files he'd examined. Apparently, it had been stolen and copied by one of Rex Austin's contacts in America. "Yeah, I saw that form."

"D-did you see question five, by any chance?" It was obvious that Hamish expected the answer to be no. When it was yes, he could hardly conceal his disappointment. "Gee," he mumbled. "You really are on the ball."

"Is Zac going to put a fake e-mail address on the application form?" Cadel hazarded, because that would have been *his* plan. And Hamish grinned.

"Fake e-mail, fake identity, fake everything," he confirmed. "Zac won't be going in as Zac." He sighed. "I wish it was me going in. I'd love to find out what happens in that place."

"You will," a familiar voice remarked, and suddenly Trader was standing beside them. "There's a debrief session after lunch, with Zac. I want everyone to attend." He studied Cadel. "How are you this morning?"

"Good," Cadel replied. He felt very small and creased and grubby next to Trader, who positively gleamed in his freshly ironed clothes. Trader smelled of cologne and toothpaste. His eyes were clear and there was a bounce in his step.

He made the kitchen look dingy.

"Aren't you eating?" he asked Cadel, just as the twins appeared. All at once the room was full of people. It was as if an alarm clock or a starter's pistol had gone off somewhere, signalling the commencement of a new day. While Hamish continued to pack toast into his mouth, Lexi and Devin started to bicker over the last of the strawberry jam. Tony Cheung sidled in to make coffee. Judith Bashford, laden down with bags of fruit, burst onto the scene like an armored tank, announcing that she had the perfect cure for Lexi's constipation. And though Trader confessed that he'd already eaten breakfast, he remained in the room, adding considerably to the noise and bustle.

Cadel didn't know quite what to do at first. He retreated to one corner, clutching a teaspoon like a shield. Then he felt Trader's arm fall across his shoulders, heavy and reassuring.

"I'm afraid it's everyone for himself at breakfast," Trader said softly. "But I'm sure you can handle it, after the Axis Institute." With a conspiratorial grin, he placed his mouth to Cadel's ear and murmured, "The good thing about Clearview House is that no one's going to poison your orange juice."

No, thought Cadel. *They'll just try and trick me into drinking ground cinnamon.* But he didn't say this aloud. Instead he took a deep breath and plunged into the milling crowd between the sink and the fridge, emerging some time later with a bowl of cornflakes. He didn't really mind all the confusion. From what he could see, it was simply the product of a general desire to get to work as soon as possible. By the time he had eaten, showered, and cleaned his teeth, everyone else was downstairs in the War Room, beavering away.

Everyone, that is, except Zac and Cliff.

According to Trader, Cliff would be monitoring Zac from a parked car during Zac's "recon of number eleven." Cliff, in turn, would be sending updates to Trader until the job was done. Zac's interview was scheduled for half past nine, so someone would have to keep an eye on the honeytoken e-mail address from that moment on—just in case it was used by GenoME.

"If it is, we might be able to capture a return address, at least," Dot advised, as the whole infiltration team clustered around Cadel, bombarding him with information. Cadel had to concentrate hard, or he wouldn't have been able to absorb everything that was thrown at him. Lexi and Hamish and Devin filled him in on what was happening, interrupting one another in their eagerness to describe their overall strategy.

Jerry, they said, had a laptop that he took home with him, but so far Cliff hadn't picked up any useful wireless transmissions. Dot's port-scanning software hadn't turned up a single useful IP address, either. The GenoME webpage had been erected in the no-man's-land between two GenoME firewalls; nevertheless, being a webpage, it had to receive http messages from the outside world. So Hamish hadn't found it hard to get through the bastion host.

Since then, however, he'd been forced to tread very carefully.

"I d-don't want to mangle the webpage, because it'll warn them we're here," he said. "And that inner firewall—it won't let *anything* in. So I'm trying to fake up a security patch that'll squeeze through and rewrite their PS."

"He might even finish the job by next Christmas," Devin sneered. And Hamish flushed.

"Just ignore D-Devin," he told Cadel. "Devin's such a script-kiddie, he couldn't write a program to save his life."

"He is *not* a script-kiddie!" Lexi protested, firing up. "You take that back!" She seized a handful of Hamish's T-shirt, almost choking him. But before she could do any more damage, Judith addressed her from the other side of the room.

"Hey!" Judith barked. "Enough of that!"

Whereupon Lexi grudgingly released Hamish.

"What if they launch a security probe?" said Cadel. Seated at his desk, hemmed in by bodies, he had been silently turning data over and over in his mind, assessing it, classifying it, and considering it from every angle. Glancing up, he addressed himself to Dot—who was standing calmly beside him. "Suppose they use Zac's e-mail address for sniffing around?" he asked. "Suppose they have a really good probe, and they get into our system?"

"They won't," Dot replied. She explained that the squad would be monitoring Zac's false e-mail address on a "discrete" machine. This machine would be used as a decoy only. It had no links to any of the other machines in the War Room.

"But what if they do sniff around?" Cadel pressed. He couldn't believe that no one had considered this possibility. "Is there anything for them to find?"

"Oh, sure." Lexi jumped in to describe how she and Hamish and Cliff had concocted an entire virtual life for Zac's alias: fake interests, fake friends, fake credit history. . . .

"No, no. That's not what I'm saying." Cadel was conscious that Trader had rejoined their group, after briefly conversing with Tony and Judith. "If they send in a probe, and do some sniffing, then you can set up a honeytoken *inside* this honeytoken. They'll be wanting to extract information and download it. We can piggyback on that. They'll be capturing our probe along with the data." Cadel gazed around at a ring of skeptical expressions. "I've done it before," he insisted. "I can set it up myself."

"We can't afford to alert them, Cadel." It was Trader who spoke. "If those GenoME people find out that we're interested—"

"They won't. I swear."

Trader and Dot exchanged glances. Then Trader checked his watch.

"We don't have much time," he observed. "They could be logging in anytime after nine thirty."

Cadel shrugged. "There's no harm in trying," he said, and Dot agreed. "We might as well," was her opinion.

All eyes were now fixed on Trader, who chewed at his bottom lip.

"All right," he said at last. "Cadel, see what you can do about tagging one of those decoy programs. Try to get the job done before GenoME uses our e-mail address. The rest of you can stick to what you've been working on."

"Oh, but *Trader*!" Lexi groaned. "I wanted Cadel to help *me*!"

"Tough luck," said Trader, shooing people away. Then he placed his hand on Cadel's shoulder and stooped until their eyes were level. "You won't let me down, will you?" he said. "If GenoME finds out about us, you'll be back at the Donkins' in no time."

"I won't let you down," Cadel replied earnestly, and Trader laughed.

"Christ," he said with a snort. "You're even better than I am, batting those baby blues." As he straightened, he released Cadel's shoulder in order to slap him on the back—so hard that Cadel nearly fell off his chair. "Well done, anyway. I knew you'd be an asset. If you have a question, ask Dot. She's coordinating the infiltration attacks."

Watching Trader walk away, Cadel thought: *Sure. I'll ask Dot. And she'll e-mail me an answer, sometime.*

But he didn't utter the words aloud.

He still didn't feel confident enough to speak his mind in such an unfamiliar environment.

SEVENTEEN

Zac returned to Clearview House after lunch. He had made his way back in a roundabout fashion, passing through shops and catching various forms of public transport. Cliff had told him to be careful, in case he was being followed.

"But he wasn't," said Cliff. "I trailed him myself, and I didn't see a soul." Glancing around the War Room, he laughed his raspy laugh and gestured at Zac. "What do you think of the glasses? They're good, aren't they?"

Zac wore ugly, black-framed glasses that had been repaired with sticky tape. His blond hair hung limp and unwashed around his ears, instead of being tied back neatly, as it usually was. His beard was untrimmed. His earring was gone. His clothes were drab and rather dirty.

"Looks desperate enough, eh?" said Cliff. "No friends. No confidence. The perfect GenoME client."

"So how did it go?" Trader was sitting with his arms folded, not far from Cadel. Everyone had stopped working. An air of excitement hung over the room. "Was there any trouble?"

"No trouble," Cliff replied. He looked enormously pleased with himself—and with Zac. "It was textbook. This bloke should have been an actor."

"It was easier than I thought," Zac mumbled. "No one tried to stop me from going to the toilet."

"Oh, you went, did you?" Trader leaned forward, his eyes narrowed. "Did you get any pictures?"

"They're downloaded," said Cliff, speaking for Zac. "You should check them out yourself. All I could see were a couple of sensors on the stairs—they must be turned off during the day." Cliff's report was directed at Trader, in a way that almost seemed to exclude the rest of the squad. "Good news is, the fire door hasn't been wired," Cliff continued. "If you head for the toilet that's in the stairwell, you could wedge open the fire door with something small, and get in after hours."

"When the sensors would be on," Trader said.

But Cliff shrugged. "If we knew what pulse those sensors were set at, we could work our way around them," he suggested. "It's just a matter of timing."

Trader seemed unconvinced. "Where are the door hinges?" he inquired. "Are any of them in the stairwell?"

"No." Cliff shook his head glumly. "We can't lift a single door off the wall. But the locks are electromagnetic. You might be able to do something with heat. A blowtorch, say."

"I don't want to brute-force anything unless I have to," said Trader. At which point Hamish interrupted. He had been getting more and more restless, his knees jigging and his fingers twitching.

"Did you see any computers?" he demanded of Zac, who pulled an apologetic face.

"Not one," said Zac. "Not on the ground floor. The receptionist didn't have one. There were no computers in the interview rooms—I had a good look, on my way to the toilet."

"The *receptionist* didn't have one?" Lexi sounded almost horrified, as if Zac had announced that the receptionist wore fetters, or a muzzle. "Why not?"

Zac spread his hands.

"I don't know," he said. "All she had was a phone and a diary."

"That's weird," said Devin. "Man, that's weird." And Cadel felt disappointed.

Was Devin really that slow?

"It's not weird," said Cadel. "It's security conscious. Anybody could walk in off the street. But if they did, they couldn't get into the upstairs offices, where the computers are. Not without a blowtorch." As everyone stared at him, he added, "Cliff just said so."

There was a pause. Then Trader remarked, "He's right. Cadel's right. This a good indication of what we're up against. Our targets won't take *any* risks." His expression was unusually serious. "We should keep that in mind, people."

"So what happened?" It was Lexi who now addressed Zac. She was obviously impatient for more details. "Did you meet Carolina?"

"No," Zac replied.

"What about Jerry?"

Zac explained that he had met only the receptionist, a lab assistant, and a potentializer called Jill, who had been pretty and friendly and sympathetic. She had offered him refreshments—tea or coffee—before conducting him into one of the downstairs interview rooms. Here she had left him to fill out an application form. "It took about an hour," he said. "I didn't move from the spot, in case there was a camera somewhere. Jill kept popping in, anyway. To see how I was getting on."

"Did you answer all the questions?" Though Trader's tone was calm, his gaze was alert, and his posture tense. "You'd better tell us if you didn't."

"I did," said Zac. "It went fine." He then related how, once he had finished his questionnaire, Jill had whisked it away while someone else took tissue samples from him. There had been a kind of medical cart in the interview room; one of the lab assistants had carried out the procedure, which had been conducted in a very professional and reassuring manner, right down to the white coat and latex gloves. Then Jill had returned, all bright eyed and bushy tailed. She had given Zac a complete rundown of the gene-plotting process and fee scale, informing him that his genetic code would be sent to "headquarters" for analysis, after which he should come back for another consultation—probably in about a week's time.

She had also persuaded him to sign some kind of waiver, which he hadn't bothered to read.

"After that, I went to the toilet," he recounted. "She didn't come with me. The bathroom was immaculate." He glanced at Cliff. "If you want to plant something in there, you're going to have to make sure it's invisible. Because whoever cleans that place doesn't miss a spot."

"The potentializers do it," said Trader. He grinned at the sight of jaws dropping and eyes widening all around him. "It's true," he insisted. "They're rostered on. One night a week each."

"The *potentializers* clean the *toilets*?" Judith exclaimed, roused from her extended silence. "Are you sure about that?"

"Believe me, it was practically the first thing we looked at." Trader rearranged his long legs, which were stretched out in front of him. "Cleaners are always the weakest link," he explained. "That's probably why GenoME doesn't contract out its cleaning."

"Man, those guys must be brainwashed," said Devin, in accents of disgust. "Or totally insane." Whereupon Lexi made a scornful noise.

"Just because *you* never clean the toilets," she said, "doesn't mean that everyone who picks up a toilet brush is crazy."

"I do too clean the toilets!" Devin snapped, firing up. And Hamish said sweetly, "She d-doesn't mean *flushing* it, Dev, she means cleaning it."

Devin opened his mouth to deliver a stinging retort. Before he could proceed, however, a piercing *beep* caused every head to turn.

The decoy computer was sounding its alarm.

"Christ!" said Hamish. "We've caught 'em!"

There was a mad rush to check the screen. Cadel couldn't compete against so many larger, heavier bodies. He hung back, reluctant to brave the scrum around the computer.

Trader also hesitated. He stood for a moment, surveying the chaos with his hands on his hips. Then he called for "a bit of calm."

"Step aside!" he ordered. "Don't touch anything!" He motioned to Cadel. "Go on, have a look," he said. "Go and stand beside Dot—she won't bite you."

Obediently Cadel joined Dot, who had bagged the chair in front of the decoy. An e-mail had arrived from GenoME.org. It was sitting in front of them like a tiny, ticking time bomb. Cadel could have sworn that every letter was pulsing ominously.

His heartbeat quickened.

"Open it," he said, and Dot obliged. Everyone squinted at the message that flashed onto the screen; it was a standard greeting, welcoming "John McDonald" to GenoME—and it had come with an attachment.

Cadel smiled.

"There it is," he muttered. "It'll be in that attachment, you watch."

"What will be?" asked Judith, and Devin replied, "The probe."

"If there is a probe," said Dot. She sat with her finger poised over the mouse, peering up at Trader. "Shall I?" she queried.

Trader nodded. And Dot opened the attachment.

There followed such a surge of activity on the decoy hard drive that Cadel could feel it through the soles of his feet. On the screen, however, all was tranquil. GenoME had sent Zac a confirmation of his next appointment, a company manifesto, a questionnaire, and a kind of sales pitch outlining all the different services that GenoME could offer, from medical screenings to family counseling.

"Leave it up," Cadel advised, upon inspecting the colorful pictures and reams of text. "We have to wait for a moment while they download . . ." He went on to explain that his probe was rather like the one designed by Hamish, except that it would disguise itself as a legitimate virus scan. Virus scans were constantly having to send out requests for virus-signature updates from the Internet. They were busy little things. That was why they so efficiently masked the activities of a program designed to dispatch regular packets of information to someone who wasn't authorized to receive them.

"And here's the source address," said Cadel suddenly. He pointed at the screen, unconsciously tensing his muscles. "Look, see? It's our target."

"So what do we do now?" Lexi asked. At which point Dot rose, abruptly vacating her chair.

"Now it's Cadel's turn," she said. And when he hesitated, Trader backed her up.

"Go on, Cadel. You found the target. You deserve the first shot."

Flushing, Cadel obeyed. He slid into Dot's seat and plunged into a virtual world of format strings and stack frames. During the next fifteen minutes, while everyone waited in silence, he surreptitiously took over the GenoME machine. But he didn't start to plunder it immediately.

"We should hold back a while," he suggested, appealing to Trader. "They'll be on high alert, while they're infiltrating a new system. It'll be safer if we take things slowly."

"He's right," Dot declared, and Hamish nodded. No one, in fact, was tempted to disagree.

So Trader ordered a thirty-minute break.

"I want this machine monitored, though," he warned. "I don't want it touched, but I want it monitored. Who's going to keep an eye on it?"

Half a dozen hands shot up, Judith's among them. Cadel hoped that she wouldn't be chosen. He wasn't sure that she had skills enough for the job.

"What about you, Cadel?" Trader was gazing down at him, smiling an indulgent smile. "Aren't you going to volunteer? It's your probe, isn't it?"

Cadel shifted awkwardly. He had a proposal to make and had been hoping to make it quietly, in a corner somewhere. He didn't want to start throwing his weight around so soon. It would look as if he were showing off.

And he knew what could happen to a person who was always showing off.

"Uh—sure," he said. "I'll do it if you like. I just . . ." He paused.

"What?"

"I just wanted to ask you something."

"Go ahead, then. Ask away." Trader nodded at Hamish. "Watch that screen for me in the meantime, will you?"

Cadel sprang to his feet, allowing Hamish to occupy the swivel chair. An inquisitive silence had fallen. Looking around, Cadel saw that everyone was staring at him—everyone, that is, except Hamish.

Hamish was staring at the decoy machine.

"It's just an idea I had," Cadel remarked hesitantly. "I've never done it before, but it should be possible."

"Go on," said Trader.

"Well—we don't know whose computer we've found. And we *won't* know until we start inspecting its files. But we do know it's got a speaker in it."

"So?" said Devin

"So if you want me to, I can reprogram that speaker and turn it into a microphone. From here." When no comment was forthcoming, Cadel added, "What I mean is, it would *receive* sounds instead of transmitting them."

Still no one responded. Cadel broke into a sweat. Surely somebody must have understood him?

"We'd be able to eavesdrop on nearby conversations," he pointed out, just as Lexi giggled with excitement. She turned to her brother.

"Can you believe it?" she squealed. "Can you believe this guy?"

Trader was frowning. The smile had been wiped clean off his face.

"Are you serious?" he said sharply, addressing Cadel. "Can you really do that?"

"I think so."

"You'd need to record it all," Hamish submitted, without taking his eyes off the decoy screen.

"I know." Cadel had ideas about that, too. "But we shouldn't rig the speaker until we've downloaded everything we can. In case there's a problem."

Lexi and Devin nodded in agreement. Tony rubbed his chin. Judith looked inquiringly at Cliff, who in turn looked at Trader.

"What do you reckon?" said Cliff.

"What do *I* reckon?" Trader's eyes creased at the corners. "I reckon we've hit the jackpot." And he whacked Cadel across the shoulder, enthusiastically.

Then he started to fire orders around the room.

"Last-minute change to the meal roster," he announced. "I want Judith and Tony taking care of dinner tonight. Dot can be in charge of data gathering, and Cadel can be in charge of Operation Microphone. Forget everything else. We want that data analyzed and we want that mike installed, pronto."

"Aye, aye, sir!" Hamish saluted.

"Zac, I want a detailed report on your visit." Trader was still reeling off instructions. "Judith, once that data starts coming in, you're going to be busy, so I want you to review all your preparations for Sonja's arrival *now.* You two . . ." He gestured at the twins. "You're in charge of data transfer. I want it *antiseptic.* Triple-checked. I don't want any direct link between this compromised computer and our own system. Is that clear? I want *air-gap protection.*"

"Yes, Trader," the twins intoned solemnly.

"All right, then." Suddenly Trader seemed to run out of breath. As the squad waited, he gazed around at everyone, expectantly. Then he flapped his hands, like someone shooing chickens. "Well?" he said. "Go on. Hop to it!"

EIGHTEEN

Cadel was waiting on the doorstep when Sonja arrived at Clearview House the next morning.

She turned up in a taxi that was designed to accommodate wheelchairs, with a convoy of vehicles following close behind. Two volunteers were driving cars packed with her belongings, and Fiona had also decided to lend a hand. The first thing that Fiona said, upon catching sight of Cadel, was, "Are you all right? You look exhausted."

Cadel flushed. He had been up very late the night before, wrestling with his microphone application and getting all excited about the GenoME computer he'd identified. E-mails stored on this machine had revealed that it belonged to Jerry Reinhard's assistant, Amy Ng. And Amy occupied a desk right outside Jerry's office, in a kind of anteroom. Everyone who entered or left Jerry's office had to go past Amy.

Trader knew this from some of the conversations he'd picked up on his eavesdropping equipment.

"It's a good place to plant a bug," he'd said. "If Jerry leaves his door open, we might hear something of interest."

Unfortunately, Jerry's computer wasn't easily accessible from Amy's. Despite the fact that she was his assistant, she didn't have his e-mail address. And she was obviously required to type his letters directly into her own machine, instead of downloading them from his. As Hamish had remarked (rather shrewdly, in Cadel's opinion), "Only someone who was up to no good would be that paranoid about security."

Jerry's security was so good, in fact, that Cadel hadn't yet found any gateway into Jerry's machine—or into the lab system, either. Amy's workstation formed part of a more vulnerable network set up for the marketing department and the five potentializers. ("Who must have their own computers somewhere," Dot had remarked. "Only not in the interview rooms, obviously.") Thanks to Cadel's probe, Genius Squad had now collected most of the data stored on this lesser network. Very little of it, however, had so far been analyzed. There hadn't been enough time to read it all. Still, everyone was hoping that once it had been checked, it would yield some clue as to how GenoME's U.S. network might be infiltrated.

There was no question that a link existed between America and the Australian lab computers. It was just a matter of tracing this link. Surely there had to be a chink somewhere in the laboratory defenses. Surely somebody would find a password, or at least a firewall vulnerability.

Cadel was determined to be the one who did. That was why he'd stayed up until two in the morning, working his way through GenoME's online records. In fact, he had fallen asleep while scrolling through endless pages of biographical detail.

If it hadn't been for Sonja's sudden appearance, he would still have been hunkered over his laptop, searching through birth dates and telephone numbers for something that would give him deeper access into GenoME's system.

"I'm all right," he told Fiona, slightly embarrassed by her obvious concern. "I'm not used to the new bed yet, that's all."

"No one's keeping you up, are they?"

"Of course not," Cadel lied. Then, to distract her, he hurried over to where Sonja was being settled into her wheelchair. "I'll take her round the back," he informed the taxi driver. "There's a ramp that leads into the kitchen."

Sonja was wearing her best flowered skirt and a pretty embroidered blouse. Though excitement was making her movements more erratic than usual, her brown eyes shone, and an irrepressible smile kept struggling across her face.

Cadel's answering smile made Sonja gurgle.

"You should see your bathroom!" he said, as she was trundled along a cracked cement path toward the rear of the house. "It's *fantastic.* And all the furniture's new. And everyone's really great—they're dying to meet you!"

Most of the squad were certainly curious, though Cadel was a little worried about one of its younger members. The previous evening, Devin had asked in his graceless way if it would be safe to allow "the spastic" near any of the computers: Was she likely to knock them about, or spew all over them? Seeing Cadel's furious scowl, Lexi had given her brother a cuff on the ear, telling him not to be so feeble. And there had followed an all-out fight, during which the twins had broken one of the stair banisters.

It was Judith who had settled that fight—much to everyone's astonishment. Though Cliff and Trader had managed to separate the twins, Judith was the one who had dragged Devin to the nearest computer and shown him Sonja's latest online discussion of pseudorandomness. Devin had stopped talking about "the spastic" after that. He had started to use Sonja's name.

Nevertheless, Cadel felt relieved that Devin wasn't around when Sonja arrived. Both Devin and Tony Cheung were, at that point, holed up in the War Room—along with Dot and Cliff. Therefore, according to Genius Squad protocol, they had to stay out of sight until every intruder was gone. Even so, quite a crowd had gathered in the kitchen to welcome Sonja. As Cadel maneuvered her over the threshold, they were greeted by a chorus of eager voices, led by the strident tones of Judith Bashford.

"Here she is!" cried Judith. "At long last!"

"Hi, Sonja, I'm Lexi. Has Cadel told you about me?"

"Lexi, you're blocking the way," said Zac. "How are they going to get in if you stand right there?"

"Nice wheels," Hamish remarked. "What's your top speed in that?"

Sonja couldn't reply, because Fiona was carrying her DynaVox. So Cadel set it up quickly while Fiona explained how it worked. Hamish was fascinated by the DynaVox. He wanted to know all about its underlying technology. When he asked if he could "give it a go," Cadel hesitated. But Sonja didn't seem to mind. Apparently she had no problem with Hamish's desire to make the DynaVox say rude words.

At last Fiona put an end to all this messing about by pushing Sonja firmly into her bedroom. Cadel was anxious that Sonja should like what she saw; he was quick to point out all the best features of the bathroom and storage facilities. Meanwhile, Judith introduced herself to Fiona and explained that Zac was one of the shift workers who would ensure that Sonja had round-the-clock tendance. "Sonja will be our main priority," Judith declared. "Trader and Cliff and Dot will take care of the other kids, while Tony and Zac and I will focus on Sonja."

Cadel devoutly hoped so. He was a little worried about exactly how much attention Sonja would be getting, if Judith and Tony became absorbed in their work. But he told himself that *he* could look after Sonja, if no one else was around. And he was reassured by the room across the hall from Sonja's. According to Judith, someone would sleep in this snug little chamber every night, ready to be of assistance. Sonja would never be left to fend for herself.

"Not that she won't have her privacy," Judith added. "We realize how important that is. Which is why we installed this intercom system." She began to demonstrate the system, as all around her the bedroom buzzed with activity. People hurried in and out, carrying bundles and boxes. Lexi was already pawing through Sonja's clothes. Hamish had pounced on Sonja's computer.

"I'll just plug this in, shall I?" he said. And Cadel frowned.

"No," he replied sharply. "*I* will."

"Shall I hang these up?" Lexi was examining one of Sonja's jumpers. "Or do you want me to throw it away? It's *so* little-old-lady."

"Lexi, leave that stuff alone!" Judith barked. "What are you doing here, anyway? You should be cleaning the upstairs toilet!"

Lexi scowled, then flounced from the room in a huff. Hamish followed close on her heels, ordered out by Judith because he had made a disparaging comment about Stephen Hawking (one of Sonja's pinups). When Sonja's possessions had all been brought in, Zac and the volunteers departed as well. Soon only Judith, Fiona, and Cadel remained to keep Sonja company.

Working together, they put away Sonja's books and clothes and electronic equipment. Judith excelled at the fiddly task of unpacking; she was very organized, and hated mess. Though her own appearance was rather messy, with her wild, wispy hair and layers of mismatched clothes, she couldn't abide messy accounts, or a cluttered kitchen, or a disorganized workspace. It was she who drew up the rosters and distributed the cleaning products at Clearview House. It was she who implemented laundry schedules, and bullied people into serving meals on time.

Cadel had learned all this after receiving exhaustive instructions from Judith on various domestic subjects such as scrambling eggs, disinfecting bathroom floors, sorting dirty clothes, and labeling leftovers. When he observed the way she made sure that Sonja's shoes were all neatly aligned, and that his best friend's clothes were distributed according to a well-conceived plan, he became even more convinced that Judith's loud and sloppy exterior concealed a true accountant's heart.

It didn't surprise him that she and Sonja seemed to click. Sonja herself had a preference for things like color-coding and correctly folded jumpers; it was torture to her when her possessions weren't put away properly. Disorder offended the mathematical precision of her mind.

So she and Judith were in perfect accord when it came to pattern groupings and tidy underwear drawers.

"Leggings," Judith mused at one point. "Would these be in the same subset as tights or trousers?"

"*That's-easy-enough,*" Sonja replied. "*If-we-classified-tank-tops-as-belonging-to-the-T-shirt-category, because-the-dominating-characteristic-was-fabric-type-rather-than-the-configuration-of-sleeves—*"

"Then leggings would be in with tights," Judith finished. "Yes. I agree. Keep it consistent."

While she busied herself with the correct gradation of Sonja's knitwear (from summer to winter), Cadel blue-tacked posters to the wall. He set up Sonja's computer and arranged her candles on the marble mantelpiece, as Fiona, in a low voice, told him that the universities were still turning him down.

"But I'm going to talk to a friend of a friend, who teaches at the University of New South Wales," Fiona informed him. "We might be able to arrange some kind of backdoor enrollment."

Cadel thanked her, though he wasn't terribly interested. University enrollment didn't seem so important anymore—not since he had joined Genius Squad. The outside world no longer mattered as much, because he had access to computers. Even Prosper English wasn't worrying him unduly. He had other things to think about.

Like his microphone application, for instance.

He was dying to tell Sonja about that. And of course he couldn't—not until Fiona had left. Cadel liked Fiona. He was grateful to her. But he grew very impatient as she hung about, fussing and fretting. It was nearly lunchtime before she finally took off, having promised to drop in the next day if she could. Judith walked her to the front door, trying not to look relieved.

Left alone at last, Cadel and Sonja knew better than to waste time. Sonja still had to visit the War Room and hadn't yet become acquainted with the whole squad. Someone was bound to burst in at any moment.

So Cadel lowered his voice and said, "What do you think?"

"*Great,*" Sonja replied, through the medium of her DynaVox.

"Is there anything we've forgotten?"

"*No.*"

"All the real work happens downstairs. There's a concealed lift, and it's big enough for your chair."

"*Hamish-is-funny.*"

"Yes." Cadel wondered what she meant by "funny." Did she think that Hamish was ludicrous or amusing? Assuming the former, he said, "Those clothes of his were Lexi's idea. She wants us to look tough."

"*Me-too?*"

"I don't know." Cadel shrugged. "She's a bit flaky. You should just ignore her when she's like that."

"But-I-want-to-look-tough," Sonja protested. Though the metallic delivery of her DynaVox was completely toneless, her face was alight with mischief. *"I-want-a-leather-jacket-and-a-nose-stud."*

"Yeah, right."

"I-do. Why-shouldn't-I?"

"No reason," Cadel muttered. He couldn't exactly say, "Because you'll look stupid." Sonja was already self-conscious about the way she looked.

Quickly, he changed the subject.

"We've cracked the first-tier network at GenoME," he said. "Zac went in there, pretending to be a new client, and planted a honeytoken e-mail address. Trouble is, we haven't found the gateway to any high-security parts of the system. So far it looks as if everything we've downloaded is just housekeeping."

"Like-what?" Sonja queried.

"Oh—marketing plans. Basic invoices. Client information." Cadel headed for the door. "Here," he said. "I'll show you. Won't be a sec."

Cadel's laptop was concealed in one of the kitchen cupboards. He'd been eating a late breakfast when Sonja's arrival had interrupted him; Genius Squad rules decreed that, in such circumstances, priority should be given to hiding all laptops. Cadel had therefore shoved his own machine behind the rolled oats and raisins before rushing out to greet his best friend.

As a result, it took him only about thirty seconds to retrieve his computer and return with it to Sonja's room. On the way, he noticed that the front door was standing slightly ajar.

He also noticed that Judith and Fiona were still chatting together outside.

"Here," he said quietly, upon rejoining Sonja. "You'll be getting these files yourself, but Judith will probably want you to look at the accounts. This is what *I've* been looking at."

"Nice-laptop," was Sonja's comment, as he placed the machine on her desk.

"Isn't it?"

"Will-I-get-one-too?"

"Your equipment's downstairs. There's a special keyboard and everything." Hurriedly, Cadel entered a series of passwords until he had gained access to his cache of GenoME client files. "You wouldn't believe what GenoME's got in here," he continued, calling up a list of file names. "They ask the most personal questions. Medical history. Marital status. Drugs taken during the last five years. I mean, GenoME doesn't need to know that kind of thing!"

"Do-we?"

Sonja's question took Cadel by surprise. He glanced at her and discovered that she was watching him intently. All at once he felt as if he had failed to pass a moral test of some sort.

"We won't be using any of this," he stressed. "Not like GenoME. They *use* it, Sonja."

"It-was-given-to-them. Not-to-us."

"So what are you saying? That we should ignore these files?" He tried to defend himself, conscious all the while that she was probably justified in airing her doubts. (GenoME might have forfeited its right to privacy, but what about its poor, deluded customers?) "I'm not paying attention to most of this," he assured her. "I'm just looking for a clue that will help me get past the next firewall." He turned back to the computer and scrolled down the list of file names. "Look," he said, "this is all I do. I call up the file—like this—and I make a note of the file number, just in case, and—"

Suddenly he stopped.

There, on the screen in front of him, was a photograph of Gazo Kovacs.

PART THREE

NINETEEN

Gazo Kovacs had been Cadel's only true friend at the Axis Institute. The last time they'd seen each other, Gazo had been trying to save Cadel from Prosper English. Poor Gazo had then been knocked out and arrested. But he had been able to escape police custody because of his unique genetic condition.

When Gazo became stressed, he exuded a stench so powerful that it could render a grown man unconscious.

Needless to say, Trader found this hard to accept. He wanted to know how Gazo Kovacs could possibly be a walking stink bomb if he was currently employed as a gardener. How could he be mowing lawns while dressed up like a spaceman?

"I don't know," Cadel replied. "Perhaps he doesn't wear his special suit anymore. Perhaps he doesn't need to, because he works in the open air."

Skeptically, Trader examined Gazo's file. In it Gazo was called Russ Adams; somehow he had managed to acquire a false identity. Cadel couldn't help thinking that Gazo must have learned a lot at the Axis Institute if he was now successfully forging birth certificates and pretending to be someone else. Gazo gave his occupation as "land care specialist." He had been hired by the University of Sydney, and worked there four days a week. Though he admitted to being an Englishman, he made no mention of the Axis Institute.

Cadel was impressed by this. At the institute, Gazo had always come across as a dunce—good-hearted but slow. Yet here he was, cleverly keeping a low profile. The only thing he'd really confessed to was his condition. He wanted his DNA profile analyzed because he needed more information about his "unfortunate handicap," and how it might be controlled.

This last disclosure touched Cadel. All at once, he was desperate to see Gazo again—to warn him against GenoME and to question him about the Axis Institute. They needed to discuss a whole range of things. Yet this could only be done if Cadel visited the university unannounced. Otherwise Gazo might get nervous and run away.

"I don't know if it's a good idea," Trader said, when appealed to. "Those coppers out there are going to be treading on your heels. And you can't afford to dodge them, or they'll wonder why."

"I wasn't going to dodge them. I was going to tell Mr. Greeniaus all about it." Cadel tried to explain his reasoning. "Gazo was at the Institute. He can confirm my testimony. Mr. Greeniaus has been looking for him, and so have I."

"But if the police start hassling this friend of yours, that might alarm GenoME. He's a GenoME client, after all." Trader winced. "Christ, he might *tell* GenoME about you!"

"He won't. He's my friend."

"If he's such a good friend, why don't you want to give him any warning? Wouldn't he be pleased to see you? Why are you worried that he'll bolt?"

"Because he's in hiding. He's afraid of my . . ." It was hard to say the word. Cadel stumbled over it. "Of my father," he finished at last, reluctantly. "Gazo's afraid of Prosper English."

"Couldn't you just ring him, then?"

"I could," Cadel was forced to concede, "if I wasn't concerned about GenoME bugging his phone."

Trader's brows snapped together. He leaned forward, his eyes narrowed. "Is there some indication of that? In the files?" he asked.

"No."

"Then—"

“I just wouldn’t put it past them,” Cadel remarked with a shrug. “Would you?”

At this, Trader relaxed slightly. He shook his head, an admiring grin creeping across his angular face. “You’ve certainly got a unique outlook on life, young Cadel,” he said. “Remarkably distrustful, if I may say so. Must be something to do with that Axis Institute training. As a matter of fact, it’s the sort of attitude we need more of around here.” And he slapped Cadel’s knee. “We’ll ask Cliff what he thinks. Maybe it’s the right thing to do after all. Maybe if the police start hassling Gazo, it’ll distract GenoME from what we’re up to ourselves.”

This, in fact, was Cliff’s view exactly. So after lunch, while Judith was educating Sonja about the squad, Cadel caught a bus to Newtown.

As did one of his bodyguards.

It was a bright autumn day. Sitting at the rear of the bus, watching the streetscape roll past, Cadel felt as if he hadn’t been outside for weeks. This wasn’t the case, of course. It was simply that his focus on Genius Squad’s mission had been so intense that he hadn’t noticed things like the weather. Even now, away from the War Room, he couldn’t quite relax. His mind was too busy. On the one hand, he kept mentally reviewing his microphone application, searching for flaws. On the other hand, he needed to plan his meeting with Gazo. There was no telling what Gazo would do when Cadel approached him. Cadel had to be prepared for a whole range of reactions.

Not that Gazo would lash out. He wasn’t a violent man. But he was bound to be edgy at first—and perhaps even suspicious.

That was one reason why Cadel hadn’t confided in Saul Greeniaus.

Saul’s mobile was sitting snugly in Cadel’s pocket. It would be used to call the detective after Cadel had spoken with Gazo. There was really no alternative; the surveillance team would alert Saul, even if Cadel didn’t. But Cadel had decided not to warn the detective about his proposed meeting, just in case Saul put a stop to it. Besides, Cadel didn’t want Saul descending on Gazo with a pack of police. Not out of the blue, anyway.

Glancing over his shoulder, Cadel checked that the unmarked police car was still following his bus. It was. Three seats in front of Cadel, a member of the surveillance team was sitting directly opposite the rear door, squashed between a teenager wearing headphones and an elderly woman with a stick. Cadel found himself eyeing the three of them, as he'd once eyed everyone who had ever come near him on a bus or a train. Gazo's sudden reappearance had resurrected old memories—and old habits. In the past, Cadel had never been free of Prosper's own surveillance specialists. Now he was reverting to his former mind-set.

It's the sort of attitude we need more of around here. Cadel remembered Trader's words and fretted over them. Prosper had taught Cadel to take nothing on trust—to be perpetually looking for a trap, trick, or loophole. Trader had endorsed that view, and it worried Cadel. He didn't know if he *wanted* to be living in that kind of world again. Not even if it was for a good cause.

He realized that the bus had reached his stop, and rose quickly. With the policeman close on his heels, he alighted from the vehicle and struck out along King Street in the direction of City Road. The air was gritty with traffic fumes. The footpaths became more crowded as Cadel drew closer to the gates of the university. He didn't look out of place among the other pedestrians, with their scruffy sweatshirts, baggy pants, and smooth young faces. If he'd been carrying a bag of some sort, he might have blended in completely.

Upon walking through the gates, Cadel didn't check to see what his bodyguard was doing. What did it matter? Whether on foot or in a car, the police would continue to dog his steps. And he didn't mind that, as long as they didn't make themselves too conspicuous. In fact, he didn't even bother to glance behind him; he was far more interested in the patches of greenery that he passed. Using a map he'd downloaded from the Internet, he intended to visit every location where his old friend could possibly be employed. Cadel expected to find Gazo mowing one of the large and manicured stretches of lawn around the campus, or perhaps shoveling fertilizer onto a garden bed.

When Cadel finally tracked him down, however, Gazo wasn't mowing or shoveling. He was planting seedlings in a damp spot overshadowed by a cluster of tall buildings. Despite the concrete benches scattered around, it wasn't the kind of place where people were destined to linger. It was more of an open-air corridor, and a dingy one at that. Tucked away at its edges were several tree ferns, and outcrops of gloomy-looking plants with leathery, underwater leaves.

Gazo was kneeling on the concrete path, dressed in blue overalls. He was alone. Cadel instantly recognized his thin, spotty face and long neck—though Gazo's tan was new, as were the tufts of hair on his receding chin. This facial hair suggested that Gazo was trying to disguise himself, but it was a failed attempt. At twenty (or thereabouts), he probably wasn't old enough to grow a proper beard.

It was a moment before Cadel could find his voice.

"Gazo," he said. And Gazo looked up.

His mouth fell open.

"It's all right," Cadel said hastily, as Gazo scrambled to his feet. "Prosper didn't send me. I came on my own."

"Cadel," Gazo breathed, in accents of astonishment.

"Can I talk to you? Would that be all right?"

"Yeah, sure." An awkward smile began to spread over Gazo's face. "You ain't grown much."

"I guess not."

"Are you a student now? At the university?"

"No." Cadel took a deep breath. "I can't get a place at university, because nobody can work out who I really am. Australia doesn't want me and America doesn't want me. Prosper English won't tell anyone where I was born." Seeing Gazo's smile dim, Cadel added, "Prosper doesn't know where I'm living, Gazo. The police have made sure of that."

"He dunno where I'm living, neiver," Gazo declared. "Leastways, he ain't tried to knock me off."

"Is that what you're scared of? Is that why you changed your name?"

"Yeah." Gazo began to remove his gardening gloves. "So you 'eard I changed me name, did ya?"

Cadel nodded.

"You was always pretty smart," said Gazo. "I shoulda known you'd find me."

"Won't you please give the police a statement, Gazo?" Cadel understood that he didn't have much time—that the surveillance team would soon be closing in and making its report to Saul Greeniaus. So Cadel couldn't afford to beat around the bush. "I'm the only one who's talked about the Axis Institute, and the police can't get any independent confirmation. Prosper's saying that I'm a liar. He says I'm making everything up—that he's not my father after all." Hearing Gazo catch his breath, Cadel said, "Didn't you hear about that? About Prosper English being my father?"

Gazo shook his head, suitably awestruck.

"I fought you were Dr. Darkkon's son," he objected.

"So did I. Then Prosper told me I wasn't. And now he won't say anything, in case it jeopardizes his defense." All this talk about Prosper was getting to Cadel. Standing in such a shadowy corner, with Gazo before him and a surveillance team hovering somewhere in the immediate vicinity, Cadel was beginning to feel as if he had returned to the Axis Institute. It was a terrible feeling. It drove the color from his cheeks and made his palms sweat. "Gazo," he went on, "you saw stuff I never saw. If you tell the police about it, you can help make sure that Prosper never gets out of jail. Because if he does . . ." Cadel had to pause a moment before proceeding. "If he does, he'll come after me. *You* might be all right, but he won't let me get away. I'm his son, you see."

There was a long silence. Gazo appeared to be softening, so Cadel made one final plea.

"Do you remember the last time we talked? In the car, near my house?" When Gazo's pale eyes flickered, Cadel knew that the exchange in the car hadn't been forgotten. "I told you to disappear, and you offered to stay. You said I shouldn't be on my own, because I was just a kid. And I said I didn't need any help." Cadel heaved a sigh. "Well, I do now. I need your help, Gazo."

"Then you've got it," said Gazo. He spoke with such surprising firmness that Cadel was taken aback. They stared at each other. Then Gazo shrugged.

"I always said I'd look after ya. It's what I wanted to do, i'n't it? Look after people." He grinned suddenly, exposing an array of stained and crooked teeth. "And if Prosper tries to find me—well, let's just say I'll kick up a big stink. Know what I mean?"

Cadel felt a prickling in his tear ducts. It was totally unexpected and horribly disconcerting.

I must be tired, he told himself. And he tried to conceal his weakness by clearing his throat.

"You can still do that, then?" he queried. "Make people pass out?"

"Oh, yeah."

"But you're not wearing a suit anymore."

Again, Gazo shrugged.

"I've learned to control it better," he replied. "If I 'adn't, you'd be out cold by now—the way you took me by surprise."

"So it's not a problem anymore? Your condition?"

"I wouldn't say that." Gazo was starting to sound more confident. Clearly, he wasn't quite the same old Gazo. Life as a gardener had made him more sure of himself. "It's still a problem sometimes," he allowed. "But what I'm doing now is I'm trying to find out more about what I got. Scientifically."

Hearing this, Cadel swallowed. It was exactly the opening he needed.

"How?" he asked. "I mean, how are you finding out more?"

"Well, it's genetic, isn't it? So I'm getting me genes sorted." From the way he expressed himself, it was obvious that Gazo didn't have a very strong grasp of exactly what gene analysis meant. "There's these people called GenoME," he said, "and you pay 'em money, and they work out what's wrong wiv your genes."

"Gazo . . ." Cadel took the plunge. "I don't think you should be going anywhere near GenoME."

Gazo frowned. "Eh?"

"GenoME was a Darkkon project," Cadel revealed. "Dr. Darkkon set it up."

His words had an immediate effect. Gazo staggered and turned white. He dropped his gardening gloves.

"Christ," he said.

"It's not a reputable company," Cadel continued. "And if you're worried about Prosper—"

"But I never seen nuffink about this!" Gazo exclaimed. "In the papers or on the telly—not a word!"

"The connection isn't well-known. That's why GenoME's still operating." It saddened Cadel to witness all the confidence drain out of his friend. "I only know myself because . . . well, because of my background," he finished, and watched a weak-kneed Gazo sink onto one of the concrete benches.

Cadel sat down next to him.

"It's a shame," Cadel said quietly. "You must want to leave all this stuff behind. I would myself, if I could. But I can't."

"Do you fink Prosper knows where I am?" Gazo rounded on him. "Will he come after me?"

"I doubt it."

"But there's a chance, right?"

"Maybe."

"So what should I do?"

Cadel hesitated. "If I was still the old Cadel," he sighed at last, "I would have told you to cooperate with the police. For your own protection. Because it would help me." He spread his hands. "But now I'm really not sure, Gazo. You'll have to decide for yourself."

Gazo studied Cadel's face for a moment, as if trying to extract an answer from it. Close up, Cadel could see a scar running across his friend's forehead. It was a nasty scar.

He wondered if it marked the spot where Vadi—Prosper's valet—had struck Gazo to stop him from rescuing Cadel.

"Let's talk to the coppers, then," Gazo suddenly declared. "Let's do it now, before I change me mind." He glanced over at the partly planted garden bed, with its freshly turned earth and tumble of empty plastic pots. "Only I gotta finish puttin' in them 'ellebores first," he concluded. "I can't let the boss down."

And he stood up to do his duty.

TWENTY

Saul Greeniaus was already on his way to the university when Cadel phoned him. Ten minutes later, the detective arrived, dressed in a neat gray suit and flanked by the surveillance team.

Cadel immediately became conscious of an unpleasant smell.

"Fertilizer?" said one of the surveillance team, screwing up his nose as he eyed the newly dressed garden bed. "I hate that stuff."

"It's me," mumbled Gazo. "I'm sorry."

Cadel was alarmed. He had experienced the impact of Gazo's gale-force stench in the past and didn't particularly want to endure it again.

"Are you going to be all right?" he asked, edging away from his friend. "Are you going to be able to control it?"

"I fink so." Gazo was still hunched on the concrete bench beside Cadel, nervously wringing his hands. "Long as they don't arrest me."

"They're not going to arrest you," said Cadel. And he addressed Saul Greeniaus. "You don't want to arrest him, do you? You just want to talk to him."

Saul's dark gaze traveled from Cadel to Gazo. His expression was impassive.

"We'd like to interview Mr. Kovacs, yes," he rejoined, in dry and formal tones. "Mr. Kovacs has a lot of questions to answer."

Cadel began to cough. The smell was getting worse; even the surveillance team retreated a few steps.

Saul's eyes widened.

"Gazo—*hack-hack!*—doesn't have to tell you anything!" Cadel spluttered. He rose and stumbled away from Gazo, who was trying to calm himself with a deep-breathing exercise. "If you scare him, he's going to end up—*hack-hack*—knocking us all out!"

Cadel had hardly finished speaking when Saul grabbed his arm. The surveillance team had already whipped out a couple of handkerchiefs to clamp over their noses and mouths. Saul was breathing in shallow little gasps as he pushed Cadel behind him.

"You'd better get out of here," the detective coughed. But Cadel shook him off irritably.

The smell was already weakening.

"Don't be stupid," said Cadel. "Gazo won't hurt me. I told you, he wants to help."

"I've got me old airtight suit at home," Gazo suddenly remarked. "Maybe I should put it on before I talk to anyone."

"That's a good idea." Cadel looked up at Saul. The detective's attitude toward Gazo didn't impress Cadel; it was little short of antagonistic. "Why don't you meet Gazo at his house this afternoon?" Cadel suggested. "Around five o'clock, say? That would give him time to put on his protective suit and call a lawyer." He turned to Gazo. "I think you should get yourself a lawyer, just in case."

Gazo swallowed. The surveillance team gagged.

For a moment, Cadel felt dizzy. He staggered, and Saul seized his arm again.

"Jesus," the detective choked out.

"I'm not saying you'll *need* a lawyer," Cadel said faintly, gulping down lungfuls of clean air. "Gazo? I'm sure you won't. But it's best to be on the safe side."

"Yeah. I understand." Gazo was beginning to sweat. "Maybe you'd better go," he advised anxiously. "Maybe you'd better *all* go. I'll be fine if I do some meditation."

“What’s your address?” rasped Saul. When Gazo gave it to him, the detective produced a mobile from inside his jacket and made a brief, one-handed entry before adding, “I sure hope I’m gonna find you there this afternoon, Mr. Kovacs. I sure hope you won’t do anything stupid.”

“Of course he won’t!” Cadel was growing cross. Why did Saul have to be so unreasonable? “If he wanted to disappear, he’d have done it already. Ow!” Saul’s grasp on his arm had tightened. “Don’t do that!”

“Is this your correct address, Mr. Kovacs?” the detective queried, ignoring Cadel. “Are you *quite* sure?”

Gazo nodded.

“And could I have your phone number, please?” Saul went on.

Gazo recited it from memory, his forehead creasing as Cadel tried to wriggle out of Saul’s iron grip. At last Gazo said, in a slightly sullen manner, “You know, Cadel’s just a kid, and he’s small, too. I don’t like it when people push ’im around.”

Saul’s reaction to this comment was unexpected. He studied Gazo in silence for a good ten seconds, then released Cadel and slipped the mobile back into his pocket.

“Point taken,” the detective replied, before shifting his attention from Gazo to Cadel. “I’ll drive you home now. Since we need to give Mr. Kovacs some space.”

Cadel blinked. “Oh, but—”

“If you stay here,” Saul interrupted, “Nick and Luca will have to stay here with you. And I think Mr. Kovacs would prefer it if they didn’t. Wouldn’t you, Mr. Kovacs?”

Gazo didn’t know how to answer. He shifted about on his seat. At the same time, the air thickened with a faint, fetid odor that sent Cadel reeling backward.

“All right,” he gasped. “Okay. Maybe that’s the best thing. Are you all right with that, Gazo?”

“Yeah,” Gazo muttered. “Sorry, Cadel.”

He lifted a hand, and the police seemed to view this action as some kind of signal. They immediately withdrew, dragging Cadel with them.

He found himself being hustled through a door, into a foyer, and then out onto a stretch of avenue—where two unmarked police cars had been left in a NO STANDING zone. He recognized one of these vehicles as the surveillance team's car. The other belonged to Saul Greeniaus.

"Get in," said the detective, disengaging all of its locks. Cadel climbed into the front passenger seat. He knew that Saul wasn't happy, but he wasn't happy himself. So that made two of them.

Saul didn't speak again until he had started the engine and was driving toward King Street.

"I hope you didn't give that guy your address," he snapped.

"No," said Cadel.

"Then don't. Not yet. Not until we've checked him out."

Cadel heaved a long-suffering sigh. "You can't arrest him. Not without gas masks," he said. When there was no reply, Cadel tried another tack. "You shouldn't be so suspicious. Gazo isn't a crook. He's just trying to help."

"You can't be sure of that, Cadel."

"Yes, I can."

"How do you know he's not working for Prosper English?" Accelerating onto King Street, Saul flicked his passenger a stern, admonishing glance. "He made contact with you, didn't he? How do you know it's not a trap?"

"Because he *didn't* make contact with me. I made contact with him." Hearing Saul's intake of breath, Cadel hurriedly continued. "I used the Internet," he volunteered. (This wasn't a lie; it simply wasn't the whole truth.) "He calls himself Russ Adams now, and that's an alias he thought up at the Axis Institute."

Suddenly the car swerved, as Saul pulled over. He stopped in a bus zone, jerking at his hand brake as if he were trying to snap it off. Then he swung around to confront Cadel, his face so pale that his eyes looked almost black.

"Do you mean to say you approached this guy?" Saul demanded. "Do you mean to say you set up a meeting without telling me first?"

Cadel flinched. But he refused to buckle. "If I'd told you first, you wouldn't have let me go," he pointed out.

Saul wasn't impressed. His voice became rougher.

"Have you any idea of the *risks* involved in what you just did?" he exclaimed, and Cadel scowled.

"Yes. As a matter of fact. I calculated them." Seeing Saul open his mouth, Cadel cut him off. "Don't you understand what I've been doing for most of my life? Don't you understand that calculating risk is what I do *best*? When I was thirteen, I even started developing a formula for predicting people's behavior." Catching sight of Saul's blanched knuckles on the steering wheel, Cadel forced himself to continue in quieter, more even tones. "Do you think I can't work out the odds of Gazo being a plant?" he said. "Mr. Greeniaus, they're negligible."

By this time Saul wasn't staring at him anymore. The detective's full attention was fixed on the windshield; a nerve was twitching high on his left cheek.

"And what about my job?" he asked, exerting enormous control over his delivery. "Is that negligible, too? I'm supposed to keep you safe. Did you take my situation into account when you did your calculations? Do you understand what I just went through?"

Cadel flushed.

"I'm sorry," he said. "I really am." Sensing that his apology wasn't accepted, he blurted out, "But you wouldn't have let me go! And if I hadn't gone, Gazo wouldn't have talked! And the whole thing would have been a disaster!" When there was still no reply, he began to lose patience. "I got you another witness, didn't I? You should be *pleased*," he protested.

Saul said nothing. He simply adjusted his hand brake and gearshift, then swung out into the traffic.

Not another word was uttered by either of them during the rest of their trip back to Clearview House.

When they arrived, Saul didn't simply drop Cadel at the front steps. Instead the detective climbed out of his car and requested a meeting with

Sonja. "I've been told that Sonja moved in today," he announced, "and I think it would be a good idea if I said hello."

"So she knows that you're keeping tabs on her?" Cadel said waspishly. The words had barely left his mouth before he regretted them. They sounded childish. Vindictive. "She's probably home," he mumbled, trying to make amends. Then it occurred to him that Sonja might be in the War Room, and he racked his brain for a story that would account for her absence if she was. "Unless Judith's taken her for a walk," he concluded feebly.

However, Sonja wasn't downstairs working. She was in her own room, and Zac Stillman was combing her hair. At least, he was trying to.

But he didn't appear to have mastered the knack.

"Here," said Cadel, upon observing the way Zac was clumsily dabbing at Sonja's head. "I can do it." He took charge of the comb and stationed himself in his customary hair-combing position, slightly to the rear of Sonja's wheelchair. Saul's brown eyes met Sonja's own as the detective quietly absorbed the scene in front of him.

Meanwhile, Zac relinquished his duties with evident relief.

"I've got to start dinner now," he said, stooping slightly to converse with Sonja. "Are you going to be all right with Cadel?"

"*Yes,*" the DynaVox buzzed.

"Good. Right." Zac nodded at Saul on his way out. "Just give me a yell if you need anything."

"We will," said Cadel, wondering how on earth Sonja was supposed to give anyone a yell. (With her intercom, perhaps?) Picking gently at a knot of food-encrusted hair, Cadel became conscious that Saul was watching him.

But when he looked up, the detective glanced away—and stepped forward to shake Sonja's hand.

"How are you doing?" Saul murmured. "Settling in okay?"

Sonja couldn't respond until he had dropped her hand. Then she asked, through her DynaVox, "*Is-that-a-gun-in-your-coat?*"

If she was trying to startle him, there was no indication that she had succeeded. Saul calmly informed her that it was indeed a gun, but that he wasn't allowed to let anyone else handle it.

"Did-you-shoot-Gazo?" Sonja inquired. Owing to the mechanical timbre of the DynaVox, this sounded like a serious question. But Cadel knew that it wasn't. He could tell by the mischievous tilt of her head and the clicking in her throat.

It was obvious to Cadel that Sonja was in an exultant mood. She must have enjoyed her day, he decided.

"She's joking," he assured the detective. "Don't be such a ghoul, Sonja." He was afraid that Saul might be offended.

The detective, however, didn't appear to notice the implied insult in Sonja's query. He was far more interested in something else.

"So you knew about Gazo, did you?" he said. Though his voice was flat, his expression was reproachful as he eyed Sonja, his hands on his hips and his posture very erect. "Didn't you realize what a big risk it was for Cadel? Going out there to meet up with Gazo Kovacs, of all people?"

"Cadel-is-an-expert-at-calculating-risk." Sonja spelled out her reply letter by ponderous letter. *"I-wasn't-worried."*

"Well, you should have been," was Saul's tart comeback. Then he softened, unable to maintain a harsh demeanor when confronted by Sonja's splayed fingers and twisted legs. "Look," he went on, "I know you can't use the phone, but you do have e-mail access. If I give you my details, could you at least text me a warning the next time he decides to do something crazy?"

"It wasn't crazy—," Cadel began. Saul, however, wouldn't let him finish.

"Everyone makes mistakes," he pleaded, still addressing Sonja. "Even Cadel. If you're his friend, you should be worried about his safety. That's all I'm saying. You should be watching his back."

Sonja had to work hard at her response. It took a while, because her muscles weren't cooperating. Nevertheless, Saul refrained from interrupting the process with further comments of his own.

Cadel noticed this with approval, even though he resented Saul's desire to co-opt Sonja as part of the surveillance team.

"Did-Gazo-threaten-anyone?" Sonja finally asked. *"Did-he-refuse-to-cooperate?"*

"No. Not at all." Cadel couldn't help sounding a touch defiant. "He told me he'd make a statement at five o'clock. At home. After he puts his protective suit on."

"So-Cadel-was-right," Sonja pointed out, her eyes straining toward the detective. *"He-wasn't-in-any-danger. If-he-had-been, I-would-have-asked-him-not-to-go."*

The detective sighed. He shook his head and checked his watch. Then he conceded defeat—albeit in a roundabout sort of way.

"Kovacs did seem pretty cooperative," he admitted. "I'm hoping we'll get some useful stuff out of him, provided he doesn't disappear in the meantime." Fixing Cadel with a severe and slightly weary look, he promised to report on his interview with Gazo. "But I'd be grateful if you didn't talk to him before I talk to you. Okay?" he requested.

"Okay," Cadel muttered.

"Thanks." The detective nodded abruptly, first at Cadel, then at Sonja. "See you later," he said, and headed for the door.

Before reaching it, however, he stopped to direct a parting shot at Cadel.

"Did you tell anyone else around here where you were going?" he asked, narrowing his eyes. Whereupon Cadel pulled his most innocent face, all crumpled brow and blank incomprehension.

"I said that I had to visit a friend," was his careful rejoinder—which seemed to satisfy Saul. The detective promptly took his leave, marching out of the house before Cadel could offer to accompany him. The front door slammed; heavy footsteps sounded on the veranda.

Cadel felt lousy. Again, he hadn't exactly lied—he just hadn't told the entire truth.

"He's-nice, isn't-he?" Sonja declared, after she had heard Saul's car drive away. *"You-can't-help-liking-him. Most-people-don't-have-the-guts-to-shake-my-hand."*

"They're probably scared it'll fall off," Cadel joked, taking refuge in flippancy to disguise his burgeoning sense of guilt. "So how did you get on with Judith?"

"Good. How-did-you-get-on-with-Gazo?"

"Good. Until Saul showed up. Then it got a bit stinky."

Sonja's chin jerked as she strained to catch his eye.

"If they'd both just relax, everything would be fine," Cadel continued. "But Saul doesn't trust Gazo, and Gazo doesn't trust Saul. Which is ridiculous."

He grimaced as he dragged his comb through Sonja's hair, distracted by the thorny issue of what would happen if Gazo's name appeared on the police network. Something like that might cause serious problems. Suppose Carolina Whitehead or Jerry Reinhard had infiltrated the police computer system? Suppose they were hunting down information about Prosper English? It was unlikely, but not impossible. If they were smart enough to hack into their clients' computers, they might be smart enough to penetrate police security. And they certainly didn't seem to mind breaking the law.

If they had been sniffing about, then they might stumble across Gazo's name. Gazo might be mentioned as a possible police informant. And how would they react then? By avoiding further contact with him? Or would Carolina try to use him in some way—by feeding him misinformation, perhaps?

Cadel decided that this last scenario was highly improbable. It was far more likely that GenoME would cut off all contact with Gazo, if he was discovered to be cooperating with the police. For this reason, Cadel decided not to interfere. He could imagine how awkward it would be, telling Saul not to post Gazo's name on the police system. The detective would naturally ask why, and Cadel would be unable to answer. Not without exposing Genius Squad.

All the same, Gazo's vulnerable situation worried Cadel. And he found that he needed reassurance about it from Sonja.

"I can't help wondering what will happen if Gazo's mentioned on the police network, and GenoME finds out somehow," he said. "I mean, surely they wouldn't do anything nasty? It's not as if he knows enough to be a threat." Hesitating for an instant, his comb poised, Cadel added, "What do you think?"

"I-think-you-worry-too-much," Sonja answered. *"If-GenoME-wants-to-harm-Gazo, we'll-have-plenty-of-warning. Until-then, you-should-forget-about-it."*

"I suppose so."

"You-know-what-your-trouble-is?" She grinned up at him, before fixing her attention once more on the DynaVox screen. *"You-did-that-World-Domination-course-for-so-long, you-think-you're-still-responsible-for-every-little-thing!"*

TWENTY-ONE

When Cadel's mobile rang the next morning, he was down in the War Room, listening to Amy Ng conducting a telephone conversation on the other side of town.

Reception was pretty good, on the whole. Cadel's bug seemed to be working. Even so, during the first half hour of its operation, nothing much had been gleaned from the snatches of dialogue overheard outside Jerry's office—except that his assistant's dog was suffering from some kind of bowel complaint.

"Yeah?" said Cadel, answering his own phone. "Who is it?"

"Saul Greeniaus," came the clipped reply. *"Have you got a minute?"*

Cadel rose from his seat and moved to a deserted corner of the basement.

"Yeah, sure," he said. "I've got a minute. What's up?"

"You'll be pleased to know that Gazo Kovacs was very cooperative," Saul announced.

"Oh. Good." (Cadel refrained from saying "I told you so.")

"The trouble is, he wants to see more of you. And I don't think that would be wise, Cadel."

"Why not?"

"Because he's gone and got himself involved with GenoME." As Cadel swallowed and glanced over to where Trader was sitting, Saul pressed for a response. *"Cadel?"*

"Yeah. I know. He told me."

"And do you know that GenoME is believed to have been Phineas Darkon's idea?"

"Of course." It was almost an insulting question, but Cadel let it pass.

"We've never been able to establish how much Prosper English was involved in its day-to-day operations, but we've been keeping a close eye on GenoME," Saul related. *"For instance, we think it's highly suspicious that GenoME should have opened a branch in Australia shortly after Prosper was incarcerated. It makes you wonder."*

"What do you mean, you're keeping a close eye on GenoME?" Cadel couldn't think of a subtler approach. And he needed an answer. Urgently. "I mean, are you tapping their phones, or what?"

"Of course we're not tapping their phones." Saul's tone implied that Cadel had been watching too many espionage movies. *"We'd need a good reason to do that, and there's no indication that anyone at GenoME has put a foot wrong so far."* A pause. *"Why do you ask?"*

"No reason," Cadel said quickly. Then, realizing how suspicious this sounded, he tried for a more plausible excuse. "I just figured that if you've been tapping their phones, you might know how interested they are in Gazo. Because if they're not interested in him, why should they find out about me?"

"Well—as I said, we're not tapping their phones. So we've no idea if they're keeping tabs on your friend. But it would be better if you didn't make contact with him for a while." A noise like a sigh reached Cadel's ear. *"Will you promise me that, please?"*

"I suppose so." Cadel realized that Trader was approaching him, looking curious. "But you've got to explain to Gazo. Explain that it's not my fault if I don't talk to him."

"I will. Don't worry."

"Will he be going back there? To GenoME?"

"It might seem suspicious if he doesn't," Saul decided. *"We'll consider it. We'll work out what to do."*

"Okay." By this time Trader was hovering nearby, his eyebrows raised, his expression vigilant. Staring at him, Cadel said, "Uh—Mr. Greeniaus?" And Trader screwed up his nose.

"What?" Saul asked.

Cadel took a deep breath. "Should you be talking to me like this? I mean—without Fiona?"

A muffled curse suggested that Cadel had hit a sore spot. *"Damn it,"* Saul muttered. *"I forgot about that."*

"Don't worry. I won't tell her."

"No. You won't. Because I'll tell her myself," Saul replied. *"I don't believe in keeping secrets."*

"So what was that about?" Trader wanted to know, when Cadel had cut the connection. He was inspecting Cadel's red face and twisted mouth.

"Oh—nothing much." Cadel decided not to repeat Saul's comment, which had struck a nerve. Keeping secrets was all that Cadel seemed to be doing lately. "Apparently the police are monitoring GenoME."

"How?"

"I don't know. Not with phone taps, anyway."

Trader pondered for a moment, rubbing his chin. Then he shrugged.

"I'll get Hamish to poke around in the police network again," he declared. "Check out what they might be up to." Seeing Cadel's bemused look, he grinned. "Unless you want to do it yourself?"

Cadel shook his head. He had never hacked into any police computers himself—and he didn't intend to, either. Not if it meant facing Sonja's disapproval. Nevertheless, he realized that Genius Squad made a habit of raiding the police system. (He himself had been tracked down after Hamish had found Hazel's address there.) So he didn't bother to voice his objections. He just waited, mutely.

"I'll put Hamish on to it now," Trader decided, glancing over to where Hamish was eavesdropping on Amy Ng's latest telephone conversation. "With any luck, he'll have something to report at the update meeting." He checked his watch. "That's at 2:00 P.M., did you know?"

Cadel nodded.

"By then we should have a pretty good idea of what we've got so far, in terms of improved access," Trader finished. "I damn well hope we'll have *something* to show for all this work. Rex Austin's been breathing down my neck."

Trader's hopes, however, were fated to be dashed. By two o'clock little progress had been made; the whole squad was still groping around in the dark, trying to find an access point into the high-security systems at GenoME. There had been a brief moment of excitement when Devin had uncovered an obscure little tax invoice, on Amy's machine, which included the IP address for a computer that appeared to be Jerry's. But as Hamish pointed out, an IP address was useless without a password.

Sitting around the kitchen table, with the dishwasher grinding away nearby, everyone struggled to come up with a new approach to the problem. Everyone, that is, except Dot.

Though the input from Cadel's microphone was being recorded, it had been agreed that whenever Amy Ng's computer was operational, somebody had to monitor what it was picking up—just in case a comment was made that required immediate attention.

So Dot was downstairs, on eavesdropping duty.

"I still say our b-best way in is through Jerry's laptop," said Hamish, who was picking at his cuticles. "He takes that home, so he must use it."

"Maybe he does," said Cliff, "but I haven't been able to intercept any wireless transmissions. Yet."

"Ten to one he's got a Virtual Private Network going," Hamish continued—almost thinking aloud. "He probably scrambles signals through a modem and has a descrambler sitting on his desk. Next to his office computer."

All eyes turned to Cliff, who folded his arms and scowled.

"We can't just nick the laptop," he said. "I've said it time and again: *No footprints.* We'd have to use it without alerting him."

"Doesn't he go anywhere on the weekend?" Zac inquired diffidently. "Could we just visit his flat while he's out for a stroll?"

Heaving a sigh, Cliff described the stringent security at Jerry Reinhard's residence. It would be impossible to get past *that,* Cliff insisted; he and Trader had already tried.

"Man-in-the-middle," squawked Sonja's DynaVox.

Instantly Cadel understood.

"What did she say?" asked Lexi. "Manny what?"

"'Man in the middle,'" Cadel repeated. "It's the sort of thing you'd use to intercept a Diffie-Hellman code." When that clarification failed to ring a bell for most of the people around him, he added, "What Sonja's saying is that instead of targeting the laptop, we should target the descrambler."

"Put in a wireless transmitter, you mean?" said Hamish. "Reroute the laptop messages through that?"

"I could do it," Cadel confessed. "We covered it at the Axis Institute. But I'd have to get at the descrambler."

"Which leaves us back where we started," Trader pointed out gently. "If we could get at the descrambler, we'd go for the work computers instead."

"What about technicians?" Judith turned to Cliff. "Couldn't we mess something up? The electricity, say, or the air-conditioning?"

"Or the plumbing!" Lexi proposed, wriggling in her seat. "What if, when Zac goes back, he blocks up the toilet and they have to call in a plumber?"

"There aren't any water pipes in Jerry's office, Lexi." Trader's dismissive tone snuffed out the spark in Lexi's eyes. "Even a computer jockey like Jerry Reinhard isn't going to fall for a plumber banging around near his hard drive."

"You know, he really *is* a computer jockey." Hamish looked up from his cuticles. "That guy never seems to lift his butt off his chair. I bet he wouldn't move just because some tradesman was drilling holes in the wall. He'd stick a pair of headphones on, or something."

"You're right," Devin agreed, gloomily. "Think of what it's been like, eavesdropping on that guy. Jerry didn't take a single phone call this morning. He never left his office. He never even went out for lunch. He was at his keyboard the whole time—*tap-tappety-tap.*"

Tap-tappety-tap.

This piece of information hit Cadel like a bullet.

He caught his breath.

"What do you mean?" he said. "You mean *you can hear him typing*?"

There was no immediate reply. However, even as Zac and Cliff and Judith peered at Cadel in astonishment, a lightbulb seemed to go off inside Hamish's head.

"Christ," he gasped. "Of course!"

"Amy was the first to arrive this morning." Cadel had already leaped up. "She switched on her computer before Jerry did."

"And we've b-been recording ever since," Hamish concluded, jumping up to join Cadel. "So it's *gotta* be on there!"

"What's got to be on where?" Trader called after the two boys, who were heading for the lift together. "Cadel? Just a minute!"

Cadel whipped around.

"The password!" he cried. "Jerry's password! He would have typed it in! Don't you see? *We'll have a recording*!"

Trader blinked. "You mean—"

"We can decode it by analyzing the sound of the keystrokes," said Cadel, punching at the lift button, which was disguised as one of the little blue wall-tiles in the pantry. He and Hamish were on their way down to the War Room before anyone else had even reached this button; the lift floor began to drop beneath their feet just as Hamish said to Cadel, with the merest trace of disappointment, "You really are good. *I* should have thought of that."

"You would have." Cadel entertained no doubts whatsoever on that score. His respect for Hamish's technical abilities was increasing by the day.

It was a pity, Cadel thought, that Hamish's personality quirks were still so challenging. When someone spent his free time substituting Gravox powder for cocoa, and maliciously reprogramming other people's cell phones, it was hard to relate to him as a friend.

Cadel could only assume that Hamish had been the butt of so many practical jokes, in his time, that the worm had turned with a vengeance.

"This isn't going to be easy," Cadel added. "We'll need some kind of program for measuring really minute differences in noise levels. We'd never be able to do it by ear."

"Leave that to Trader," said Hamish. "If there's one thing he *does* know, it's how to interpret recordings." When the lift bounced to a standstill, and its doors slid open, he rubbed his hands together. "Quick," he urged. "Let's get started, b-before those Wienekes try to muscle in!"

"But aren't we supposed to be working as a team?" Cadel objected.

Hamish, however, wasn't listening. He had stopped in his tracks and was staring at Dot—who sat with her back to him, a pair of padded headphones clamped over her ears. She hadn't even turned her head at the sound of the lift's arrival.

Clearly, she was deaf to everything but the noise from Amy's computer bug.

"Jeez," Hamish spluttered, transfixed by the images displayed on Dot's laptop screen. Even from where he was standing, Cadel could see pearl-colored satin and filmy lace. He realized that Dot was scrolling through a very fancy underwear catalog, full of languorous, shiny-haired, full-lipped women who didn't look at all like Dot.

As Hamish pulled a comical face, Dot became aware of his presence. To Cadel's surprise, however, she didn't expunge the flashy garments with one click of her mouse. Instead she slowly turned her head and regarded the two boys without a trace of expression while she removed her headphones. If she was embarrassed, she didn't show it. In fact, it was Hamish who blushed. He seemed lost for words.

Cadel was the one who finally spoke.

"We need to listen to the first hour of that recording," he told Dot, trying not to look as startled as he felt. Why on earth should someone like Dot be interested in exotic lingerie? Surely she must be shopping for a gift? Surely she couldn't be buying it for *herself*?

Or was she simply mooning over items that she didn't have the courage to wear, like a kid with her nose pressed against the window of a toy shop?

Whatever the explanation, it suggested that there was more to Dot than met the eye. In fact, if she had been anyone else, Cadel might even have felt a bit sorry for her. But her stolid, inscrutable demeanor was off-putting. It repelled sympathy. And it was so profoundly at odds with the pictures on the screen that Cadel couldn't help being slightly rattled.

"We're—um—going to listen for keystrokes," he continued, wishing that Hamish would say something. Dot gave a nod. Wordlessly she offered up her headphones, before calmly exiting the lingerie site.

Only when the array of distracting, skimpy products had disappeared did Hamish find the courage to blurt out, "Special occasion?"

Dot fixed her impassive gaze on him.

"What would you know about special occasions?" she replied, with a lack of emphasis that was somehow more insulting than a sneer.

Then the lift doors opened again, and the rest of Genius Squad spilled out.

TWENTY-TWO

By the end of the working day, Genius Squad had captured Jerry Reinhard's password.

They had been lucky. Amy's computer had picked up the sound of Jerry's initial keystrokes when he'd first arrived that morning. These soft little clicks had then been microanalyzed. By half past four, Dot's infiltration team had isolated the eight-letter key to GenoME's high-security network and had used it, in combination with his IP address, to break into Jerry's computer.

The next step would be to mount an attack on GenoME's heavily fortified American system. But it wouldn't be easy. No one knew exactly what kind of access the password would provide, or exactly how much time would elapse before it was changed.

No one wanted to trigger any alarms.

Cadel was eager to participate in the initial assault on GenoME's inner defenses. He felt that his skills would be needed. Throughout the day, everyone in Genius Squad had played his or her special part in the infiltration process; while Trader had analyzed keystrokes, and Devin had plundered the potentializers' machines, and Sonja had helped Lexi with the decoding, Cadel had worked side by side with Hamish on various tasks, including a privilege-escalation plan. It seemed to Cadel that he was an indispensable cog in the Genius Squad machine.

But apparently he was mistaken. Because to his immense chagrin, he was required to eat dinner with Saul Greeniaus—who had phoned after lunch to ask if Cadel would join him for an evening meal.

"I have to update you on a few things," Saul had said, *"and Ms. Currey isn't free until seven. So I figured we could eat while we talked."*

"Couldn't we just talk now?" Cadel had protested. "Over the phone?" But Saul had been adamant.

"Face-to-face would be best," he'd replied. *"Ms. Currey needs to be present, remember?"*

Cadel hadn't dared raise any further objections, in case the detective became suspicious. But he wasn't happy. For one thing, he wanted to help his fellow squad members. And for another, he was worried about Sonja's well-being.

Though she'd assured him repeatedly that she was fine without him, Cadel wasn't entirely convinced. Tony was efficient but inexperienced; he hadn't yet learned to anticipate her needs. Zac was kind but distracted. Only Judith inspired Cadel with any confidence.

He didn't mind leaving Sonja with her.

But the evening promised to be a busy one, and Cadel feared that Judith would find herself too preoccupied to keep a close eye on Sonja. In the end, Trader had to put his foot down. "If you don't go," Trader said, "then Greeniaus is going to stay. And we don't want him here—not tonight. There's too much at stake." Flinging a casual arm around Cadel's shoulders, Trader attempted to lighten the mood. "Think of this as a diversionary tactic," he suggested whimsically. "Your job is to keep that copper off our backs, okay? And if you succeed, we'll give you first dibs on Jerry's files."

Still Cadel hesitated. He would have preferred almost any other job, but he didn't really have much choice. He grudgingly complied after Hamish had looked up from his computer and said, "Let's face it, Cadel—once the staff at GenoME go home, there won't be much we can do, anyway. Not with all their systems switched off. They even disconnect their bloody *routers*, for god's sake!"

It was true. Unless the systems were live, nothing of great importance could be gleaned from them. So at seven o'clock, when everyone else was beavering away in the War Room, Cadel found himself standing on the front veranda of Clearview House, shielding his eyes from the blaze of Saul's headlights.

He climbed into Saul's car quickly, before the detective could even think about getting out.

"Hello." Saul sounded surprised. "What's the rush?"

"I'm starving." When Cadel slammed the front passenger door, Saul raised an eyebrow. But he didn't comment. Only when they were cruising down Parramatta Road, heading east, did he ask if Cadel liked Italian food.

"Yes," said Cadel.

"We're meeting Ms. Currey at the restaurant," Saul explained, with a sidelong glance that was unreadable in the dimness of the car's interior. "Until then, I should probably keep my mouth shut."

"Who's paying?" Cadel said rudely. Whereupon a corner of the detective's mouth twitched.

"Don't let that worry you," he replied. "I'm thrashing it out with Ms. Currey. We'll settle it one way or another."

Something in his tone sparked Cadel's interest. It sounded as if Saul and Fiona were at loggerheads.

"Is there a problem?" Mentally reviewing the events of the past two days, Cadel drew the obvious conclusion. "Did you get in trouble for talking to me?"

Saul flicked another look at him but didn't answer. In fact, they both remained silent until they reached their destination.

Marco's Restaurant and Pizzeria was situated on Parramatta Road, in a row of small shops that had a dark, forlorn appearance at that hour of the night. Only Marco's was lit up; when Saul parked outside it, Cadel spotted Fiona through the restaurant's big front window. She was sitting at a table, examining a plastic-covered menu. Hers was the only occupied table in the whole establishment. Apparently, the midweek dinner hour wasn't a busy time at Marco's.

Fiona smiled as Cadel approached her. "I'm sorry I haven't dropped by," was the first thing she said. "I've been frantic, you've no idea. How's it going, Cadel? Are you settling in okay?"

"Yes," he replied, dropping into the seat next to her and burying his face in a menu. "I think I'll have pizza."

"Good choice. This place does excellent pizzas." Saul unbuttoned his jacket before sitting down, his attention fixed on Fiona. "I know it's an imposition, dragging you out here," he said, "but at least it's a tasty imposition."

"It's not an imposition, Mr. Greeniaus; it's my job," Fiona retorted. She was so curt that Cadel felt almost sorry for the detective, who reached quietly for a menu, absorbing her rebuke without a trace of resentment.

"You shouldn't get mad at him," said Cadel. "It wasn't his fault about Gazo. It was my fault, really."

Fiona blushed. "I'm not mad," she mumbled. "I'm just—I've had a hard day." Laying a hand on Cadel's arm, she added, "There's still nothing from Mel Hofmeier, I'm afraid. The department's dragging its feet."

Cadel shrugged. He hadn't been expecting good news. They all three studied their menus, made their choices, and placed their orders; it wasn't until the waiter had departed that Saul fixed his dark eyes on Cadel and announced, in a low voice, "I've got some disturbing information about Prosper English."

Cadel stiffened. His stomach seemed to do a backflip.

"There's been an incident at the prison where he's being held," Saul continued softly. "One of the guards was found dead this morning, with an empty envelope in his possession. The envelope had Prosper's name typed on it." Saul hesitated for a moment, then muttered, "We think the guard may have been poisoned, but we're not sure how yet. There's a fragment of skin adhering to the glue on the flap, so we'll get that analyzed. If it doesn't belong to the guard . . ."

He stopped and scanned Cadel's face intently. Cadel licked his dry lips. He could feel a nerve jumping in his jaw.

Fiona pressed his hand.

"Don't worry, sweetie," she said, without much conviction. "You'll be all right."

"Did—did—" Cadel couldn't spit out the question that he wanted to ask. Fortunately, he didn't have to. Saul knew what he was thinking.

"We're not sure if Prosper's responsible," the detective admitted. "It's hard to see how he could have done it, because of various circumstances that I won't go into." All at once he dropped his gaze and rearranged his cutlery. "The thing is, Cadel . . . I know I shouldn't be asking, and this is entirely off the record, but did you see anything like this when you were at the Axis Institute?"

Fiona's mouth tightened. So did her grip on Cadel's hand.

"Mr. Greeniaus—," she began, but Saul cut in, harshly.

"This is *off the record,* I swear to you! On my *life.*" All at once he stopped, as if regretting such an uncontrolled burst of emotion. After a moment, he proceeded more calmly. "You should know by now that the last thing I want is to harm Cadel in any way. I just need to know if there's something I've missed." He leaned forward. "Please."

Cadel tried to think. Fear never sharpened his wits, but always blurred and smothered them like fog; he had to push that fog aside before he could reason clearly. As the waiter placed a bowl of garlic bread in front of him, Cadel concentrated on what he had just heard. Poison. The Axis Institute.

He was determined not to dwell on the dead guard.

"They taught poisoning at the institute," he said at last, "but I never did that course." He cleared his throat before continuing. "I knew some girls who put poison under their fingernails and scratched people."

Conscious that Fiona was grimacing with disgust (as she always did when the Axis Institute was mentioned), Cadel shifted uncomfortably, retrieving his hand from her grasp. He reached for a piece of garlic bread.

Saul was frowning at the tablecloth.

"You see, if Prosper did this—well, that's one thing," he observed. "The trouble is, I can't understand how he managed it. And if he didn't manage it, then it's possible that someone might be trying to kill *him.*" He raised his eyes. "I don't suppose you've any idea who that someone might be?"

Cadel tore off a hunk of garlic bread and popped it into his mouth. Slowly, he shook his head.

"It could be anyone," he mumbled.

"It could be," Saul agreed. "In fact, it could be anyone who's afraid that Prosper might break down and testify. Including Earl Toffany."

Cadel stopped chewing.

"Who's Earl Toffany?" asked Fiona. And Saul replied, "The head of GenoME," before turning back to Cadel.

"We thought it was a strange coincidence, the way GenoME opened a branch here right after Prosper was arrested," the detective went on. "We were wondering if there were plans for a jailbreak. Now we're wondering if the plan is to kill Prosper because he knows too much." He pinned Cadel down with a speculative stare. "You must have been wondering that yourself, surely?"

Cadel couldn't swallow his bread. If he'd tried, he would have choked. His heart was hammering against his rib cage.

He found it impossible to speak.

"This isn't right," Fiona said, breaking into the conversation. She didn't seem angry—just tired. Tired and disappointed. "Cadel shouldn't have to deal with this. He's been through enough. I mean, I know you're doing your job, but does it have to be at Cadel's expense?" She leaned across the table so that she wouldn't be overheard by any restaurant staff. "Don't you realize how hard he finds it to cope with the whole *issue* of Prosper English?" she implored. "I've been trying to get him counseling for that very reason."

Cadel gasped, then began to cough. He'd inhaled a bread crumb. As Fiona patted his back, he spluttered, "I'm not scared of Prosper! I'm *not*!"

"Of course you're not," Fiona replied soothingly. "I just don't think you should be made to feel responsible for interpreting his actions, or assessing his state of mind. It isn't fair." She turned to Saul. "Cadel's already conflicted—he doesn't need the extra pressure."

"All right." Saul raised a hand. "Point taken. I'm sorry."

"This isn't the department talking," Fiona insisted. "I'm just concerned about a child who's been pushed around from pillar to post—"

"But I'm fine!" Cadel exclaimed. "God! Will you please stop *worrying* about me?" The more they both fretted, the more guilty Cadel felt. And the more guilty he felt, the crosser he became. "I don't care about Prosper! Why should I? He doesn't matter to me one bit, so you can ask all the questions you like! Just stop making such a *fuss*!"

As soon as the words had been spoken, he realized how infantile they made him sound. Saul's expression confirmed it. The detective bit his lip.

"I'm sorry, Cadel," he said at last, quietly. "You're so smart, I keep forgetting how young you are. We won't talk about Prosper. Not unless we have to."

"But I don't *care*!" Cadel cried—then cringed as two waiters peered at him from the kitchen door. Lowering his voice, he hissed, "Prosper doesn't care what happens to me, so why should I care what happens to him?"

"Because he's your father," Saul rejoined. "Of course you care. I'd think less of you if you didn't." Saul's melancholy regard was deeply unsettling. "And in case you're worried, let me inform you that Prosper's fine. He's bearing up extremely well. Better than you are, in fact." With a wry twist of the mouth, Saul added, "You'd never think he was in prison, the way he talks."

Cadel winced. He'd forgotten that Saul had been talking to Prosper English. The whole idea was dreadful. Cadel didn't even want to picture them both in the same room; he had a horrible feeling that Prosper would somehow threaten Saul's very existence.

"Please be careful," he begged the detective. "Please don't tell him you see me. Because he'll hate that. He'll hate *you.*"

"It's all right." Saul sounded far too confident. "I can handle Prosper English."

"No, you can't. No one can."

"Cadel—"

“You can’t trust him an inch! He’s too clever!”

“Cadel.” Saul reached over to lay a steady hand on Cadel’s wrist. “Prosper English isn’t going anywhere. Believe me.”

Cadel subsided. He wasn’t convinced, but he could see that it would be pointless to continue. In fact, he didn’t say much after that. Neither did Saul. They ate their meals in almost complete silence, though Cadel had lost his appetite. He wanted to blurt out everything he knew about GenoME and Genius Squad. He wanted to ask a hundred questions about Prosper English, Earl Toffany, and the guard who had died. But he couldn’t. He couldn’t tell the truth.

Instead he had to sit there, feeling like a complete fraud, until finally—mercifully—Fiona offered to drive him home.

TWENTY-THREE

When Cadel arrived back at Clearview House, he found it very dark and quiet.

At first glance, there didn't seem to be anyone around. No one answered his hail. His footsteps echoed on the bare boards of the hallway as he made for the kitchen, wondering if absolutely everyone was in the War Room. Or had something unexpected occurred? Had there been a mass evacuation?

If so, the exodus must have been made on foot; he had seen at least three cars parked out front. Fiona had seen them, too, and had driven away quite satisfied that the house was fully staffed.

Cadel, however, wasn't so sure; if there *were* any supervisors on the premises, they were making themselves pretty scarce. Having checked the kitchen, he was about to make his way downstairs when he heard the hiss and crackle of amplified breathing. Then a voice addressed him from the microphone that was hidden away behind an electrical socket.

Clearly, Cadel's entry must have triggered the internal alarm.

"Cadel! Is that you?" It was Hamish. "Come down, quick! We've done it!"

Done what? thought Cadel. But there were rules that governed the intercom system. No one was allowed to use it for long conversations, just in case a stranger happened to approach the back door, glance through the kitchen window, and see somebody talking to a wall. So Cadel took the lift downstairs, where he was greeted by a breathless chorus.

"There you are! Terrific!"

"You should see all this stuff!"

"We've got through to the lab!"

The War Room was buzzing with excitement. Cadel looked around. He saw little clumps of people everywhere: Sonja and Lexi in one corner; Cliff and Judith in another. Hamish was huddled with Dot and Devin around a single computer screen, like chilly people crouched around a fire.

As soon as he caught sight of Cadel, Hamish jumped to his feet.

"I got through!" he exclaimed. "I got into the lab computers! Jerry's been working late, so I got through!"

"Oh, yeah?" said Cadel. Though he hadn't yet recovered from Saul's news and was still feeling shaky, he tried to respond with a show of enthusiasm. "Did you use Jerry's password?"

"That's all we needed! It was a cinch!" Hamish cried. "Now we can run a piggyback op!"

"It's just as we thought," Dot added, more coolly. She went on to explain, for Cadel's benefit, that the lab computers did indeed dispatch regular deliveries of genetic information to GenoME's American network, where each electronic packet was broken down, analyzed, and interpreted. From the information contained in these packets, GenoME could produce a series of client reports, which were swiftly sent back to the Australian branch.

In other words, every time a packet left for America, the lab computers received another by return post.

"So it's perfect for us," Cadel muttered. He was trying to concentrate on what he'd just been told. "We can disguise our probes as DNA profiles, and the information we get back will look like client reports."

"Exactly!" Hamish chirruped.

Dot pointed out that the setup was ideal, because the Australian lab technicians weren't security conscious. Once their data had been entered into GenoME's system, the process was largely automated. Packets went out and packets came back in. The technicians didn't appear to worry about what happened in between.

"They're probably too busy," Cadel remarked. And Hamish said, in tones of withering scorn, "If those lab computers got up and went to the toilet, no one would notice."

It certainly seemed as if the lab machines were the weakest link in the GenoME network. So when Cliff strolled over and suggested piggy-backing on Jerry's e-mails, Hamish shook his head.

"Uh-uh," he replied. "Jerry sits on that machine all day. It's going to b-be hard enough downloading his files. We don't want to wander in and out of there too much."

"Jerry's got intuition," Dot confirmed. "Like Cadel. As for Carolina, she's paranoid. She checks and double-checks everything." According to Dot, while Carolina's machine was now wide-open, it was also more closely observed than the laboratory computers. "We should concentrate on those," Dot declared. "They're our best chance of penetrating the American firewalls."

And that was that. Cliff didn't argue. He did, however, insist that someone should also inspect Carolina's computer files, very carefully. "Because we can't afford to overlook anything," he growled. "I want her e-mails monitored. And Jerry's, too."

"Oh, we'll do that," Hamish assured him. "We've already started." Turning back to Cadel, Hamish revealed that, since Carolina and Jerry had *both* put in a late night at the office, large amounts of data had already been extracted from their well-protected hard drives. "Trouble is, most of it's encoded," said Hamish. "Which is where Lexi and Sonja come in. Decrypting is *their* job."

Cadel glanced across at Sonja, who was struggling to bash something out on her modified keyboard. Her movements had become quite erratic, as they always did when she was tired. Her eyes were ringed with dark circles.

"It's getting too late for Sonja," he said abruptly. "She ought to be in bed."

"Oh, she's all right." Cliff waved a careless hand. "She couldn't be happier."

But Cadel disagreed.

"She's worn out," he insisted. "I'll take her upstairs."

"No. *I* will." It was Judith who spoke; she had been poring over her laptop, absorbed in some kind of number-crunching exercise. Now she straightened, and stretched, and hauled herself out of her seat with a great popping and cracking of joints. "We have to talk about something, anyway," she observed, and approached Sonja's wheelchair. Her heavy, rolling gait made her look as unstoppable as an armored tank. "You come with me, love, and I'll get you sorted," she told Sonja. "You should have been in your pj's an hour ago."

"But we're not finished!" Lexi complained. "We haven't got to the subkeys yet!"

"And you won't. Not tonight," Judith said firmly. "You can do them tomorrow."

Cadel watched as Judith seized Sonja's wheelchair and pushed it toward the lift. He didn't know whether to feel relieved or resentful. On the one hand, it was nice to see someone else taking responsibility for Sonja—especially since he himself was almost dropping with fatigue. (It was never easy lifting her out of that wheelchair, even at the best of times.) On the other hand, he couldn't quite see why Sonja and Judith got on so well. They were both mathematicians, of course, but Sonja's attitude toward numbers was very pure and refined, whereas Judith regarded them merely as a means to an end—like a jimmy in a burglar's tool kit. For Judith, numbers were for sabotaging corporations, and plundering offshore bank accounts.

Cadel wondered if Judith's wealth could be part of the attraction for Sonja. Could Sonja be angling for a ride in Judith's lightplane, perhaps? Or a weekend at Judith's beach house?

But he immediately dismissed the idea. Sonja wasn't like that.

"So what did your copper friend have to say?" Cliff gruffly inquired, as the lift doors closed. He fixed his small, muddy eyes on Cadel. "Why did he want to have dinner with you? Any particular reason?"

"Oh . . ." Cadel shrugged. He didn't want to talk about Prosper English. "Just some fuss at the jail."

"What fuss?" said Hamish.

"What jail?" said Devin.

"Anything we ought to know about?" Cliff queried.

Cadel wiped a hand across his face. He was conscious of Lexi, sulking in the background. He was aware of his own confusion. Data was raining down on him from all sides; what he needed was some peace and quiet, to sort it out properly. To decide what was important and what could safely be ignored.

He was about to say as much when the intercom spluttered and Judith's voice rang out, distorted by feedback.

"Get up here," she squawked. "Something's going on."

There was a moment's stunned silence. Then Cadel found himself caught up in a stampede. Still somewhat dazed, he allowed Cliff to hustle him into the lift, which was a very tight squeeze for six people. Squished between Dot and Lexi, he was almost suffocated by the sickly musk of Lexi's cheap perfume.

When the lift door slid open, after a brief but uncomfortable ride, Cadel spilled out along with everyone else. The kitchen was dark. It was hard to see. Nevertheless, he could just make out Judith's bulky shape beside Sonja's wheelchair.

"What the hell—?" Cliff began. But Judith wagged a finger at him.

"Shh!" she hissed. "Listen! There's someone outside!"

Sure enough, distant shouts could be heard, issuing from somewhere in the enormous, parklike grounds. There followed a faint thumping noise and the crunch of footsteps on gravel.

"I can see a light," Judith whispered, squinting through the slats of a venetian blind that hung crookedly at the window over the sink. "I think someone's got a flashlight—"

"Everybody upstairs!" Cliff instructed, striding toward the back door and flinging it open. But not a single person obeyed this directive. Even Dot pressed forward, keen to see what was going on.

As Hamish and Devin clustered around Judith, blocking Sonja's view through the window, Lexi and Dot headed for the door. They jostled Cliff, trying to peer past him.

Cadel wasn't about to fight for a vantage point. Instead, sensibly, he flicked the switch that turned on the outside lamps.

"There! Look!" squeaked Lexi. "I see someone!"

"Is that guy wearing a *tie*?" Devin yelped, and Cliff said, "Cadel. Come here." Reaching back, he grabbed Cadel's arm. "That's one of your stakeout goons, isn't it?"

Dragged through a tightly packed scrum, Cadel became wedged between Cliff's flank and Lexi's. Before him lay a stretch of mangy lawn, bathed in electric radiance. Beyond it, a bobbing beam of light marked the passage of a heavy man in a dark suit, who was running so fast that his tie streamed over his shoulder, snapping in the breeze.

He was attempting to train his light on the figure tearing along some ten meters ahead of him.

"Well?" Cliff snapped. "Is it the police, or isn't it?"

"I—I think so," Cadel stammered. "I can't really see . . ."

"Oy!" the formally dressed runner yelled. But he was yelling at his mysterious quarry—not at the people in the kitchen. He didn't even glance their way. *"Oy! Police!"*

"It's a cop," the twins chorused, just as the shadowy fugitive was swallowed up by darkness, vanishing around the northernmost corner of the house. His pursuer was close on his heels.

Cadel realized that they were both heading for the gate.

"Veranda!" Hamish cried, whereupon there was another stampede—this time down the hallway. Hamish and the twins all thundered toward the front door, jabbing each other with their elbows, while Cliff slammed the back door and locked it.

"Get her out of the way," Cliff ordered, jerking his chin at Sonja as he addressed Judith. "Into the bedroom. Don't stand near any windows." Reaching for a high cupboard, he directed his next command at Cadel. "You—upstairs."

"But—"

"*Upstairs,* Cadel!" Cliff pulled down a large plastic jar. In the dim light, Cadel couldn't tell if the jar was full of raisins or coffee beans. "Your copper friend will gut me if anything happens to you," said Cliff. "I want you out of harm's way."

"But—"

"Go on, love," Judith urged stoutly. "I'll look after Sonja."

"Just *go*!" Cliff barked, fishing around in the jar. And Cadel went—not because he had any intention of heading upstairs, but because a sudden whoop from the front of the house indicated that something of interest had happened.

When he joined Hamish and the twins, they were bouncing around like cheerleaders, beside themselves with the thrill of the chase.

"There! There!" Lexi shrieked. "Get him, quick!" The boards of the veranda shook beneath her. "Oh my god, he's getting away!"

"No he's not—look!" Devin pointed. "There's another copper!"

Lurking behind them both, Cadel saw enough to give him a reasonably good idea of what was going on. Two wavering flashlight beams were now visible; with their assistance, and in the milky radiance of a nearby streetlight, Cadel could make out a dark silhouette pounding along the pale ribbon of the gravel driveway. Having outrun the first policeman, the fugitive had made a mad dash for the front gates—hoping, perhaps, to squeeze through them, or climb over them. But the sight of another flashlight-bearing, suit-wearing policeman just beyond those gates caused the fleeing trespasser to change his mind. He swerved back toward the house instead.

"He's heading this way!" Lexi screamed. Cadel grabbed her arm, to pull her inside.

At which point Hamish darted onto the driveway, with a shrill: "Come on!"

Cadel was gob smacked. He realized that the fugitive, in desperation, was setting his course for one of the parked cars—and that Hamish was trying to intercept him. Behind Cadel, Cliff cried, *"Hamish! Come back here!"* Then Lexi took off, disengaging herself from Cadel's grip.

Almost everyone in sight seemed to be converging on the stocky, black-clad stranger, who—propelled by his own momentum—slammed into Cliff's car before frantically jiggling the door handle.

"Get back!" yelled the closest policeman, making wild gestures at Hamish. *"Stop! Get back inside!"*

Hamish, however, was in a frenzy of excitement and didn't seem to hear. As his quarry broke away from Cliff's car, Hamish made a clumsy attempt to tackle him. It wasn't a successful maneuver. Hamish ended up on the ground, with his hands over his nose. He had been kicked in the face.

"Oh my god," said Cadel, and started forward.

But Cliff snatched at his collar, yanking him back. At the same instant, Lexi jumped out in front of the briefly delayed fugitive, blocking his planned trajectory. For some reason, he hesitated; possibly he was intimidated by her sturdy build, or her leather gear, or her eyebrow stud. At any rate, he stopped for a moment—allowing the first policeman to catch up.

It was immediately obvious that this particular law enforcer really knew how to bring someone down. He threw himself at his target like a first-grade rugby player; the noise of the impact made Cadel wince. There was a howl of pain from the trespasser and a delighted screech from Lexi. She began to perform a kind of war dance, punching at the air and springing from foot to foot.

"We-did-it! We-did-it!" she sang.

The policeman glared up at her, panting. "You get back inside!" he roared. "Are you crazy, or what?" He was holding his captive in a painful-looking armlock. His flashlight lay discarded on the grass.

Its steady beam was aimed directly at a damp, flushed, contorted face that Cadel recognized instantly.

"Mace!" he gasped.

TWENTY-FOUR

"Who?" said Lexi. And the breathless policeman croaked, "You know this guy?"

Cadel nodded. He was vaguely aware that Cliff had released him; that the second policeman was hurriedly approaching; that Hamish was gingerly dabbing at his split lip with one sleeve. But Cadel's overriding interest in Mace caused him to disregard these events.

Mace was wearing a black beanie, black gloves, and a black nylon tracksuit. There were dark smudges on his cheeks and forehead. As he lay there, his chest heaving, he swore at Cadel—who retreated a step.

"Okay, that's enough," the breathless policeman warned Mace. "You're only making it worse for yourself. What's your name? *Hmmm?*"

The sole response was a four-letter word, crudely placed in front of a three-letter one.

"He's called Thomas," Cadel said quickly, before the breathless policeman could lose his temper. "Thomas Logge."

"Isn't that the kid from your last billet?" inquired the second policeman, who had suddenly materialized out of the shadows, waving his flashlight. Cadel knew him. It was Mick Mattilos.

"Yes," Cadel mumbled.

"Watch it, Glen, he's a juvenile," Mick said to his partner. "Go easy, for Chris'sake."

Glen immediately rose. He hauled Mace up, too, neatly sidestepping a couple of flailing kicks in the process. Hamish, meanwhile, had also staggered to his feet; his nose wasn't bleeding, but his lip was.

"Are you all right, Hamish?" asked Cliff.

"He kigged be in the bouth," Hamish complained, his voice snubbed and muffled. "I could have lost a tooth."

"You shouldn't have tackled him," was Cliff's unsympathetic response. "I told you to stay put."

"I was tryig to *help,*" Hamish whined. And Mick said, "You'd better get a doctor to look at that. We might need photos, too—depending on the outcome."

"What the hell do you think you were playing at?" Glen demanded of Mace, who stubbornly refused to answer, pulling against the policeman's iron grasp instead. "Is this some kind of prank? Eh? Some kind of practical joke?"

"Do any of you kids know anything about this?" Mick added, surveying the assembled company with a gimlet eye. He looked from Hamish to Lexi to Cadel; when his gaze reached Cadel, it lingered on his face. "This isn't some lunatic role-playing scenario, is it? Some trick you're all in on?"

"No!" Lexi yelped, convincingly outraged. But then she undermined her show of injured innocence by turning to Cadel and saying, "Was it your idea?"

Cadel shook his head. Cliff growled, "I bloody hope not." Glen, who had been expertly frisking the uncooperative Mace, suddenly pulled something from a pocket in the black nylon tracksuit pants.

It was a little velvet-covered box.

"Uh-oh," said Glen. "Does this belong to anyone?"

His partner frowned. "But we caught him coming *in*!" Mick protested, as Mace bucked and jerked like a dog on a rope. In the process of tightening his hold on the prisoner, Glen dropped the velvet box—which was pounced upon by Lexi.

She immediately opened it, then proudly displayed the antique fob watch that was nestled inside.

"Looks like real gold," she declared.

"It's nod mine," said Hamish.

"Here," Mick commanded. "Give that to me."

His tone must have caused Lexi some offense, because she shut the box with a *snap* and tossed it at him, bridling. He only just managed to catch it. Cliff said, "Do you recognize it, Cadel?"

Again, Cadel shook his head. He was mute with shock. Nothing made sense; he couldn't quite believe that Mace had turned up, at Clearview House, so late at night. It seemed so risky. So *enterprising*. How had Mace managed to track him down? And for what purpose?

"No weapons," Glen concluded, after completing his search of Mace's pockets. "Unless you count a Swiss army knife."

"We'll have to get to the bottom of this," said Mick. "I suppose I'd better call the boss." And he produced a mobile phone from somewhere inside his jacket.

Hamish, by this time, was lurching toward the veranda. He announced that he was going to wash off the blood, but was promptly advised by Cliff to "put some ice on it first." Devin was eyeing Mace with frank curiosity. Lexi sidled up to Cadel and said, "Did you actually used to *live* with that guy?"

"Yes," Cadel murmured.

"In the foster home?"

"Yes."

"So that's how he knew where to find you?"

It was a good question. As far as Cadel was aware, no one had mentioned his new address to Mace. In fact, Saul had been trying to ensure that Cadel's whereabouts remained a well-kept secret.

How had Mace, of all people, learned that secret?

"All right, everyone inside," Cliff ordered. "Lexi—Cadel—it's time for bed. Dot, will you get them upstairs, please?"

Cadel realized suddenly that Dot had joined them, looking almost eerily detached. Hamish had disappeared into the house. Mick was muttering into his cell phone. As for Mace, he had stopped fighting when threatened with a pair of handcuffs. “It’s up to you, mate,” Glen had warned him. “It’s your choice.”

Mace had chosen the sensible course.

But he still refused to speak. And he glowered at Cadel in such a ferocious way that even Dot reacted, nudging Cadel in the ribs.

“You heard Cliff,” she said. “Go to your room.”

“The boss says he’ll meet us,” Mick declared. He was addressing his partner. “Says he’ll make the necessary calls. We’re to wait in the car till backup arrives. He says to be sure our subject’s well clear of the scene.” Mick turned to Cadel. “That’s you, kid. You’d better go upstairs, right now.”

Cadel didn’t argue. Though his gaze was riveted to the spectacle of Mace in burglar’s attire, he wrenched himself away without too much effort, trudging numbly back into the house. His last glimpse of Mace was a flash of snarling teeth and frightened eyes, briefly spotlit as Glen retrieved his flashlight.

Judith was hovering in the doorway of Sonja’s room, looking worried.

“It’s all right,” Dot announced, without waiting to be asked. “Everything’s under control. Where’s Hamish?”

“In the bathroom,” Judith replied. “What happened?”

“It was just some kid,” said Dot, and Lexi added, “It was some loony friend of Cadel’s.”

“He’s not my friend,” Cadel countered. “He hates me.”

“Perhaps he came here to kill you, then,” Devin observed, in a dispassionate tone. Judith frowned.

“Devin!” she snapped. But no one else reproved him. On the contrary, Lexi became quite excited.

“Oh my god!” she exclaimed. “Do you think so? Do you think that’s what the pocketknife was for?”

“Upstairs,” Dot said firmly. “Go on. All of you.”

“I just want to talk to Sonja—,” Cadel began. Dot, however, wouldn’t hear of it.

"Later," she said. "You can talk to her later. Right now, Cliff wants you up in your room."

Cadel balked. He regarded Dot sourly for a moment, wondering what gave her the authority to tell *him* what to do. Certainly he wasn't in her debt; he had twice approached her for information about her brother, only to come away unsatisfied. Either she distrusted him, or she simply didn't like talking to people.

Her brother hadn't. He had been almost incapable of communicating with other human beings. Dot wasn't nearly as antisocial, but she was still very aloof and taciturn; perhaps it was a family trait.

"Before I go—when did you last see Com?" asked Cadel, and Dot sighed. Her manner suggested that she recognized a trade-off when it was presented to her so bluntly.

She wasn't by any means stupid.

"I saw him the day after the Yarramundi campus blew up," she replied. "He came to my house and asked for some money. Then he stayed one night and went out the next day to make some calls from a phone booth. I never saw him again after that."

"Did he take the money with him?"

"Yes. Now, go up, or do you want me to call Cliff?" She paused for an instant, as if wearied by the tiresome job of fastening words together into sentences. "It's the police who want you to do this, Cadel."

"I know," he acknowledged, and began to climb the stairs. It had occurred to him that he could easily communicate with Sonja online; his intention was therefore to fish his laptop out of his underwear drawer and send her a reassuring message.

But he hadn't reckoned on the Wieneke twins and their insatiable curiosity.

"So what did you say this guy's name was?" Lexi inquired, as she followed him up to the top floor. "Maze, was it?"

"Mace. But his real name's Thomas."

"And why exactly does he hate you?"

"I don't know." Cadel wasn't about to tackle the endless saga of the sabotaged monitor and the bike magazines. "Because he's stupid, I guess."

"Oh, yeah." Devin's tone was sarcastic. "A person would *have* to be stupid to hate *you*. I mean, what's to hate?"

"Don't take any notice of him," Lexi urged Cadel, scowling at her brother (who was in the rear of the procession). "He's just jealous, that's all."

"I am not!"

"Because you're so smart and good-looking, with such great skin," Lexi continued remorselessly, still addressing Cadel, "and he's such a *loser.*"

"Says the fat slut with bad breath!"

"Oh, *don't,*" Cadel begged. He had reached the top-floor landing and couldn't bear the prospect of even one more carelessly traded insult. "Stop fighting, will you? I thought twins were supposed to stick up for each other. You're lucky you've even got any family. I wish I did."

"Would you like me to be your sister, Cadel?" Lexi threw her arm around his neck just as Cadel pushed open his bedroom door. "I'd rather have you as my brother than this loser over here."

While the twins traded more insults, Cadel wriggled out of Lexi's grip. All he wanted was some peace and quiet, so he could send a message to Sonja. But before he could suggest that the twins return to their own rooms, Hamish suddenly called to them from the floor below.

"Hey, you guys!" he exclaimed. "Whad are you doig?"

"None of your business," was Devin's sour response—which didn't deter Hamish in the least. His heavy boots mounted the stairs at a rapid pace; within seconds he was in plain sight, a disheveled figure holding a packet of frozen peas over his nose and mouth.

"Hey," he said eagerly, "did you see whad Cliff had? Cliff had a gun!"

"What?" Devin immediately brightened. "You're kidding."

"No. I saw id. When he chegged by lip, I saw id under his jumper. Tugged into his waisdband."

Cadel suddenly understood why Cliff had stopped to poke around in a jar of coffee beans. (Or had they been raisins?)

"Oh my god!" Lexi breathed, wide-eyed. "Do you think he would have shot that guy, if the police hadn't come?"

"Of course not," Cadel said crossly. He felt that there was enough melodrama in his life; it annoyed him that Lexi should feel the need to manufacture even more. "He's not an idiot, you know."

"He might have," Devin opined, with obvious relish. "If that Mace bloke came here to kill you, Cliff might have had to use the gun in self-defense."

"Against a penknife?" Cadel scoffed. And Lexi said, "What if the cops see his gun? What if they arrest him? What if they come in and search the place, looking for more?" She lowered her voice until it was just an overwrought whisper. *"What if they find the War Room?"*

"Lexi, Cliff's a private detective." Cadel was trying to snuff out her mounting excitement. "He's probably licensed to use a firearm. They can't arrest him if he has a license."

"Yes, but is he *supposed* to be a private detective?" Devin asked. "I thought he was meant to be a youth worker. I thought that was his cover story."

Cadel and Hamish exchanged glances. Then Hamish said, "He's subbosed to be a former private detegtive turned youth worger. Id's all on file. Didden you look?"

Hamish went on to explain that Cliff claimed to have grown disillusioned with apprehending criminals and was now—according to his faked-up curriculum vitae—devoting himself to crime prevention by helping troubled youth. This was obviously news to the twins. It soon became apparent that they hadn't done much research on the Clearview House staff, either before or after moving in.

Not like Hamish and Cadel.

"Jesus," said Hamish, juggling his packet of frozen peas, "you bean you didden run a few chegs first? Livig dangerously, Devin."

Devin shrugged. "We figured it had to be better here than it was at

Gran's, no matter what was going on," he retorted. "At least no one here's got dementia."

"Not that there were any red flags," Cadel conceded, recalling the searches he'd run through various databases. None of the Clearview House staff appeared to have a criminal record, for instance; all of them had managed to pass themselves off as trained youth workers, either by forging their qualifications or by producing a genuine certificate of some sort. (Zac, for instance, had studied welfare work right after leaving university.) "Still, you ought to be more careful," Cadel added. "You should always do your research—you shouldn't take *anything* on trust."

"Oh, and what makes you such an expert?" Devin sneered, bristling. "How come you're my boss, all of a sudden?"

"Because he's smarter than you," said Lexi, at which point Devin hit her. She instantly hit back, triggering a fight that sent them both reeling into poor Hamish, who nearly fell down the stairs. Cadel cried, "Stop it!" Hamish retreated. Then Judith's voice came echoing up from the hallway.

"Oy!" she bellowed. *"What's going on up there? Why aren't you kids in bed?"*

Cadel took the hint. He escaped into his room, shut the door, and locked it. Being small and weak, he had always found physical violence a very disturbing—and alien—concept. Though his upbringing had been warped, it had never involved slaps or punches. No one had ever raised a hand to him during his early childhood, because Prosper would never have allowed such a thing.

The twins, however, had quite clearly been raised in a far more volatile environment. Devin, in particular, seemed to be quite an angry sort of person. As for Hamish, though he was as sharp as a tack in many ways, he could also be immensely childish in others. And his taste for practical jokes made Cadel uneasy.

Many of the students at the Axis Institute had been fond of vicious practical jokes, often involving concealed razor blades and poisoned fingernails.

Extracting his laptop from his underwear drawer, Cadel decided that Genius Squad wasn't going to be the answer to all his prayers. It was a pity; he'd never in his life before found a group of people who were not only his own age (more or less), but who shared many of his interests. At first glance, the squad had looked so promising.

But he didn't feel comfortable with its younger members. Lexi was overwhelming, Devin was unnerving, and Hamish—well, Hamish was ever so slightly off balance. It was hard to imagine that any of them would ever become a really good friend.

Not like Sonja.

Cadel sent a message through to her as quickly as possible, knowing that it was her habit to check her e-mails every night before going to bed. He told her that Mace had scaled the garden wall, not realizing that the place was being staked out. He also assured her that Mace had been apprehended and was now in custody—along with the mysterious gold fob watch.

I know it didn't belong to Mace, he wrote, *because if it had, I would have seen it before. He might have extorted it off some poor kid at school and can't bear to part with it, even when he's conducting home invasions.* Cadel thought for a moment, reviewing all the possibilities. *On the other hand,* he continued, *it might have been stolen from another house around here. Or it might have been payment for what he was about to do. Or he might have found it somewhere. Or his brother might have given it to him. There are any number of explanations that fit the case.*

Indeed, there was one explanation that Cadel didn't even want to air, because it sounded so mad. Rather than come across as completely paranoid, he withheld it from Sonja, going on to ask her how she was.

I hope you aren't too worried, since it wasn't Prosper after all. And I know that Mace can't be working for Prosper, because Prosper never hires people that stupid. He always used to tell me: "Choose the correct tools"—

and Mace must be the bluntest tool in the toolbox. Conscious of an all-too-familiar banging and yelling somewhere below, Cadel concluded with the words: *I won't come down just yet—not until I get permission. If Saul shows up, I don't want him getting mad at Cliff for not making me stay upstairs; it's bad enough that Mace found out where I was. I just hope Saul doesn't decide to take me away. That would be a disaster. Anyway, see you soon.*

And he signed off using the nickname she'd once given him: Stormer.

Then he waited.

Her answer was a long time coming. The Wienekes had calmed down—and slammed into their separate bedrooms—at least ten minutes before Sonja's message finally dropped into Cadel's in-box. He even had time to run a computer check on Mace's brother. (Sure enough, Scott Logge had been jailed for several break-and-enter offenses.)

But when at last Cadel opened up Sonja's reply, he found only a numerical sequence: *44-9/01-1-126/90-60-232/04-53-32/06.*

Decoding this sequence wasn't too hard. He recognized it instantly as an example of their very own periodic-table code, devised while he was still being closely monitored by Prosper English. To break it, one merely needed a thorough knowledge of the various atomic numbers and weights.

And since Cadel knew all those by heart, he was able to translate Sonja's response without delay.

The first number in any periodic table sequence was always an atomic number, and 44 was the atomic number of ruthenium (Ru). Then came a weight: in this case, 9.01, which happened to be the atomic weight of beryllium (Be). Next came hydrogen (H), which had an atomic number of 1; iodine (I), which had an atomic weight of 126.90; and neodymium (Nd), which had an atomic number of 60.

The final elements were thorium (Th), iodine once again, and sulfur (S). So the complete sequence read: *Ru-Be-H-I-Nd-Th-I-S.*

Are you behind this?

Cadel gasped. The question hit him like a punch in the solar plexus; he couldn't believe that Sonja was even asking it. Automatically, he sent back the atomic number of nobelium (No), adding several explanation points for emphasis. But he was so shaken by Sonja's suspicion that he couldn't think clearly. He couldn't piece together a single line of code before Sonja's next message came through: *1-74/92-39-167/26-9-126/90-7-72/6-68-140/91-49-47/88-90-126/90-7-39/1.*

Cadel spelled it out to himself: *H-As-Y-Er-F-I-N-Ge-Er-Pr-In-Ti-Th-I-N-K.* In plain English, Sonja was saying that she thought the whole situation had his "fingerprint" on it.

How can you say that? he typed furiously, abandoning the periodic-table code in his eagerness to defend himself. *What are you talking about?*

Her coded rejoinder was astonishingly swift. It was another sequence of numbers, which—when translated—read: *I-Fm-Ac-Er-O-B-Be-Dy-Er-La-S-Th-O-U-Se-S-O-He-Cd-P-La-N-Ti-Ti-N-Th-I-S-Ho-U-Se-S-O-Y-O-U-Cd-Be-B-La-Md . . .*

If Mace robbed your last house so he could plant it in this house so you could be blamed . . . Like Cadel, Sonja had envisaged a really crazy scenario. Unlike Cadel, however, she had been brave enough to put it into words.

She was wondering if Mace had been planning a setup.

How could that be my fault? Cadel demanded, refusing to use the code. *You think I encouraged him to come here? So he'd be caught doing something illegal? Is that it?*

He didn't care about security. He didn't care that someone might read their exchange, and understand it, and accuse him of framing his foster brother.

He was past caring.

Seeing this, Sonja lapsed back into plain English. *You got someone else to ruin Mace's magazines,* she reminded him. *And from what you've said, he doesn't seem bright enough to have found your address on his own. I just wondered if maybe you put the idea in his head.*

Well, I didn't, Cadel countered.

Okay, was her quick response.

Do you believe me?

Yes.

Feeling slightly better, Cadel was willing to concede a point. *I can see what you mean, though,* he acknowledged. *About Mace. It doesn't seem like his kind of revenge.*

Have you run the probabilities? Sonja wanted to know. When Cadel confessed that he hadn't, she continued: *Then you should. Because it's all very peculiar, don't you think?*

Cadel agreed. It was very peculiar.

It didn't feel right.

TWENTY-FIVE

The next day, Genius Squad began to turn GenoME inside out.

It was a complicated job, requiring a range of skills. While Lexi and Sonja toiled away over ciphers and subkeys, Tony helped Judith to review the financial data that had already been decoded. And while Hamish and Cadel busied themselves with the American interface, Dot and Devin were supposed to be keeping an eye on local activity.

Cadel's piggyback operation was short-lived; it stopped altogether, once the American operation had shut down for the night. But before that occurred, he discovered (to his surprise) that the online Hamish was a very different animal from Hamish in the flesh. Cadel would have picked Hamish for an e-prankster, continually planting booby traps and careening messily through databases with no thought for the chaos that he might be wreaking. Oddly enough, however, the virtual Hamish wasn't like that at all. On the contrary, he prowled around networks like a cat, silent but deadly.

Cadel was most impressed.

He said as much to Trader just before the afternoon update meeting. This took place in the kitchen and was attended by everyone except Zac—who was on eavesdropping duty downstairs. The proceedings opened with a brief status report from Trader; having first delivered Cadel's news about the dead prison guard (for the benefit of those who hadn't already heard it from Cadel), Trader then gave an account of his own recent telephone conversation with Saul Greeniaus. According to Saul, Mace hadn't been trying to remove anything from Clearview House.

On the contrary. Having stolen Hazel Donkin's grandfather's fob watch, Mace had intended to plant it somewhere in Cadel's new residence.

"I gather he wanted you blamed for the theft," Trader told Cadel, with barely suppressed amusement. "Obviously not a very bright lad, in many ways."

"What's going to happen to him?" Cadel inquired. "He's not going to be charged, is he?"

Trader shrugged. "I'm not sure," he admitted. "But whatever does occur, it's not your problem. *Your* problem is breaking into GenoME's American network." He offered up his most encouraging smile. "Have you done that yet?" he asked.

Shifting slightly in his chair, Cadel was forced to confess that so far, he and Hamish had only just managed to infiltrate the node-code analysis program. Nevertheless, they were hoping to use this program as a platform for conducting raids on the rest of the system, once the computers in California were operating again.

Trader seemed to accept this. At any rate, he moved on, questioning Dot about the contents of Jerry's computer files. Had any further progress been made? When Dot revealed that most of the GenoME's Australian profits were going straight to a company in the Cayman Islands, Trader glanced at Judith.

"You might want to look into that," he said. Judith's response was to rub her hands together, eagerly. Tony couldn't suppress a smile of satisfaction as he scribbled in a memo book with his gold fountain pen. (Being a methodical and precise sort of person, he was the only member of Genius Squad who ever took notes during meetings.)

"We've also worked out that Carolina's been keeping tabs on Prosper English," Dot continued—and all eyes immediately swiveled in Cadel's direction. He felt his face grow hot.

"What—what do you mean?" he stammered.

"She's got a file full of newspaper downloads," Dot replied. "Articles about Prosper's arrest. That sort of thing. Plus a collection of stuff that's been lifted directly off the police system."

"The police system?" said Judith, sounding alarmed. And Lexi exclaimed, "Does that mean she knows where Cadel is?"

Sonja began to grunt as she flailed around in her wheelchair. Cadel saw that she was trying to use the DynaVox, so he reached over to steady her arm; his gentle grip gave her the support she needed to spell out the words *"There's-nothing-about-Cadel-in-her-files."*

"She might not have found his stuff yet," Hamish remarked, pushing his glasses up his nose. "The last time I looked, he was in a high-security part of the Federal Police d-database."

There was a pause. During it, Trader tapped at his teeth with one finger, in a meditative fashion, while Cadel sat dumbly, trying to process what he'd just heard. At last Trader said, "It's no big deal. Carolina can't get at Cadel while he's in here. Our security's too good—and besides, we'd find out what she was doing before she did it." Having aired this opinion, he proceeded to another topic. "What *I* want to know is: Was she behind that prison-guard business?" he demanded. "Was she trying to kill Prosper English, or what?"

He looked to Lexi for an answer. But Lexi seemed uncertain. "I don't think so," was all she would say, as she glanced at Sonja—whose own response was made slowly and clumsily.

"Carolina-knows-about-the-dead-guard," Sonja confirmed, *"but-she-found-out-from-hacking-the-police-system. She-wasn't-involved."*

"Really?" Trader was now drumming his fingers on the tabletop. "Are you sure?"

"Positive. She-sent-her-findings-to-Jerry-via-e-mail. Her-covering-note-was-very-surprised."

"What a pity," Trader lamented. "If GenoME had tried to kill Prosper English, we might have been able to use that against Earl Toffany. As the company boss, Earl would have to be implicated somehow." He raised an eyebrow at Cadel's shocked face. "What?" he pressed. "You're not worried about Prosper English getting killed, are you? I thought he put a gun to your head?"

"I don't—," Cadel began, but couldn't find his voice for a moment.

Trader's careless, offhand manner had chilled him. It had put him in mind of other discussions, about other deaths. "I don't want anyone *killed,*" he gasped. "That's the way people used to talk at the institute!"

There followed a long, embarrassed silence, during which Trader scrutinized Cadel with less than his usual insouciance. It was Cliff who changed the subject.

"Anything else?" he queried. "Has anyone found out anything about Rex Austin's son? Or Fountain Pharmaceuticals? Or NanTex?"

No one answered. Not immediately, at any rate. Finally Sonja remarked, through the agency of her DynaVox, *"One-odd-thing."* And then she hesitated.

"What?" said Cliff. But still she seemed reluctant to talk. It was Lexi who finally said, "That guy, you mean?"

"What guy?" Trader wanted to know. At which point, high and piercing, the alarm shrilled—making everyone jump.

"Shit." Cliff bounced to his feet. "Who could that be?" He moved to the bulletin board hanging on a stretch of wall near the pantry and pushed it aside to reveal a CCTV screen. "It's bloody Saul Greeniaus!" he protested. "For Chris'sake, Cadel, what does he want *now*?"

"I don't know." Cadel resented being asked. "How should I know? Maybe he's got some news about Mace."

"Lexi, tell us about your guy—quick," Trader snapped. And Lexi shrugged.

"Jerry's got a file on him," she explained, as various people whisked their laptops out of the kitchen. "He's not staff, and he's not a client. He may have had something to do with GenoME once, but nowadays he's just working in a bank."

"Show me the file," Cliff ordered, propelling Lexi toward the lift. Trader called after them, "Make it snappy, please!" then grabbed Cadel's arm.

"You need to take care of this." Though Trader's tone was pleasant and easy, the pressure that he applied to Cadel's wrist suggested that he wasn't as tranquil as he appeared. "See if you can't get rid of Greeniaus quick-smart—we don't want him hanging around."

"Okay, okay," Cadel muttered. He was still trudging down the hallway when the doorbell rang again. Trader had already vanished; Cadel didn't know where he'd gone. Only Judith remained in the kitchen with Sonja.

Cadel checked his watch. It was 2:38 P.M.

Upon opening the front door, he found Saul Greeniaus waiting on the veranda. "Hello," said the detective, who looked as dark and straight and narrow as a stick of charcoal in his gray suit. "Should you be answering the door by yourself, do you think?"

Cadel sighed.

"Should you be *speaking* to me by yourself, do you think?" he retorted, and glanced around in a pointed manner. "Hasn't Fiona come?"

Almost at once, he regretted having lost his cool—because Saul studied him thoughtfully, eyes narrowed.

"Something bothering you, Cadel?"

"No," Cadel replied.

"You aren't being hassled by anyone?"

"No!" Cadel retreated into the dimness of the hallway. "Come in, if you like. *I* don't care. I just figured you wouldn't want to get in trouble, that's all."

His words were convincing, but his tone was wrong. And he could see how Saul took note of this even as he crossed the threshold at Cadel's invitation.

"Fiona won't be coming," the detective announced, surveying his immediate vicinity. He was carrying a large yellow envelope. "This will only take a minute. Is there someone here who could stand in for Fiona? A concerned adult?"

"Um . . . well . . . Judith's in the kitchen." Cadel wondered where Trader had disappeared to. "If you don't mind Sonja being there as well."

"I imagine you probably tell Sonja everything you hear from me, anyway," Saul said dryly, and followed Cadel to the back of the house. Here Judith had been busying herself with various innocent-looking jobs around the sink; she bustled up to the detective, wiping her plump red hands on a tea towel. The word *harmless* was practically tattooed on her forehead.

"Would you like something?" she offered. "Coffee or tea?"

"No, thanks," Saul replied. "I won't be long." And he nodded at Sonja. "Hello, Sonja," he said, moving toward the table. "I'm sorry to interrupt."

"Is-it-about-Mace?" was Sonja's response. Whereupon the detective paused, clearly thrown off balance.

It was apparent that the previous night's events were not uppermost in his mind.

"Oh," he said. "Yes. I mean—no." He turned to Cadel. "Have you not heard about that? Mr. Lynch called me . . ."

"I've heard that Mace wanted to get me into trouble for stealing Hazel's watch," Cadel confirmed. "But how did he find me? How did he even get here? It's *miles* away from the Donkins' house."

"He was visiting his sister-in-law, who lives near here," Saul explained. "He does that sometimes—takes off after school, and stays the night. Or so Mrs. Donkin says."

Cadel nodded. It was true. And Hazel had always regarded these infrequent excursions quite favorably, because she approved of Mace's sister-in-law. Alone of all the Logge relations, this sister-in-law was a kind, decent, hard-working woman—despite (or because of) the fact that her husband was in jail.

"It was very unfortunate," Saul added. "That other kid at the Donkins' . . . What's his name?"

"Janan," Cadel supplied.

"Yeah. Well, he asked Mrs. Donkin for your address. So he could write and remind you about something. Something to do with chocolate-bar wrappers?"

"Oh. Right." Cadel felt a pang of guilt. "I promised to send him some."

"Did you? I wish you hadn't." The detective went on to describe how Hazel had seen no harm in allowing Janan to correspond with Cadel, though she wouldn't have dreamed of allowing Mace to do the same. "She should never have been given this address in the first place," Saul declared, and it was obvious from the detective's tone that the idea hadn't been his. "When she wrote it down, Thomas must have seen it, and that was that. I only hope he doesn't shoot his mouth off. Because if he does, you might not be safe here."

"Oh, surely it isn't *that* bad!" Judith objected. And Cadel asked, "You mean you think Mace is working for someone else?"

"Someone else?" Saul blinked in surprise. "Hell, no," he said, without hesitation. "I think this whole thing was the dumb plan of a dumb kid. But if the news spreads, someone might hear it who isn't so dumb."

Cadel bit his lip. He wasn't convinced that Mace's actions had been completely without sense or forethought. Nevertheless, he refrained from commenting—and Saul seemed to regard this silence as evidence that Cadel agreed with him.

"Anyhow," said the detective, "it's no big deal. No matter what kind of penalty Thomas Logge is given, it won't make any difference. He'll end up in prison one day, just like his brother. It's probably where he *wants* to end up. Kids like that—they can't imagine anything else." Saul reached into his yellow envelope and produced a small photograph, which he placed on the tabletop. "Here's something far more important," he assured Cadel, indicating the picture. "Do you know this girl?"

Cadel stepped forward. He found himself staring at a snapshot of two people: a man and a woman. The man was big and beefy, with a crew cut. The woman was small and pretty, with dyed red hair.

Cadel knew that it was dyed, because he knew the woman.

He stepped back abruptly, as if he'd been burned.

"That's her," he gasped, his heart hammering. Saul frowned.

"That's who?" he asked.

"Niobe! That's Niobe, from the institute! Remember? She was one of the twins—they were assassination students." Seeing the detective's pinched expression, Cadel grabbed his sleeve. "Where is she? Have you found her?"

"Not yet," was Saul's calm response, as he disengaged himself from Cadel's grasp.

"Where did you find the photo?" Judith interjected.

"This photograph was in the dead guard's apartment." Saul didn't even glance at Judith. He hadn't taken his eyes off Cadel. "Your old friend appears to have been living with him. But now she's packed her bags and gone."

"It was her," Cadel croaked. The scenario was unfolding in his head, so quickly that his tongue could hardly keep up with it. "She tried to kill Prosper, because she blames him for what happened to her twin," he gabbled. "I bet that's it. She can't stand the guilt of having fractured her own sister's skull, so she must have decided that Prosper was ultimately responsible. And she only shacked up with the guard to make sure he'd deliver Prosper's letter. But the guard got worried about what was inside. That's why he opened the envelope—and was hit by whatever she put in it." He appealed to Saul. "Some kind of chemical, maybe? One that would react with the air?"

Saul placed a hand on his shoulder.

"Sit down, Cadel," the detective advised. "You don't have to worry."

"Would-she-know-about-Cadel-being-Prosper's-son?" Sonja asked. She tried to say something else as well; her muscles, however, wouldn't oblige. They began to work against her, contorting uncontrollably.

"Niobe won't go after you, Cadel," Saul insisted, reproving Sonja with a grim look. "She doesn't know where you are, to begin with. Unless someone in Clearview House has spilled the beans."

"Oh, no." Judith had been inspecting Niobe's photograph; now she raised her head, becoming quite defensive. "No, we've all been warned about Cadel's situation. No one here would put him at risk."

"I hope not," Saul dourly observed. Turning back to Cadel, he said, "We have you under surveillance. Niobe can't get near you—as long as you don't open any mail."

Cadel was studying Niobe's two-dimensional face. It had changed a lot since their first meeting. Back then, Niobe had been bubbly and affectionate. But the institute had warped and twisted her personality. It had taught her to do more than lie and cheat.

It had taught her to kill.

"If she ends up killing Prosper, it'll serve him right," Cadel declared. Though he made an effort to sound untroubled, his voice cracked before he could finish.

Saul's grip on his shoulder tightened.

"I'm sorry, Cadel." It was a gruff but heartfelt apology. "I'd have asked Gazo to identify her, except that we don't know if he's still connected with this woman."

"He isn't," said Cadel. "He never liked her much." After fingering the photograph for a moment, he passed it to Saul. "She was quite nice, really. Until they screwed her up at the institute."

Silence fell. Saul returned the snapshot to its envelope. Sonja was fighting a muscular spasm. Judith was trying to calm her down.

Cadel stood irresolute. He still felt shell-shocked.

"I won't bother you anymore," Saul finally announced. "I'll just tell you that Prosper English will be appearing at the Coroner's Court on Monday, in relation to this death. As a witness. Of course his connection seems pretty tenuous right now, but it's the coroner's job to investigate all deaths that aren't from natural causes, so Prosper really has to be questioned. To establish if any charges should be laid . . ." Saul shrugged, in a resigned manner. "You mustn't worry, though. He'll be closely guarded. I'll make sure of it."

When Cadel didn't reply, or even acknowledge this news with a grunt, Saul murmured, "Will you be all right, Cadel? Do you want me to call Ms. Currey?"

"I'll be fine," said Cadel. Then it occurred to him that Trader would probably want Saul escorted from the house. (What if the detective decided to poke around on his own?) So Cadel gestured at the back door. "You can leave this way, if you want," he said, adding, "There's something I want to ask you."

Saul didn't object. At least, he didn't give Cadel one of his quizzical looks. Instead he bade a polite farewell to Sonja, thanked Judith, and followed Cadel outside.

Together they walked around to the front of the house, Saul keeping his eyes peeled, Cadel racking his brain for a convincing question to ask. It wasn't until they had reached Saul's car that Cadel finally spoke up, having experienced a last-minute flash of inspiration.

"You told me that you were analyzing the envelope with Prosper's name on it," he said. "Does that mean you've done a matching DNA test on Prosper?"

Saul paused in the act of unlocking his driver's door.

"We can't use that sample for a paternity test. Not without permission," he said, reading between the lines. "I'm sorry."

Cadel shrugged. "I figured you couldn't, or you would have told me."

For some reason, this careless remark made a big impression on Saul. He pondered it for a while, his expression serious. At last he said, "You're right. I would have told you. There are people who believe you should be shielded from this kind of stuff, but . . . if I keep things from you, you won't have all the facts. And without the facts, you won't be able to protect yourself." He lifted an eyebrow. "I know you're smarter than most of us. That's why I figure, when it comes to the crunch, you'll be safer if you're properly informed. Don't you think?"

Cadel nodded, speechless.

"Okay, then. I'll keep you posted." Without further ado, Saul climbed into his car and slammed the door. Revving his engine, he flapped his hand at Cadel, urging him to step aside.

But Cadel didn't obey. Moved by an obscure impulse, he leaned down and tapped on the driver's side window—which was immediately lowered.

"What?" asked Saul.

Cadel took a deep breath. "You don't need to worry," he said. "I'll be careful from now on. I won't do anything stupid."

At which point, for the very first time, Saul smiled at him.

"Well, of course you won't," the detective replied. "I think I've worked *that* out by now."

And he roared off toward the front gates.

TWENTY-SIX

The next morning, news of Prosper's impending court appearance hit the GenoME system.

It was Devin who first alerted Cadel to this flurry of e-mails. Devin had been given the task of monitoring Jerry's e-mail traffic—and according to Devin, the local computers were running hot.

"They found out about Prosper from the police network," he said, "and now they're forwarding the information to America." He spoke sullenly, looming over Cadel's workstation with his hands in the pockets of his baggy jeans and his black beanie pulled down low over his forehead. Cadel knew perfectly well that Devin resented having to concentrate on local activity. Hacking into GenoME's American system was the glamor job of their operation; Devin made no secret of the fact that he would have preferred working alongside Hamish and Cadel.

As a result, the atmosphere of the War Room no longer crackled with excitement. Instead, a kind of gloomy impatience had infected the air, thanks to Devin's hisses and sighs and restless fidgeting.

Lexi, on the other hand, was completely absorbed. Now that she had so much decrypting to do, she'd stopped wandering from workstation to workstation, snapping rubber bands between her fingers and commenting on people's outfits. She didn't have the time.

"Well," Cadel remarked, giving Devin his full attention, "we know that Carolina's interested in Prosper English. She's got that file on him, remember?"

"Yeah, but there's something going down," Devin insisted. "It feels like they're a bit frantic suddenly. Like they're up to something."

"Maybe they are," Trader suddenly observed, from behind him. "But we won't know unless you keep an eye on them." Draping an arm across Devin's shoulders, he flashed his movie-star smile, which was beginning to look slightly frayed around the edges. Like most of Genius Squad, he hadn't been getting much sleep. "So why don't you concentrate on your work, instead of distracting these people? *Hmmm?*"

"I was just *telling* them," Devin growled, before shrugging off Trader's arm and stomping back to his desk.

Trader turned to Cadel.

"What about your side of things?" he asked. "Any developments?"

"Yeah," Cadel conceded. He had been picking his way through the GenoME node-code analysis program and had discovered two interesting features. One was a series of regular, automated downloads to an outside system. The other was an archive full of past node-code reports, dating back several years.

"Hamish has been checking it out," Cadel reported, "and he's found ten names linked to another database that we haven't got into yet. It's heavily protected."

"One of the ten names is Jimmy Austin," said Hamish, adjusting his glasses. "You know—Rex's son. And one belongs to that guy Lexi mentioned. The guy who works for a b-bank."

"Really?" Trader frowned. "Any idea what that's about?"

"Not yet," Hamish admitted. "Like Cadel said, I haven't got into the linked site."

"Give it all you can, then," said Trader, after a moment's intense thought. "And distribute that list of names. In fact, I might do a bit of research on them myself." Again, he addressed Cadel. "What about the outside downloads? Do you know where they're going?"

Cadel shook his head. "But it won't be too hard to find out," he surmised.

"Do it," said Trader. "That's a priority. Because I wouldn't be surprised if those downloads were going straight to Fountain Pharmaceuticals. What kind of stuff are we talking about?"

"Genetic data," Cadel replied. And Trader nodded.

"See, it makes sense," he mused. "Chester Cramp's in charge of Fountain Pharmaceuticals, and I've always had a sense that he calls the shots when it comes to process. Because GenoME's gene analysis system probably came straight out of NanTex, and NanTex used to be run by Chester. In fact, as far as I'm concerned, Fountain Pharmaceuticals is just NanTex under another name." He clapped Cadel on the shoulder. "If we can get into the Fountain system, then we'll know for sure," he finished. "I'm counting on you for that, Cadel. You, too, Hamish. Don't let me down."

"Don't let me down," Hamish mimicked, after Trader had withdrawn to the other side of the room. "Yes, *suh*! Roger, wilco!" And he snorted. "I hate all this team-building crap, it's so b-bogus. Like we're stupid enough to need it, for god's sake."

Cadel said nothing. He had vowed to concentrate on his work, because if he kept himself busy enough, he wouldn't fret about other things.

Unfortunately, Hamish wasn't being very cooperative.

"So what do you reckon?" he asked, with a sly, sidelong glance. "Why are all these e-mails b-being fired off, suddenly? Why is Jerry so interested in Prosper's court appearance?"

Cadel shrugged. He didn't want to think about Prosper English. Or Niobe. Or anyone else associated with the Axis Institute.

"I can't answer questions like that," he said. "There's no point running probabilities, because I don't have enough information."

"D-do you think GenoME actually *hired* that poisoning girl to kill Prosper?"

"How should I know?"

"Because you've met her, that's why." Hamish leaned toward him. "What's the d-deal with her, anyway? Someone told me she killed her own twin sister."

"Not exactly. I mean—it was complicated. You wouldn't understand." An image flashed into Cadel's mind: a memory of his last meeting with

Niobe. It had occurred on the institute campus, quite late at night. Niobe had been dressed in a black turtleneck, black pants, a black vest, black gloves, and a black balaclava. She had been on her way to the microbiology labs, where she had subsequently fractured her twin sister's skull in hand-to-hand combat.

Cadel closed his eyes. He took a deep breath to steady himself.

"Look—I don't want to talk about it, all right?" he snapped. "It's pointless! This whole discussion is pointless! Why don't you just wait until Lexi and Sonja have finished decoding? Then we might actually have some *data*!" And he resumed his work, conscious of Hamish's disappointment. By directing all his energy at the computer screen, however, Cadel was able to block out the frustrated pout next to him, just as he was able to block out Devin's restlessness, Lexi's occasional bursts of excitement, and Judith's loud comments about money laundering. Having thrown himself wholeheartedly into GenoME's system, Cadel tried again and again to piggyback on those mysterious downloads.

By lunchtime, he had succeeded. And he had also confirmed Trader's suspicions.

GenoME was sending genetic data through to Fountain Pharmaceuticals.

"I knew it," said Trader, upon being informed. His eyes glittered and his teeth gleamed; his exultation was infectious. "Didn't I tell you? It's NanTex under another name." He ruffled Cadel's hair. "Well done. Well *done.* That's what I like to see!"

"Most of the system's off-line now," Cadel remarked. "Things have shut down for the night over there."

"But you can pick it up again tomorrow?"

"Yes."

"*Attention, people!*" Trader spun around to address the other occupants of the War Room. "You'll be pleased to know that Cadel's through to Fountain Pharmaceuticals! From now on, he'll be in charge of finding out what Chester Cramp is up to!" Cadel flushed as Devin slowly and mockingly applauded. Even Judith's murmur of approval seemed rather weak. But Trader didn't allow this muted response to intimidate him. On the contrary, he beamed at Devin and added, "Meanwhile, Hamish and Devin can focus on GenoME's American network."

Devin's jaw dropped. Hamish scowled. Trader declared, "Never say I don't care about my team, Devin," and waited for a response.

Devin scratched his chest awkwardly.

"Uh—thanks," he said at last.

"But I want to make one thing clear," Trader continued, raising a finger. "You do what Hamish tells you to do. He's your boss on this." Before Devin could protest, Trader warned sweetly, "You're a ram-rodder, Devin. I need more subtlety than you can offer, I'm afraid. And if you don't like it, you can go back to Jerry's e-mails. All right?"

In the sudden silence that ensued, Cadel heard a strangled grunt. One glance told him that Sonja was struggling to speak.

He was about to draw attention to this fact when Lexi gave a yip and swiveled around to face the rest of the room. She had been attending to her computer, oblivious to everybody else.

"Oh my god!" she cried. "Trader, listen!"

"I'm talking, Lexi."

"Yes, but—"

"In a minute, please."

"But *they're planning to free Prosper English!*"

Everyone was struck dumb by this announcement. Even Trader fell silent. Dot blinked. Hamish gasped. Tony's eyebrows climbed his forehead until they almost disappeared into his hairline.

Cadel sat quite still, speechless with shock, as Sonja rolled an anxious pair of eyes at him.

At last Trader recovered. Crisply he demanded an explanation, which Lexi was eager to provide.

"We've been lucky," she said, "because Carolina must be out and about. Instead of calling Jerry, she's e-mailed him. Maybe she trusts firewalls more than she trusts mobile phones." Gesturing at her computer screen, Lexi added, "It's all here. Laid out in dot points."

"What is?" said Trader.

"Her plan to kidnap Prosper English. When he arrives at the Coroner's Court." Lexi was bobbing up and down in her seat, unable to keep still. "That Gazo guy is supposed to stink up the whole courthouse, so everyone will pass out except the GenoME people. They'll be disguised as journalists, and they'll have gas masks and stuff." Lexi's frantic gum-chewing started to slow as her brow creased. "I guess they'll be dragging Prosper out to a car, or something," she speculated. "It doesn't say here. Maybe she hasn't worked that out yet."

"Wait—wait a minute." Cadel couldn't believe it. He had to swallow hard before continuing. "Gazo can't be doing that," he whispered. "He *wouldn't* do that."

"Carolina thinks he will. She'll threaten to expose him if he doesn't. By telling the police who he really is." Lexi consulted her data. "Which means that she must have worked out who he really is herself. Somehow."

"Her husband would probably have known about Gazo," Trader mused. "Chester Cramp used to run NanTex, remember. He'd be familiar with all of Darkkon's genetic mutants. I'm sure Gazo's problem must have rung a few bells for Chester, when it turned up on Gazo's application form."

"Yeah. I guess. Except that I can't find any e-mails from Chester on the subject," Lexi pointed out.

"Maybe he phoned her."

"Maybe."

"If she's threatening to expose Gazo, then she doesn't realize that the police have already b-been told about him," said Hamish. "So either Gazo hasn't been mentioned on the police system yet, or she hasn't found him there." He scanned the room. "Somebody ought to check."

Cadel realized that he was on his feet, though he had no memory of rising. Sonja watched him with evident concern.

Trader was deep in thought.

"It's all a bit rushed," he said, stroking his chin. "I'd be surprised if they could pull it off. Though if they do, we're in luck." He glanced at

Judith. "As long as we can prove that the orders came from America. Otherwise Earl Toffany could say that it was all Carolina's idea. He could blame her and get off scot-free." Feeling a tug at his sleeve, Trader rounded on Cadel. "What? What is it?"

"We have to tell the police," Cadel insisted.

"Oh no." Trader was adamant. "And tip them off about what we've been doing? Not likely."

"But—"

"Gazo will tell them." Trader spoke with a careless confidence that Cadel found abrasive. "He's on the side of the angels now, isn't he? Or isn't he?"

"If-Gazo-tells-the-police-about-Carolina's-plan, someone-might-report-it-on-the-police-system," Sonja unexpectedly interposed. *"And-Carolina-has-access-to-that."*

"She's right," agreed Devin. He seemed startled to hear these words issuing from his own mouth, but plowed on, anyway. "Sonja's right. If Carolina learns that the cops know what she's going to do, she'll think up another plan," he said. "Without telling Gazo about it."

"And-she-might-try-to-silence-him," Sonja added. *"Because-he's-the-only-witness-who-can-testify-that-she's-arranging-to-have-Prosper-abducted."*

As far as Cadel was concerned, Sonja had hit the nail on the head. Gazo *was* in danger. Clearly, Carolina hadn't yet stumbled on evidence of his cooperation with the police. But this was no guarantee that she wouldn't come across an incriminating e-mail in the future.

"I need to tell Gazo," Cadel declared. "Right now. I need to tell him that Carolina's been spying on the police." He raised his voice, forestalling Trader's objection. "Gazo can warn Saul Greeniaus about what GenoME's doing," he said, "as long as we pretend that he got all his facts from GenoME. Not from me. That way, the squad will be protected."

"Cadel—"

"I'm going to do it!" Cadel clenched his fists. "You can't stop me, Trader!"

A hush fell. The only movement was Sonja's juddering; the more she tried to subdue it, the worse it became. Everyone else remained motionless, gaping or wincing or (in Lexi's case) dimpling with glee. Even Trader seemed taken aback.

"I'm not going to stop you," he said finally. "I'm going to ask you to think. You were told not to contact Gazo. Suppose the police are tapping his phone? Suppose they're watching his house? How are you going to get in touch without alerting them?" Seeing Cadel frown, Trader pressed his advantage. "What if they get suspicious?" he continued more quietly. "First you contact Gazo, after being warned not to. Next thing he's on the phone, telling police to keep his name off their computers. Isn't it possible that they might put two and two together?"

"No." Cadel stood firm. "No, they won't," he said. "Because they won't know I've been anywhere near Gazo."

Trader clicked his tongue and shook his head.

"How do you propose to manage that?" he inquired. "There are two coppers sitting outside the gate as we speak, Cadel. You're not going to get past *them.*"

"Oh, yes I am," said Cadel, with absolute certainty. "Just watch."

TWENTY-SEVEN

Lexi was only too delighted to help with Cadel's costume. She threw open her wardrobe, dragging out armfuls of unsuitable clothes: black net tank tops, black vinyl miniskirts, black leather pants covered in oddly placed zippers. No matter how many times Cadel stressed that he was trying to *avoid* being noticed—that a black lace corselette or a T-shirt covered in fake blood spatters was likely to attract unwanted attention—Lexi kept pleading with him to "at least try this on."

"But you'll need a jacket!" she would say, holding up a shaggy black vest made of artificial fur, or a trailing black velveteen cape trimmed with red satin. "Go on, please? It'll look *fabulous* on you!"

Cadel, however, refused to oblige. The more Lexi begged, the more uncooperative he became. "I just want ordinary stuff," he insisted. "Don't you have any ordinary stuff?" In the end, he chose a black cotton skirt, a black lace bra, and a pair of black tights. Combined with one of his own white T-shirts—worn beneath Sonja's embroidered pink sweater—the skirt didn't look too outlandish, though its hem was slightly asymmetrical.

On his feet he wore Judith's ankle-boots. These boots had high heels and added greatly to the overall effect, Cadel thought. Luckily, he and Judith shared an identical shoe size.

He turned down Lexi's offer of black nail polish.

"How am I supposed to get it off afterward?" he said. "I'll be doing a quick change, Lexi. I can't be messing around with nail-polish remover." Nor did he favor lipstick that was deep purple, or fire-engine red. Secretly, his aim was to imitate Dot, whose bland appearance meant that she never stood out in a crowd. Everything about her was neutral—even her lipstick. And it was Dot's lipstick that Cadel eventually borrowed, much to Lexi's disgust.

He had decided not to worry about jewelry. Managing hair clips would be fiddly enough. By tying his hair back tightly, he flattened out most of his curls; the bouncy little ponytail that resulted from this maneuver could be wound up and pinned down into a kind of bun, which could then be concealed beneath a large silk flower attached to a comb. Sonja contributed the comb. It had been a Christmas gift from her friend Kay-Lee, but Sonja had never worn it.

"*You-look-better-than-I-do-in-most-things,*" she said. "*Even-silk-flowers.*"

Gazing into Lexi's mirror, Cadel couldn't disagree. He was almost disappointed to see that he still made a pretty convincing girl—at least from a distance. Up close, his budding mustache was perhaps a little too heavy, and his jaw a little too angular. It was also just as well that Sonja's sweater happened to have a high neck.

Nevertheless, his transformation was so remarkable that Trader gasped at the sight of him.

"Good god," said Trader. Then he burst out laughing.

"Isn't he gorgeous?" Lexi crooned. "Don't you like what I did with his hair?"

They were standing in Sonja's bedroom, surrounded by heaps of Lexi's discarded clothes. Trader shook his head in wonder as he eyed Cadel from every angle.

"I honestly wouldn't have recognized you," Trader admitted. "Is this something you learned at the institute?"

"More or less," said Cadel.

Trader cocked his head to one side, his smile still plastered across his face. "It's a great disguise," he conceded, "but I still don't understand how you're going to get out of here. The coppers will be suspicious because they won't have seen you come in. Not dressed like that, anyway."

"I won't be dressed like this when I leave," Cadel informed him.

"Then they'll follow you."

"I know."

"You can't hide in the back of the van," Lexi pointed out. "If they're looking through the gates, they'll see you climb into it."

"Don't worry," said Cadel. "I know what I'm doing." Once again, he addressed Trader. "I just need Hamish and Devin to help me. It won't take more than four hours, tops."

With the American system shut down for the night, Hamish and Devin were at a bit of a loose end. So Cadel wasn't surprised when they agreed to accompany him to the cinema. Zac volunteered to drive there and might even have stayed to watch the movie if its subject matter had been more to his taste.

"I'm not a big fan of horror films," he remarked, tapping the entertainment page of Judith's newspaper. "Couldn't we see this one instead?"

"No," said Cadel. "It's all a matter of timing."

"What about me?" Lexi plaintively demanded. "Why can't I go?"

"Because you have decoding to finish," Trader rejoined, and that was the end of that. No further discussion was entered into. By two o'clock Cadel was sitting in Zac's battered old van, heading for the city. On his knee he was nursing a backpack that contained his bulky girl's costume, as well as a packet of crisps protruding artfully out of one side pocket. This chip packet was another part of his disguise.

"There has to be a reason for bringing such a big bag," Cadel had explained, after insisting that Hamish load up his own backpack with lemonade and caramel popcorn. "The police have to think we're smuggling cheap snacks into the movie."

"You mean those guys actually *think*?" had been the response from Hamish, who was almost too enthusiastic about Cadel's plan. Cadel worried that the surveillance team might start to wonder why Hamish kept prancing from foot to foot and breaking into giggles. Would they grow suspicious? Or would they look at those massive biker's boots, and that unsuccessful buzz cut, and decide that Hamish was just a harmless flake?

Cadel certainly hoped so.

Before leaving Clearview House, Cadel had donned one of Devin's beanies, as well as a pair of blue jeans and a red top. Devin himself was already gone by then; he'd caught the 1:07 bus (as instructed) wearing an outfit similar to Cadel's—minus the beanie. Cadel made sure that Zac's van arrived at the Broadway cinemas with barely enough time to spare. Knowing that the police car was on his tail, Cadel wanted to be able to charge inside at top speed without giving the impression that he was running away from his bodyguards.

As Cadel had told Zac, it was all in the timing. When Zac entered the multilevel car park and pulled over, Hamish and Cadel immediately jumped out. This ploy took the police by surprise. They obviously weren't prepared for such a quick drop-off, though it didn't take them long to react. By the time one of them had climbed out of their vehicle, however, Cadel and Hamish were already through the exit door and halfway up a flight of stairs that led to the cinema complex.

Cadel tore off his beanie in the stairwell. At the top of the stairs, he punched through another door to find himself just around the corner from the cinema box office. Devin was waiting for him, tickets in hand. Cadel exchanged the beanie for a ticket while he and Hamish and Devin raced around the corner. It was at this point that Devin donned the beanie.

Then they separated. Cadel plunged into the ladies' restroom while Hamish and Devin sprinted toward cinema number three. Cadel was sure that the usher had seen only two boys, one dressed in a gray beanie, a red top, and blue jeans. If given a description, she would direct the police toward cinema three—where Hamish and Devin would be sitting in the dark, at the very back of the theater.

Here they would remain for the next two-and-a-half hours.

Cadel surprised one little girl when he crashed into the ladies' toilets, but didn't try to explain himself. As she stared at him, openmouthed, he scurried past her and shut himself in a cubicle. Then he changed his clothes, waiting several minutes (until the coast was clear) before emerging to slap on makeup. He was interrupted during this process by a middle-aged woman in a tracksuit. By that time, however, he was wearing lipstick, so she didn't give him a second glance.

He had already concealed his backpack inside a larger plastic bag, which he'd brought with him for that purpose. And he knew that the ankle boots made him look taller than usual. Nevertheless, when he finally emerged from the restroom, he did so with a wildly beating heart and a high color.

Sure enough, one of his bodyguards was sitting on a bench not far from cinema three.

Cadel recognized him as the driver of the car that had followed Zac's van from Clearview House. The other policeman was probably inside cinema three, sitting somewhere near Hamish and Devin. Devin had been told to stay slumped in his seat, thereby giving the impression that he was fairly short. He was also supposed to be keeping his mouth shut and his face lowered. Cadel hoped that he would remember to do this. There was a risk that the movie might distract him.

Marching past the bored police driver, Cadel busied himself tucking Sonja's hairbrush into Lexi's shoulder bag. This activity was supposed to divert attention from his face to his hands. But he wasn't too worried. Having timed his exit to coincide with the end of another film, he was carried along in the tide of patrons spilling from cinema four, and managed to lose himself in the crowd pretty quickly. With so many people to look at, the policeman didn't appear to notice Cadel—who slipped out of the cinema complex into the larger, brighter expanse of an adjacent shopping mall.

From there, he descended to street level and made for the university. It took him about ten minutes. But it was another hour before he located Gazo. In fact, he was just beginning to wonder whether he should risk making inquiries at the main university office when he spied a man pruning a hedge near the entrance to St. Paul's College.

Cadel recognized his friend instantly. Rather than calling out Gazo's name, however, he scanned the immediate area for any suspicious-looking people who might be loitering on benches or sitting in cars. There were cars aplenty, and even a scattering of people, though Cadel decided that they probably weren't police officers or GenoME surveillance scouts. For one thing, they were all very young. And for another, they were all on the move, walking briskly past Gazo on their way to a library or a bus stop, their backpacks laden with books, the noise from their iPod earphones blocking out the roar of traffic and the chatter of birds. Every one of these busy pedestrians seemed as harmless as a drink of water.

Even so, Cadel approached his friend with great care. Clacking along in his high-heeled boots, he pretended to catch sight of Gazo when they were only five or six feet apart. Gazo was wielding a pair of hedge trimmers. His attention was fixed on the foliage in front of him, so he didn't notice Cadel at first. Not until Cadel had muttered his name.

"Gazo? Is that you?"

Gazo turned, his face a mask of astonishment. He looked even more surprised when he saw Cadel, whom he clearly didn't recognize.

"Remember me?" Cadel continued, with what he hoped was an alluring smile. "Ariel?" he said, and winked.

Ariel was the alias that Cadel had used in his disguise course at the institute. Hearing it, Gazo gasped. His eyes widened. Before he could speak, however, he was interrupted.

"Someone might be watching," Cadel said softly. "Just smile and look bashful, okay? I don't want to advertise the fact that I'm here."

Gazo nodded. His answering grin was a little agonized, but all the more convincing as a result. Cadel was sure that if a *real* girl had accosted Gazo in the street, she would have received a similar kind of grin.

"Has GenoME contacted you?" Cadel asked. "About helping at the Coroner's Court?"

Gazo's bewildered expression was as revealing as any spoken response.

"Fine," said Cadel. "That's all right." And he went on to explain that GenoME was planning to abduct Prosper English, using Gazo as a secret weapon. "I've been hacking into the GenoME system," Cadel explained hurriedly, without mentioning Genius Squad, "and I don't want the police to find out what I've been up to. But I *do* want them to stop GenoME from freeing Prosper. That's why I was wondering if you could warn the police, as soon as you're approached. You will, won't you?"

"Of course," Gazo replied, in a dazed fashion.

"I figured you would." Cadel tried to adopt a flirtatious pose, putting a hand on one hip. He was hoping that, from a distance, he had the appearance of someone who was teasing Gazo about not showing up at a party. "The thing is, you'll have to tell Saul not to send any e-mails about this," he went on, "because GenoME has been hacking into the police computer system." Seeing Gazo's furrowed brow, Cadel decided to spell out exactly what he wanted his friend to do. "If anything gets onto the police system, it might tip off GenoME. So you'll have to pretend that GenoME was your source about the hacking, as well. You can't mention my name. All right?"

Gazo hesitated, still absorbing this torrent of information. At last he said, "Sorry . . . When will I be hearing from GenoME?"

"Soon. Prosper's going to court on Monday. Which means GenoME will probably call you today sometime. Or tomorrow."

"I don't get it." Gazo began to frown and shake his head. Then it must have occurred to him that he was supposed to be bantering with a girl, because he slapped on his tortured grin again. "Why would them people at GenoME fink I'd help break the law?" he demanded.

"Because they know who you are, Gazo. They'll probably threaten to tell the police where you're hiding if you don't help out. And they might offer you a lot of money, as an incentive." Cadel laughed a mirthless laugh. "Not that you could trust them to give it to you."

"I wouldn't take it, even if they did. *I* don't want Prosper outta jail."

"No. Neither do I."

They stared at each other for a moment, in perfect accord. Then Cadel said, "I'd better go. I shouldn't hang around for too long."

Gazo licked his lips. "Are the coppers following you?" he queried.

"I don't think so. But they might be following you." Struggling to project an air of playfulness, Cadel delivered his final instructions. "As soon as you hear from GenoME, give Detective Greeniaus a call. He'll tell you what to do. And remember—don't mention my name."

"No. I won't."

"Mr. Greeniaus told me how helpful you've been." It occurred to Cadel that his friend deserved a pat on the back. "Thanks so much for talking to him. I really appreciate it."

"He's a nice enough bloke," Gazo said with a shrug. "I reckon he'll do the right thing."

"I know he will," said Cadel. And he took a deep breath, conscious of the minutes ticking by. He couldn't afford to linger. "Bye, Gazo. Sorry I can't stay."

"Bye, Ca-Candy."

Cadel was impressed. He would never have expected such a quick recovery from Gazo, who had corrected his slip of the tongue just in time. But then again, Gazo had been a student at the Axis Institute. Like Cadel, he had grown accustomed to being watched.

Perhaps he had grown accustomed to dissembling, as well.

They parted breezily, Gazo with a wave, Cadel with a smile. Anyone observing them would have seen no backward glances as Cadel bustled away, his whole attention focused on putting one high-heeled boot in front of the other. It wasn't easy, walking in those boots. And he didn't want to arouse suspicion by turning an ankle, or tripping over a crack in the pavement.

Upon reaching King Street, he doubled back, returning to Broadway through the park in front of Sydney University. He reached the cinema complex with nearly an hour to spare; the police driver, he saw, was still sprawled on a bench near cinema three, bleary-eyed with boredom. The only other people in sight were a couple of ushers, looking almost as bored as the driver.

This, Cadel thought, is going to be difficult.

He went to the snack bar and made two purchases: a can of soft drink and a bag of mixed sweets. While passing the bodyguard, he took a swig from this can, tilting his head back and concealing part of his face. The sweets were supposed to act as a diversion. Their bright colors and seductive textures must have proved more fascinating than Cadel's profile, because no sharp inquiry followed him into cinema three.

Fortunately, there were still a lot of spare seats in the theater. Cadel picked out Hamish and Devin in the back row, simply because he had told them to sit there; it was so dark that they were barely visible. For the same reason, Cadel found it hard to identify the other bodyguard at first. Only after positioning himself at one end of the back row did Cadel recognize the close-cropped skull stationed two rows in front of him.

Yes, he decided, this is *definitely* going to be difficult.

During the next hour, very slowly and carefully, he changed his clothes: first the shoes, then the skirt, then the sweater. He wiped off his makeup, and unpinned his hair. All the while, he kept a close eye on the policeman; whenever that nuggetty head in front of him swiveled, Cadel would lower his own chin and slide down deep into his chair. Finally, Devin passed him the beanie. After Cadel had yanked it on, the two of them performed a quick switch while Cadel's bodyguard was watching the big screen.

Then, as soon as the credits started to roll, Cadel and Hamish made a hurried departure. Leaving a hatless Devin to skulk in the back row, Cadel lured his bodyguard outside, where Zac was waiting. "How was it?" asked Zac, in a loud voice. Whereupon Hamish replied, "Too long," and giggled.

"I fell asleep," Cadel said.

"He missed the b-best bit," Hamish added, and giggled again. "The bit with the eyeball. The rest was crap."

"I told you it would be," Zac admonished. "Horror films always are."

On their way to Zac's van, Cadel and Hamish made desultory conversation about the movie—conscious that they were being followed. But once they were actually *in* the van, and heading for home, they were able to let their guard down. Cadel began to massage his temples. Hamish began to wriggle about in his seat.

"Oh my god!" he erupted. "That was *so awesome*! I can't b-believe it actually *worked*!"

"Do you think it really did work?" asked Zac, addressing Cadel.

"I hope so," Cadel replied. He was feeling the reaction already; his hands were beginning to tremble, and he'd broken into a sweat. "If it didn't, I'll probably hear about it soon enough. From Saul Greeniaus."

"Of course it worked!" Hamish insisted. And Zac said, "Did you speak to Gazo Kovacs?"

"Yes," said Cadel, staring out the window.

"Is he going to cooperate?"

"Yes." Preferring not to elaborate, Cadel cleared his throat and changed the subject. "Did anything happen while we were out?"

"Only one thing." There was a pause as Zac negotiated a rather tricky bit of traffic. At last he sighed, then said, "Sonja finished decoding one of Carolina's old e-mails. And it turned out to be an eye-opener. Apparently, the Australian branch was opened for just one reason: so that GenoME could get hold of Prosper English." He cut a quick glance in Cadel's direction. "That's what Carolina implied, anyway."

"Oh shit," Hamish breathed.

"If only Earl Toffany had agreed with her—in writing—we'd be able to pull the plug on GenoME right now," Zac concluded. And then he shrugged. "As it is, we've still got some digging to do."

TWENTY-EIGHT

"All right," said Trader. "Let's consider our current status here."

It was Saturday afternoon, and Genius Squad had gathered around the kitchen table. No one was absent, because no one was on eavesdropping duty. With Amy's computer turned off for the weekend, the bug inside it couldn't be used.

"Cliff and I have discussed the situation," Trader announced, "and we think that measures will have to be taken vis-à-vis this kidnapping attempt. It's going to cause a bit of a problem for us, unless we move fast." He glanced over to where Cliff was sitting. "Care to expand on that, Cliff?"

"Uh, yeah," Cliff rumbled, leaning forward. He looked very tired—and he wasn't the only one. Cadel could hardly keep his eyes open, having been awake since 3 A.M. He had risen early to give himself extra time for trawling through the American systems, which were now shut down for the night.

Cadel worried that he might fall asleep where he sat.

"Okay," said Cliff. "First off, for those who haven't been told, the police are aware of GenoME's plans because Gazo Kovacs has alerted them."

"I *think* he's alerted them," Cadel amended, stifling a yawn. "I'm not sure yet. When Saul rang me this morning, he didn't go into specifics. He just wanted to know if he could come round at four o'clock. He said it was very important, and it had to do with Prosper English." Cadel shrugged, in a resigned manner. "Maybe he's just going to bawl me out for visiting Gazo yesterday."

"Well, let's assume he wants to tell you about the proposed breakout," said Trader. "We can't be sure about that, because there's no mention of it on the police systems—"

"Which is a good thing," Judith interjected.

"Which is, as you say, a good thing," Trader agreed. "But if Gazo *has* told the police about GenoME's plan to abduct Prosper, we have to ask ourselves: What happens if the cops now decide to raid the Australian branch? Or arrest Carolina? You can bet Jerry Reinhard has a contingency plan in place."

"He does," Cliff gloomily confirmed. "He has a whole policy document."

"As well as a red button," added Hamish, who was chewing on a piece of Lexi's bubble gum. This gum kept sticking to his braces, but he refused to spit it out. "*You* know," he said, when he saw Trader frown. "I mean a self-destruct program. To trash all their computer files and slam the door to America."

"Then we have to tackle that program ASAP." Cliff thumped a fist on the tabletop. "God forbid Jerry gets nervous and destroys valuable data."

"You can sabotage a self-destruct program, can't you, Dot?" Trader inquired. "There must be a virus you can install, or something?"

"Oh, sure," Hamish butted in airily. "I can do it myself." As he picked bits of gray goo off the metal in his mouth, Cliff regarded him without expression. Dot sniffed.

Trader turned to Cadel, who was rubbing his eyes.

"Cadel, I need you to find out what the coppers are up to. Since they won't be discussing their plans online, you'll be our only conduit. And we have to know what to expect."

Cadel grunted. It was bad enough lying to Saul Greeniaus about Genius Squad. Pumping the detective for information would be even worse.

"Now what about Carolina's e-mails?" Trader continued, throwing the question at Dot. "Have any more come through?"

Dot was the only squad member who didn't look tired. Her smooth, round, small-featured face was as implacable as ever. She sat like a carved Buddha, calm and solid in her neatly pressed clothes, not a hair out of place.

"There's been nothing in the past few hours," she said. "What came through earlier is still being decoded. But the arrangements for Monday seem to have been finalized."

"With Earl Toffany's input?" Trader sounded hopeful. Dot, however, shook her head.

"Not so far."

"You know, me and Sonja are really overworked," Lexi suddenly complained. Like Hamish, she was chewing gum; her bare feet were propped against the edge of the table, and she was playing fretfully with a rubber band. "There's heaps and heaps of decoding to do—I don't know why Devin or Tony can't take over some of the basic stuff." She directed her next comment at Tony Cheung. "You can decrypt Vigenère ciphers, can't you?" she whined. "It's just a lot of frequency analysis: *Anyone* can manage that." As he opened his mouth to reply, she plowed on, addressing Trader. "Anyway, I won't be working the whole weekend, that's for sure. I wanna go to the movies, like Devin did."

"You can go to the movies all you want, after Monday," Cliff growled. "Until then, we need to milk those systems as dry as we can." Without waiting for Lexi's protest, he shifted his attention to Sonja. "Anything more on that encrypted American link?" he demanded, and Judith said, "What encrypted American link?"

Cliff had been referring to the mysterious, heavily protected GenoME database discovered the previous day. When reminded of this, and of the ten client names linked to it, Judith smacked her forehead. "Oh, right," she mumbled. "Of course."

"*It's-a-challenge,*" Sonja remarked, using her DynaVox with some difficulty. "*It's-going-to-take-time, getting-in.*"

"How long, do you think?" Trader queried.

"*I-don't-know.*" There was an extended pause as Sonja struggled with her uncooperative right hand. At last Cadel had to put his own hand over hers and apply a comforting pressure.

"Don't hound her," he said crossly. "She gets really tired."

"I'm not hounding her," Trader said.

"She has to work extra hard, you know. Harder than anyone else. Just *sitting* there takes it out of her."

"I'm aware of that, Cadel."

"Anyway, she's been doing stuff for Judith this morning."

Trader blinked, and peered at Judith. "What stuff?" he inquired.

Judith began to chuckle.

"Oh, you'll love this," she said. There followed a ten-minute digression on the subject of Cadel's latest discovery. A series of payments had been made to Fountain Pharmaceuticals by a company in the Cayman Islands. Though this company wasn't the same one receiving money from GenoME's Australian branch, Judith was convinced that the two organizations were closely connected. "They've got a couple of directors in common," she explained. "I'm still working out the exact relationship."

"Well, you'd better hurry up, then." Cliff's tone startled everyone; it was harsh and abrupt. Even Trader stared at him in surprise, prompting Cliff to thump the table again. "If the police decide to raid the Australian branch on Monday, we'll be left high and dry!" he barked, swinging his head from side to side like a bull in a ring. "Rex Austin wants to know what happened to his son, people! That's why we're here! And we might only have a day or so left to find out!"

A chill ran down Cadel's spine. The words "only a day or so left" sounded distinctly ominous to him. He sat up straight, and saw that other people were doing the same. Sonja lurched in her wheelchair, her hand writhing beneath Cadel's.

Trader shot his second-in-command a fierce, narrow-eyed look.

"For god's sake," he hissed, but wasn't allowed to finish. Lexi prevented him.

"What do you mean by that?" she asked Cliff, her chair tipping forward, her feet hitting the floor. "Why do we only have a day or so left? No one told *me* about any deadlines!"

"You said we'd be working on this project for months," Devin added. And Hamish said, "You're not planning to *close Clearview House,* are you?"

"No, of course not," Trader hastened to assure them. "What Cliff's trying to say is that we'll find it much harder to complete our mission if the Australian branch shuts down and we don't have access to the American system anymore." His gleaming smile flashed out yet again. Wielding it, he made a solemn promise. "Believe me when I tell you that Genius Squad will continue to exist," he declared, "just as long as GenoME is a going concern."

"Which won't be for much longer," Cadel remarked flatly. "Not if Sonja cracks that database."

He was feeling unsettled, and anxious, and guilty about Sonja—who had dark circles under her eyes. He was also sluggish with fatigue. His early awakening had been preceded by a restless night full of ominous dreams involving poison, jailbreaks, and Prosper English. He didn't want to interrogate Saul. He didn't appreciate being treated like an idiot. And he was beginning to wonder if he'd made a big mistake, coming to Clearview House.

More and more, as the days passed, he sensed that he was being manipulated.

"Haven't you been researching those ten client names I gave you?" he continued, irritated that his last observation had elicited from Trader only a puzzled look. "Jimmy Austin? Jenny Jarvis? Michele Sapone? It's easy enough to run an Internet check. I did it this morning and found six of them. *Six names.* In about two dozen newspapers." He glanced around the table. "You know why? Because they were all found dead, with severe head injuries—Jimmy Austin included. Though of course they didn't all die in the same place, or at the same time." Something occurred to him. "Which might explain why no one's made the connection before now," he mused.

"Oh my god," said Hamish. Blinking rapidly, he pounced on this tidbit like a kitten on a cockroach. If he'd had any fears about being evicted, Cadel's news had driven them straight out of his head. "So you think those six people might have been *murdered* by GenoME?"

"Yes," Cadel replied.

"What about the other four? The ones who aren't dead? How are they connected?"

"I don't know," Cadel admitted. "But the database might tell us why, when we finally get into it."

"Cool," said Devin. He, too, had been momentarily distracted from the problem of his own uncertain future. Even Lexi had brightened up.

It was amazing, Cadel thought sourly, how a little blood and gore always raised their spirits.

"Well, this is more like it," said Cliff. "If we can prove that Earl Toffany is a murderer, our job's done."

"Our job's *also* done if we can prove that Earl Toffany is behind the plan to abduct Prosper English," Trader retorted. "Trouble is, Earl's watching his back. He's delegating his decisions." Dragging his fingers through his hair, Trader let his smile slip sideways. "All we need is evidence of *one illegal act* that he's been directly involved in. Otherwise he can start blaming subordinates."

"*And-that's-not-good-enough-for-Rex-Austin?*" Sonja piped up. Whereupon Trader shook his head.

"There's a history between Rex and Earl," he divulged. "Rex is looking for a trophy. He wants Earl's head on a platter. It's personal."

Personal? Cadel sucked air through his teeth at the sound of that word. Destroying a dangerous corporation was one thing; personal vendettas were another. Cadel knew that when things got personal, they got obsessive. And vindictive. And blinkered.

"You told me that Rex Austin wanted to bring down GenoME," he objected, breaking into the discussion. "You didn't say he wanted to bring it down on top of Earl."

Trader's eyebrows climbed his smooth, tanned forehead. Then he made a dismissive gesture.

"Well," he began carelessly, "since we can't really accomplish the first objective without achieving the second—"

"But we can!" Cadel's tone was sharp. "Of course we can! We could almost do it now, with what we've already got." Cadel scanned the faces around him, frustrated that most of them wore bored or puzzled expressions. Only Sonja seemed uncomfortable—but then, Sonja always seemed uncomfortable. (She was continuously fighting with her own limbs, after all.) "If we crack that database, and it shows that those six dead people were murdered by GenoME, what's our plan if Earl isn't implicated? Keep digging?" As Trader opened his mouth to reply, Cadel added, "Suppose GenoME kills somebody else in the meantime?"

"Listen, son." All at once Cliff took over. He held up a hand, to stop Trader from muscling in. "It's not a matter of what we decide to do. It's a matter of what Rex Austin *wants* us to do. He's the one paying us, so he calls the shots. Understand?"

The implication hanging in the air was that if Cadel didn't like it, he could always leave. Trader must have sensed this, because he intervened quickly.

"Not that we don't value your input," Trader insisted, crinkling his crow's-feet at Cadel in a reassuring display of advocacy. "God knows, we wouldn't have come this far without you. And of course, if we uncover any indications that GenoME's going to commit murder, then the police will be told about it."

"Yes, but—"

"We're not going to let GenoME get away with anything, believe me." Trader's indulgent little laugh grated on Cadel's nerves. "That's the whole point of this operation."

"Yes, but what about *us*?" Cadel snapped. "You said that Rex Austin has a personal grudge against Earl Toffany. Well, that's his business. But is it ours?" Ignoring Sonja's garbled attempt to intervene (her DynaVox squawked "*cat*," for some reason), Cadel clutched the edge of the table with white-knuckled fingers. "I mean, exactly how far would Rex Austin be willing to go to get his revenge? And how far would *you* be willing to go to satisfy him? Because it might be a lot further than I'm comfortable with."

The silence that followed was so taut—so tense—that everyone jumped like rabbits when the alarm sounded. Trader glanced at his watch. Cadel cursed under his breath.

"Four o'clock, on the dot," Trader said dryly. "That copper of yours is certainly reliable."

Reliable. It was another loaded word, and it snagged Cadel's attention. He sat for a moment, lost in thought.

Saul was reliable, all right. He was a man to be relied on.

Unlike Trader Lynch.

"Well, go on." Trader was unusually abrupt, as if slightly disconcerted by Cadel's absentminded air. "You'd better talk to him, don't you think? Before he calls in a SWAT team?"

"Yeah." Cadel stood up. "Yeah, I'll go and talk to him."

TWENTY-NINE

Saul and Fiona had come in the same car.

Cadel noticed this instantly. He also noticed that they were both wearing jeans and sneakers. But neither of them looked particularly relaxed as they trudged across the gravel driveway. And when Lexi screamed, they stiffened.

"It's all right!" Cadel assured them. Glancing over his shoulder, he saw Devin chase Lexi out of the kitchen into the living room. There followed a series of violent thumps and yells; clearly, one of the twins had said something unforgivable to the other.

With a sigh, Cadel stepped onto the veranda and shut the front door behind him. "Can we go somewhere?" he pleaded, hoping to forestall any inquiries about the noise.

Saul and Fiona exchanged startled glances. Then the detective said, "Go where?"

"I don't know. Anywhere." Cadel winced at the sound of another faint scream. He was suddenly desperate to escape. "Maybe we could take Sonja for a drive. She hasn't been out since Tuesday."

Having made this suggestion, he regretted it almost immediately. He knew that the wheelchair wouldn't fit in Saul's car. He knew that they wouldn't be able to set up Sonja's DynaVox. There would be discussions, and disagreements, and loads of fuss, and it would mean going back inside. . . .

"Forget it," he said abruptly, thinking, *Judith's here. Judith will take care of her.* "It doesn't matter. Let's go. Let's just go."

But Saul didn't move. He stood quite still, regarding Cadel with his usual solemn intensity, while Fiona frowned and fidgeted, her attention divided between Cadel and Clearview House.

"What's wrong?" she asked. "What's happening in there?"

"Nothing." Cadel brushed past her, heading for the car. "Where shall I sit? In the backseat?"

"But Cadel," said Fiona, pursuing him, "if something's wrong, we might be able to help. Is it the other kids? Are they picking on you?"

"No." Yanking open one of the car doors, Cadel caught sight of the detective's thoughtful expression and cried, "I'm nervous! That's all. I'm nervous about what you want to tell me. Is it bad news?"

"Oh, no!" Fiona exclaimed. "I have some *great* news!" She put an arm around Cadel's shoulder. "And you don't have to worry about Saul's—I mean, Mr. Greeniaus's news. It's not going to affect you at all, really. Is it?" she added, turning to Saul.

"I hope not," the detective replied. He cocked his head. "What about a park?" he inquired, without taking his eyes off Cadel. "Would you like to go to a park?"

"Okay." All at once, Cadel found himself longing for open space, green lawns, scattered trees. . . . "By the water," he proposed. "A harborside park." At this hour, so late in autumn, the harborside parks wouldn't be very crowded.

Saul gave a nod. Then he slid behind the steering wheel, while Fiona climbed into the backseat, beside Cadel. Though he would have preferred to sit alone, Cadel didn't protest. He remained silent as they rolled down the drive and pulled into the street.

Only when they were well clear of the automatic gates did Fiona feel free to talk.

"The good news is that I've made some progress with one of the universities," she announced, her cheerful tone undermined by her creased forehead. "I met a man at dinner the other day, and he teaches at the University of New South Wales. He runs a cryptography and security course, and he doesn't mind if you sit in. Unofficially. You won't get any course credits, but it'll be something interesting to do while . . ." She hesitated a moment. "While we're sorting things out," she finished.

Cadel didn't know how to reply. A university course was out of the question, at least while he was a member of Genius Squad. He could only hope that Fiona's plan would take some time to arrange—because he couldn't refuse to cooperate. Not without arousing suspicion.

"Oh," he said faintly. "That's good." Catching sight of Saul's narrowed eyes in the rearview mirror, Cadel tried to change the subject by asking the first question that occurred to him. "Is this university guy your new boyfriend?"

Fiona blushed. "No!" she spluttered. "Of course not!"

"Oh." Cadel was surprised at how sharp her reaction was. "Sorry."

"It was a birthday dinner." Fiona directed this remark at the driver's seat. "There were about twenty people. I'd never met him before." She cleared her throat. "Anyway, he's married."

Saul nodded, but said nothing. Cadel glanced from the detective to Fiona and back again, wondering if he was imagining things. When Fiona fell silent, staring red-faced out the window, he decided that he probably wasn't.

Normally, he would have given the subject his full attention. He would have tried to calculate the odds of a union between Saul and Fiona. But though he was conscious of being vaguely pleased, he couldn't dredge up much interest.

He had too many other things on his mind.

The trip to Glebe Point park was a quiet one. Saul wanted to concentrate on his driving, while Fiona appeared to be speechless with embarrassment. When they reached their destination, however, something about the golden light and crisp afternoon air loosened their tongues. The park was almost empty. A few people were walking their dogs along the foreshore; half a dozen kids were playing soccer under the trees. The sun was so low that even garbage bins and benches cast long shadows across the grass.

A pink-and-white ice-cream van was parked nearby.

“The surveillance team didn’t follow us,” Cadel observed, as he scrambled out of the car.

“No.” Saul was inspecting the ice-cream van. “I told them to watch the house for intruders. I can take care of you myself.” He looked from the van to Cadel, and then to Fiona. “Would you care for a soft serve? My treat.”

“Well, I shouldn’t . . . ,” Fiona began, before capitulating. “Oh, all right. Thank you. Single scoop for me. Vanilla.”

Cadel requested two scoops of vanilla, and Saul contented himself with a can of lemonade. Having equipped themselves with their treats, they wandered over to a bench near the water, scaring off a couple of seagulls as they did so. Before them Sydney Harbor glittered like a sequinned cape beneath the lazy sweep of Anzac Bridge. Even the dockyards looked picturesque.

Cadel found himself sitting between Fiona and Saul. Both of them were beginning to relax. The lines on their faces had smoothed out.

“I heard somewhere that this stuff is made out of pig fat,” said Fiona, through a mouthful of ice cream. “Amazing how nice pig fat can taste.”

Cadel grunted. Saul gave a half smile. When he didn’t comment, Cadel examined his clean-cut profile and said, “So what did you want to tell me?”

The detective sighed.

“To be honest, Cadel, I don’t *want* to tell you at all,” he confessed. “But I promised I wouldn’t keep you in the dark.” Dragging his gaze away from the shifting, gleaming surface of the harbor, he fixed it on Cadel. “Remember how suspicious I was about GenoME setting up a branch in Australia? Remember how I thought it might have something to do with Prosper’s arrest?”

Cadel nodded, thinking, *He doesn’t know about my talk with Gazo yesterday.*

“Well, I was right,” Saul went on. “We’ve just received word from Gazo Kovacs that he’s been approached by GenoME to take part in a plot involving Prosper English.” After a moment’s careful scrutiny, he added, "You don't look very surprised." And Cadel realized that he should have been guarding his expression, which was much too calm.

He shrugged. "You always said that it couldn't be a coincidence," he rejoined, inwardly cursing his own stupidity. Saul seemed to accept this explanation, though he continued to watch Cadel in a pensive sort of way.

"Apparently GenoME is planning to assassinate Prosper at the Coroner's Court. With Gazo's help. I'm pleased to say that Gazo came straight to us with the information." Saul frowned suddenly. "What's wrong?"

"Ass-assassinate?" Cadel stammered. *"Assassinate?"*

"Yes," Saul replied. "It was in the cards. I daresay Earl Toffany wants to be his own man, without having to run errands for Darkkon or Prosper English. Darkkon's dead now, of course, but there's always a chance that Prosper might be acquitted—or that he might escape. Or even that he might rat on Earl Toffany. Stranger things have happened." Saul heaved a sigh. "Anyway, whatever the reason, some of those GenoME drones are going to shoot Prosper when he's in the courtroom." Lunging forward, the detective caught Cadel's ice cream as it slipped from his fingers. "Cadel? Look at me. It's *not going to happen.*"

"Oh dear." Fiona laid a hand on Cadel's back. "Put your head down, sweetie. Take a deep breath."

Cadel felt sick. He lurched to his feet, staggered a few steps, and vomited all over the grass.

By the time he'd finished, he was slumped on the ground, dazed and blinking. Fiona was wiping his mouth with a tissue; Saul was swearing somewhere behind him.

"Water," Fiona said. "Empty that can and get me some water." She must have been addressing Saul, because when Cadel started to get up, she forced him back down. "It's all right. Everything's all right."

"It must—it was the ice cream." Cadel croaked.

"I know."

"Pig fat . . ."

"*Shh.* Take it easy." Her cool hand was on his forehead. "Did you eat any lunch?"

"Uh . . . no." He had been too busy. "But I'm okay now."

"Give it a minute," Fiona advised. "Saul's bringing some water for you."

Cadel couldn't believe what had just happened. His whole body was trembling. He was racked with shame. How could he have been so feeble? What on earth was the matter with him?

"Here." Saul thrust the lemonade can under Cadel's nose. "Rinse your mouth out."

"He doesn't have a fever," Fiona murmured. "But he didn't eat any lunch. And then with the ice cream on top of that, and the shock . . ."

"Can you move, Cadel? You don't want to be sitting here; it's a mess."

Cadel struggled to his feet, appalled at how shaky his knees were. After collapsing onto the bench, he looked up to see Saul and Fiona hovering over him, wearing identical expressions of sympathy and concern. Fiona was bent almost double. Saul was holding the lemonade in one hand and a melting ice-cream cone in the other.

It was terrible to observe their compassionate faces and to know that they were being deceived. Cadel had never before felt so bad about misleading anyone.

Tears sprang to his eyes.

"Oh, sweetie." Fiona smoothed his hair. "It's all right. You mustn't fret."

"We've got it all arranged," Saul hastened to add. "The court will be staked out, and so will the GenoME building. Gazo won't lift a finger to help; he'll disappear just before the action starts, so he won't be in harm's way—and won't, with any luck, be stressed enough to lose control of his stench. As for the hired guns, we'll have to catch 'em in the act. With their gas masks. Otherwise we have nothing but Gazo's statement, and he can't name any names, or give us any descriptions. Since he was contacted by phone." Seeing Cadel wipe his wet cheeks, Saul relinquished the can of lemonade and pulled a neatly ironed handkerchief from his hip pocket. Passing this handkerchief to Cadel, he said, "We won't let your dad get hurt, Cadel."

"I don't *care* about him!" Cadel cried—though of course he was lying. The surge of emotion that he'd experienced at the mention of Prosper's death had actually turned his stomach.

I must be tired, he thought desperately. *I must be worried about Sonja. I shouldn't have eaten that pig-fat ice cream.*

"I don't care about him—why should I?" he insisted, furious with himself for succumbing to his own capricious feelings. He didn't want to care about Prosper. He wanted to hate Prosper. "Anyway, for all we know, the whole shooting story is a lie," he went on, thankful that his brain was beginning to work again. "Gazo wouldn't want to see Prosper released, and the GenoME people might realize that. Maybe they're lying about wanting to shoot Prosper, just so Gazo will cooperate. And maybe, once Prosper's out, they'll shoot Gazo instead. So Gazo won't have a chance to rat on them when he sees that Prosper wasn't killed." Certainly there had been no mention of killing Prosper in Carolina's e-mails. But then again, Sonja hadn't decoded every one of them yet.

Cadel didn't know what to believe.

"If Prosper *is* freed, I'm in big trouble," he remarked unsteadily. Then, at the sight of Fiona's pitying glance, he shrilled, "I'll shoot him myself if I have to!"

"Listen." Having shoved Cadel's ice cream into Fiona's free hand, Saul placed his own hand on Cadel's, crouching down in front of him. "There is no way on earth I'm going to let Prosper English anywhere near you," the detective sternly declared. "Even if he escapes—which he won't—and even if he finds out where you are—which he won't—he's not going to get past me, I promise."

Cadel studied the weary, anxious, fine-drawn face in front of him. Then he conjured up a memory of Prosper's foxy smile and bright black gaze. The comparison was enough to make anyone flinch.

"Don't," he said. "Please don't get in his way. Prosper wouldn't hurt me, but he'd hurt you. I know he would."

Saul didn't argue. All he said, after a moment's silence, was, "It's all right, Cadel." Then he stood up. "Let's get you home," he suggested.

Home. Cadel couldn't help reacting to this word. And something about his tight mouth and sagging shoulders alerted the detective, who squinted at him.

"What is it now?" Saul asked.

"Nothing." Cadel shook his head.

"Don't you feel at home in Clearview House? Is there a problem with that place?"

"No." Cadel rose abruptly, turning to Fiona. "Can we go, please?"

"Oh! Yes, of course." Fiona sounded flustered. " Just let me get rid of these ice creams," she said, and made for the nearest garbage bin.

When she was out of earshot, Saul leaned toward Cadel.

"I know damn well something's wrong," the detective muttered. "But if you don't tell me what it is, I can't help you. Cadel," he growled. *"I just want to help."*

Cadel stared at him, and was sorely tempted. The relief of unloading every nagging concern—of trusting someone besides Sonja—would have been indescribable. Besides which, Cadel hated lying to Saul. Of all the people Cadel had ever met, Saul was the hardest to lie to.

But Cadel knew that he had to fight the urge to confess. Because, after all, what kind of help could Saul really offer? Could he give Cadel a place to live? Could he give *Sonja* a place to live? No, he could not.

Thinking about Sonja, Cadel stiffened his resolve. What would happen to Sonja, if Genius Squad was disbanded? So far, she and Cadel had received only a tenth of their fifty-thousand-dollar payout—and they wouldn't be receiving any more if the job wasn't finished. At this point, if Sonja lost Clearview House, she would find herself back in her old haunts, with inadequate nursing care and a shared bathroom.

"Sonja's the one who needs help, not me," he said at last, looking Saul Greeniaus straight in the eye. "She can't even go to the toilet by herself. She has to wear diapers to bed." Seeing the detective blink, Cadel took a deep breath. "If you can't help Sonja, you can't help me," he said flatly.

Then he headed back to the car.

THIRTY

When Cadel returned to Clearview House, he informed Genius Squad about the plan to kill Prosper English. He mentioned that the police would be staking out GenoME's Australian branch on Monday, while the matter of the dead prison guard was being discussed at the Coroner's Court. But he didn't tell anyone that he'd lost control of his stomach.

He didn't even admit it to Sonja—not until the next morning, when he took her for a walk around the neighborhood. Then, at last, he felt free to talk without running the risk of being overheard.

"I felt so bad," he finally confessed, as he maneuvered Sonja's wheelchair around a raised crack in the footpath. "The two of them were being so nice to me, and I sat there and lied. I'm sure that's why I threw up. Not because I was worried about Prosper, or anything." When Sonja didn't reply, he added, "It was the guilt. The guilt made me sick."

"*Maybe,*" was Sonja's cautious response.

"It's funny, because I never used to be like this. I never used to mind lying." Cadel glanced behind him at the surveillance team's car. This car would drive for a hundred yards or so, then park and wait until Cadel had passed it, before trundling forward another hundred yards—only to park and wait once again. "You know what worries me?" he said softly. "What worries me is what'll happen if Saul finds out about the squad. He's going to be so mad. So disappointed." Cadel pulled a face. "I don't even want to think about it."

"*What-worries-me-is-finding-another-place-to-live,*" Sonja rejoined, jabbing at the DynaVox screen very slowly, and with great difficulty. *"If-Clearview-House-closes."*

"Trader said it won't. Not yet."

"I-know." There was a long pause. *"But-do-you-trust-him?"*

Cadel hesitated. They had come to an intersection, and he stopped at the curb, peering up and down a wide, empty street.

At last he said, "No. Not really."

"Me-neither."

With a heave, Cadel steered Sonja's wheelchair onto the road and crossed both lanes at a brisk pace. Only when he had reached the other side, and negotiated the gutter, did he remark, "I always feel as if he's hiding something. But I don't know what it could be. Do you?"

"Maybe-he's-just-ruthless," Sonja proposed. *"Maybe-he-doesn't-care-what-happens-to-us, even-though-he-pretends-to."*

"Maybe that's it."

"Judith-cares." After a momentary battle with her own skittish body, Sonja continued in a voice that might have been defiant if it hadn't been electronically generated. *"I-like-Judith."*

Cadel grunted.

"She's-an-embezzler, but-she-has-principles." Suddenly Sonja rolled her eyes, as if embarrassed by her own lame rationalization. *"This-is-so-hard,"* she spelled out. *"Isn't-it?"*

Cadel knew what she meant. Nothing seemed clear-cut; everything was unsettlingly ambiguous. But he didn't say anything, because they were passing an elderly dog-walker.

This woman was the first pedestrian they'd encountered since setting out. It was very quiet. Though the noise of a nearby highway occasionally drifted across the lichen-encrusted roofs of neighboring houses, the atmosphere was as hushed as a church or an art gallery. Cadel felt that he was walking through a kind of oasis, cut off from the harsher, louder, brighter districts not far away.

"What was going on last night when I got home?" he asked, to change the subject. "What was all the fighting about?"

After a brief flurry of movement, during which Cadel had to resettle her in the wheelchair, Sonja informed him that Hamish had played a trick on Devin. *"Hamish-said-that-he'd-reprogrammed-Devin's-iPod-with-lots-of-old-fashioned-music,"* Sonja explained, *"and-Devin-hit-the-roof."*

"But Hamish didn't really do that?"

"No." According to Sonja, the truth was that Hamish had acquired an iPod identical to Devin's (*"Which-wasn't-hard, when-you-consider-that-Devin's-taken-the-serial-number-off-his"*) and had spent hours downloading *"sad-old-fart"* songs onto it. Then he'd swapped the two machines.

"Imagine-putting-in-all-that-time," Sonja marveled, *"just-to-piss-off-Devin. It-doesn't-make-sense."*

But it made perfect sense to Cadel. In fact the whole scenario was ominously familiar. "Hamish is bored," he sighed. "GenoME's shut down for the weekend, so he's bored." Something occurred to Cadel suddenly, and he considered it for a short time before continuing. "The strange thing is that Hamish won't mess with people's computers. He'll play stupid practical jokes in real life, but he won't do it in virtual space. It's like he's only grown-up when he's online."

"He's-certainly-not-grown-up-about-money," Sonja observed. *"He-won't-have-any-left-if-he-keeps-buying-iPods."*

"Better than stealing them."

"True."

"Though I'm not sure if Devin really stole that iPod of his. I know he claims he did. I know he says that's why he scraped off its serial number. But sometimes I wonder if he got rid of the serial number just to make himself look tough. To make it *look* as if he's a hardened criminal."

Sonja snorted. *"You-have-a-suspicious-mind,"* she said, and Cadel shrugged.

"On the contrary, I'm giving him the benefit of the doubt."

"You-never-give-anyone-that," Sonja ploddingly countered. *"You-were-brought-up-not-to."* Then, to Cadel's astonishment, she said, *"I-think-we-should-go-back-now."*

Cadel stopped in his tracks.

"Why?" he demanded.

"I-have-decoding-to-do."

"But it's Sunday. It's our day off."

"I-like-decoding. It's-fun." When Sonja craned around to look at him, her head wouldn't cooperate. She couldn't quite meet his eye. So she gave up.

"You'll tire yourself," he objected. At which point a thought struck him. "Do you need to go to the toilet?" he asked.

"No." The serene tone of the DynaVox was contradicted by the abrupt, almost violent manner in which Sonja attacked it. Clearly, this question had annoyed her. *"I-want-to-get-back."*

Cadel sighed. He knew that he couldn't exactly take the moral high ground, when he himself had been working until the early hours of the morning. And he *certainly* couldn't say that Sonja needed more rest than he did. Any suggestion of that kind would infuriate her.

So he began to execute a wide and gentle U-turn, causing the surveillance-team driver to rev his engine. There was a prolonged silence. At last the DynaVox squawked, *"Are-you-mad?"*

"No." To prove it, Cadel added: "Why should I care what time we get back? Besides, Fiona said she might drop in today, so I ought to be around when she arrives. Because Trader won't want her poking around."

"Isn't-this-the-second-Sunday-she's-given-up-for-you?" Sonja inquired. *"She-must-care-about-you-a-lot."*

"I guess."

"You're-lucky. My-social-worker-doesn't-care-about-me."

Cadel couldn't contest this claim. He *was* lucky. Fiona really did care about him; he wasn't just another file number to her. And when he gave the matter some consideration, he realized that Sonja was no longer his one true friend. Sonja wasn't the only person who would be upset if anything happened to him. Fiona would mind, too. As would Saul Greeniaus. The trouble was that Cadel hadn't been truthful with either of them, so he couldn't really derive much comfort from their obvious concern. The more sympathetic they became, the worse it made him feel.

At least with Prosper he had never felt guilty about lying. On the contrary, Prosper had always encouraged him to lie. With Prosper, Cadel hadn't been obliged to pretend that he was a good person.

Quite the opposite, in fact.

As he pushed Sonja's wheelchair along the uneven footpath, Cadel tried to concentrate on what she was saying. He listened to her account of how she had traced the differential characteristics of the database cipher by "trying each possible final-round subkey with a number of input pairs satisfying the first-round differential." Cadel had no trouble following Sonja's narrative. He was interested in the entire process. Nevertheless, even while he nodded, and grunted, and made occasional comments, his thoughts kept drifting toward Prosper English.

He didn't want to think about Prosper. Every time he did, his stomach would churn. But he realized that his stomach was trying to tell him something. And he was forced to admit that, despite all his claims to the contrary, he *did* care about Prosper. Because he was convinced that Prosper cared about him—albeit in a warped, enigmatic sort of way.

No one believed it, of course. Though Cadel had insisted, over and over again, that Prosper would never harm him, the general consensus was that Cadel had been brainwashed by a ruthless manipulator. *"Just-because-he-didn't-shoot-you,"* Sonja had once remarked, *"doesn't-mean-he-didn't-regret-it-afterward."*

But she was wrong. Cadel knew it. And he couldn't banish from his heart every faint, lingering trace of regard for the first person who had ever exhibited any real affection for him.

If it hadn't been for Prosper, he might never have learned how to love at all. Because the ability to become attached to people was something that you had to exercise at an early age, if you didn't want to lose it altogether.

And Cadel had exercised his on Prosper English. For want of a better alternative.

"Isn't-that-Fiona's-car?" Sonja suddenly inquired. Sure enough, Fiona Currey's vehicle was passing through the Clearview House gates, immediately ahead of them.

Cadel cursed aloud.

"It's-all-right," Sonja assured him. *"No-one-will-be-doing-any-work. Everything-will-seem-pretty-normal."*

She was right. When Cadel and Sonja arrived back at the house, they discovered that Genius Squad had succumbed to the prevailing Sunday-morning atmosphere. Dot was absent. So were Trader and Tony. Cliff was on lunch duty, firing orders at Hamish. Judith was hanging out laundry, whistling in the sunshine. Devin was hunched over his iPod. Zac and Lexi were playing pool.

It was as if every one of them had been carefully briefed beforehand. Had they all been discussing a church picnic, they could not have made a more thoroughly disarming impression on the visiting social worker. Fiona was relieved. Though she tried to hide it, Cadel could see her getting more and more cheerful every time they encountered another harmless scene in another tranquil domestic setting. She smiled at the slouching, uncommunicative Devin. She helped Judith to hang out the clothes. She even played pool for about ten minutes.

Then she gave Sonja a bath, laid the kitchen table, and engaged Cadel in a long, earnest discussion about his private affairs.

"Mel's been looking into that sample collected from Prosper English," she related. "The one they took to see if it matched the skin on the envelope found with that poor dead guard. Apparently it didn't; there's no proof that Prosper ever went near the envelope. But Mel's hoping that we might be able to use your dad's sample for a paternity test."

"I thought we needed Prosper's permission for something like that?" Cadel inquired, and Fiona shrugged.

"Maybe. All I know is that Mel's hoping to force the issue. Though we can't expect an answer very soon." She hesitated before adding, "Even if we do run a paternity test, it might not advance your case. You know that, don't you, sweetie?"

"Yes," said Cadel.

"Because you don't want to end up in Scotland. As a worst-case scenario." Fiona went on to announce that she had been speaking to her friend about his cryptography and security course. "The problem is, it's on a Monday evening," she said. "And I don't like the idea of you riding around in buses at that time of night. Though of course those policemen will be watching you." Fiona sighed. "Which raises another problem. Your attendance at the university is supposed to be unofficial. What happens if it's recorded somewhere in the police files? I don't want my friend getting into trouble, just because he helped us out."

Cadel said nothing. He was at a loss for an answer, since he knew that he wouldn't be attending any evening courses for quite some time. Not until GenoME had been dismantled, anyway.

Fortunately, Fiona didn't seem to expect any useful suggestions from him.

"Don't worry," she said. "I'll figure something out. Meanwhile, how have you been? Are you feeling better now?"

"Better?"

"You haven't thrown up again?"

"Oh." Cadel winced. He was ashamed of his weak stomach. "No, I'm fine."

"What did you eat for breakfast?" Fiona asked, as if she really cared. Then, apparently satisfied with his response (which was "scrambled eggs"), she glanced around his room. "And what have you been doing with yourself?" she wanted to know. "Have you been able to use that computer in the office?"

"Sometimes." Cadel realized suddenly that no one in Genius Squad had arranged a fake computer schedule to cover the office machine, which was supposed to be the only computer in the place. It was a dangerous oversight. Suppose he claimed that he had access to the office computer on Tuesdays and Thursdays only? What if Fiona should hear something different from another member of Genius Squad?

If that happened, he would be caught out.

"Sonja's been teaching me a really neat cipher," he quickly remarked, to distract Fiona's attention. "It's called the Solitaire Cipher, and it lets you communicate with another person in a really complex code without using a computer. All you need is a deck of cards."

He went on to explain, in minute detail, how the Solitaire Cipher worked. Fiona smiled and nodded, and made an effort to understand. She didn't try to interrupt or turn the conversation. Nevertheless, she looked deeply grateful when Hamish eventually announced, from the bottom of the stairs, that lunch was ready.

Cadel's ploy had succeeded. After her long struggle with the cutting and counting of cards, Fiona had forgotten all about Cadel's computer schedule. He had successfully bored her into a state of partial amnesia.

"Okay," she said, almost jumping to her feet. "I suppose I'd better go. Have you spoken to Mr. Greeniaus since yesterday?"

"No." Cadel was carefully shuffling his cards. In a bland voice he added, "Have you?"

Fiona colored slightly.

"No," she said. "But he did say that he'd be at the Coroner's Court tomorrow, for your dad's appearance. Just to make sure that nobody shoots anybody. So you're not to fret. Because Mr. Greeniaus has everything under control."

Cadel remained silent. Sitting cross-legged on his rumpled bedspread, he quietly cut and stacked the deck of cards, his eyes cast down.

"Cadel?" A pause. "What's wrong?"

"Nothing."

"Yes, there is."

Cadel raised his head, as a terrible thought struck him. "*You're* not going, are you?" he demanded. "To the Coroner's Court?"

"No, no. Of course not."

"That's good." The prospect had filled Cadel with dread. It was bad enough that Saul Greeniaus should be exposed to Prosper English, but Fiona Currey? "Don't go. You mustn't. Prosper mustn't find out about you, not *ever.*"

"Sweetie, we discussed this when we first met. Your case file is restricted. How could Prosper English find out about me?" Fiona gently patted his arm. "You've got enough to worry about. Don't concern yourself with me, or with Mr. Greeniaus. We're grown-ups—we can look after ourselves."

Cadel disagreed. Fiona, he knew, wouldn't stand a chance against Prosper English. But he refrained from making the obvious comeback. Instead, he rose and accompanied her downstairs, where he waved her out the door just as Trader's car pulled up alongside the front steps.

There was a brisk exchange of compliments. Trader flashed his gleaming smile and indulged in his usual bantering tone. Despite this jovial facade, however, Cadel sensed that he was deeply agitated.

Sure enough, Fiona's car was no sooner heading for the front gate than Trader sighed and said, "Thank Christ *she's* gone. We need to talk."

"Why? What about?" asked Cadel.

"I'll tell you in a minute. Where's Judith? Is Tony here yet? It's time we had a confab." Trader barged across the threshold, his smile extinguished, his eyes glittering. "I might be wrong," he said, "but I think I'm on to something. Something big."

THIRTY-ONE

"Okay," said Trader. "This is what I want to tell you. I've put two and two together, and come up with an idea." He glanced around the kitchen table, making sure that he had everyone's full attention. "At the moment, Sonja and Lexi are trying to penetrate a well-protected database that Cadel discovered in the GenoME sytem," he announced. "You might remember that ten names are associated with this database, among them Jimmy Austin's. You might also remember that only four of these ten people are still alive. Well . . ." He took a deep breath. "I think I can guess why the six dead people were actually killed."

The reaction was muted. Hamish continued to pick food out of his braces. Lexi gnawed at an apple. Devin belched noisily, as if he'd swallowed too much air while he was eating. Perhaps he had. Lunch had been a hurried affair, with little time provided in which to digest.

Dirty dishes were still strewn across the tablecloth.

Some of the squad hadn't eaten at all. Poor Tony Cheung had been dragged away from a family beachside barbecue, in response to Trader's urgent summons. Even Dot was back. She had appeared in the kitchen so suddenly that she gave the impression of having been teleported.

Now she stood in one corner, because all the chairs were occupied.

"You see, Tony's been doing some research on that Cayman Islands company," Trader continued. "The one that's been sending money to Fountain Pharmaceuticals. Do you all remember that?" Nods from the assembled squad. "Well, he's discovered that it's a subsidiary of something called NeuroSolutions. And you'll never guess what NeuroSolutions is involved in."

"*Electrode-implants,*" Sonja piped up—much to everyone's surprise. Even Cadel turned to stare at her.

"That's it," said Trader, before she could elaborate. "Basically, we're talking about a brain-machine interface. There's been a lot of research into how you can help quadriplegics run robotic arms without pushing buttons. By implanting electrodes into their brains." He proceeded as if oblivious to the sympathetic looks that were being cast in Sonja's direction. "That's what NeuroSolutions has been doing—ostensibly," he said. "Trying to interpret brain signals, and transmit them to computers. I've been reading about it on the Internet."

And so has poor Sonja, Cadel thought, but remained silent. He knew that Sonja couldn't bear to be pitied.

"On the one hand, therefore, we have NeuroSolutions, which is somehow connected to Fountain Pharmaceuticals," Trader said. "And on the other hand, we have our ten mysterious names. Which I've been investigating." Trader leaned forward, instinctively lowering his voice. "Cadel has already pointed out that six of these people died of head injuries. What he didn't pick up, however, is that all of them were behaving erratically before they died. All of them were complaining about headaches. And all of them were booked for psychiatric evaluations."

"Wait a minute." Zac straightened, apparently jolted out of a well-fed daze. "How do you know that? Surely that's medical data? How did you find out?"

"I have my methods." Trader flapped an impatient hand. "What's important is that those head injuries were severe. I mean, *severe.* They were so bad that if anyone had tried to remove some kind of implant, it wouldn't have been noticed." As Judith gasped, and Lexi's mouth dropped open, Trader hurriedly argued his case. "I'm ninety percent sure," he said, "that the encrypted database we've been trying to unlock contains information about experiments conducted on GenoME clients like Jimmy Austin—experiments involving electrode implants. I think that those six dead people were killed because their electrode implants malfunctioned." There was a brief, stunned silence. Then Hamish chuckled.

"Oh, man," he said. "That is *so* cool. A zombie brigade!"

"Hang on a minute." It was Judith who spoke, loudly and skeptically. "Is this just a guess, or do you have any proof?"

"We'll have proof when we get into that database," Trader replied, turning to Sonja. "And we need to get in before the court hearing tomorrow. Otherwise, if GenoME tries to kill Prosper English, the police will raid the Australian branch. They'll arrest all the staff, and the whole Australian system might self-destruct, to stop the police from getting into it. In which case we'll have to start all over again."

In response, Sonja groped toward her DynaVox screen. But Cadel—who was becoming increasingly annoyed with Trader's high-handed treatment of Sonja—spoke for her, in a sharp, combative tone.

"Then I guess we'll just have to start all over again." Seeing Trader's mouth tighten, Cadel folded his arms. "We can't get anything useful out of that encrypted database until tomorrow night, because that's when they'll switch on the U.S. system after the weekend."

"Yes, but—"

"Ask Hamish. Ask Dot. They'll tell you the same thing. Even if Sonja does work out all the codes, it won't do us any good before tomorrow night."

During the pause that ensued, Hamish screwed his face into an apologetic expression, while Dot's head moved up and down. Neither of them uttered a word, however. Zac was the one who finally addressed Trader, hesitantly.

"If what you say is true," he said, "there are still four people wandering around out there with electrodes implanted in their brains. Including that fellow who's working for the bank. Am I right?"

"Possibly."

"Which begs the question: Why aren't *they* dead?"

Trader shrugged. "Perhaps their implants aren't malfunctioning yet," he rejoined. "Or perhaps the other six changed their minds about having implants. It's even possible that none of these people were told about the implants; they might have had routine surgery for something else, and been used as guinea pigs. But the ones who ended up dead might have begun to realize that something was wrong. They might have started to kick up a fuss. Who knows?" He spread his hands. "We can't be sure until we check that database."

"We-should-warn-the-four-people-who-are-still-alive," Sonja's DynaVox slowly enunciated. And all eyes swiveled toward Trader.

"Not yet," was his decision. "It might tip off GenoME."

Zac looked pained. "But there's a moral imperative—," he began, before Trader interrupted.

"Right now, our moral imperative is to get the guy who's ultimately responsible: namely, Earl Toffany. If I'm right about the implants, then he must have known the truth—and there could be proof of that in the encrypted database." Trader took a deep breath. "However," he continued, "if we don't get into that database before Prosper English arrives in court tomorrow, we might lose our chance."

"Not necessarily." Hamish was frowning, his glasses sliding down his nose. "Even if Jerry d-does panic, and tries to pull the plug on his system, we've sabotaged its self-destruct program. Just like you told us to. We should be able to stop him from destroying his files."

"Yeah, but he can still smash the machines," Cliff objected. And Cadel pointed out that even intact machines would be useless, once it became known that the police were investigating GenoME's Australian staff.

"If the Australian branch goes down, all the passwords will be invalidated," he said wearily. "We won't be able to piggyback on the DNA reports anymore, because you can be sure that no one in the American office will be accepting *any* data packets from here, no matter who's supposed to be sending them. Not if there are concerns about the police. We'd have to find another route." He rubbed his eyes, which were prickly with fatigue. "It's like Trader says," he allowed. "We'd have to start all over again."

Hamish subsided, biting his thumbnail. Whereupon Cliff took charge of the conversation.

"Okay," he growled, "let's forget about that database. Let's forget about police raids, and passwords, and what Jerry might do if he panics. Let's focus on the main issue here: *We need to pin something on Earl Toffany.* So does anyone have any ideas?" He scanned the faces around him; when there was no immediate reply, he snarled, "Come on, people, this is supposed to be Genius Squad!"

Cadel began to knead his temples. The situation was beginning to overwhelm him; he wanted the meeting to finish so that he could assess matters in peace.

"You'll have to fake an e-mail," he remarked with a sigh. And Trader tensed.

"What?" said Cliff.

"You'll have to fake an e-mail," Cadel repeated. "It's all you can do. Make up an encoded e-mail from Carolina to Earl, and be sure he can't answer it without incriminating himself." Cadel lifted his head. "It'll be risky. If it doesn't work, they'll know that we're into their system. They'll shut it all down. But if they're going to shut it down, anyway, we don't have much to lose . . ."

He trailed off, suddenly depleted. For several seconds no one spoke. Lexi, who had finished her apple, tossed its soggy core into the bin. Devin burped. Zac coughed.

"What would we put in the e-mail?" Trader said at last.

"I don't know." Cadel gestured vaguely. "Something about Prosper English? Something about killing him?" All at once his gut began to heave in a familiar way; he became conscious of a vague unease that wasn't quite nausea. "I need to go to the toilet," he announced, rising abruptly. His chair tipped over as he bolted for Sonja's bathroom, afraid that he might be about to vomit again. But it was a false alarm. By the time he'd reached his destination, his stomach was already starting to settle.

So he washed his face and sat for a while, taking deep breaths as he stared down at the gleaming tile floor.

He was scared. That was his problem. He was scared that Prosper might escape from the Coroner's Court, or—even worse—that someone might be killed. And it troubled him profoundly that the prospect of bloodshed didn't seem to concern Cliff or Trader in the slightest. They hadn't even blanched at the thought of a perverse brain-implant experiment. And they had brushed aside any suggestion that lives might still be saved.

Cadel recognized that mind-set. He had encountered it at the Axis Institute.

It reminded him of Prosper English.

Cadel would have liked to stay in the bathroom, where he felt safely shielded from outside interference. But he knew that Sonja would be wondering what had happened to him. Therefore he rose and trudged back into the kitchen—where he discovered that the meeting had begun to break up. Various members of the squad were milling around, clearing the table. It appeared that a decision had been reached.

"*Are-you-all-right?*" asked Sonja, upon catching sight of Cadel. She was part of a small cluster that also comprised Judith and Lexi.

"I'm fine," said Cadel. "What's going on? Are we all done?"

"I bloody *hope* so." Lexi groaned. "My *butt's* gone to sleep." And in a piercing voice, designed to be heard from some distance away, she added, "I thought this was supposed to be our *day off*!"

Trader ignored her. But Judith said, "It is. And I don't see why it shouldn't be. GenoME isn't going to shut down in America just because things go wrong over here." She gave a sniff. "It's not like you can't find some other way into the American network, surely? I admit I'm not a computer person, but I don't understand why everyone's so frantic."

"It's the passwords." Cadel cut her off. "The passwords and all the encryption keys. Didn't you hear what I said before? They'll get changed in the States if there's a problem over here; at least, they will if Earl wants to keep the police out of his system. Ten to one he'll overhaul the entire network, just to be on the safe side. And if he does, we'll be back at square one, looking for a new entry point." He fixed his attention on Sonja once more. "So what's happening tomorrow? Are we going to send an e-mail, or not?"

"*Ask-Trader,*" came the reply. And Lexi drawled, "Yeah, it's no good asking us. We're just the decoders. It's total job demarcation in this place."

"I think Dot's taking care of it," Judith volunteered. She jerked her chin, and Cadel squinted across the room to where the rest of the squad's infiltration team were gathered around Trader. Even as Cadel approached it, however, this group dispersed. Dot marched off toward the lift. Hamish hurried after her. Devin made for the fridge, leaving Trader to address Cadel's concerns.

"You look a bit white," said Trader, with a very convincing degree of solicitude. "You're not sick, by any chance?"

"No. I always look white." Cadel dodged Trader's encircling arm. "So what's happening with this e-mail, then?"

"Ah." Trader nodded, before going on to describe how a fake e-mail would be the squad's "last-resort scenario." He and Cliff would devise the message, while Dot and Hamish would be handling the technical side of its dispatch. "We have to encrypt it properly, and send it in exactly the right way," he said. "And, of course, we have to be extremely careful about the timing. That'll be your call. Yours and Dot's. I'm putting you on eavesdropping duty, Cadel."

Eavesdropping duty? Cadel peered up at him in confusion. But Trader seemed oblivious, breezily proposing that Cadel listen to every conversation being held in the vicinity of Jerry Reinhard's office the next morning. In the event of a sudden alert or panic, Dot would immediately fire off the fake e-mail.

"Dot and Hamish will be monitoring local e-mail traffic for the same reason," Trader said. "But that'll take more time, because of the decrypting. You're the one who'll most likely notice the first signs of agitation."

Cadel was genuinely puzzled. He knew that he was the best hacker in the squad. Why on earth did Trader want to saddle him with a job that could be done equally well by Zac, or Tony, or Judith?

"Are you sure you don't want me online?" he said. "I mean, if something unexpected crops up, I might be able to stop it."

"*Mmmm-mmm.*" Trader patted Cadel on the back, in a mildly condescending sort of way. He even produced one of his movie-star grins. "What bothers me, Cadel, is that you're going to be a bit distracted, what with Prosper's court appearance, and everything." As he cocked his head, his smile seemed to curl at the edges, like burnt paper. "I mean, I don't want you rushing off to the toilet in the middle of a job that no one else can finish," he gently concluded. "It might make all the difference between success and failure."

Cadel flushed, then set his jaw and glared. But Trader's expression remained perfectly benign. Sympathetic, even. Cadel couldn't detect a trace of calculation or contempt.

He wondered if there was some other reason why he wouldn't be allowed online. Or whether it was simply because he had displayed signs of jangled nerves.

Either way, he wasn't going to throw a tantrum. That would just confirm that he was unstable.

"Fine," he said shortly, and turned on his heel.

Later, in Sonja's bedroom, he pondered recent events while he helped her to drink a cup of tea.

"What do you think of Trader's idea?" he finally asked. "I mean, about the brain implants?"

Sonja stabbed at her DynaVox several times before making contact, laboring away for a minute or so to spell out the reply: "*It-makes-sense.*"

"Yeah. I know." Cadel couldn't really find fault with the proposal.

He just wondered how Trader had thought of it, since he himself would never have made the leap from NeuroSolutions to dead people. "I guess I'm not so smart after all," he muttered.

At which point Lexi stuck her head around the door and hailed them both. "Oy!" she said. "Are you guys coming to the movies, or what?"

THIRTY-TWO

Cadel could feel a tension in the air when he came down to breakfast the next morning.

He discovered Judith in the kitchen, blearily preparing Sonja's porridge. Hamish was also present, munching through what looked like half a packet of cornflakes. But Lexi and Devin were still in bed, having stayed out much too late the night before.

According to Hamish, the twins were now scared to emerge from their bedrooms.

"Trader's going to flay them alive," he announced gleefully. "I'm glad *I* wasn't stupid enough to go."

"So they didn't end up asking him?" said Cadel, who'd refused to accompany the twins upon discovering that they hadn't sought permission for their night out at the cinema. ("Why give Trader a chance to say no?" had been Lexi's attitude.)

"Nope. They didn't ask anyone." Hamish grinned. "And now they're in *big* trouble."

"Trader's got more important things to worry about than those two," Judith growled, spooning porridge into a plastic bowl. "He won't even be here this morning."

"Why not?" Cadel inquired. "Where is he?"

"Hanging around the Coroner's Court. And Cliff'll be watching number eleven with Zac. So it's going to be me in charge of everything." Judith jabbed her spoon at Cadel. "That's why I need you to help feed

Sonja. *And* get her dressed. You've got about an hour before you can start eavesdropping."

"Is Dot here?" Cadel asked.

"Downstairs." Judith shoved the bowl of porridge into his hands, before wiping her own hands on her baggy old sweater. "If you need me, I'll be kicking a certain pair of slackers out of bed," she concluded.

Feeding Sonja wasn't easy. Sometimes, if her spasms were very bad, two people were required for the job. On this occasion she managed with only one helper—Cadel—but by the time he had fed her and cleaned her up, brushed her hair and teeth, dressed her and wheeled her into the War Room, it was nearly half past eight. He didn't have a chance to comb his own hair or clean his own teeth before Amy's computer sprang to life, far away in her downtown office.

From that moment on, Cadel had to keep his ears cocked for any disturbing noises or comments from the GenoME branch. Other people had to fetch him food and drink. He couldn't even empty his bladder without first appointing a temporary replacement. And when his mobile phone trilled, he had to beg for assistance while he spoke to Saul Greeniaus.

Tony obliged, as Cadel withdrew to a quiet corner.

"*Just rang to see how you are,*" the detective announced, through a fuzzy, unstable connection.

"I'm fine," said Cadel. "Where are you?"

"*At the prison,*" Saul replied.

"Oh."

"*Everything's under control. You don't have to worry.*"

"Um." Cadel wasn't so sure about that. "Is—is Prosper with you now?"

"*No.*" Saul sounded terse and preoccupied. Cadel wondered what he was doing. "*Is Ms. Currey with you?*"

"Fiona?"

"*She said she'd drop by to see how you were.*"

Cadel could hardly suppress a groan. He screwed up his face and clawed at his tangled curls.

Hamish glanced over, mouthing the words: *What's wrong?*

"She doesn't need to drop in," said Cadel, trying to keep the edge of desperation out of his voice. "I'm fine. Didn't she tell you? Everything's fine."

"Well, you can take that up with her." Saul's tone was noncommittal. *"Meanwhile you should stay where you are, and I'll call you again when I'm done. You're at Clearview House now, aren't you?"*

"Yes."

"Good."

"Saul—I mean, Mr. Greeniaus . . ."

"You can call me Saul."

"You're not going to be handcuffed to Prosper, are you?" Cadel's dreams the previous night had been laced with this fearful image. "You're not going to be driving in the same car?"

"I won't be anywhere near Prosper English," the detective assured him. *"I'm not a prison officer."*

"Oh. Okay."

"I've gotta go now, Cadel. Say hello to Ms. Currey for me. And don't get yourself all worked up—there's no need."

"Yes, but . . ." Cadel wanted to explain why the utmost caution was *vital* when dealing with Prosper English. But he quickly realized how futile such an exercise would be. No one else knew Prosper as well as he did. No one else could really appreciate how much of a threat the man posed. "Please be careful," was all that he could find to say, in the end. "You have to be really, really careful."

"I will. It's my job."

And Saul broke the connection, leaving Cadel to face a barrage of inquiring glances.

Apologetically, he delivered the bad news.

"Fiona might drop in again," he said, and Judith cast up her eyes.

"Oh, man," said Hamish. "Just what we need."

"Any particular reason?" Judith wanted to know. "For Chris'sake, she was only here yesterday."

"She must be in love with Cadel," Lexi muttered, casting a sly look at Sonja. "I guess she's not the only one."

"Don't be stupid!" Cadel snapped, but was distracted by Judith's next question, which concerned the timing of this proposed visit. When exactly could they expect Fiona? Cadel had to confess that he wasn't sure.

Judith sighed. "If we're expecting your social worker," she said, "then we should send Sonja upstairs right now. We'll never get her out of the War Room soon enough, otherwise. There won't be time once the alarm's tripped."

"But Sonja can't sit upstairs by herself!" Cadel objected.

"Of course not." Judith seemed miffed at the very idea. "I'll send Tony with her. And if this woman shows up, Devin can take your place under the earphones. But you'll have to move like greased lightning—I don't want a sticky beak from DoCS trailing around the house looking for you."

Cadel agreed to this plan, since he couldn't think of an alternative one. And after Sonja had been wheeled into the lift, he spent about an hour listening to clunks and clicks and creaks, interspersed by the occasional outbreak of uninteresting dialogue. If anything was happening at GenoME's Australian branch, he decided, it certainly wasn't happening in Jerry's office. Nor in Amy's, for that matter. He often heard her yawn and crack her joints between bursts of typing.

She answered the phone only once, to confirm a lunch date.

GenoME's e-mail traffic was equally tedious. Devin reported messages about interviews, supplies, and accounts, but not a single mention of gas masks, getaway cars, or Prosper English. Cliff was no luckier. According to Judith, who had been receiving regular updates, he was in Zac's van with a piece of Trader's spyware, measuring vibrations on window glass. Nothing he'd picked up so far impressed him as the least bit peculiar.

In addition to which, every GenoME staff member was at his or her normal post.

"They must be using hired goons for the job," Hamish observed at one point. This was after Devin had remarked that it seemed to be business as usual at number eleven, judging from the e-mail exchanges. "They must want alibis, or something."

"But if they'd hired someone, there would be some kind of record," Judith objected. "I would have found something in the branch accounts."

"Maybe the payments are being sent from America," said Cadel, drawn into the discussion despite himself. It was hard not to be distracted when so little was happening in Amy's office. "Maybe Carolina has a private account that we don't know about."

If there was any kind of response to his proposal, Cadel missed it. Because suddenly the sound of a ringing telephone reached his ears—all the way from Jerry Reinhard's office. Cadel listened, totally absorbed, as Jerry answered the call. Though he could hear Jerry's muffled voice, he couldn't distinguish any actual words. It was Jerry's abrupt and urgent delivery that worried Cadel.

Normally, Jerry Reinhard spoke in a very soft, deliberate sort of way.

"I think something's going on," Cadel began, addressing no one in particular.

Then the alarm buzzed.

There wasn't a moment to lose. Ripping off the headphones, Cadel sprang to his feet. He didn't stop to receive orders or ask questions. He didn't even fling a warning at Judith. He simply charged into the lift at top speed.

When he charged out again, he found himself face-to-face with Sonja and Tony, who were waiting nervously in the kitchen.

"You'd better hurry," Tony advised. "Or she might start peering through windows." It was a measure of his apprehensiveness, perhaps, that he had spoken at all—since he rarely ever did.

"Something's up at GenoME," said Cadel, who was bursting with the news. "Jerry's beginning to freak over there."

"Why?"

"I dunno why." Without pausing to elaborate, Cadel headed for the front door. He pulled it open just as Fiona was about to press the doorbell again.

She looked almost as flushed and disheveled as Cadel did.

"Oh!" Her surprise was evident. "Hello. Sorry, have I interrupted something?"

"No." Cadel's reply was too quick, and he secretly cursed himself for it. But Fiona didn't seem to notice.

"Well—that's good," she said. "So you're not busy?"

"Um . . ." Cadel hesitated. "Sort of."

"I just wanted to see if you were keeping yourself occupied. Instead of sitting around wondering what's going on at the Coroner's Court." Fiona squinted over his head, into the murky depths of the house. "Is Sonja here?"

"Yes."

Fiona nodded. "So you've got someone to talk to?"

"Uh-huh." Cadel had begun to feel increasingly awkward. He knew that the longer he stood guarding the threshold, the more suspicious his behavior would appear.

He also knew that if he *did* invite her in, the whole of Genius Squad would throw a collective fit.

"You don't have to worry about me," he said, trying to inject a cheerful note into his voice. "I've been doing computer stuff. When I'm on the computer, I completely forget everything else. So I haven't been thinking about Prosper at all."

"You haven't?"

"No."

But Fiona wasn't convinced. She studied him skeptically, and may have questioned him further if his phone hadn't rung.

As he answered the call, she stood patiently on the doorstep.

"Hello?" he said.

"Cadel?"

"Yeah."

"It's Saul. Are you still at home?"

"I'm at Clearview House, if that's what you mean."

"Who else is with you?"

"Why?" Cadel's heart skipped a beat. "What's happened?"

"Just answer the question, please!"

Cadel swallowed. He had never heard the detective speak so urgently before.

"Uh . . . Sonja's with me. And Mr. Cheung. And Fiona. She just arrived."

"Put her on."

Cadel took a deep breath. "Tell me what's happened first," he insisted.

"I'll tell you when I get there. Now put her on."

"You're coming here?"

"PUT HER ON, WILL YOU?!"

Wide-eyed, Cadel handed the phone to his social worker. He had no doubt that Saul's outburst and Jerry's telephone conversation were closely linked. Something had happened. Something *nasty* had happened.

Cadel was desperate to return downstairs.

"Yes. Okay. No, it's not a big problem." Fiona was gripping the cell phone so tightly that her fingers looked bloodless. Nevertheless, she was doing her best to remain calm. "All right," she said into the mouthpiece. "Yes, I will. Of course. Don't worry." She signed off, then passed the phone back to Cadel. "Mr. Greeniaus will be coming over in about thirty minutes," she informed him. "I'm supposed to stay until then."

Cadel couldn't stop his shoulders from slumping. Bad news was being piled on top of bad news—and he *still* didn't know what happened. Except that Saul himself was alive.

But what about Prosper English?

"There's nothing we can do until we know what's going on," Fiona pointed out, laying a hand on Cadel's arm. "So why don't we go inside and have a cup of tea, and you can show me that card trick again?" With a lopsided smile, she added, "Who knows? I might even understand it the second time round."

"Oh," said Cadel. "Right. Yes. Okay." And he stepped back to let her in.

Because he didn't really have any choice.

THIRTY-THREE

The next half hour was torture.

Cadel knew that all hell must be breaking loose downstairs. Yet he had to sit glumly at the kitchen table, drinking orange juice and discussing his legal status with Fiona. At one point Tony left the room for five minutes (to make an urgent phone call, he said) but Cadel wasn't in a position to ask about this call when Tony returned. He was merely able to deduce, from Tony's slightly withdrawn expression, that the call had probably been made to Trader, or to Judith. And that the news at the other end of the line had been disturbing.

At last the doorbell rang.

Fiona wouldn't let Cadel answer it alone. She accompanied him to the door and was standing beside him when he admitted Saul Greeniaus—who looked terrible. The detective had shed his jacket to reveal a rumpled, sweat-stained shirt and a shoulder holster. His tie was hanging askew. His hair was in disarray, and his eyes were red-rimmed.

He stepped across the threshold briskly, before anyone had the chance to issue a formal invitation.

"Don't come near any entry points again," he warned Cadel, banging the door shut behind him. "Not unless I'm with you. And stay away from the windows, too, if you can." Glancing toward Fiona, the detective added, "We'll need to draw the curtains. All of them."

Cadel was examining Saul's face, which was full of grim lines and dark shadows. It told a very clear and frightening story.

"Prosper's escaped, hasn't he?" said Cadel. "You don't know where he is."

For a moment Saul didn't reply. Seeing him hesitate, Fiona gasped. She covered her mouth with both hands.

Saul's heavy gaze seemed weighted down with contrition and self-disgust.

"I'm sorry, Cadel. We blew it. *I* blew it." A muscle twitched in his cheek. "There's no excuse for what happened. But we'll find him."

"What *did* happen?" Cadel inquired, feeling strangely calm. Saul shook his head.

"I don't know," he admitted. "I had everything under control and then: *Bang!* He disappeared." Once again, the detective turned to address Fiona. "You can go now. Thanks for your help. I'm sorry I screwed up your schedule."

"It doesn't matter." Fiona waved the apology aside. "This is an emergency. I'll stay."

"No." Saul was adamant. "You can't stay."

"Yes I can. I'll ring up and cancel—"

"Listen." Saul took a deep, steadying breath before attempting to outline his position. "We both have our jobs to do. Mine is to minimize risk. And you'll be making it a lot easier if you keep clear of this house for a while." As she hesitated, he appealed to her. "Please," he begged. "Please don't make me argue."

It was clear that she had reservations. Biting her lip, she fixed her eyes on his shoulder holster. "You're not bringing that gun in here?" she protested.

"Fiona—I'm sorry—I have no choice," he said.

"But this house is full of children!"

"Exactly."

"Can't you take the poor boy to a police station, or something?"

"And put him where? In a cell?" Saul placed a hand on Cadel's shoulder. "This house should be as safe as any hotel or police station. It has an alarm system. There's a surveillance team outside. Prosper English doesn't know where it is." Seeing Fiona flinch, Saul quickly tried to reassure her. "Not that Prosper will come for Cadel. He wouldn't be that stupid. But it's best to take precautions. That's all I'm doing—taking precautions."

Fiona sighed. Not being a police officer, she was in no position to argue. And she must have realized this, because she nodded in a resigned fashion before kissing Cadel on the brow. Then she took her leave. "I'll call you!" was her final promise, made as she retreated to her car.

Saul was careful to watch her until she had passed through the gates. Once she'd gone, he closed the front door, locked it, and asked Cadel who was at home. "Not Trader Lynch, obviously," the detective remarked. "I've had reports that he hasn't come in yet. Neither has Zac Stillman. But Ms. Bashford came in early. Where can I find her?"

Cadel blinked. He was still reeling from the shock of Saul's news and had to think for a moment before a suitable lie occurred to him.

He had forgotten that the police were monitoring all traffic into and out of Clearview House.

"I'm—I'm pretty sure Judith's upstairs," he stammered. "In the office."

"Well then, I'd better warn her," Saul decided, and began his ascent. But when Cadel didn't follow him, he stopped. "What is it?" he asked, glancing back.

"Oh, I-I just have to tell Sonja. She's in the kitchen." Cadel almost blushed at how lame this excuse sounded. To his astonishment, however, it seemed to work. Without even hesitating, the detective offered to "bring everyone else down," since Sonja couldn't come up.

"We need to run this past all of you," he explained. "Because it's going to involve the whole house."

Cadel knew that he didn't have much time. Once he was certain that Saul had reached the first landing, he galloped into the kitchen and pounced on the intercom socket. "Judith?" he gasped. "Come up, quick! *Now!* Saul knows you're at home!" Then he swung around to confront Tony and Sonja. "I'll keep him out of here as long as I can, but it won't be easy. We need to make sure he doesn't see anyone using the lift."

"*What's-happened?*" Sonja demanded.

"Later. Ask me later."

Retracing his steps, Cadel could hear Saul's raised voice as the detective called for Judith. It wouldn't take long to search the top two floors. Cadel realized that he would have to initiate some sort of delaying tactic.

So when he reached the second landing and found himself face-to-face with Saul, he plunged straight into the topic that would have been uppermost in his mind had he not been worried about evacuating the War Room.

"How did Prosper get away?" he asked. "I thought you had it covered."

"We did." Clutching the banister, his brow furrowed, Saul seemed anxious to unburden himself. "Everything was going like clockwork. There were three GenoME suspects, and we picked 'em out of the crowd straight off; gas masks are pretty bulky things. Gazo Kovacs didn't so much as fart. The whole thing was handled beautifully. Prosper hadn't set foot in the courtroom, and our suspects were already in handcuffs. It was textbook. Absolutely textbook."

"So what happened?"

Saul shook his head, shoulders sagging. "It was an inside job," he muttered. "It had to be. Prosper just . . . just *walked* out of a holding room. The guard with him must have been dirty. They walked out together while we were arresting the other three, and they got into a paddy wagon and drove away." It was apparent that Saul hadn't fully recovered from the shock of this maneuver. "I still can't work out if Prosper organized the escape, or if it was part of GenoME's plan," he said, almost as if he were talking to himself. "I keep thinking: If it was GenoME's doing, then why wasn't Prosper killed right there in the holding room? Because it was supposed to be an assassination attempt, not a breakout. And if GenoME *did* abduct Prosper from the holding room, then why didn't he kick up a fuss? He was told what GenoME intended to do. He was told to expect a bullet in the brain if he was stupid enough to play along with any so-called abduction." The detective sighed. "Unless, of course, he was being held at gunpoint . . ."

"Perhaps it *was* Prosper's idea," Cadel suggested dully. "Perhaps he was improvising. If he saw his chance, and fooled the guard—"

"No." Again Saul shook his head. "There was nothing improvised about this. Someone tampered with the custody protocols. Someone made sure that the guard was allowed to evacuate him in the event of a problem. A problem like those arrests we made." Saul clenched his fists. "That's how the two of them got out," he spat. "They had clearance."

"You mean, it was a computer glitch?"

"More or less." Hearing Cadel click his tongue, Saul peered down at him. "Can you think of anyone who might have caused it? Anyone you know?"

Cadel shrugged. He was finding it hard to concentrate. "I'd have to look at the system with the glitch in it. The Corrective Services system," he said, though his thoughts had turned, inevitably, to Dr. Vee. A renowned hacker, Ulysses Vee had also taught a whole classful of malicious hackers at the Axis Institute. And after the institute's destruction, he had disappeared into thin air.

Could he have resurfaced, to help his old friend Prosper English?

"Christ, I'm sorry." Saul thumped a fist on the handrail. "I should have checked everything. *Everything.* You warned me, and I didn't listen."

"Who was the guard?" Cadel inquired, disregarding these apologies. He was following his own train of thought. "The one who went with Prosper? What was his background?"

"We're looking into it. First things first, though. I can't find Ms. Bashford."

"Oh." Emerging from a state of absorbed reflection, Cadel had to change tack so abruptly that he stumbled over his response. "I came—I mean, they're all downstairs. Judith was in the laundry," he said.

Saul grunted.

"But what are you going to do?" Cadel continued, stalling for time. It was almost a relief to focus on the problem of keeping Saul away from the lift. By busying himself with this minor logistical challenge, Cadel was distracted from the question that had begun to encroach on his peace of mind like a threatening thundercloud, namely: What would Prosper do next?

"I'm going to stay with you," Saul announced, brushing past Cadel on his way back to the kitchen. "I'm not taking any more chances."

"But—"

"It's nonnegotiable. The staff here will just have to deal with it. If possible, the other residents should move out." Arriving at a bend in the stairs, Saul glanced up, to catch sight of Cadel's dropped jaw. "It's a short-term solution," the detective said. "I don't like it, either. The trouble is, it's all we have."

"But you can't stay *here*!" Cadel spluttered, too horrified to dissemble. "Not in the *house*!"

"I'm afraid that's nonnegotiable, too," Saul declared. Upon reaching the kitchen—and finding a slightly breathless crowd gathered there—he stated his case without apology. He would be staying. There could be no arguments. Though threatened with lawyers, journalists, and the New South Wales ombudsman, he refused to budge. Not even Judith could persuade him to change his mind. "Your boss can take it up with my boss," was his flat rejoinder when she objected.

"And in the meantime?" Devin growled. "What are we supposed to do in the meantime?"

"Either sit tight or get out." Saul spoke so quietly and calmly that this piece of advice didn't sound nearly as offensive as it actually was. "I'll try not to get in anyone's way. I won't interfere with the schedule. But I have to be here. All night, if necessary. Until we have a better idea of what's going on."

Hamish groaned. Lexi swore. Her loud abuse, however, bounced off the detective like handfuls of popcorn. As for Tony Cheung's murmured protests about procedures and supervision, they were carelessly waved aside.

"When Mr. Lynch returns, I'll take it up with him," Saul countered. "Until then, you should all just go about your business."

Surveying his fellow squad members, Cadel realized that they would, in fact, be *unable* to go about their business. As long as the detective was hanging around, no one would be able to return to the War Room. No one would be able to monitor GenoME's activities.

Except possibly Cliff and Zac, from their parking spot near number eleven.

"I tell you what," Cadel said slowly, his mind working away at top speed. "Why don't I . . . Why don't I spend the day on the computer, upstairs? It's what I'd like to do, and it would mean that Mr. Greeniaus could keep out of everyone's hair." He smiled crookedly at the detective. "No offense, or anything."

"None taken," Saul replied (as if he meant it). "But I don't want you on the computer, Cadel. And I'll have to do regular reconnaissance patrols of the whole house. Just to keep an eye on things."

"How regular?" Hamish demanded, and Saul shrugged.

"I don't know. Once an hour?"

There was a slight ripple of movement, which Cadel interpreted as a sign of dismay. He knew that everyone in the kitchen—except Saul—must be acutely anxious about urgent jobs waiting to be finished downstairs. He also knew that none of these jobs could now be his. He was stuck with Saul Greeniaus, and would be for the rest of the day. Saul had become his allotted task.

Not that he cared much. Prosper's escape had suddenly made the whole GenoME infiltration scheme seem strangely unimportant.

"Well, I'm sure we can arrange things," said Judith, trying to adopt a cheerful manner—without quite succeeding. "It's not the end of the world, and we're all resourceful people. In the meantime, why don't I give Trader a call?"

But there was no need. The words were hardly out of her mouth when the back door burst open and Trader Lynch strolled in. Unlike Saul, he presented a serene and perfectly groomed appearance. His smile gleamed. His eyes sparkled. With one sweeping glance, he noted and assessed every person occupying the room.

Then he flung out his arms and cried, "Here I am! Not to worry! Now—what seems to be the problem?"

THIRTY-FOUR

It was impressive, the way Trader took charge of everything. First of all, he swept Saul off to a "private interview" in the upstairs office. This tactic allowed the rest of Genius Squad to return to the War Room, while Saul was out of the way.

Unfortunately, Cadel had to stay with the detective, who seemed reluctant to lose sight of him.

Then, during the interview itself, Trader astounded Cadel with his rapid footwork. After listening carefully to Saul's list of demands, Trader indulged in a short period of reflection before announcing, "There *is* such a thing as emergency accommodation. I'll see if I can set something up for the other kids overnight." He sprang to his feet suddenly. "Just let me make a couple of calls," he said. "I won't be long. Cadel, this computer will be yours for the rest of the day." He tapped the hulking monitor that occupied most of the desktop around which they were gathered. "You can log on now, if you like," he finished. "Show Mr. Greeniaus what you can do."

This wasn't a suggestion. It was an order, though it happened to be phrased in the chirpiest of voices. Cadel understood that Trader didn't want Saul leaving the office anytime soon. No doubt Trader was intending to rush straight down to the War Room with further instructions for the rest of Genius Squad. Cadel didn't know what those instructions might be; something to do with a mass evacuation, possibly. Perhaps Trader had access to a "fallback" residence where the squad could reassemble in peace, far away from Saul's prying eyes.

Whatever Trader's plans were, however, they couldn't be carried out if Saul was in the immediate vicinity. So the detective had to be detained upstairs. Cadel had to move fast, before Saul decided to get up and go.

"I might be able to trace that computer glitch," was the most diverting observation that Cadel could think of. He produced it just as the door was closing behind Trader. "You know—the one that changed the custody protocols at the Coroner's Court? I could find out who was responsible."

Saul's eyes widened. "Really?" he said, and Cadel shrugged.

"I could give it a try."

Saul pondered for a moment. Then he shook his head. "No," he decided. "It *would* be useful, but we can't risk it. I told you before—I don't want you on the computer."

"But—"

"No."

To Cadel's alarm, the detective rose from his chair. *Not yet,* Cadel thought. *Trader needs more time.* And aloud he said, "So did you arrest everyone at GenoME? You told me you were staking the place out."

Saul hesitated. Then he sighed, and collapsed back onto his seat. "Yes, there was a raid," he glumly admitted. "The staff are being questioned—all except one. She managed to slip away just before we moved in."

Carolina, Cadel deduced. *Carolina escaped.*

"How?" he asked. "I mean, if the police were watching the building . . ."

Saul described how a motorbike courier had arrived at the GenoME branch shortly before the first arrests were made. This courier had entered the reception area wearing his bike helmet, and five minutes later had apparently emerged again, carrying a large package.

"But it wasn't him," Saul disclosed. "He was found later, tied up in a toilet cubicle. That woman we're looking for—Carolina Whitehead—must have driven off in his gear."

"And you still haven't found her?"

"Not yet." Saul began to drag his fingers through his hair. "She's the one we need," he fretted. "She must know *something,* if she's on the run.

So far we've got nothing on the rest of 'em. The thugs we picked up in court are just local muscle, as far as I can see. Guns for hire . . ." He broke off abruptly as his eyes met Cadel's. "Sorry. I'm unloading, and I shouldn't be. This isn't your problem; you've got enough of your own. Anyway, I can't afford to waste time. I have things to do. Calls to make." The detective stood up, laying a hand on the computer. "Meanwhile, I want you to promise that you won't touch this thing."

Cadel opened his mouth. Before he could lodge a protest, however, Saul said gravely, "If Prosper's looking for you, he'll start online. You know that."

"But he won't find me," Cadel objected. "I won't let him."

"Maybe not," the detective had to concede. "Maybe you're too smart. Let's not forget, though: Prosper has someone on his payroll who hacked into the systems at Corrective Services and changed the custody protocols. How hard would it be for that same person to track *you* down?" Without waiting for an answer, Saul hammered his point home. "What if we're talking about that guy from the Axis Institute? Ulysses Vee? Vee knows you, Cadel. He knows your style. And he's pretty sharp—you said so yourself. Are you absolutely sure he won't pick up your trail?"

Cadel scratched his head. It was true: Dr. Vee *did* know him. And Dr. Vee was also a first-class hacker. However unlikely it might be, there was an outside chance that Cadel would somehow give himself away, if he logged on to the Net.

"But what am I supposed to do all day?" he groaned. "If I can't go out and I can't use the computer, how am I going to stay busy? Because I have to stay busy. I *have* to." Though he didn't point out that he needed to keep his mind off Prosper English, the implication was clear.

Saul must have picked it up, because he wrinkled his brow in a fleeting demonstration of concern. "Well . . . I guess you can show me your playing-card trick," he proposed. "Ms. Currey told me about that. It sounds pretty neat."

No doubt he meant well, but the detective could have been talking to an eight-year-old.

Cadel was offended.

"You don't have to call her Ms. Currey anymore," he snapped. "I mean, I know you're going out with her, so why pretend? I'm not stupid."

Saul raised one eyebrow. He was about to speak when the door burst open and Trader walked in. Trader's expansive smile seemed to light up the whole room. Even his hairstyle was reassuring.

"That's settled," he said. "I've found emergency accommodation for Hamish and the twins, down in Maroubra." He went on to explain that Judith would transport the three evicted teenagers in her car. "Unfortunately, no one can take Sonja for the night," he continued, "but that's okay. I'll sleep here myself and make sure she's looked after properly."

Saul grunted—apparently satisfied—but Cadel could hardly contain his amazement. Was Trader really going to uproot Genius Squad at such a time? Was he really going to dump Hamish and the twins in some kind of refuge, when there was so much work to be done?

"Are they all going to be together?" Cadel asked, trying not to sound as anxious as he felt. Whereupon Trader tipped him a surreptitious wink.

"Oh, yes," said Trader. "It's a great big house near the beach. They'll love it."

At this point Cadel remembered that Judith lived in Maroubra, where she had bought herself a sprawling seaside mansion. With all the money she'd made plundering offshore bank accounts, she had also purchased a vineyard, a lightplane, a country house, and a safe full of gold ingots.

Cadel relaxed slightly. He was sure that Judith's mansion would offer every kind of facility required by Genius Squad, from Internet access to spa baths.

"And *you* can help those kids pack," Trader added, still addressing Cadel. "God knows, they'll need all the help they can get. Hamish couldn't pack a lunch box, let alone an overnight bag. And I don't want Lexi bringing her whole bloody wardrobe along." Having provided Cadel with a plan of action, he turned back to Saul. "Now," he said, "you were wanting a quick rundown of the alarm system?"

Cadel had to admire Trader's cunning and self-confidence. Even the detective fell into line, reluctantly giving Cadel ten precious minutes in Hamish's room. While Trader lectured Saul on sensor pulses and power grids—dragging him all over the house to examine various junction boxes—Cadel caught up on the latest news, which Hamish delivered in a whisper as he drifted around his bedroom, trying to decide what to pack.

"It's such b-bad luck," he lamented softly. "We're really going to need you, and you'll be stuck here with that dickhead in the stupid tie." Hamish went on to say that the forged e-mail had been sent to Earl Toffany, but that no reply had been received; that Jerry had anticipated the police raid by a minute or so, disconnecting every machine so that no one could eavesdrop on the action; and that Dot was still in the process of collating what had been salvaged from the havoc wrought by Jerry's self-destruct program, which had been more of a challenge than anyone could have anticipated.

"It was like *Alien* in there," Hamish concluded, referring to his most recent virtual patrol through the GenoME network. "You could practically see all the lights flashing and the gases venting. *'Self-destruction in T minus ten seconds'*—that kind of thing. Boy, I had to be quick."

"It's a bloody mess," growled Devin. Like his sister, he had made a beeline for Hamish's bedroom the minute Saul was out of sight. "No one knows what's going on anymore. The last we heard from Cliff, he was still outside number eleven, trying to see who the police were pushing into their cars."

"I can tell you that myself," Cadel hissed, with a nervous glance toward the closed bedroom door. "They picked up everyone except Carolina. She escaped."

"Really?" said Devin. "Shit. That's bad."

"Not as bad as Prosper English," was Cadel's view. But neither Hamish nor Devin seemed interested in Prosper English.

Only Lexi sympathized with Cadel's concerns.

"Poor Caddy," she crooned, winding her plump arm around his shoulders. "I guess you're really freaking out, eh? With Prosper on the loose, and all. Do you think he'll try to find you?"

"Yes," Cadel replied shortly, sliding out of her grasp.

"He'll be stupid if he does, with that copper hanging around," she said. Whereupon Devin turned away from Hamish and demanded of Cadel, in a dour tone, "How long is that cop going to stay here, for god's sake?"

"I don't know," said Cadel.

"I hope he stays for a week," Lexi chirped. "Judith's house sounds *fantastic.* She's got a pool and a home theater and everything! She's got a wide-screen TV in *every* bedroom!"

"Shh!" warned Devin. And Cadel said, "Keep it down!"

He had barely spoken before footsteps sounded on the stairs, heralding Saul's return. Devin swore under his breath, while Lexi assumed the challenging pose with which she usually confronted Saul, arms folded, lips arranged into a sneer.

Hamish didn't react at all. He was standing with a mismatched sock in each hand and a look of confusion on his face. "Are these my socks?" he asked, as Saul entered the room.

And that was the end of the informal debriefing.

Over the next half hour, Cadel began to feel increasingly isolated. He had nothing to do but watch Hamish and the twins running around with T-shirts and toothbrushes, while downstairs the squad's computers were quietly smuggled into Judith's car. Lots of noisy squabbles were staged for the purpose of distracting Saul. Lexi threw a brief tantrum after being told to remove eight pairs of shoes from her suitcase. Devin sulked when Trader insisted that he would need to pack more than just his iPod and a pair of boxer shorts.

Trader even had the brilliant idea of asking Saul to help Hamish, who was utterly incapable of logical thought when it came to filling a toiletry bag or anticipating the need for sleepwear. Because he was busy with Hamish, Saul didn't notice the way various members of Genius Squad kept disappearing into the War Room, loaded down with the quilts and pillowcases needed to disguise their computers. Nor did he query the presence of so much bed linen in Judith's car. "It's best to be on the safe side," was Judith's rather feeble explanation, which Saul accepted without a murmur.

By two o'clock, the evacuation was complete. Cadel wasn't allowed to wave good-bye from the garden. He couldn't even watch everyone leave from inside the house, which was stuffy and dark now that all the curtains were drawn. All he could do was sit in the kitchen with Sonja, listening as first Judith's car, then Tony's, roared off down the driveway, taking with them Hamish, Lexi, Devin, Judith, Tony, and Dot.

Suddenly, the house seemed very quiet. Even Trader's lustrous personality couldn't lighten the morose atmosphere. Neither could a scrappy lunch of baked beans and tinned pears. After lunch, Trader had to go out for a while. Cadel assumed that he was tracking down Cliff, or perhaps visiting Judith's house to oversee the installation of a temporary War Room. Whatever the reason for his absence, however, he was sorely missed. Sonja was never chatty at the best of times (because communicating was such an effort for her), and Saul couldn't seem to concentrate on any topic for more than a few minutes. His ear was always cocked for suspicious noises, and he kept leaping up to check windows or make phone calls.

In the end, Cadel read to Sonja for most of the afternoon. He also played a bit of Hackenbush, and gave Saul a demonstration of the Solitaire Cipher. As the hours rolled by, and Prosper remained at large, Cadel grew more and more depressed. Saul received regular updates about the progress of the police investigation, but they weren't particularly encouraging. Jerry Reinhard refused to talk. The hired thugs had said only that they'd received their instructions over the telephone, from "a woman with an American accent." Carolina still hadn't been located. As for the rest of the GenoME staff, they appeared to be totally clueless.

When Trader returned, it was time to cook dinner. Saul took charge of the preparations, rolling up his pin-striped sleeves to produce a very tasty pasta sauce. Cadel peeled the vegetables while Trader threw together a salad; it was Trader who also insisted on feeding Sonja, while his own meal grew cold. "That's what microwaves are for," he said, with a display of indestructible vivacity. He even did most of the washing up and was a huge help in getting Sonja ready for bed.

All in all, he gave a terrific impersonation of someone born to be a professional caregiver. Anyone less attentive than Cadel would have been fooled. But Cadel noticed that Trader was always hyperalert, constantly focused on the detective and what he was doing.

Saul missed this; he was too preoccupied. And whenever he *did* turn his attention to the people around him, it was focused almost exclusively on Cadel. He was worried about Cadel. That much was obvious from the questions he asked, and the manner in which he asked them.

"Do you want to talk to Ms. Currey?" was his first, tentative inquiry. "You can call her now if you like. It's not too late."

"No, thanks," said Cadel, who had just emerged from the second-floor bathroom—towel in hand—to find Saul leaning against the banisters outside. "Um . . . I'm finished in there, if you want to use it."

But the detective ignored this offer. His face looked drawn and bruised. "Have you discussed all the recent developments with Sonja?" was his next question. "She might have something useful to contribute. You can stay in her room tonight—we could arrange it."

"No. That's okay."

"She'll be all right here. You both will." Saul jerked his thumb. "There's been a change of shift outside. Jack and Luca are on the job now—they're top guys. Really reliable. *Nothing* will get past them."

Cadel nodded. He didn't know what to say.

"And if anything does get past them, I'll be here. Guarding your door. So you mustn't be nervous." After a brief pause, during which Saul continued to regard Cadel with discomforting gravity, the detective said (for perhaps the fifth time in as many hours), "It's only a precaution, though. You realize that, don't you? I'm not expecting Prosper to show up." He cocked his head. "Our latest reports indicate that he might have headed south. Do you have any idea if he has a boat stashed down near Wollongong somewhere?"

"No." said Cadel. By now he had noticed the kitchen chair stationed outside his bedroom. And he pointed at it. "Is that where you're going to sit?" he asked.

"Yes."

"All *night*?"

"That's the plan."

"But when are you going to get any sleep?"

Saul hesitated. His gaze slid away toward the darkening stairwell. "I don't sleep much," he finally divulged. "Not when I've got things to think about." Then he glanced back at Cadel. "I hope *you* get enough sleep tonight, though. I don't want you lying awake worrying. Because there's no need."

"Oh, I'll be all right," Cadel insisted, knowing full well that he wouldn't be.

Sure enough, he found himself tossing and turning once he did go to bed, his head full of fearful possibilities. He could never rest easily now—not as long as Prosper was at large. Not as long as his own details were drifting around on the police computer system. It was no good relying on systems like that. It was no good relying on anything or anyone—not where Prosper was concerned.

My only chance of keeping safe, Cadel thought, *is to disguise myself and disappear. Vanish off the radar. Change my name. Take my money and run.*

But what would happen to Sonja if he did that? He couldn't leave Sonja. And he couldn't take her with him, either—not if he wanted to pass as someone else. Because Sonja would be impossible to disguise.

Oh god, he thought, *this isn't fair. What shall I do? How am I going to solve this? There* must *be a solution!*

And he racked his brain, finding no comfort in the muffled coughs and sighs that announced Saul's proximity. Saul was yet another problem, because he had to be shielded from Prosper English. If the two men were ever to confront each other, Saul was bound to come out worse. He would be lucky to survive, in fact.

Cadel was calculating the detective's chances when, suddenly, at about eleven o'clock, sleep overtook him. He fell into a restless doze, during which he dreamed that he was a little kid again, riding in a train with his nanny, looking for weaknesses in the rail network. Peering through a window, he caught a glimpse of a familiar face on a station platform. It was Sonja's face, wearing a lost expression. Before he could wave, however, the train slid past, gathering speed.

And he pressed his forehead against the cold glass, straining to look back.

"Cadel."

He opened his eyes. He was awake. But he could still feel something cold on his forehead.

With a lurch of his heart, he realized what it was.

"Wake up, Cadel," a familiar voice drawled. "Time to go."

PART FOUR

THIRTY-FIVE

I'm dreaming, thought Cadel. *This is just another bad dream.* And he shut his eyes again, willing himself to wake up.

"Come on, now. Don't dawdle." The cool, precise voice sounded faintly amused. "We're not out of the woods yet."

Cadel recognized the unmistakeable diction of Prosper English, and it made the blood turn to ice in his veins. But the silhouette hanging over him wasn't like Prosper's. It looked far more like Zac's, with its long, straight hair and loose garments.

Confused, Cadel squinted toward the open door of his bedroom, through which artificial light was streaming. He couldn't see anyone beyond it.

"Up you get," said Prosper—and this time there could be no doubt. His smooth tones were issuing from the lank-haired, hemp-clad figure beside the bed. "Don't bother making a fuss, either, because it's pointless."

"Saul." Abruptly, Cadel's head cleared. He sat up straight, careless of the gun aimed at his temple. "Where's Saul?"

"Shh."

"*What have you done?*" Fear rose in Cadel's throat like some kind of black bile. "Where is he?"

"In the storage cupboard." As Cadel caught his breath, Prosper added, "He's not dead, if that's what you're worried about. We couldn't risk damaging his clothes, so we used chloroform." Prosper gestured with the handgun. "Speaking of clothes, I want you out of those pajamas. Quick-smart." And he snapped on the bedside lamp.

Instantly, his face became visible—and so did the fact that he was disguised as Zac Stillman. His mane of graying hair had been tightly confined beneath a blond wig. His thin lips were framed by a false mustache and beard. His bony feet were shoved into scuffed brown sandals.

From a distance, he was probably convincing. Up close, however, there was no mistaking that sharp black gaze or imperious nose.

"I realize this must be a shock," he purred, "but you're going to have to speed things up. We haven't got all night." And he reached for a discarded sweatshirt, which he tossed at Cadel. "We have a long drive ahead of us."

Cadel didn't ask "Where to?" Of the fifty or so questions that had popped into his brain, he picked the most urgent one.

"Where's Sonja?" he demanded, fumbling with his pajama buttons. "Where's Trader?"

"You don't have to worry about Trader," was Prosper's careless reply. "Trader won't get in our way."

"What do you mean?"

"I meant exactly what I said. Trader won't get in our way. We had to tie him up, though. To make it look good." When Cadel froze, Prosper gave an impatient hiss. "Hurry, please, or I'm going to lose my temper."

Cadel was stunned. He wanted to protest but couldn't speak, let alone move. Then he heard another voice from somewhere out on the landing, and his heart skipped a beat.

"*Saul?*" he croaked.

"*Shh!*" Prosper repositioned the gun barrel against Cadel's brow, listening intently. Cadel, for his part, was so frightened that he could no longer hear anything except the loud thudding of his own pulse.

At last Prosper relaxed. "No," he said. "That's just Alias, making a phone call." He stepped back. "Get up. Now. I won't ask you again."

Clumsily, Cadel scrambled out of bed. As he shed his pajamas and put on his clothes, Prosper kept talking.

"You need a haircut," he remarked, "which is probably fortunate, all things considered. Good thing you haven't grown much. I'll just check those pockets, if I may. We wouldn't want you messing with a cell phone."

"Where's Sonja?" Cadel repeated, peering into the long face that hovered above him.

"Are those your shoes? Really, Cadel, what disgusting objects."

"Where is she?"

"In bed. Asleep. Presumably." With one foot, Prosper pushed the shoes toward Cadel. "I must admit, I'm looking forward to meeting the famous Sonja."

Cadel swallowed. "You leave her alone," he said hoarsely.

Prosper raised an eyebrow.

"My dear boy, do you really think that's an option?" he murmured. "She *can't* be left alone. That's the whole point, isn't it? And since Trader will be tied up for the next few hours, we're going to have to take her with us. Otherwise she might hurt herself. Fall out of bed, or something." He glanced impatiently at Cadel's illuminated bedside clock, which displayed the digits 11:53. "Besides, she's our cover story. We're supposed to be whisking her off to the hospital."

"They'll never believe it." Cadel spoke as calmly as he could, though his hands were beginning to shake. "Those police will never let you walk out of here with me. Not even if you *are* disguised as Zac Stillman."

"Is that so?" Prosper said, before raising his voice. *"How's it going, Alias?"*

"Nearly there," came the reply. And suddenly a figure appeared, framed in the doorway.

It was Saul Greeniaus.

For a split second, Cadel lost his bearings. He was disoriented. Then Saul said, "What do you think?" and Cadel realized that he wasn't looking at the detective after all.

On the contrary, he was looking at a very good impression of Saul. A pseudo-Saul, complete with shoulder holster.

"Not bad," was Prosper's opinion. "What do *you* think, Cadel? You know the man. Is there anything we've missed?" When Cadel didn't respond, Prosper studied his stricken face. "What's the matter? You're not going to be sick, are you?"

"Hello, Cadel." It was unutterably strange to hear Alias's bland voice issuing from Saul's mouth—though, on closer inspection, that mouth was just a little too wide to be Saul's. And those eyes weren't really big enough. "Nice to see you again, after all this time."

Alias was wearing brown contact lenses, a special wig, and thick-soled shoes, to give him height. He was also wearing Saul's shirt and trousers.

At the sight of these garments, Cadel nearly lost control.

"I take it you used *his* phone?" Prosper was addressing Alias, who nodded. "Good. Excellent. And the *polizei* didn't seem suspicious?"

"Not really," Alias replied. "A bit startled. I told them to stay put and watch the house."

"Well done."

"I told them Cadel insisted on coming with us."

"Well, let's hope there isn't some kind of clearance code that we should know about." Prosper nudged Cadel in the ribs. "Is there?"

Cadel was so preoccupied with his own despair that he'd missed the previous exchange. He had to clear his throat before answering.

"Is there what?" he said.

"Does your friend Saul Greeniaus use some kind of password when he's giving orders?" asked Prosper, and Cadel mumbled, "I don't know."

"We'd better get a move on, then." With a second nudge, Prosper urged Cadel forward. "This whole thing could blow up in our faces any minute."

Together they moved out of the room and onto the landing. Here Cadel discerned a very faint, vaguely chemical smell that reminded him of something. He also spied a stack of strange boxes near a puddle of familiar clothes.

These clothes came as such a shock that he lurched to a standstill.

"Cliff!" he breathed, then rounded on Alias. "You came here as Cliff!"

"Dyed my crew cut," Alias agreed cheerfully. "And stuck a bit of padding here and there."

"Where is he? Where's Cliff?"

"For god's sake, Cadel!" Prosper snapped. "We can talk later! Right now we have to go."

On his way downstairs, Cadel tried desperately to think. But fear was clogging his brain paths. And he was distracted by the nasty, nagging, chemical odor, which seemed to follow them as they descended, and which made him feel slightly ill. It wasn't until he had reached the ground floor that he finally realized what the smell was.

Having once been exposed to a rag soaked in chloroform, he wasn't about to forget the stink of it.

"Right," said Prosper. "Now, where's Sonja? In there?"

"No!" Cadel halted again. He felt the gun barrel prod at his spine. "Please. Just leave her."

"I can't. I'm sorry."

"Please." Cadel's voice cracked, and next thing he knew Prosper's left arm was draped around his shoulders, while Prosper's gun had come to rest against his cheek.

"Don't be silly," Prosper gently advised. "She'll be perfectly safe with me, as long as you do what you're told." Seeing Alias pause just ahead of them, Prosper barked, "Go on, then! Go and get her!"

"Oh. Right," said Alias, and disappeared into Sonja's room.

"So this is the plan," Prosper continued, turning back to Cadel. "We're going to walk out of here and get into the policeman's car. Alias will be driving. I'll be holding Sonja. If you do anything to alert that surveillance team, it's Sonja who's going to suffer." Without warning, he lowered his gun and inserted it into his waistband without engaging the safety catch. Cadel realized, with astonishment, that the safety catch had never been *dis*engaged. "I'm not going to shoot you," Prosper confessed, a little ruefully. "I couldn't bring myself to do anything of the sort. But

I'll happily shoot Sonja if you give me the least bit of trouble. You understand that, don't you?"

Cadel nodded.

"Good." Prosper stooped, so that his mouth was almost level with Cadel's ear. "Incidentally, you can look as distressed as you like—don't worry about that. You're supposed to look distressed when your best friend's being rushed to the hospital."

"You didn't hurt Saul, did you?" Cadel couldn't restrain himself. The question erupted out of him, despite all his best efforts.

Sure enough, Prosper didn't like it. He narrowed his anthracite eyes. After a long pause, he said, "What if I did?"

Cadel bit his lip. Though he remained silent, the answer was written all over his face.

"As a matter of fact, I didn't need to hurt him," Prosper revealed. "Alias always gives a flawless performance, and we were both of us hiding behind armfuls of boxes. Your friend didn't suspect a thing—he opened the cupboard door for us. I just had to jump him from behind with my chloroform." Prosper's sneer exposed one razor-sharp canine tooth. "What a fool."

Cadel said nothing. To argue would have been risky—and in any case, he was concerned about what was happening in Sonja's bedroom. A loud *clunk* worried him so much that he started forward. But he didn't get very far. Prosper caught and held him before he'd advanced more than a few steps.

"Easy now," said Prosper.

"I just want to go in!"

"You don't have to. They're coming out." Prosper's embrace was like a harness or a straitjacket, encircling Cadel from behind. "See? Here they come."

Cadel gasped. Alias had emerged from the bedroom with Sonja, who was dangling from his arms like a wet towel. Every muscle in her body was limp. Her head lolled, and her eyes were closed.

She was unconscious.

"What have you done?!" Cadel cried.

"Shh!" Prosper braced himself as Cadel tried to break free. "A touch of chloroform. That's all."

Cadel caught his breath. *"Chloroform?"* He was appalled.

"It makes her easier to manage," Prosper explained. "She'll be awake in a couple of minutes. So calm down and be good."

"I couldn't spare the time to put on her street clothes," said Alias. But Prosper appeared to take this unfortunate development in his stride.

"That's okay," he said. "Pajamas will be more realistic. Are you all set?"

Alias gave a nod.

"Cadel? Are you going to behave?" Prosper muttered. "It wouldn't be very nice for anyone if we ended up besieged in this place, would it?"

Cadel shook his head. He couldn't speak.

"Right, then. Let's go." Prosper shifted his grasp, so that he once more had his arm draped around Cadel's shoulders. When they emerged through the front door together, it must have seemed—from a distance—that he was trying to comfort the anxious Cadel, who kept glancing back at Sonja in a very convincing way.

Their hurried exit was also convincing. (As Prosper said, during their sprint toward Saul's car, "You don't muck around in a medical emergency.") Within seconds Sonja had been loaded into the backseat and Cadel had followed her. Alias then started the engine. Prosper joined Cadel in the rear of the car.

Zac's van was parked nearby, but Cadel didn't get a chance to comment on this until they were rolling down the driveway.

"You took Zac's van," he said.

"It's very distinctive," was Prosper's reply.

"How did you take it?" Cadel was dazed. He couldn't imagine the hijack scenario. "What did you do to Zac? And to Cliff?"

Prosper sighed. He was sitting directly behind Alias, with Sonja's head pillowed in his lap. Her feet lay across Cadel's knees.

"You don't give me much credit, do you?" Prosper's eyes were riveted to the gates ahead, which were illumined by the headlights of Saul's vehicle. "I didn't do anything to anyone. I didn't have to. I simply called Trader and made a request." He lowered his voice suddenly, addressing Alias. "There they are. Our *polizei* friends. Do you see them?"

"I see 'em," Alias confirmed. Glancing up, Cadel spotted an unmarked police car under a streetlight. Both car and streetlight were visible through the wrought-iron framework of the gates, which were slowly starting to swing open. But he didn't spare the police more than a moment's thought, being far more interested in Sonja's breathing. It was harsh and labored. He didn't like the sound of it.

Then her eyelids fluttered.

"She's waking up!" he exclaimed. "Sonja! Can you hear me?"

"Don't acknowledge them," Prosper ordered. He was speaking to Alias. "They're supposed to be incognito. And *we're* supposed to be in a rush." As Saul's car swept past the surveillance team, gathering speed, Cadel saw Prosper checking a side mirror. "They're not moving," Prosper said. "They haven't moved. No—their lights are still off."

"So far, so good," Alias remarked.

"Step on it until we turn the next corner. Then make sure you keep to the speed limit." Prosper's gaze dropped from the mirror to Sonja's head, which had moved slightly. One of her hands was beginning to twitch. "After all," he observed, "we don't want to make ourselves conspicuous, do we?"

"What if she starts throwing up?" Cadel demanded. He could remember vomiting after his own first encounter with chloroform. "Is there a plastic bag in here, or an old towel?"

"My dear boy, how would I know? It's not my car," said Prosper. He turned toward Cadel, smiling one of his slow, secretive smiles. His eyes glittered in the dimness. "You'd know better than I would. I gather you're quite familiar with this vehicle, after all your little outings."

Cadel stiffened. He dragged his attention away from Sonja and fastened it on the shadowy face beside him—which, though familiar in every curve and hollow, looked slightly odd without spectacles. The straggling wig gave it an uncharacteristically rakish air.

"Has Trader been spying for you?" asked Cadel, in a very small voice.

"Oh no. It's Dot who's been spying for me." Seeing Cadel's mouth fall open, Prosper chuckled. "Didn't you work that out? My goodness, dear boy—we *do* have a lot to catch up on."

THIRTY-SIX

There was something surreal about that drive. At times Cadel wondered if he had woken up at all. Having been abruptly wrenched from his warm bed, he now found himself gliding along in a dimly lit car occupied by Alias (disguised as Saul Greeniaus) and Prosper (disguised as Zac Stillman).

It was hardly surprising that the whole experience had a dreamlike quality.

"Yes, Dot's the one I hired to keep an eye on things at Clearview House," Prosper remarked, surveying Sonja's restless form with obvious misgivings. "Apparently Dot has a hard time holding down a *normal* job, because she finds it so hard to relate to people. And she was in dire need of money after her share portfolio went belly up. Never mortgage anything to buy stock, Cadel—it's a mug's game." He jerked his head back, as Sonja's arm flicked toward it in a sudden muscular spasm. "Dear me," he said. "Is this normal? Or is something wrong?"

"She's always like this." Cadel leaned over and caught Sonja's wayward hand. Her eyelids were beginning to flutter. "Can you hear me, Sonja? Are you feeling sick?"

At that instant she kicked out, catching him in the stomach. It wasn't a forceful blow, so it didn't hurt much. Nevertheless, Prosper was displeased.

"Get up front," he said to Cadel.

"Oh, but—"

"*Get up front.*" Though Prosper spoke in a measured and deliberate fashion, his tone made Cadel's palms sweat. "She'll break your nose if you stay there."

"I'll hold her down! She'll be all right, see? I've got a firm grip now." Cadel wanted to be close to Sonja when she woke. He knew how frightened she would be even if he *was* nearby. And if he wasn't . . . "She might hurt herself, otherwise. It gets worse when she panics."

"My dear boy, I'm not worried about her. I'm worried about you." Prosper aimed his gun at Sonja's head. "Now, get up front, please—I won't ask you again."

Cadel clenched his teeth. Prosper's close proximity filled him with a strange, almost illogical fear, which paralyzed his thought processes and had its roots somewhere deep in his subconscious. Nevertheless, at the sight of that gun barrel resting against Sonja's skull, his fear was submerged in a tide of hot anger.

All at once, his mind cleared.

"You'd *better* be worried about her," he snapped, "because she's the only thing keeping me in line. That's why you brought her along, isn't it? So I wouldn't try to escape?" Receiving no response, Cadel peered into the semidarkness. "You can't seriously think I want to be here? With *you*?" he spat. "If you do, you must be delusional."

The flicker of a streetlight briefly illuminated Prosper's crooked smile. "I did think it likely that you might still be nursing that unreasonable grudge of yours," he admitted, seizing one of Sonja's flailing arms. Then, in a sharper voice, he said, "It's nice to see that your unfortunate taste for the company of policemen hasn't destroyed your ability to think in a strategic manner."

Cadel's heart sank. He knew that Prosper was referring to Saul Greeniaus. There could be no doubt whatsoever that Prosper knew all about Saul, and about Saul's dealings with Cadel.

It was grim news. For Saul, more than anyone.

"What's that to you?" Cadel cried. His dismay and impotent fury turned the question into a broken wail. "Why can't you just *leave me alone*?"

"Because you're my son."

"Oh, really?" Cadel couldn't contain his scorn. "Why wouldn't you admit it, then?"

"And have you spirited away by my abominable cousin Bernard? To a Scottish pig farm?" Prosper shook his head. "Believe me, Cadel, there are worse fates than a spell at the Donkins' house. I was only thinking of you." Then Sonja gave a high-pitched squeal, and he winced. "For god's sake, aren't we there yet?"

"Not far now," said Alias, as Cadel reached across to stroke Sonja's face. But her head wouldn't keep still.

"Sonja, it's me. Cadel. I'm right here. You don't have to worry."

"Watch that foot," warned Prosper.

"Can you hear me? Sonja? You have to calm down. You have to stop thrashing about, or you'll hurt yourself."

"Yes indeed," Prosper drawled. "We wouldn't want this gun to go off accidentally."

Cadel gasped. "Shut up!" he exclaimed. If his hands hadn't been fastened to Sonja's uncontrolled limbs, he probably would have struck Prosper. "Don't you *dare* threaten her!"

"I wasn't threatening anyone," Prosper replied coolly.

"She's not deaf, you know! She's not stupid! But you didn't bring the DynaVox—she can't *talk* without her DynaVox!"

"Which is probably just as well," Prosper observed. "Since I can't imagine she has anything of interest to say."

There was so much careless contempt in this remark that it left Cadel momentarily speechless. Though shaken, however, he wasn't surprised. Clearly, Sonja hadn't been forgiven for making friends with him. It was Sonja, after all, who had changed his understanding of the world. It was Sonja who had set him on the straight and narrow.

He realized that if he did anything reckless, he would put Sonja at risk. Because Prosper would not hesitate to kill her. He had killed Cadel's mother, after all. So why not Sonja?

Cadel took a deep, steadying breath.

"I hate you," he said evenly. And once again, Prosper smiled.

"Yes, I know," he rejoined. "You mentioned that at our last meeting. Just before I heard you begging the police not to shoot me." Without waiting for a reply, he leaned forward to address Alias. "Is this it? We should be close now."

"We are," said Alias. "It's just around the corner."

"What is?" Cadel demanded, and Prosper said, "We'll be making a switch. You know the procedure." Then he wrinkled his nose. "What's that smell?"

Cadel flushed. "It's Sonja," he revealed. "She can't always—I mean, she has to wear a diaper."

Over in the driver's seat, Alias almost choked on a cough. Prosper's raised eyebrow was visible for an instant in the glow of someone's passing headlights.

"Good god," he said. "Well, there's no accounting for tastes, I suppose."

Then they swerved into a side street.

Cadel was so preoccupied with Sonja that he didn't pay much attention to his immediate surroundings. He was conscious of a narrow lane lined with brick walls and wooden fences. He noticed the fluid shape of a cat darting behind a Dumpster. But by the time Saul's car had rolled into a poky concrete garage, Cadel's attention was focused exclusively on Sonja's face. So he didn't pick up many clues as to the building's exact location.

It was somewhere in Sydney's western suburbs. That was all he knew.

"Out," said Prosper, once Alias had cut the engine. As Cadel opened his mouth to protest, Prosper forestalled him. "Just do it, will you? And I'll take Sonja."

"But—"

"I won't hurt her, Cadel, if that's what you're worried about." Adjusting his grip on Sonja's arching torso, Prosper added, "She's far more likely to hurt *me,* at this rate."

"Did I hear somebody mention diapers?" asked Alias, who had already climbed out of the car. "We don't have any of *them,* you know."

"We'll improvise." Prosper pushed open the door next to him. "Give me a hand here, will you? Cadel, let go of her feet."

With an overhead light now illuminating the car's interior, Cadel had a clear view of Sonja's face. Her wide, staring eyes were straining toward him. Her mouth was working furiously. She began to make piping noises.

"It's all right," he pleaded. "No one's going to hurt you. Ow!" He had relaxed his grip on her slightly and a muscular contraction had driven her knee up into his jaw.

Seeing this, Prosper scowled.

"Get out of the car!" he snapped, before turning to Sonja. "And if you do that again, my dear, I'll cheerfully repay the compliment."

"She can't help it!" Cadel could hardly speak; he was nursing his throbbing chin. "Why don't you listen? If you scare her, she'll only get worse!"

Prosper studied him for a moment, apparently pondering this advice. At last the impenetrable black gaze shifted from Cadel's face to Sonja's, and Prosper began to address her in the tranquil, pleasant tones with which he had so often beguiled his teenaged patients—not to mention the staff and students of the Axis Institute.

"Sonja, let me introduce myself," he said. "I'm Prosper English. You must have heard about me. I'm sorry we have to meet under these circumstances, but I've brought you here to make sure that Cadel doesn't escape, since he wouldn't dream of running away and leaving you." A quizzical smile touched the corner of his mouth. "Now, I'm reliably informed that you're an intelligent girl. So I'm sure you've already deduced that if I were to kill you, it would be defeating the purpose of your abduction. That's why there's really no need for you to panic. All I ask is that you cheer up and calm down. At the moment, you're just worrying Cadel, and we neither of us want to do that, I'm sure."

Something about the slow, silky rhythm of his delivery was having an effect on Sonja. Though still nodding and trembling, she seemed slightly more tranquil. Her brown eyes searched his face, while her tongue butted at the back of her crooked teeth.

Prosper caught her gaze and held it.

"You're very fond of Cadel, aren't you, my dear?" he said, and continued as if he had received an answer. "Well, so am I. That's why he'll be perfectly safe with me. It's also why *you'll* be perfectly safe with me, as long as he's around. Because I don't want to upset him. And if you get hurt, it's going to upset him." A soft chuckle. "God knows, I've upset him enough already. I don't want to make things worse."

Sonja honked then, and he looked to Cadel for a translation. But none was forthcoming.

"I don't know what she said," Cadel confessed miserably. "I can't tell without the DynaVox."

"Well . . . we'll sort that out later," Prosper decided. "Right now, we all have to change our clothes. Cadel can do that first, and then he can help you with your outfit, Sonja. After he's fixed his hair and put on his makeup." Even to Cadel's jaundiced eye, Prosper's sympathetic expression was very persuasive. "You can cope with a short absence, can't you? He'll only be in the next room."

Another honk.

"Blink twice if you agree. Can you do that?" When Sonja blinked twice, Prosper smiled again. "Good. Excellent. I felt sure we'd come to an understanding. Now, see if you can put an arm around my neck, and I promise I won't drop you."

Cadel wanted to warn Sonja that such a promise was worthless—that Prosper simply couldn't be trusted. But a warning of that kind would only serve to frighten her. And if she became frightened, she would start to thrash about.

So Cadel held his tongue. He followed Alias through a door at the rear of the garage into a small kitchen. Here the counters were strewn with open chip bags and used coffee cups. In the living room beyond, dirty dishes shared the pale pink carpet with a sleeping bag, a scattering of newspapers, and a portable television.

It was obvious that someone had been camping in this unfurnished house, which looked like a cheap rental accommodation. Everything in it was grubby and battered, from the tired old light fixtures to the damaged venetian blinds. After giving the place a quick glance, Cadel decided that nothing about it alarmed him.

Then he checked over his shoulder and was relieved to see Prosper edging through the kitchen door, with Sonja writhing away in his arms.

"Come on," said Alias. "Your stuff's over here." He conducted Cadel into the bathroom, which was pink like the carpet (where it wasn't black with mold). There was no shower curtain. The bone-dry bath was full of clothes.

When Cadel saw all the cosmetics and prosthetics laid out on the fake-marble vanity, he recognized many of them from his days at the Axis Institute. The mustache kit, for example. The collection of fake fingernails.

Cadel had always liked Alias. While most of the institute staff had behaved in a way that was both disturbed and disturbing, Alias had been consistently cheerful, supportive, and matter-of-fact. For all his clandestine talents, he'd never quite fitted in. He was simply too pleasant.

"Why are you doing this?" asked Cadel, studying the face that was almost—but not quite—the face of Saul Greeniaus. "Why are you helping Prosper English?"

Alias shrugged. To his credit, he looked slightly embarrassed.

"Money," he replied. "I'm on the run. It's hard to find work."

"Were you the guard who helped him to escape? The guard at the Coroner's Court?" Cadel wanted to know, and Alias nodded.

"I was his lawyer, too. Some of the time." Alias began to paw through the pile of clothes in the bath. "I acted as the go-between, though he did set up a *Reader's Digest* sweepstake code. He'd get some of his information through fake junk mail. Ah." With a flourish, Alias produced a long, filmy skirt and padded bra. "Here you go."

"I'm supposed to be a girl, am I?"

"That's the idea. Just put those on, and I'll do your makeup."

"Whose idea was the junk-mail code?" Cadel inquired, and Alias scratched his neck, grimacing.

"I dunno if I should tell you that. Prosper hasn't given me clearance."

"Was it Vee? Did Vee get into the prison network?" Kicking off his shoes, Cadel continued to pepper Alias with questions. "Did he change the protocols and let you walk out of the Coroner's Court? Did he set up the Genius Squad War Room?"

"Hell no!" Alias seemed quite shocked. "Vee's had nothing to do with Genius Squad. Now, what do you think—should we shave your legs? They're getting a bit shaggy down there, but I've seen worse on many a hippy chick. And they'll be hidden by the skirt." He tapped his chin thoughtfully. "Maybe we'll risk it. You're still pretty enough to carry it off—though I think you should wear a turtleneck. And I might give your mustache a bit of a tweak. Thirty seconds with the tweezers should sort it out."

"Alias." Cadel took a deep breath. "Did Prosper hurt Saul Greeniaus?"

Alias blinked. Then he sighed. Then he pulled a wry face, his expression half sheepish, half impatient. "You know me, kid," he retorted. "If I were a violent man, I wouldn't be a master of disguise, would I? Do you see any blood on this shirt?" He plucked at one pin-striped sleeve. "We used chloroform. We didn't even use a gag. He'll be fine."

"Truly? Please tell me the truth."

"It's the truth, Cadel." Alias was certainly convincing—perhaps because he looked so much like Saul. "We were on a tight schedule, remember? We honestly didn't have time to rough him up."

Cadel nodded. He pulled on his skirt as Alias reached into the bath for a sweater.

"A word in your ear, though," Alias added. "If I were you, I wouldn't keep talking about that cop. He's a bit of a sore point, for some reason." Seeing Cadel's brow crease, he made haste to offer reassurance. "Not that Prosper's a man who'll lose his temper. I'm not saying that. It's just—well, we want him to keep a clear head. We don't want things getting too personal, do we?"

"No," said Cadel. "You're right. We don't."

THIRTY-SEVEN

When Cadel emerged from the bathroom about thirty minutes later, he was sporting a plum-colored rinse in his hair. He was also wearing a pair of pink trainers, a mauve angora sweater, a long black skirt with an elastic waist, and masses of expensive makeup.

At the sight of him, Prosper froze in his tracks.

"What do you think?" said Alias. "Not a bad job, is it?"

There was no immediate reply. Studying Prosper from between mascara-caked, kohl-encircled eyelashes, Cadel was at first confused to see nothing but a blank look. It wasn't until Prosper's gaze slid uneasily away from his own that Cadel realized.

Of course.

"Do I remind you of my mother?" Cadel asked maliciously.

Prosper narrowed his eyes but directed his next remark at Alias.

"You don't think he's too . . . memorable?"

Alias frowned.

"Too much of a stunner, you mean? Not really." He scanned Cadel from top to toe. "If he was taller, perhaps. Or blond. But personally I think he's less noticeable when he's dressed as a girl. There are lots of pretty girls, after all. You just don't see too many boys with features like that."

"Where's Sonja?" said Cadel. He had realized that she wasn't in the living room. "Where have you put her?"

"In there." Prosper waved his hand. "Where the mattress is." Watching Cadel hurry away, he added, "She's under sedation."

Cadel whirled around.

"What?"

"She's sedated. For the trip. It'll be a long one, and I don't want her braining somebody." As Cadel charged out of the room, Prosper raised his voice to insist that there was no need to panic. "Barbiturates won't do her any harm! Not in the correct dosage!"

But Cadel wasn't listening. He had already reached Sonja and had dropped to his knees beside her motionless body. She was sprawled across a soiled, queen-sized mattress, which lay directly on the carpet. Her eyes were closed and her mouth hung open.

She still wore her pajamas.

"Sonja?" said Cadel.

There was no reply.

"Sonja?" When Cadel shook her, she grunted and moved her head. But she didn't wake up.

He checked her pulse and was relieved to find it reassuringly strong.

"She must have been pretty tired," Prosper remarked from the threshold. "She had an empty stomach, too, I daresay. Makes for rapid absorption."

Cadel didn't raise his eyes. He kept them lowered while he stroked Sonja's arm, trying desperately to control his jagged breathing.

"She'll be all right," Prosper continued. He strolled over to where Cadel knelt. "Look at her color. It's perfectly healthy. Look at her fingernails—pink as your shoes." Receiving no answer, he tried again. "What's wrong? Are you sulking?" He bent down, to get a better view of Cadel's expression. "Don't cry, or your mascara will run."

"I'm not crying!" Cadel exclaimed fiercely. And he wasn't. He was enraged. "I'm *sick*, if you want to know! Sick to my stomach! You make me want to *throw up*!"

"Ah." Prosper straightened. "Well, if you could throw up into the toilet before we leave, I'd be grateful. Because I don't want you being sick while we're on the road."

"What road?" Cadel still wouldn't look up. "Where are we going?"

"You'll see."

"Will Judith be there?" Cadel almost hoped that she would be. He almost hoped that she *was* employed by Prosper English. Because she was the only person—besides Cadel himself—who could be trusted to take care of Sonja.

"My dear boy." Prosper tugged playfully at Cadel's ponytail. "You seem to be laboring under a misapprehension. I told you, I hired Dot, not Judith. I had nothing to do with the creation of Genius Squad. It was already up and running by the time Trader approached me—or rather, by the time he approached his old mate Alias and made inquiries about me. I gather Rex Austin asked Trader to sound me out, just in case I had any dirt on GenoME. So Alias passed on the message, and I agreed to supply Rex with information. In exchange for which, of course, I made a few requests of my own." When Cadel lifted his gaze at long last, startled into reacting, Prosper smirked down at him. "I requested that Trader expand his team to include you, Dot, and your crippled friend," Prosper explained. "He wasn't too happy about Sonja, but I couldn't be sure that you'd agree to sign up unless she came with you. We had to provide a little extra motivation—I knew you wouldn't be able to resist living in the same house. And it's not as if she isn't useful, in her own way."

Cadel swallowed. A great weight seemed to settle onto his shoulders, like a heavy iron chain. He suddenly realized that he had been living a life of illusion—that, despite appearances, he had never really escaped from Prosper English.

Prosper's peculiar genius was to create misleading scenarios. Cadel had thought that in joining Genius Squad, he was securing for himself a certain amount of freedom, away from the restrictions imposed by Hazel Donkin and the police.

But he had actually been walking into a trap.

"So—I mean—who else knows about this deal of yours? On the squad?" Cadel stammered. (Had *everyone* been lying?) "Trader and who else?"

"Dot," Prosper replied. "I told you. As it happens, she was in my debt. Because I helped her brother to skip the country."

Cadel's heart sank. "What?" he spluttered, followed by, "When? When did you help him?"

"Oh, before my arrest. When the institute started to collapse." Prosper went on to explain that, although "dispensing with" Com might have expunged a potential witness, it was never a wise policy to throw away really useful and intelligent tools like Com. "Waste not, want not," Prosper said with a smile. "If I'd got rid of Com, I would never have secured Dot's services. Though needless to say, she's not immune to the lure of a big payoff. Not since her stockmarket reverse."

"But I don't understand." Cadel was almost reeling with shock; he couldn't get things straight in his head. "Why would Trader even *want* to break into the GenoME system? Why bother with Genius Squad when *you* were around to dish up all the dirt on Earl Toffany?"

"Because I didn't have much dirt to dish," Prosper admitted. "To be honest, I've never been terribly well informed about Earl's activities. He was always a bit of a problem, was Earl. A bit of a maverick. I used to say as much to Phineas, but he wouldn't listen." Something about Prosper's flattened tone suggested that this hadn't been an unusual state of affairs. "At any rate, keeping tabs on GenoME was difficult. Earl is rather paranoid about me—that's one reason why his security is so tight. He seems to think I'm a *threat*."

As Prosper's lip curled, Cadel felt a chill run down his back like a trickle of cold water. For someone who frequently (and without difficulty) passed himself off as a mild-mannered professor of cultivated habits, Prosper could be remarkably menacing when he let his guard drop.

"So what kind of information *did* you give to Rex, then?" Cadel inquired, and Prosper shrugged.

"Oh, a few choice tidbits. Naturally I spaced them out, so that Trader wouldn't be tempted to renege on our deal." Prosper's sneer became more pronounced. "Let's see. What did I tell him? I told him that Fountain Pharmaceuticals is just NanTex under a different name. I told him about the faulty brain implants—"

"I knew it!" Cadel cried. "I knew Trader never worked that out for himself!"

"I was half afraid he wouldn't believe me," Prosper confessed. "The brain-implant project was a joke. A fiasco. I could hardly believe it myself when I first heard about it." He shook his head in disgust. "Needless to say, it was one of Darkkon's little pet projects. Darkkon's and Chester Cramp's. It had something to do with mind control, but I can't be more specific because they didn't choose to pass on the details. Not to me, at least. No doubt they were anticipating . . . shall we say . . . an unfavorable response from this quarter?" And he laughed.

Cadel frowned. He rubbed his forehead. "So you made a deal with Rex and Trader," he said. "And you hired Dot to keep an eye on me, as a condition of the deal."

"In a nutshell. Yes."

"And they're the only ones who know about it? Trader and Dot and Rex Austin?"

"The only ones."

"But how did you find me in the first place? Was it Trader who told you where I was?"

Prosper's disappointment showed in his exasperated air. "Give me a little credit, Cadel. I've always known where you were," he said. "Since the day you arrived in Australia, I've been monitoring the Department of Community Services. Or Vee has, anyway. He set up the department firewalls, so it wasn't hard for him to get in."

"You mean—"

"Originally, when you were much younger, I had to make sure that your status wasn't being questioned by the authorities. I had to stamp out any fires. Then, when I was arrested . . ." Prosper shrugged. "Let's just say I didn't want to lose track of where the department had put you."

"So you knew about the Donkins? From the very beginning?" Cadel croaked.

"Yes. And I'm sorry I didn't get you away from them sooner." Prosper sounded genuinely apologetic. "There was a communication problem. It was lucky that Trader and Alias had worked together once, or I might never have heard about Rex Austin's plans at all. Because no one on Genius Squad could ever have risked approaching me directly. Not in jail. As I said, it had to be done through Alias."

Cadel wasn't listening. He was thinking about Sonja, and how he had led her straight into a lion's den. Saul, too; by making friends with Saul, Cadel had effectively painted a target on the detective's back. And Gazo . . .

"Gazo's all right, isn't he?" Cadel cried, aghast at his own stupidity and negligence. Thanks to him, Gazo was in serious danger—because Prosper was now free to eliminate anyone who might testify against him. "Gazo's no threat to you. Not now you're out of prison," Cadel insisted breathlessly. "He can't be a witness if you never go on trial!"

Cadel was prepared to defend this position with the full force of his considerable intellect. He owed it to his friend. But he wasn't given the opportunity; Prosper interrupted, sighing and shaking his head in an irritable manner, as if Cadel was being deliberately perverse.

"I've never understood your attachment to that noxious, dim-witted freak," Prosper complained. "Why do you have such a taste for the company of all-around *losers*? First Gazo Kovacs. Then Sonja Pirovic. Then Saul Greeniaus, who strikes me as being sadly deficient in brains."

"He's not!"

"Clever people don't end up hog-tied and shut in storage cupboards," was Prosper's disdainful response. "I honestly despair of you sometimes. Do you really want to spend the rest of your life with people like Hazel Donkin and that ludicrous Currey creature? Or are you *trying* to annoy me, because you've entered your rebellious teenage phase?"

Slightly winded by this accusation, Cadel struggled to comprehend Prosper's outlook—which was so different from his own. The contrast between their views of the world was stark enough to make Cadel dizzy, as if he were trying to peer through somebody else's prescription glasses.

How could such a bright man have such a blinkered attitude?

"I like to think that underneath all this silly acting-out, you fully grasp your situation," Prosper went on. "You're not stupid—you must see that I'm the only one who can offer you any kind of life. What can you look forward to otherwise? More foster homes? Extradition to my cousin's pig farm? A dreary existence spent looking after all the rejects you've managed to collect along the way?" Before Cadel could protest, Prosper hammered home his argument, point by point. "What makes you think I'll *allow* you to waste your talents? You know perfectly well that you're a shining star. I'm not about to let you hide your light under a bushel."

Deeply discouraged, Cadel gazed up into Prosper's clever, confident face. It looked implacable. But Cadel remembered when he himself had believed what Prosper believed. Surely there had to be some small chance of convincing Prosper that his reasoning was flawed? That it didn't take certain things into account?

"You don't understand," Cadel began. "I know you want the best for me, but you don't understand how I feel—"

"Of course I do." Prosper wouldn't let him finish. "I realize you must have felt abandoned over the past few months. It was unfortunate, and I'm sorry. Though, if it hadn't been for *your* actions, I would never have been locked up in the first place." His lips twisted into a reluctant smile. "But that's all water under the bridge for me. And for you, too, I hope. My point is that I never lost sight of you, or stopped working to improve your situation. I've been watching your back, Cadel." Suddenly his smile turned wolfish. "Do you think that your friend Mace would have received his just deserts if it hadn't been for me?" he said.

Cadel gasped.

"Come now," Prosper chided, as Cadel struggled to draw breath, "surely you must have worked *that* out?"

"How—how—"

"My dear boy, I can't tell you how many complaints have been lodged against that deplorable child, by various parties—your social worker, for one. It was in the system: Vee found out what Mace had been doing, then passed it on to Alias, who passed it on to me. So when I happened to encounter your antagonist's brother in the prison exercise yard, I struck up an acquaintance." Prosper shook his head, as if the sheer depths of human ignorance continued to sadden and astonish him. "*What* a fool. He was actually under the impression that *you* had been tormenting *Mace*—what with the magazine incident and so forth."

Prosper went on to explain, with a glint of cold malice in his hooded eyes, that Mace's brother had sought advice as to how Mace might engineer his revenge against Cadel. Whereupon Prosper had suggested "planting evidence," in the sure and certain knowledge that Mace would be caught by the police surveillance team if such a ploy was ever attempted.

"I even proposed encouraging that other kid—the little one—to ask for your address," Prosper smugly revealed. Then his smile faded suddenly; his expression became serious. "Because I've always looked after you, Cadel, and I always shall," he concluded. "I'm your father. You have to come to terms with that. You have to understand what it means."

There followed a long pause, during which Cadel had to wrestle with his conscience. Prosper was so *persuasive.* So self-assured and articulate. So proud of his only son.

Defying him seemed not only ungrateful, but oddly churlish. Especially for someone like Cadel, whose life had never been exactly well stocked with doting family or friends. In holding fast to new loyalties—in choosing to trust Sonja and Saul—he had to pull against a strong, dark undertow of attachment.

He had to fight against his own heart.

"Prosper?" It was Alias who finally broke the silence—or at least, it was Alias's voice. But the figure standing in the doorway didn't look like Alias at all. When Cadel turned, he saw only a fat, middle-aged woman with lots of graying hair, and egg stains on her cardigan.

The transformation was so complete that Cadel peered past her as he tried to locate Alias. Then she spoke again, and he realized who she was.

"What do you think?" said Alias. "Best I can do, at short notice."

"Very impressive," was Prosper's opinion. "In fact, you're making my skin crawl."

"Your own stuff's laid out," Alias declared. "But you'll probably need my help with it." He cast a troubled glance at Cadel. "Unless you don't want him here on his own. Only, I'm not sure we'll all fit in the bathroom . . ."

"Don't worry about Cadel," said Prosper, with absolute certainty. "Cadel wouldn't leave his little friend in *my* tender care—would you, dear boy? And he knows that he wouldn't get far if he tried to take her along." Without waiting for a response, Prosper began to exit the room, tossing suggestions to Cadel over his shoulder as he did so. Why not indulge in a short nap? Or watch a little TV? Prosper would be busy for a few minutes, but when he had finished disguising himself, they would all be ready to hit the road.

"I'm sorry I can't offer you a laptop," he added. "I'm afraid I wouldn't trust you with a computer just now. But rest assured that when you finally come to your senses, Cadel, you shall have all the technology you need. In fact, I'll build you your *very own* War Room, if that will make you happy."

Then he disappeared, taking Alias with him. And Cadel found himself in a wholly unsupervised state, free to walk out of the house if he so desired.

Except, of course, that he wasn't free. Not as long as Sonja needed his help. Not as long as he continued to play what was undoubtedly an important role in Prosper's plans for the future (whatever they might be). All his life, Cadel had been shackled by one restraint after another: high expectations; constant surveillance; his own reputation for mischief; even the carefully constructed destiny imposed on him by manipulative men with warped morals. Never once had he felt unsupervised, even when he was completely alone. Never once had he viewed his existence as anything but a locked room with bolted windows.

I'll never escape, he thought. *How can I, when Prosper's in my blood?* This awful insight made him want to scream aloud with fury and frustration. To pound his fists on the floor.

Before he could vent his feelings, however, his gaze fell on Sonja's wasted physique. And for perhaps the fiftieth time, he reminded himself that compared to his best friend, he was as free as a mountain eagle.

THIRTY-EIGHT

Cadel was familiar with the tactic of switching cars. It was a ruse much favored by Prosper, who had often used it to good effect. Cadel himself had once taken part in an elaborate escape from a police headquarters, involving several changes of vehicle. On that occasion, however, there had been no garment-switching. No one had changed so much as a pair of socks in order to avoid detection.

This time, it seemed that Prosper was leaving nothing to chance. The four people who emerged from his secret safe house at around three o'clock on Tuesday morning bore very little resemblance to the four people who had arrived some two hours earlier. Cadel had been transformed into an auburn-haired young girl. Alias had assumed the appearance of a blowsy, overweight housewife. As for Prosper English, he was no longer an imperfect replica of Zac Stillman. Instead he was pretending to be a harmless old grandpa, with white hair and a white goatee, broken veins across his cheeks and nose, lousy teeth, bifocals, a bad stoop, and a shabby tweed jacket.

Only Sonja remained unchanged. According to Alias, there was very little point in trying to disguise her. "You can't pass her off as anything but a spastic," was how he bluntly put it (much to Cadel's disgust), before adding, "On the plus side, though, people often can't tell the difference between one spastic and another. So we might just pull this off. Because the police will be looking for a cripple with three men, and she'll be a cripple with one man and two women."

Prosper sniffed. "I very much hope that by the time the police start looking for *anyone,* she'll be a cripple safely tucked away out of the public eye," he said. But in case he was being unduly optimistic, he decided to put her on the floor of their getaway car and cover her with a sleeping bag.

"You can't do that!" Cadel protested. Even Alias pointed out that if the police should stop them, a concealed body was bound to look suspicious. "The trick is to make everything seem totally aboveboard," he said. "That's why I didn't choose a van. Coppers don't like vans because they can't see what's going on inside."

His plan, he explained, was that everyone in the getaway car should give the impression of being part of a family. And no normal family would hide one of its members under a sleeping bag. Regardless of how deformed she might be.

But Prosper wouldn't be persuaded.

"She's drugged," he said. "It's obvious. Besides, I'm not sitting around while the police search this car. If they get close enough to see Sonja, they'll also be close enough to talk to Cadel. And I don't suppose *he'll* keep his mouth shut." Placing a long, bony hand on the back of Cadel's neck, Prosper outlined his strategy. "The purpose of using these disguises is to discourage the police from pulling us over in the first place. We have to make sure that we *don't attract attention.* Which means staying under the speed limit. And wearing our seat belts. And behaving"—he smirked—"like a family on a road trip."

Cadel wondered sourly what someone like Prosper could possibly know about families on road trips, but said nothing. After everyone except Sonja had paid a final visit to the bathroom, the whole team bundled into a blue four-wheel drive that was parked at the rear of the house, concealed from public view by a tall fence. Cadel was instructed to sit beside Sonja's swaddled form, in the back of the car, and pretend to be asleep. He was also told to keep his mouth shut.

Then Prosper (who was in the driver's seat) engaged the safety locks.

"We don't want you jumping out and hurting yourself," he remarked. "Nor do we want you signaling for help. That's why you should put this up." And he passed Cadel a shirt on a hanger, to suspend from the handle above the window next to him. "It'll give you a little privacy."

"I think *I* should be on the nod, too," Alias suggested, from the seat beside Prosper's. "It would look more realistic at this hour of the morning." In a slightly anxious tone, he observed that a car full of party animals would have been even more realistic, and possibly a better disguise. Only he'd been worried about the effect it might have on any passing police officers.

Prosper assured him that the right choice had been made. "Your execution has been flawless," said Prosper, as he turned the key in the ignition. "So—are we ready now? Have we put out the garbage? Locked all the doors? Fed the fish?" He grinned mischievously. "Yes? Good. Off we go, then."

And off they went. Before long they had traversed the surrounding labyrinth of suburban streets and were cruising down a freeway, heading west, toward the mountains. Cadel was mystified by this tactic. He had expected that Prosper would attempt to flee the country in some kind of seagoing vessel. By traveling inland, they were not only abandoning the coast and all its possibilities, but were leaving behind them almost every international airport in Australia.

Unless they were making for Perth? Or Adelaide?

"Where are we going?" Cadel queried.

"You'll see," Prosper replied.

"To the mountains?" said Cadel.

"You'll see."

"Is Dot going to be there?"

Prosper sighed impatiently, as if he were being importuned by a fretful toddler wanting ice cream.

"You asked me that question before," he said. "I was astonished to hear it then, and I'm doubly astonished now. I can only assume that you're tired." He glanced into the rearview mirror. "What do *you* think, Cadel? Do you think Dot is going to be there?"

Cadel pondered this inquiry, which had been delivered in a very patronizing tone. "I think she'd be stupid if she was," he said at last. "If she disappears now, the police are bound to suspect her. But if she stays put and pretends to know nothing about you . . . well, she might just get away with it."

"She might," Prosper agreed, without taking his eyes off the road.

"I guess that's what Trader will do, too." Cadel was thinking aloud. "I guess he'll pretend you took him by surprise. It might even work, if nobody finds out about the War Room."

"My dear boy, why should anyone find out about that?" Prosper seemed to be enjoying Cadel's step-by-step display of logical analysis. "After all, nobody's actually looking for it."

"The trouble is, Saul will wonder how you tracked me down," Cadel continued. "He'll be suspicious of everyone who knew where I was. He'll be asking a lot of questions." A vivid mental image of Saul's face suddenly assailed him like a blow, so that he flinched, and shut his eyes briefly. The pictured face wore a grimly determined expression. "You shouldn't underestimate Saul," he added. "I know him. You don't. You're basing your conclusions on incomplete data."

"No, dear boy, that's what *you're* doing," Prosper declared. He then proceeded to explain that, when they came to investigate how he had walked unopposed out of a holding cell, the police would discover certain carefully placed clues. "They'll realize that the same hacker who broke into the computer system of the Department of Corrective Services *also* broke into another database containing your DoCS case file," he related. "Which, of course, happens to include all your contact details. And since the hacker in question doesn't have anything to do with Genius Squad . . ." He shrugged. "Well, let's just say I've illumined one particular line of inquiry. While the road to Clearview House remains shrouded in darkness."

"Vee was the hacker, wasn't he?" Cadel demanded. "Vee's still around."

"As far as I know, Dr. Vee is somewhere in the northern hemisphere," was Prosper's oblique response.

"Yes, but that doesn't mean anything. Not if he's got a modem." Cadel leaned forward, grabbing at Prosper's headrest. "Who else is still around? What happened to Dr. Deal? I know he escaped from prison the day you were arrested—did *you* organize that? Do you have him stashed somewhere?" Another, even more staggering thought occurred to Cadel. "Did Luther Lasco *really* die in that explosion? Or did you manage to save him?"

Over in the front passenger seat, Alias snorted. "Jesus," he said, without opening his eyes. Prosper sucked in his breath, before letting it out again very slowly. When at last he spoke, his voice trembled with suppressed amusement.

"I'm pleased to know that you've retained enough respect for your poor old dad to credit him with an almost *superhuman* level of ingenuity," he drawled. "Makes me feel a lot better about the way I brought you up."

"But—"

"Go to sleep, Cadel. You're overtired. You're losing it." Prosper reached back and squeezed Cadel's hand, which was still gripping the driver's headrest. "I'll wake you when we get there."

"Get *where*?" asked Cadel.

"You'll see when we arrive," said Prosper.

But Cadel soon realized that they wouldn't be arriving anywhere in a hurry. They drove and drove, along a freeway dotted with gigantic road trains. They drove past Blacktown, through the outskirts of Sydney, and over the Nepean River. They were in the lower reaches of the Blue Mountains when Cadel finally fell asleep, lulled into a restless doze by a very dull, late-night radio discussion about fishing quotas.

He woke more than an hour later, bleary and confused, as they hit a pothole. Around him, dawn had begun to creep across towering crags and rolling, bushy slopes. He couldn't believe his eyes.

"What—how—where are we?" he mumbled.

"Ah." Prosper was still driving. "You're awake, at last."

"We're in the country!"

"A brilliant deduction."

"I need a drink." Squinting down at Sonja's pale face, just visible above the folds of the sleeping bag, he saw that her mouth and jaw muscles were starting to quiver. "Sonja needs to get out of here."

"Not long now," Prosper said, and turned to Alias. "Are you sure this is the road?"

"Positive," Alias replied.

"Bit rough, isn't it?"

"That's the whole point," said Alias. "It's a weekender. A track like this keeps people away. So no one'll rob the place."

Prosper sighed. "I just hope there's an inside toilet," he remarked, sounding unimpressed, and Alias stared at him in amazement.

"Are you kidding?" said Alias. "There's a bloody *spa bath*!"

By this time Cadel's head had cleared, somewhat—and he realized, with a sinking heart, that he had no idea where they were. Peering out from behind the shirt that flapped and swayed on its hanger as they bumped along, he could see only thick, scrubby forest beside the road. Sometimes there would be a flash of smoke-blue ridge beyond a smudge of distant grassland. But, for the most part, his view was of tumbling rocks and twisted white tree trunks.

"Left up ahead," said Alias, whereupon the car slowed. Craning his neck, Cadel spied a mailbox. It marked the beginning of a precipitous track that plunged headfirst into the nearest gully.

"Jesus Christ," said Prosper.

"It's better than it looks," Alias assured him.

"Why would anyone in their right mind want to spend a weekend out here?" Prosper demanded, and Alias shrugged.

"I don't know. Trout-fishing, perhaps."

"Do they have winged trout in this neck of the woods?" Prosper grimaced, nosing his way down the track toward a half-concealed roof that appeared to be positioned directly underneath them. "We'll have to rappel in a minute!"

"Bird-watching, then." Alias pointed. "See that? It's the garage. You can hide the car in there."

Cadel had already noticed a power line, which had been strung perilously between clawing branches and across rocky clefts. It was attached to the eaves of what looked like a superior kind of a cedar cabin. As Prosper rolled to a standstill, Cadel ran a calculating eye over the building's woodpile, chimney, and outside fuse-box, all dimly visible in the murky light. A security sticker had been placed in one of the windows, warning that the house was equipped with a monitored alarm system.

"Hang on," said Alias, and jumped out of the car to push open the garage doors. Prosper then eased their vehicle into the space beyond, which was dim and generously proportioned.

Cadel unbuckled his seat belt.

"No silly tricks, now," Prosper warned, watching him in the rearview mirror. "Sonja's not really portable for someone your size. You wouldn't want to be dragging her through the bush in some fruitless attempt to escape."

"I know," said Cadel.

"Don't try to lift her. You'll only hurt yourself." Having satisfied himself that Cadel was making no move to disobey, Prosper slipped from behind the steering wheel, raising his voice to address Alias. "Where's Vadi's car?"

"I'm not sure," Alias replied, pitching his own voice very low. "It should be here."

"What if the alarm's on? Can you actually get inside this place?"

"Oh, yeah." Alias nodded. "Trader gave me his code."

"*Trader?*" gasped Cadel. "This is *Trader's* house?" He would have said more if Sonja hadn't groaned suddenly. Concern for her well-being drove every other thought straight out of his head; he had to be dragged from his seat.

"Wait! Stop! She's waking up!" he protested, but to no avail. Prosper kept a firm grip on his arm, and Cadel soon found himself being nudged toward Alias—who was still stationed at the garage door, all drooping hems and sagging bulges.

"I'll bring Sonja," Prosper said firmly. "Cadel, you get into the house."

"But—"

"Don't annoy me, please. It's been a long night." Prosper then gave Alias *his* instructions, clearly and crisply. "Don't let this child out of your sight for one instant," he advised. "And don't let him near any phones. Is there a computer in the house?"

"Uh—yes—"

"Don't let him anywhere near that, either." Prosper pinched Cadel's earlobe. "I've already paid a very high price for underestimating my son. Rest assured, I won't be doing it again."

Cadel wanted to hang back and satisfy himself that Sonja was being properly treated. But he wasn't given the chance. Alias immediately hustled him across a brick walkway toward the cabin's main entrance, where Cadel committed to memory the key code that Alias punched into the alarm panel. Being a six-digit code, it occupied Alias for just long enough to give Cadel time for a quick look at the system's fire-alarm component—which remained operative after the burglar alarm had been turned off.

He filed this fact away in his head, for future reference.

"*Hello? Vadi? Are you here?*" Alias called, upon entering the house. There was no reply. Cadel glimpsed a pair of grubby women's sandals lying in the entrance hall, but was quickly guided past them into a lofty and spacious living room, containing—among other things—a cathedral ceiling, a slow-combustion stove, and a whole wall of windows.

The rose-tinted view from these windows was spectacular.

"Nice, isn't it?" Alias flicked on some halogen lights. "I like the built-in couch, especially."

"This isn't Trader's." Cadel had observed a pile of well-thumbed financial reports on the coffee table. Together with the dirty old sandals—and a framed newspaper article about corporate fraud—they told him all that he needed to know. "This house belongs to Judith Bashford, doesn't it?" he said. "Trader managed to get the alarm code off her, somehow."

Alias smiled and shook his head in amazement.

"You're really something else," he remarked.

"She doesn't know that you're here, though. Does she?"

"Look!" said Alias, attempting to change the subject. "There's a wide-screen TV! Do you want to watch it?"

"I think he'd be better off taking a nap," Prosper submitted, from behind them. But Cadel didn't turn around. He had just seen something that interested him far more than Prosper's whereabouts.

On a shelf beneath the TV, directly beside the DVD player, sat a video-game console.

THIRTY-NINE

Cadel had never been much interested in computer games. They had always seemed to him rather restrictive and futile; he preferred to manipulate reality, not a computer-generated facsimile of the world.

Nevertheless, he was by now fully acquainted with every characteristic of every console in the known universe, thanks to Hamish. In Hamish's opinion, there were few topics as interesting as the relative merits of Sony, Microsoft, and Apple gaming products; he had lectured Cadel on the subject more than once, over breakfast. So Cadel was able to tell, literally at a glance, that the console beneath the television had online gaming capability. In other words, it could be connected to the Internet.

The question was: Had Judith availed herself of this feature?

"What about diapers?" he demanded, wrenching his gaze from the console and fixing it on Prosper's flushed face. "Sonja needs diapers."

Knowing that this remark would irritate Prosper, Cadel had used it to distract him. Because the last thing Cadel wanted was to advertise his keen interest in Judith's console. If he did, someone might realize how important it was.

If he didn't, on the other hand, he might get lucky.

Cadel knew that people of Prosper's generation weren't accustomed to regarding computer games as portals to the Internet. To such people, the world was a place where each piece of technology had a single, defined function: where phones and computers were communication devices, while gaming consoles were for pitting yourself against the machine in front of you. There was a good chance that Prosper had never heard of multiplayer gaming—that he might view the console as essentially harmless.

But his suspicions would be aroused if Cadel demonstrated more interest in the console than in Sonja's well-being. So Cadel began to fret about diapers. He was convinced that such fretting would annoy Prosper, who would see it as a sign of weakness. And if Prosper became annoyed, he was less likely to concentrate on the bits of equipment scattered throughout the house.

Sure enough, Prosper's flush deepened.

"First things first," he said through his teeth, adjusting his grip on Sonja—who was beginning to grow restless. "Where are the bedrooms? Through there?"

"Through there," Alias agreed. "The main's got a bathroom off it."

"Wait a minute." Cadel was thinking furiously. "Couldn't we just put her in here? I mean, we *are* going to give her some breakfast, aren't we? And let her watch television? It's bad enough that she doesn't have her DynaVox."

"Fine," Prosper snapped. He crossed the room in three long strides and dropped his burden onto the sofa. "Now, where are all the phones?"

"There's one in the kitchen," said Alias, "and one in the study, and one in the main bedroom."

"Go and get them," Prosper ordered. "Every phone and every modem. Now."

Obediently, Alias scurried off. Meanwhile Cadel had crouched beside Sonja, who was restless but not fully awake. Her eyes were half closed and didn't focus properly when Cadel murmured in her ear.

"Sonja? Can you hear me? It's all right. Don't worry—I'm with you." He looked up. "How much of that drug did you give her?"

"She'll be fine," said Prosper—and stiffened suddenly, lifting his chin.

Then Cadel heard it. The purr of a distant engine.

"Damn," Prosper breathed, grabbing Cadel's arm. Caught in a grip like a tourniquet, Cadel was hauled upright and out of the living room almost before he knew what was happening. He nearly tripped on the hem of his skirt.

"Wait!" he gasped. "Sonja—"

"Shh!" Prosper had once again produced his handgun. He dragged Cadel over to a small window near the main entrance of the house, from which vantage point they both had a clear view of the almost perpendicular driveway.

The noise of the engine was growing louder.

"Prosper?" Alias called, from somewhere out of sight. *"Is that Vadi?"*

"I don't know!" Prosper replied, disengaging the safety catch on his gun. It was clear that if the driver of the approaching vehicle wasn't Vadi, he or she was in grave danger of being shot.

This thought had barely crossed Cadel's mind when a familiar green hatchback bounced into view.

"Oh no!" he gasped—having recognized Judith's car. Before he could scream a warning, however, two unexpected things happened. He heard Prosper reengaging the pistol's safety catch, and he saw who was driving the green hatchback.

Not Judith, that was for certain.

"It's Vadi!" Prosper loudly informed Alias, and moved toward the front door. Cadel was compelled to stumble after him.

"You—you stole Judith's car?" Cadel stammered, astonished that anyone could be so stupid. A stolen car would be reported, after all. A stolen car was bound to attract attention.

But Prosper clicked his tongue.

"For goodness sake," he said, sliding his gun into his coat pocket and pulling open the front door, "do you think I'm a fool? Of course it isn't Judith's."

"The plate number—"

"Is a forgery. So is the car. And not a bad effort, either." Prosper addressed the man who was climbing out of the hatchback. "Good job, Vadi. Well done. Any trouble?"

Vadi shook his head. He was slim and young, with dark, oily skin and sleek black hair. At first glance he seemed to be quite normal; it was only after a few moments that his webbed hands, pinched nostrils, and slightly odd blink became evident to the casual onlooker.

Cadel, who had always found Vadi's presence deeply disturbing, refused to acknowledge it with a nod or a glance, staring down at the floor instead.

"Sorry I'm late." Vadi's delivery was soft and thick. "The plates weren't ready on time."

"Come in." Prosper stepped back, his bony fingers still fastened around Cadel's wrist. "You remember my son, don't you?"

"Of course."

"You'll be pleased to know that the car fooled him," Prosper announced, "so we've cleared our first hurdle. Now for the second." Releasing Cadel, he strode toward the living room. "Just keep an eye on things here, will you? I won't be a minute. Alias needs help." Disappearing around a corner, he added, "Find my son something to eat."

There followed a brief silence, during which Prosper's retreating footsteps seemed very loud. Then Vadi—who had quietly closed the front door—said, "What would you like to eat, sir?"

Cadel's heart skipped a beat. He couldn't help glancing up, convinced that Vadi was taunting him with that suavely respectful "sir." But the smooth, dusky face displayed not a trace of animosity. It was expressionless.

Cadel swallowed. Confronted by Vadi, of all people, he found himself unable to speak. Vadi's unchanged appearance brought back a host of bad memories, because Vadi had once been employed as Prosper's servant, in a house that sat high on a cliff above the sea. All kinds of traumatic things had occurred in that house. It was where Prosper had first acknowledged that Cadel was his son. It was where Prosper had confessed to murdering Cadel's mother. And it was where Prosper had first put a gun to Cadel's head, threatening to shoot him.

Vadi, moreover, was aquagenic—a genetic mutant. Beneath the high neck of his sweater, a rudimentary set of gills was concealed. And though he didn't smell fishy, or leave slimy marks on surfaces, something about him had always made Cadel's skin crawl.

It was an instinctive reaction to adulterated humanity.

"Have you had breakfast?" Vadi inquired, after failing to elicit any kind of response with his first question. "No? Then I'll make some for you. Toast, perhaps? An omelette? No mushrooms, as I recall."

"I don't want you touching my food!" Cadel blurted out. "And I don't want you touching Sonja!"

Vadi blinked, in a manner suggesting that he had more than his fair share of eyelids. Backing away, Cadel braced himself. But Vadi simply inclined his head.

"There are Pop-Tarts," he went on. "And cornflakes. I checked the supplies when I was here earlier."

"I'm not hungry," said Cadel. He turned on his heel and marched back into the living room, casting a furtive glance at the console as he did so. Yes: There was an Internet cable. The machine was set up for multiplayer gaming.

In which case, it would also have a messaging facility.

Kneeling beside Sonja, Cadel furiously reviewed his options. He knew that they weren't extensive—that the console's Internet connection would only allow him to communicate with other players, unless various time-consuming adjustments were made to its programs. And how would he ever persuade some anonymous, Californian gaming geek to make contact with Saul Greeniaus? How could a message even be *dispatched,* if Cadel was kept under surveillance?

"Right," said Prosper, upon reentering the room. He was carrying an armful of telephone handsets, and a sprinkling of modems. "I'm going to lock these in the garage," he announced, smirking at Cadel. "It wouldn't be fair, leaving them around to tempt you."

"What about diapers?" Cadel retorted. He had been rapidly reviewing every aspect of his current predicament and trying to project possible outcomes. "We're going to need diapers."

Prosper's eyebrows snapped together.

"For god's sake—," he began.

"We need them! For Sonja!" Squeezing her hand, Cadel added, "How far do you think we'll get without them? She doesn't have much control, you know! Over *anything*!"

Prosper hesitated, chewing his bottom lip. Vadi said, somewhat obscurely, "There's nothing on the way there."

"Nothing?" Prosper frowned. "No pharmacy? Not even a gas station?"

Vadi shook his head.

"Where *are* the nearest shops?" Prosper inquired—then rephrased the question when Vadi cast a sidelong, speculative glance at Cadel. "I mean, how long would it take?"

Vadi shrugged. "Maybe . . . thirty minutes. Each way." As Prosper checked his watch, Vadi proceeded to offer advice, choosing his words with great care. "It could be done. There's no point leaving here for another ninety minutes, at least. The . . . ah . . . facilities won't be available."

"Are you sure about that?"

"Oh, yes. I couldn't get an earlier booking."

"Pity," said Prosper. He wore a sour kind of look, as if he'd bitten into a lemon. After a moment's consideration, he nodded at Vadi. "Okay. Do it. Take the four-wheel drive—there's a gun in the glove box. And make sure you're only carrying cash. No ID, just in case."

Vadi seemed to accept this ruling. He immediately started to empty his pockets, which yielded up a wallet, a bunch of keys, a cell phone, a Chap Stick, a pair of sunglasses, and an electronic organizer in a case—all of which he deposited on a nearby side table. "Can I keep this?" he asked, picking up the cell phone.

If there was a reply, Cadel missed it. A rush of adrenaline had temporarily affected his hearing; by concentrating fiercely on Sonja's face, he hoped to exert some control over his rapidly escalating heartbeat. *Please,* he thought, *please, please, please don't get antsy.* He was afraid that an anxious blush might color his cheeks and give him away.

"Hmmm," said Prosper, peering suspiciously at the electronic organizer now sitting on the side table.

Vadi hastened to reassure him.

"That's an old PalmPilot. It has no wireless connection."

"Then what do you need it for?" Prosper wanted to know. And Vadi became slightly defensive.

"Scheduling," he replied. "Contact details."

"That's what brains are for, aren't they?" said Prosper, with ironic emphasis. "Data dumps are an awful *risk,* Vadi. Very insecure."

"Which is why there is no wireless connection." Vadi's response was bland. Uninflected. "I'm not smart like you, sir. My brain isn't big enough for all the instructions you give me."

The two men surveyed each other for a moment, as Cadel watched them, holding his breath. Then Prosper abruptly off-loaded his collection of equipment, piling it into Vadi's arms.

"You can take these," he ordered. "Put them in the garage. That cell phone isn't yours, I presume?"

"No," said Vadi.

"Nothing on it to worry about? You haven't entered any numbers, or names?"

"I picked it up this morning," Vadi replied, sounding faintly self-conscious. At which point Cadel realized that the cell phone had, in fact, been stolen.

"All right." Prosper seemed to approve. "You'd better take it along, then, but don't use it unless there's an emergency. What's the number, in case I have to call you?"

"Uh . . ." Vadi jerked his chin at the organizer. "I put it in there. I'm not good at remembering."

"Never mind. Cadel can get it if I need it." Prosper began to guide Vadi toward the front door. "The keys to the four-wheel drive are in the ignition. Off you go, and get a good supply of incontinence products for our *guest.*" Prosper's sarcastic pronunciation of the word "guest" made Cadel want to hit him. "No dawdling. But no speeding, either. Is that understood?"

Vadi nodded. "What else should I buy?" he asked, and Prosper paused, turning to Cadel.

"Anything else she might need, dear boy? Baby food, perhaps? A teething ring?"

It was such a cheap shot that it enraged Cadel, who narrowed his eyes. "I hope you end up in a wheelchair one day," he answered unsteadily, "so I can laugh at *you.*"

"Oh, I'm not laughing. In case you haven't noticed, I'm *extremely* annoyed." Prosper's tone was suddenly ice-cold. "Now answer me. Is she going to need anything else?"

"A comb. A toothbrush—"

"Apart from the obvious."

Cadel toyed with the notion of asking for a sippy cup, which would certainly make everyone's life easier. But after that snide remark about teething rings, he simply couldn't do it. So he said, "No."

"Good." Once again, Prosper addressed himself to Vadi. "I'd send Alias, if I could, but he's busy with his disguise. And I don't want him wandering about the local shops when he's all kitted out, in case . . . well, in case he's recognized. So to speak."

Vadi nodded. "I understand."

"Just do your best and keep a low profile. You must have heard Alias on the subject often enough." As Vadi made for the door, Prosper darted ahead to open it for him. "I'm sorry about this," Prosper observed, as the overburdened Vadi edged past, "but I'm afraid it's unavoidable. Bad smells will always attract unwelcome attention."

With a grimace, Vadi acknowledged the truth of this remark. Then he left. Prosper didn't wait on the threshold to monitor his movements, but shut the door and returned to the living room, where he took up a position near the sofa.

"Now," he said, "since I've been deprived of all my staff, temporarily, I suppose the ball's in my court as far as housekeeping goes. So tell me, Cadel: What would you like for breakfast?"

"Pop-Tarts," said Cadel, who had been running feverish calculations in his head. And he looked up at Prosper with wide, blue, innocent eyes.

FORTY

Upon entering the kitchen, Cadel took careful note of where the toaster, blinds, and smoke detector were situated.

He was pleased with what he saw.

"My word," Prosper remarked, gazing around at all the stainless-steel appliances and expanses of granite countertop, "no expense spared, I see."

"Vadi said there were eggs." Cadel opened the fridge. "I could scramble a few for Sonja."

"My dear boy, are you mad? I wouldn't let you anywhere *near* a pan full of hot eggs! Might as well give you a deep-fat fryer and have done with it." Prosper sounded amused. "I'll cook the breakfast. You can take care of your Pop-Tarts—whatever they might require. Nothing that involves an exposed flame, I trust?"

"You stick 'em in a toaster," Cadel replied. He had relinquished the fridge to Prosper, and had moved to the pantry cupboard—where an unopened box of Pop-Tarts was sitting on the bottom shelf. They were cherry-flavored.

He didn't much like cherry-flavored food of any description, but that didn't matter. Under the circumstances, he resolved to force down as much as he could.

"Let's see." Prosper reached into the fridge. "Milk. Butter. Bacon. Eggs."

"I'll get the frying pan," Cadel offered.

"You'll do nothing of the sort." Prosper's whiplash response made Cadel start. "You'll stay away from anything remotely resembling a kitchen utensil—I don't care what it is. Just stand there. Right there. And don't move."

Cadel froze, still clutching the packet of Pop-Tarts. He waited while Prosper produced from various kitchen drawers a spatula, a mixing bowl, a frying pan, and a whisk. At no point during this process did Prosper lose sight of Cadel for more than two or three seconds at a stretch.

"I promise I won't stick a paper towel in the toaster," Cadel said at last, sarcastically. And Prosper smiled.

"No chance of that, dear boy," he declared, cracking eggs with a breezy confidence. "I've got my eye on you."

"So what about my Pop-Tarts? Can't I heat them up? Will I have to eat them cold?" Cadel rattled the box under Prosper's nose. "They *are* meant to go in the toaster, see? It says so right here."

Prosper set down his last broken eggshell. Then he took the box and scanned the instructions printed on its back. "How many do you want?" he queried, ripping it open.

"Uh . . . two?" Cadel suggested.

"Two it is." Having crossed to the expanse of gleaming counter that separated the sink from the stove, Prosper deposited two Pop-Tarts into the four-slice toaster and pressed down the switch. He left the box on the counter before returning to his mixing bowl. "There are plates in that cupboard," he said. "Get out three. But no funny business—I didn't get much sleep last night."

Cadel refrained from commenting. As he retrieved three plates from a low shelf, Prosper studied him, adding milk to the eggs. "You're very quiet," Prosper finally observed. "Isn't there anything you want to ask?"

Cadel carefully laid three white plates beside the toaster. "Will you tell me where we're going?" he said when he'd finished.

"No."

"Well, then." Cadel shrugged. "Not much to talk about, is there?"

"Don't you want to talk about Niobe?" Seeing Cadel stiffen, Prosper gave a wicked grin. "Yes," he said, energetically whisking. "I thought you might be wondering about her."

Cadel swallowed. "You haven't—?"

"No. I have not." Prosper dumped his egg mixture into the pan. "Yet."

"It wasn't your idea, then? That whole—assassination attempt?"

"Oddly enough, it wasn't. Though of course I took full advantage of it." Prosper was awkwardly placed. Because of the way the stove was positioned, he couldn't scramble his eggs in comfort if he wanted to watch Cadel at the same time. Doing both meant facing away from the pan, and cutting quick glances back at it occasionally. "We didn't have much notice, what with one thing and another, but I think we did very well. Considering all the time constraints."

"What about Niobe?" Cadel demanded, though not because he cared. He was trying to engage Prosper's attention while he himself absent-mindedly picked up the box of Pop-Tarts. "Where is she now?"

"That I can't tell you."

"Can't or won't?"

"Can't. At this stage."

"She did you a favor," Cadel opined, easing more Pop-Tarts out of the box. After removing one from its plastic packet, he began to fiddle with it in a distracted kind of way, squeezing it, twirling it, tossing it from hand to hand. All the while, he didn't take his eyes off Prosper. "If she hadn't killed that guard, there would never have been a hearing at the Coroner's Court. And you would never have escaped."

"Of course I would have escaped. Do you think I'm a fool? There would have been other opportunities. I had several irons in the fire; if I hadn't, I never would have been *able* to take advantage of that fortuitous visit to the Coroner's Court." Prosper frowned suddenly. "For god's sake, will you stop playing with the food? It's very ill-bred. Not to say irritating."

Cadel put down the Pop-Tart with some deliberation, noting as he did so that the nearby electric kettle was full of water.

Good, he thought.

"Bring me two of those plates," said Prosper. "Put them right here. That's it. Will your little friend be having bacon?"

"No." Cadel cleared his throat. "She's not very good at chewing meat."

"Ah."

"She can have toast, though. If it's cut up into pieces and has lots of butter on it." Glancing toward the kitchen door, Cadel was shaken by an unexpected stab of guilt. "Can't I just go and check on her?" he pleaded.

"All in good time."

Prosper scraped his eggs onto the two plates. Then he proceeded to fry bacon with a careless ease that both surprised and impressed Cadel, who had somehow never imagined Prosper cooking, any more than he would have expected to see the Devil watering houseplants.

Cadel was about to remark on this when the toaster ejected his Pop-Tarts with a soft *clunk*. It was the signal he'd been waiting for.

The success of his plan now depended on split-second timing.

"So are you going to let us watch television?" he asked, moving toward the toaster. "Or do you think I'm going to—ow! Ouch!" He dropped the first Pop-Tart (which was, indeed, very hot), so that it landed on the counter. "Damn!"

"Don't burn your fingers," Prosper warned. "Just wait a moment."

"No, no. It's all right." Grabbing a tea towel, Cadel used it to pick up his fallen Pop-Tart. Simultaneously he retrieved the unheated Pop-Tart, hiding it beneath the limp screen of checked cotton in order to transfer it to the toaster. He did this under the pretext of collecting his other toasted Pop-Tart, which soon lay on his plate beside Pop-Tart number one.

Prosper didn't appear to notice Cadel's sleight of hand. Perhaps he was too busy turning rashers. Certainly the sizzle of frying was so loud that it completely masked the muffled *clunk* of the toaster switch being reset; Cadel didn't have to cough or speak to conceal the telltale noise that occurred as he put down his tea towel—which he left precisely where it would conceal the depressed switch.

But the trickiest step was still to come.

"Don't even think about eating that yet," Prosper recommended, lifting his pan off the stove. Immediately the splutter of hot fat died away. "You'll burn your tongue."

"I'll just try it."

"Cadel—"

"I'm *hungry,*" Cadel snapped, and bit into a Pop-Tart. "Aagh!"

This time there was no pretense; he really did burn his tongue on the sugary filling. Spitting it onto the counter was more of a reflex action than a well-considered ploy.

"There. What did I tell you?" said Prosper.

"Sorry." Cadel returned the offending Pop-Tart to his plate and began to wipe up the mess. In doing so, he had to retrieve the tea towel and shift the electric kettle slightly, until the bottom edge of its handle was resting on the depressed toaster switch.

Then he discarded the tea towel and took possession of his plate.

"Can I go back in now?" he lisped, pointing at the door to the living room. He was anxious that Prosper should follow him. But Prosper said, "Wait."

There was a nerve-racking delay while he distributed rashers of bacon and searched through the cutlery drawer for knives and forks. It looked as if he might even cross to the sink with his dirty frying pan—and perhaps spot Cadel's trick on the way. To prevent this, Cadel began to edge out of the room.

He felt as if he was trying to haul an enormous fish into a rowboat. *Come on,* he prayed. *Come on, come on!*

"You do realize that Sonja's not actually going anywhere, don't you?" Prosper drawled. With a plate in each hand, he approached Cadel, who was standing on the threshold, trying not to look as nervous as he felt. "I can't understand why you're so worried. It's not as if she can get into any *mischief.*"

"She'll be scared," Cadel countered. He didn't know exactly how long it would be before the Pop-Tart caught fire. On the Internet, the timing of Pop-Tart blowtorch experiments varied enormously—owing, perhaps, to the difference in toasters or fillings. It could take up to eleven minutes for the sugar to ignite, or as little as two minutes.

Cadel was also concerned about the smell. He thought it unlikely that the rich aroma of bacon and eggs would long disguise the stench of burning. But he didn't want to shut the kitchen door, lest Prosper become suspicious.

So he resigned himself to an uncertain outcome and settled himself on the floor beside Sonja—who flung out an arm toward him.

Her wide, fixed gaze left him in no doubt as to how she was feeling.

"It's all right," he said, abandoning his plate to catch at her hand. "I'm here. Don't worry."

"I hope you're not expecting *me* to feed her?" Prosper drawled. He was standing over them both, still holding plates like a waiter. "If so, you're about to be sadly disappointed."

Cadel couldn't suppress a sniff. "You?" he scoffed. "I wouldn't trust you to tie her shoes, let alone feed her." And he was startled to see Prosper smile.

"How well you know me, dear boy." Stooping to rid himself of her plate, Prosper addressed Sonja with veiled malice. "You shouldn't expect any help from me," he said. "For instance, I shan't be changing your diapers. That will be Cadel's job. So don't be surprised if he starts to display a little less enthusiasm for your company in the future. You couldn't exactly blame him, could you?"

Sonja's eyes filled with tears. Cadel saw them, and his rage nearly choked him—because certain subjects were of such unspeakable delicacy that Cadel had never raised them with Sonja. Instead, they were simply handled in silence. As if they didn't relate to her at all.

Cadel had to control his breathing before he could say, in threatening tones, "Back off."

Prosper raised his eyebrows. "I'm just stating the facts."

"Don't you dare."

"Bit of a touchy subject, is it?" Prosper slyly observed, and Cadel lost his cool.

"*Shut up!*" he cried.

"Hey." A bewildered voice interrupted them. "What's going on?"

It was Alias speaking. But when Cadel swung around, he saw Judith standing nearby.

His heart leaped.

"Ah." Prosper straightened. "Excellent. Really excellent."

"I stuck with the same padding," said the long-haired, brightly colored, generously proportioned figure across the room. And Cadel realized that, once again, he was looking at a demonstration of Alias's remarkable skill. "We're lucky she likes such distinctive clothes."

At that instant, Sonja's grip on Cadel's hand tightened convulsively. Turning to look at her—seeing her writhing lips and staring eyes—he realized that she didn't understand. So he tried to clarify matters. "It's not Judith," he said quickly. "It's not Judith; it's Alias. I'm sorry. I'm so sorry."

"Jesus Christ!" Prosper exclaimed, high above his head, with a quite disproportionate degree of frustration. "Would you please stop apologizing? It's such an annoying habit, and one that I utterly abhor!"

Cadel blinked. Even Alias seemed taken aback. Finally Cadel quavered, "That's because you don't have a conscience."

Then something went *WHUMP* in the kitchen.

Prosper didn't hesitate. Instant comprehension was written all over his face; without directing so much as a snarl at Cadel, he flew out of the room, yelling, "Stay there!" over his shoulder.

Cadel was frantic. He jumped up, edging toward the side table. But he couldn't do anything useful, because Alias was still around.

"Extinguisher! Where is it?" Prosper bellowed, from the kitchen doorway. He was addressing Alias, who winced. Then the fire alarm began to squeal, and Alias put his hands over his ears.

"Oh, shit!" he said.

"Get the extinguisher, damn you!"

Alias disappeared. Prosper rounded on Cadel, his eyes blazing, his teeth exposed in a carnivorous sort of grin.

"Nice try!" he shouted, over the deafening noise. "Bad news is, I'm not stupid! I had Vadi disable the service connection! There's no one monitoring that alarm, and no one close enough to hear it!"

Cadel tried to look disappointed. It wasn't hard. Despite the ominous crackling sounds issuing from the kitchen, Prosper seemed determined to remain where he was—at least until Alias came back.

Cadel was desperately afraid that, despite all his efforts, he wouldn't win for himself a single, unsupervised minute.

"Here! Here it is!" Alias burst onto the scene again, wielding a fire extinguisher. He thrust it at Prosper, who vanished into the kitchen.

It was at this point that Prosper made a mistake.

In the heat of the moment, he didn't tell Alias to stay put. So Alias followed him, leaving Cadel alone with Sonja. It was the window of opportunity that Cadel had been waiting for.

Without a second's delay, he pounced on Vadi's PalmPilot. The case remained where he'd found it, so that no one would realize that its contents were missing. But he whisked the organizer over to where he could attach the appropriate cable. Then he began the clumsy process of entering his message, driven almost to distraction by the outdated equipment's ponderous speed.

"Come on," he whispered. "Come on, *come on . . .*"

No one in the kitchen could hear him—not through the wail of the fire alarm. Of that he felt sure. But he was terrified that Prosper might return at any moment.

So he tried to be as brief as possible.

"At Judy's cabin. Cadel." was the message that he tapped out, before sending it through to Fiona's mobile. Each step in the download seemed to take a hundred years. He wasn't even sure that his brilliant idea would actually work. And he wouldn't be in a position to run any checks, either.

But in one respect he was very, very fortunate. By the time Alias had appeared, ordered back into the living room by Prosper, Vadi's little PalmPilot was tucked away behind the television.

And Cadel was sitting beside Sonja, gamely munching on his Pop-Tart.

"Bloody hell," sighed Alias. He was able to speak at a normal volume, because the fire alarm had been turned off. "You're a charming guest, I must say."

"What happened?" asked Cadel.

The response from the kitchen was a bark of mirthless laughter, which he found very unsettling. It also seemed to disturb Alias, who glanced uneasily at the kitchen door and lifted an admonishing hand when Prosper staggered into view.

"Now—let's not get overexcited," Alias beseeched. "There's been no harm done. I mean, nothing that a paint job won't fix . . ."

Prosper ignored these feeble attempts at conciliation. Tossing aside the extinguisher (which hit the floor with a mighty *CLANG)*, he marched right up to Cadel, his hands on his hips.

Sonja whimpered. Cadel held his breath.

Prosper pursed his lips, then shrugged.

"Not a bad effort," he said. "That blind must have been coated in retardant, or we would have had a bit of a mess on our hands."

Then he bent down and patted Cadel's pale cheek.

FORTY-ONE

Cadel's penalty for lighting a fire was to eat every single scrap of the cherry-flavored Pop-Tarts cooling on his plate. "Since they'll probably give you food poisoning," Prosper decreed, "I'd certainly classify them as a slap on the wrist." He seemed to think that feeding Sonja her scrambled eggs also constituted a suitable punishment. ("I can't imagine anything more revolting," was how he put it, much to her evident distress.) And he refused to let Cadel watch TV.

"You should take a nap," was Prosper's opinion. "You've had a long night, and it's affecting your tactical abilities." He obviously enjoyed rubbing Cadel's nose in the fact that the fire alarm had not been monitored. And he also may have felt that making Cadel lie on the couch, with absolutely nothing to do, was yet another way of exacting revenge.

Cadel didn't mind, though. He had plenty to think about. In fact, he appreciated having the *time* to think. Since leaving Clearview House, he'd been too rushed and panic-stricken to concentrate. Nothing had made much sense, because he'd been worried about Sonja and preoccupied with getting a message through to Saul. . . .

That message had been sent, at any rate. Not directly to Saul, because Alias had taken Saul's mobile, but to Fiona Currey. With any luck Fiona would transmit the message to Saul as soon as possible—if, that is, she had received it in the first place. Cadel couldn't be sure that the text had been transmitted. He didn't know if Judith, when asked, would choose to reveal the address of her cabin—though he couldn't imagine why not.

And even if she did, how long would it be before Saul finally reached this place? More than an hour, certainly.

Perhaps he would call on some local police to raid it for him.

Cadel flicked a glance at Prosper, who was playing poker with Alias at the dining table. In Cadel's view, the match was hardly a fair one; even if Alias *could* beat Prosper, would he really want to? In light of everything? Cadel thought not.

His gaze then traveled from Alias to Sonja, who was lying on the opposite couch. Cadel was very, very anxious about Sonja. He had a horrible feeling that she would be jettisoned, without ceremony, as soon as Prosper thought it safe to do so. In the bush somewhere, perhaps? On a beach? The location would depend on Prosper's escape plan, which Cadel still couldn't fathom. If it involved a sea voyage, why go inland? If it involved a plane trip, why not head for a nearby airport?

Unless . . .

Cadel gasped. *Of course!* He sat bolt upright, propelled by the force of his own excitement, and twisted around to address Prosper.

"Are you going to steal Judith's plane?" he demanded. "Is *that* somewhere nearby?"

Prosper didn't so much as lift an eyebrow. He kept staring at the cards he'd been dealt, as if Cadel hadn't uttered a word. It was Alias who reacted. Though he didn't speak, his head jerked up. And he looked to his boss for guidance.

"I'm right, aren't I?" Cadel continued. "She must have bought this place because it's close to some little country airstrip!"

"You're supposed to be asleep," said Prosper, in an absentminded fashion. He was rearranging his cards. "You're so exhausted, you're not thinking straight."

"Yes, I am." In fact, Cadel was thinking with great clarity. "But a lightplane won't get you *that* far. Is there going to be a fuel stop? Do you have a boat stashed somewhere really remote? Down on the south coast, or something?"

"An interesting scenario," said Prosper, sounding deeply bored. Then Alias turned his head.

"Shh," he whispered. "Listen."

Everyone fell silent. Sure enough, the hum of an approaching car engine was faintly audible.

Prosper checked his watch.

"That's probably Vadi," he observed. "Still—it's best to be on the safe side." Whereupon he set down his cards and picked up his gun.

Watching him leave the room, Cadel tried not to look as frightened as he felt. When Vadi returned, he would want his electronic organizer. But Vadi's organizer was still sitting behind the TV—because Cadel hadn't been given a chance to retrieve it.

Judith's airplane, Cadel fretted. *I need to tell Saul about Judith's airplane.* By leaving an encoded message, perhaps? Using Judith's deck of cards, and the Solitaire Cipher?

Of course, he might not have to leave a message. Not if Saul asked Judith for the address of her cabin and Judith mentioned the nearby plane. Then Saul might put two and two together and realize what was going on . . .

Whack! A large, light, plastic-covered bundle suddenly bounced off Cadel's skull.

"There," said Prosper, from the doorway. "There are your diapers. Now what are you going to do with them?"

"Uh . . ." Cadel hesitated.

"What if I carry her into the main bedroom?" Alias was trying to be kind. He rose from his chair, laying his cards facedown on the table. "Would that help?"

Cadel wondered if there were any locks on the bedroom doors.

"I guess so," he said, thinking hard. "But she won't want anyone else there when I—when she—well, you know."

Then his stomach turned over, as he saw Vadi approach the side table.

"I'm afraid you've forfeited your right to privacy, dear boy," Prosper declared. "Since you can't be trusted not to abuse the privilege."

"But Sonja—"

"Can blame *you* for any embarrassment she has to endure." Peering across at her, Prosper frowned. "By the by," he remarked, "you might like to tie her down before you attempt anything. She appears to be having some sort of tantrum."

It wasn't a tantrum, however. It was a convulsive, muscular response to seeing Vadi pick up his organizer case. Cadel reached for Sonja's hand just as Vadi said, "Where's my PalmPilot?"

After which, for five full seconds, silence reigned.

Slowly, Prosper turned his head. Vadi and Alias followed suit until they were all three staring at Cadel—who lifted his chin defiantly, his face as white as salt.

Sonja began to make little chirping noises.

"Where is it?" Prosper finally asked.

"Where's what?" said Cadel. He was only buying time; he knew that he wouldn't be able to stall Prosper for very long. In fact, he doubted that much advantage would be gained from a delay—especially if Prosper started to throw his fists around. Cadel half expected it, bracing himself for a slap on the face, at the very least.

Instead, Prosper seized a handful of Sonja's hair.

"You know," he said, in conversational tones, "if I was to dislocate her spine, she wouldn't be hugely inconvenienced."

"It's there." Cadel pointed. "Behind the television." While Vadi was crossing the room, he added, "I sent a message. Don't hurt her—"

"What message?" Prosper interrupted, his grip on Sonja's hair tightening.

"I said I was here." Cadel's voice shook. "If you hurt her, I'll kill you. I will."

"It's plugged in," said Vadi, yanking his organizer free of its connection. "There's a cable back here—I don't know what it's for."

Cadel was poised to hurl himself straight at Prosper, whose gun was almost certainly tucked away in his clothes somewhere. There was a very slim chance that Cadel might be able to reach it before its owner did, if Sonja's life was threatened.

But Prosper didn't move. He didn't so much as shift his weight.

He seemed to be reviewing their predicament, his dark gaze blank and impenetrable.

"The fire," he said at last. Then he examined his watch again. "Damn it."

"I don't understand how you could get this to work," Vadi muttered, gingerly nursing the rescued organizer. "It's so *old.* It wasn't designed to link up with the Internet. Was it?"

"It's an information delivery system," Cadel replied. "You just have to know how to unlock the right doors—"

"Okay, listen." Prosper released Sonja's hair, so that her head fell back onto the sofa cushions with a soft *thud.* He spoke crisply and rapidly. "This is going to be tight, but we might just make it. As long as we leave right now."

Alias gawped at him.

"But—"

"*Now!*" Prosper barked. "Into the car! Everyone!"

"But my message might not have got through," said Cadel. "You might be safe. I'd have to check."

It was a last-ditch effort, and it was futile. Vadi hissed in disbelief. Prosper narrowed his eyes, not the least bit amused by Cadel's clumsy attempt to get back online.

"You'd be better employed keeping your mouth shut and your hands to yourself," was Prosper's recommendation. "I'm beginning to lose patience with you, I really am. You're pushing your luck." He grabbed Cadel's collar. "Now get into the car, or I'll *drag* your friend there by one foot."

"Which car?" said Alias, and Prosper bared his teeth in an impatient snarl.

"The hatchback," he snapped. "What else?"

"But we'll be early," Vadi objected.

"Then we'll improvise."

"But my stuff!" cried Alias. "All my makeup and prosthetics!"

"Leave them." Seeing Alias hesitate, Prosper slid his free hand into the pocket of his jacket. "I can't let you get caught. You do realize that, don't you?"

It was a none-too-subtle threat, which Alias understood perfectly. His eyes widened. He retreated a step.

"I'll take the girl," Vadi offered. "Alias can drive."

"No. You drive," said Prosper. As Vadi opened his mouth to remonstrate, Prosper overrode him. "Forget the plan. The plan has changed. Speed is essential. That's why we have to get going! *Right now!*"

So they left. Vadi took Sonja, and Alias took the diapers. Prosper kept his hand firmly clamped around Cadel's collar until they were all safely bundled into the green car—where Cadel found himself in the backseat, wedged between Sonja's lolling form and Prosper's rigid one. Then Vadi took off, accelerating up the driveway and veering onto the road. Cadel had driven with Vadi once before, in a sleek and stately BMW. It had been such a smooth ride that Cadel had spent at least half of it dozing.

But when pressed for time, Vadi had a lead foot. And though Cadel shut his eyes quite often during this second trip, it wasn't because he felt drowsy. It was because he didn't have the courage to open them.

Vadi drove like a Formula One racer.

"Jesus!" gasped Alias, after a particularly close shave. "You're going to kill us!"

"No he's not." Prosper spoke calmly. "He's had special training."

"Yes, so you said!" Alias squeaked. "But we're not on the plane yet, for god's sake!"

Prosper laughed. He seemed genuinely amused. All he said, however, was, "Do you still have that gun, Vadi? Give it to Alias, then. He can return it when we arrive." As Alias craned around to look at him, wearing a pained expression, Prosper remarked, "I don't want to be stopped for speeding."

Strangely enough, they weren't. Though Vadi drove like a maniac, bouncing through potholes and screeching around corners, no flashing lights or wailing sirens intruded upon their frantic journey. In fact, they hardly saw any vehicles at all; the crumbling country roads over which they skimmed bore very little traffic. Once they passed an old pickup, heading in the opposite direction. Once they overtook a brand-new Range Rover, which sounded its horn at them. And once they nearly collided with a truck full of sheep. But for the most part, their passage was unobserved.

Vadi barreled along without hindrance, answering questions in a distracted sort of way, both his hands on the wheel.

"She has leased space in a hangar," he explained, for Prosper's benefit. "There aren't many buildings there. One belongs to a glider club. It's only busy on the weekend."

"So what kind of interference can we expect?" asked Prosper. Then, with a wry half smile, he added, "Besides the police, of course."

"Maybe an airstrip manager," Vadi replied. "It might be too late to avoid him now. If we're lucky, there will be no one."

"Why didn't we just break in overnight?" Alias queried. "Is there an alarm system or something?"

"No," said Prosper. "But most regional airstrips only operate during daylight hours, and I didn't want to alert people. Besides, we're neither of us too confident about flying at night. Are we, Vadi?"

"That's not the main reason," Vadi retorted, a little put out. "You told me to book a time. So I did."

"Yes," Prosper agreed. "Because a stolen aircraft would have created a ruckus. I wanted to keep things as quiet as possible for as long as possible." His gaze slid sideways toward Cadel, who hunched his shoulders. "Unfortunately, now that our cover's blown, there's not much point trying to play by the rules."

"This place is hard to find," Vadi said. "That might work in our favor."

"It might." Prosper didn't sound very sanguine. "We still have to rethink our second leg, though."

Vadi grunted, and Cadel wondered what exactly this "second leg" might entail. But Prosper's whole body was as taut as a guitar string, and Cadel didn't want to make inquiries—just in case they triggered an outburst.

If Prosper lost his temper, Sonja would be his prime target.

All at once the car began to slow, as it approached a modest T-junction. The sign that marked this intersection was so badly scarred by lead shot that it had been rendered illegible; nevertheless, the very existence of a sign indicated that something important must lie at the end of an otherwise unpromising side road. Certainly Vadi didn't hesitate over his choice of routes. He turned straight onto the rough dirt track, which wound through several hectares of level, scrubby land, much of it covered with stands of ironbark and grevillea. Mysterious bits of rusty casing were scattered here and there. Parakeets fled from the roar of the engine.

After about five minutes, Alias had to get out and open a barred gate.

At last, however, they reached cleared countryside and saw—across a flat expanse of yellowish grass and macadam—the distant gleam of metal roofs. Beyond these roofs more bush seemed to jostle against a perimeter fence. And beyond the treetops a low hill reared up, half shorn of its timber.

"There it is," said Vadi. "And that's the manager's car."

"Keep going," Prosper advised. "Don't slow down."

"What if they've already called this manager guy? The police, I mean? What if they've warned him?" Alias demanded. To which Prosper replied, "If they'd warned him, he wouldn't be here. I'm armed and dangerous, remember? They wouldn't have let him stay." With another quick glance at Cadel, he murmured provocatively, "We seem to be in luck, don't you think?"

No one said anything else—at least not for several minutes. As Vadi drove briskly around the edge of the airfield, Cadel spied a wind sock flapping away on top of a pole. A single-engine aircraft was tethered near one of the steel sheds grouped to the north of the wind sock. The smallest of these sheds, which boasted several windows and an air conditioner, also bore a large sign that said OFFICE.

A white station wagon was parked directly under the sign.

"There he is," said Vadi. "There. See? The airstrip manager."

Sure enough, a man was climbing out of the white car. From a distance, it was hard to make out what he looked like. But his interest in the approaching hatchback was evident from the way he turned to peer at it, shading his eyes from the early-morning sun.

"Is this the only road in?" asked Prosper, and cursed under his breath when Vadi answered that it was. By now they were close enough to see the manager's brown hair and mustache. He wore a pair of jeans under a plain khaki jacket.

"He's just arrived. Look. He's still got his keys out," said Alias. And Cadel instantly realized what *that* meant.

Any warning issued by the police might very well be sitting on the office voice mail, waiting to be heard.

"Okay," said Prosper. "I can't see any more cars, so this won't take long. Vadi stays here with the kids until I say otherwise. Alias, give that weapon to Vadi. And remember: I want to get as close to this guy as possible before throwing my weight around, or he might try to run. Cadel . . ." Prosper's dark glare was like a double-barreled shotgun, aimed straight at Cadel's forehead. "You keep your mouth shut, or people are going to get hurt. Understand?"

Mutely, Cadel nodded.

"Right. Stop here." Prosper unbuckled his seat belt as Vadi stamped on the brake. "This is close enough. Okay—are we all clear about what's going to happen? Vadi stays put. Cadel shuts up. And Alias . . ." Prosper inclined his head. "Alias, it's over to you now."

FORTY-TWO

The poor airstrip manager didn't stand a chance. He smiled broadly as soon as Alias emerged from the car. In fact, judging from the enthusiastic reception that Alias received, Judith Bashford was a familiar and welcome sight around the airstrip.

Then Prosper climbed out of the backseat and joined Alias. Cadel watched the airstrip manager stride toward them. Clearly, there was nothing alarming about Prosper's wispy white hair and tweed jacket. If there had been, the airstrip manager would surely have faltered a little, his smile fading. He wouldn't have hurried so eagerly to close the gap between himself and his visitors.

Cadel looked away. He couldn't bear to witness the inevitable moment when realization dawned.

He didn't dare raise his eyes again until Vadi gave a grunt and murmured, "Good job." This remark prompted Cadel to glance up—by which time Prosper had drawn his gun. Shell-shocked, the poor airstrip manager was standing with his hands in the air, stammering out answers to Prosper's questions. From inside the car, Cadel couldn't hear exactly what was being said.

He could, however, see Alias detaching a bunch of keys from the airstrip manager's belt. Shortly afterward, all three of them—Prosper, Alias, and their unfortunate captive—began to move toward one of the large tin sheds. Upon reaching it, they stopped for a minute or two. (Cadel speculated that this delay was caused by a search for the right key, but couldn't be certain because they were so far away.) Then Alias dragged open one big aluminum door and vanished into the shed's murky interior with his two companions.

"Can you see?" Cadel whispered to Sonja, who was slumped against him. When she managed a nod, he pressed her hand.

Over behind the wheel, Vadi sighed. It was obvious that he didn't like waiting. He kept consulting his watch and nervously scanning the horizon. His muddy skin gleamed with perspiration; his breathing didn't sound quite right.

It worried Cadel that someone so jittery should be holding an automatic pistol.

"Is that safety catch on?" he asked, and Vadi jumped in his seat.

"What?"

"Have you engaged the safety catch on your gun?"

"No talking, please, sir."

At that moment Alias appeared again, pushing open the second aluminum door to reveal the pale outline of a small plane inside the tin shed.

Then he beckoned to Vadi. But when Vadi tried to climb out of the hatchback, Alias shook his head, miming a steering wheel.

"You're supposed to drive over," Cadel pointed out. He had to acknowledge that using the car to transport Sonja from one location to another was a good idea. And when Alias waved them straight into the hangar, Cadel realized that Prosper had been thinking strategically.

With the green car tucked well out of sight, there was no indication that Prosper had even arrived at the airfield. Not from a distance, anyway.

It was a smart move.

As Vadi switched off the engine, Cadel scanned his surroundings in amazement. He was impressed by the sheer size of the hangar, which was certainly large enough to accommodate both a car and a plane—with plenty of room to spare. In one of the vacant corners, Prosper stood with his gun trained on the airstrip manager, who was being forced to remove his clothes. Not far away, Alias was also undressing. Apparently he intended to disguise himself as the airstrip manager, despite the fact that he had left his makeup kit at Judith's house.

Cadel was about to observe to Sonja that the mustache problem might prove to be insurmountable when something else caught his eye. Frowning, he peered more closely at the airplane. It was a neat little machine, as white as a cloud, with three wheels, one propeller, and a three-door cabin. Everything about it looked stylish; Cadel recalled that Judith had mentioned paying close to $100,000 for her "four-stroke Jabiru," and this particular aircraft had JABIRU painted on its tail.

But from what he could see, it contained only four seats.

"That's not ours, is it?" he demanded of Vadi, who was now exiting the car. "Hey! *Hey!*"

Vadi, however, didn't seem to hear. He pocketed his pistol and slammed the driver's door shut behind him.

So Cadel pushed open his own door.

"There are only four seats in that plane!" he cried, scrambling out. To which Prosper replied, "Get back in the car."

"Who are you going to leave here?"

"Get back in the car."

When Cadel hesitated, reluctant to comply, Vadi grabbed his arm and tried to enforce Prosper's request. Alias, meanwhile, had unstrapped his padding.

"I'll need some water," he suddenly announced. "I can't do this without water. Or scissors, for cutting up the wig. And maybe some paste, or correction fluid."

"Where's your bathroom?" Prosper asked the airstrip manager. "Over in that office?"

The response was a wordless nod. Prosper then turned to Vadi, who was still struggling with Cadel.

"You can't leave Sonja here!" Cadel exclaimed. "Not on her own! You *can't*!"

"Shh," said Prosper, before addressing Vadi. "I want you to check out that office. There'll be water, and maybe duct tape or electric cables—something you can use on this one." He jerked his chin at the airstrip manager, whose horrified expression seemed to amuse him. "Not for

torturing you, Eric, don't worry. For tying you up. These great hawsers lying around here simply won't do."

"You want Alias to go with me?" said Vadi, seeking clarification. He now had Cadel in a headlock.

"I want you to escort them both—Eric and Alias," Prosper explained. "Eric can help you with the keys. Can't you, Eric?"

Another nod from the dazed airstrip manager. By now he wore only his boxer shorts; Alias had even taken his socks.

"Meanwhile, I'll prep the plane," Prosper continued. "*And* keep an eye on my son here. Are you sure this is the right key, Eric?" Holding aloft a rather ordinary-looking ignition key, Prosper subtly adjusted the position of his gun until its barrel was pointing straight at Eric's heart. "You wouldn't be mucking me about, would you?"

"Of course not!" Eric quavered. "It's the spare! She left it herself!"

"Good," said Prosper, returning the key to his pocket. "Then off you go with Vadi. That's it. Don't dawdle. We haven't got all day."

With a shrug, Vadi released Cadel and used his gun to shepherd Eric out of the building. Alias trailed behind them, clutching his wig in one hand and Eric's keys in the other.

Cadel rubbed his bruised throat, trying not to cough. He felt Prosper's hand on the back of his neck.

"Now," Prosper said, "let's see how big this plane is, shall we?"

He yanked at Cadel's collar with such force that Cadel almost tripped, and had difficulty staying upright as he was hauled in the direction of Judith's airplane. "Wait—please!" Cadel gasped. "We have to talk about— Ow!" Prosper had relinquished his turtleneck, only to grab his ponytail instead. The pain was excruciating. "Ow—ow—"

"So sorry, dear boy." There wasn't, however, a trace of regret in Prosper's languid delivery. "I have to put this gun away, and I know how tricky you can be, if given half the chance."

Cadel's eyes were so full of tears that he could hardly see what was going on. But he assumed that Prosper was trying to get into Judith's airplane. And he was right; before long the tight grip on his hair relaxed, as he was bundled through a cabin door and pushed into a very comfortable, upholstered seat. The smell of new carpet and old exhaust fumes made him feel nauseous.

Or perhaps he was just sick with fear.

"Listen," he gabbled, "you can leave her here as long as you tell someone where she is."

"Oh, I can, can I?" Prosper's tone was absentminded. He was surveying the instrument panel. "Nice to have your permission, I'm sure."

"Please. *Please.*" Cadel's voice cracked. "If you call someone about Sonja, I promise I'll be good. I *swear* I will. I'll do everything you say." Hearing Prosper snort, he leaned forward, fists clenched. "I mean it," he pleaded. "This isn't a trick. Please believe me, I'm telling the truth. Word of honor."

"Word of honor?" At last Prosper's interest was piqued. He turned away from the instrument panel and fixed Cadel with a bright, steely, penetrating look. "What are you talking about? You wouldn't know what that means."

"Yes I would! I'm different now! I keep my promises!" When Cadel saw Prosper's face harden, he realized that this wasn't a piece of information likely to please someone who had once been involved in founding a University of Evil. So he did something he'd never, ever thought he could bring himself to do.

He swallowed and said, "Please, Dad. I'm begging you. I won't cause you any more trouble for the rest of my *life,* if you just do this one thing."

Prosper frowned. Deep within him, some kind of seismic disturbance caused his features to shift like a subsiding wall. There was a hint of irresolution in the set of his mouth—a puzzled look in his eyes.

Before he could utter a word, however, he was distracted by a distant growl, wafting through the open door of the cabin.

It was the growl of an approaching car.

"Shit," he said.

For one instant, he and Cadel stared at each other. Then Prosper sighed.

"You're not going to keep quiet, are you?" he muttered. Before Cadel could think of a response, Prosper was looming above him, poised to pounce.

There followed a short, sharp scuffle.

Pulled from his seat and thrust toward the rear of the cabin, Cadel found himself faced with a closed hatch in an upholstered bulkhead. "No!" he cried, instantly comprehending. "No! *No!*" And he lashed out wildly, having no wish to be locked in the baggage compartment.

But Prosper had the advantage over him in height, weight, and reach. Within seconds the open hatch gaped before them; though Cadel planted his feet against its rim, Prosper simply knocked them aside with his own foot, while his hands were engaged in gagging Cadel and pinning down his arms.

"It won't be for long," Prosper gasped. "You're not going to suffocate."

"N-n-n-h!"

"It's really very roomy—look." With a full-body heave, he shoved Cadel into a long, dark hole. "I'll be back soon."

"No!"

The hatch slammed shut, leaving Cadel in total darkness. "Now don't make a fuss," said Prosper, his voice muffled by the intervening bulkhead, "because no one's going to hear. Just sit tight and be good. I won't leave without you."

"Wait!" Cadel punched at the hatch, which wouldn't open. It didn't seem to have a handle on the inside. *"Don't! Come back, please!"*

There was no answer.

"Don't leave me in here!" Cadel screeched, kicking and pounding. He threw himself against the bulkhead. He bounced from one end of the compartment to the other, casting about for another exit. But he was completely enclosed in a narrow, upholstered drum. He couldn't even stand up straight; he had to crawl around on his hands and knees.

"Okay. Okay." *Stay calm,* he thought. It was already hot, and he had no idea how well ventilated this stowage hold might be. Panicking wouldn't help. Throwing a fit wouldn't help. If he screamed too much, he would lose his voice. If he kept blundering about, he would hurt himself.

So he wrenched off one shoe and began to hit the floor with it, rhythmically. *Bang-bang-bang. Bang-bang-bang.* Physical activity of this kind helped him to keep his fear in check. He was so desperately afraid—for Sonja, for himself, for the newcomers in the approaching car—that he couldn't concentrate. Little surges of hysteria kept making his heart race and his hands tremble.

A sob escaped him, followed by another.

He clenched his teeth.

No, he thought. *Don't let it get to you. Don't, don't, don't.*

He tried to ignore the fact that he was trapped in a small, confined space. He tried to stop gulping down air so frantically, because the noise of his panting made it hard to hear what was going on outside. Not that he had the slightest chance of hearing much, anyway, through the layers of bulkhead and padding—not unless someone came really close to the plane and raised his or her voice. If that happened, then his banging might become audible to the newcomers, whoever they might be.

Bang-bang-bang! Cadel drummed on the floor with all his might, before it suddenly occurred to him that he was being overly optimistic. There was very little chance that anybody *would* approach the airplane—not if Alias was successful. Providing that his disguise was good enough, Alias might be able to convince the new arrivals that he really was Eric the airstrip manager, and send them away—especially if they weren't the police. And if they were, they might believe his claim that no one else had approached the airfield that morning.

Of course, even Alias wouldn't persuade the police to leave. That much was certain. They would want to stay, no matter what they were told, just in case Prosper should appear. For that reason, too, they would probably evacuate Alias. And if he had any sense, Alias would immediately take off in Eric's car, before anyone saw who was lurking in the office.

Cadel groaned. The entire scene had flashed into his head: Alias vanishing down the road; the police lulled into a false sense of security; one policeman heading for the office and carelessly opening the door. . . .

What if that policeman turned out to be Saul Greeniaus?

"Don't panic," Cadel told himself, his ears cocked for the rattle of gunfire. "Keep calm. It might not happen." The police might not have arrived. Or if they had arrived, Vadi might have escaped already, by climbing out of a window during Alias's chat with them. In which case Prosper would surely have followed Vadi's example and slipped away quietly, instead of firing at the police from behind the hangar door.

Unless, of course, only a couple of police officers had shown up. Faced with such a modest force, Prosper might choose to risk a shoot-out for the sake of stealing Judith's plane. . . .

Cadel didn't know what to think. He wasn't in the right frame of mind to calculate probabilities. He could hardly control his breathing, let alone the direction of his thoughts.

Then he heard a dull *crack* from somewhere outside.

At first he held his breath. He listened hard, his ear pressed against the bulkhead. But when nothing else reached him, he couldn't contain himself. He beat his fists against the floor, screaming.

"Help! Help! I'm here! Let me out!"

It was a crazy thing to do. All he gained from it was a pair of sore hands. As he fell back onto his haunches, however—dejected and defeated—he noticed a slight tremor in the fabric of the airplane, which had responded to his shifting weight. And he realized that, since it wasn't a big machine, the impact of something heavy might rock or shake it a little.

So he began to hurl himself against the curved wall in front of him, conscious that the space it encompassed was becoming very stuffy.

"I'm in here! Let me out!" he bawled.

Sonja knew where he was. But Sonja couldn't talk—not without her DynaVox. Prosper also knew where he was, but Prosper might have escaped.

Oh god, thought Cadel. *Oh god, oh god, what if everyone goes away and leaves me?*

At the top of his voice, he bellowed, *"I'M IN HERE!"* Whereupon the plane juddered.

He could feel it through the palms of his hands. A kind of lurch, as if someone was climbing on board.

"Hel-hello?" he squeaked.

And he received an answer. It was faint and distorted, but it was still an answer.

"Hello? Who is that? Where are you?"

The accent was Canadian.

FORTY-THREE

"Saul!" Cadel hammered on the hatch. *"In here! It's me!"*

The hatch was yanked open. Light flooded into the compartment, momentarily blinding him. He shielded his eyes.

"Oh, my god," Saul croaked.

Two hands seized Cadel, one on each arm. He was pulled through the hatchway. Next thing he knew, he was nose to nose with a crouching Saul Greeniaus.

The detective's eyes were red. He was pasty, unshaven, and rumpled. He wore a stained white T-shirt.

"Are you all right?" he demanded, his voice raw with emotion.

Cadel couldn't speak. Instead, he nodded.

"You're not hurt?" Saul seemed to need reassurance. "He didn't hurt you?"

Cadel shook his head. A lump in his throat prevented him from speaking.

"Thank Christ." Lunging forward, the detective hugged him. "Thank *Christ.*"

Saul's grimy T-shirt smelled of shoe polish, or something similar; Cadel realized that the garment must once have been used as a cleaning rag, and had probably been picked up at Clearview House. Chances were good that Saul hadn't stopped to change or eat or do one single thing for himself since waking up on the floor of that storage cupboard.

Cadel didn't want to let him go.

"I found Sonja. She's fine. She's in my car," Saul continued, a little unsteadily. "I'm going to get you both out of here. Right now. Is that okay with you?"

Cadel made a huge effort and forced out a husky "*Prosper . . . ,*" at which point Saul pulled away.

"Where *is* Prosper?" he said, seizing Cadel by the elbows. "Did *he* shut you up in here?"

Cadel's heart sank. He closed his eyes briefly.

Oh no, he thought. And aloud he croaked, "You mean you didn't get him?"

"No." The detective sounded enormously tired. "Why? Was he here with you?"

"He . . . he . . ." Cadel had to stop for a moment. He swallowed, and licked his dry lips, before continuing. "He heard a car. I think it was yours." Seeing the detective frown, Cadel nodded toward the rear of the hangar. "There's a back door. If you didn't see him, he must have gone out that way."

Saul's whole body sagged. His head drooped. But he didn't let go of Cadel.

He seemed to be thinking.

"What about the other two?" Cadel asked, in a bloodless voice. Saul immediately raised his head again.

"You don't have to worry about them," he replied. "We got both of them—whoever they are."

"You did?" Cadel was astonished. "Even Alias?"

"Alias?"

"The one disguised as the airstrip manager." As Saul blinked, Cadel added, "I told you about him. He used to teach me at the Axis Institute."

"You mean we have *Dean Tucker* out there?" Saul exclaimed.

"Who?"

"Dean Tucker! That guy! The disguise expert!" Saul's grip tightened. "Are you sure? Really sure?"

"I . . . I guess so." Confused, Cadel tried to recall some of Alias's false identities. "Though I've never heard him called Dean Tucker before."

"That's his real name." Saul sat back on his heels, craning around to peer through a window. "I don't believe it," he said. "Dean Tucker. We got *Dean Tucker.*"

"How?" Cadel urgently needed to know. It was clear that events hadn't unfolded according to his predictions. And he was anxious to discover why. "How did you get him? What happened? Didn't he try to fool you?"

"Oh, yeah." Without releasing Cadel, Saul began to shuffle backward out of the cabin, shoulders bowed, knees bent. "And he almost succeeded."

"So what did he do wrong?" Cadel inquired, matching the detective's pace. "What happened?"

Saul reached the cabin door and halted there, hunkering down to check that the coast was clear. Then, upon catching sight of Cadel's face, he heaved a sigh and continued.

"Tucker said he was Eric Rowley. Told us he hadn't seen anyone else this morning. I asked him to go, for his own protection. And he got into that white car." One side of the detective's mouth lifted. "Then I saw him adjust the driver's seat."

"Oh." Cadel understood. If no one else had been at the airstrip, why would Eric have needed to adjust the driver's seat in his own car?

It seemed that Prosper had been wrong about Saul Greeniaus.

Saul wasn't a fool, after all.

"That's when I told him to put his hands up," Saul went on. "We were lucky. The other guy could have fired on us at that point, but he was halfway out a window, and we caught him in the act. One warning shot was all it took. If we hadn't been on the alert, we might have missed him." Saul jumped down from the plane, landing lightly on the floor of the hangar. *"Sergeant Cope!"* he cried. *"Over here!"* And he reached back to help Cadel.

"So no one was hurt?" Cadel demanded, fumbling his own jump slightly.

"No one was hurt."

"Did . . . did Fiona pass on my message?"

Saul's arm encircled Cadel's shoulders. "Do you think I'd be here if she hadn't?" he said, before turning to confront the owner of the heavy boots galloping toward them.

These boots belonged to a very large, uniformed policeman.

"Is that him?" the policeman panted. "Or is it a her?"

"Yeah." In his oversized T-shirt, Saul looked rather fragile next to the big and beefy Sergeant Cope. "But we just missed Prosper English."

"Bloody hell."

"He's out there, somewhere." Saul pointed at the little door behind the airplane. "He must have taken off—when? About ten minutes ago?" With a raised eyebrow, he sought confirmation from Cadel.

"Something like that," Cadel agreed. (Though he couldn't be sure, because he didn't have his watch.)

"So he can't have got far," Sergeant Cope speculated.

"No," Saul agreed.

"Then we'd better start searching." Plucking his two-way radio from his belt, Sergeant Cope began to retrace his steps. But he froze when Cadel blurted out, "Be careful. He's armed."

"Who?" The sergeant turned back. "You mean English?"

"He's got a gun," said Cadel, and Saul observed, "It's probably my gun." As his audience gaped at him, Saul could only offer up a bitter and humorless smile. "Prosper English took my gun," he admitted, in a tone suggesting that he wasn't about to defend himself against charges of unacceptable negligence.

Sergeant Cope looked embarrassed. Cadel, however, was reviewing the night's events. As far as he could recall, Alias had been wearing Saul's shoulder holster at Clearview House—and in the car afterward. The holster had been quickly abandoned, but not the gun extracted from it, which had been placed in the glove box of the four-wheel drive.

The four-wheel drive used by Vadi.

"No. It wasn't yours," Cadel told Saul. "Prosper always had his own gun. He gave yours to Vadi—that guy in the yellow shirt. Vadi has it."

Saul glanced at Sergeant Cope, who said, "Not anymore, he doesn't. We disarmed him."

"Where's the gun?" Saul wanted to know.

"With Cam." Sergeant Cope started to move again. "Didn't you see him take it? You must have been heading over here at the time." And he barked a series of call letters into his two-way radio.

Saul followed the sergeant, taking Cadel with him. Outside, the sun was dazzling. It was a moment before Cadel could see, because his eyes still hadn't adjusted fully to daylight after his long spell in the baggage compartment.

"Which one's your car?" he asked, squinting across a wide expanse of concrete toward the office. A police car was parked beside Eric's station wagon; an unmarked, bronze-colored sedan stood nearby, partially blocking the road out. All of these vehicles appeared to be empty, however. Though one uniformed officer was stationed next to the police car, most of his colleagues were clustered around Vadi and Alias, who were sitting on the front steps of the office, wearing handcuffs.

"My car's just over there." Saul indicated a silvery four-wheel drive that had been positioned behind him, close to the hangar. "Sonja's safe inside it, don't worry. I gave her a drink."

"Where's Eric?" asked Cadel.

"In the bathroom. Throwing up."

By this time the four policemen in front of the office had swung around to face Sergeant Cope, who was jogging heavily toward them. Though Cadel assumed that these four men were police officers, only one wore a uniform. The others possessed a kind of dense, serious, no-nonsense quality, which he recognized from countless surveillance teams.

Saul moved to join the group.

"I just want to get my gun," he informed Cadel, in a low voice. "I shouldn't leave here unarmed—not if Prosper's hanging about."

"Where are we going?" Cadel queried. And Saul fixed him with an enigmatic look.

"I don't know," the detective replied. "Somewhere that's not Clearview House is what I'd recommend."

Cadel flushed. He would have liked to speak—to apologize, perhaps—except that he couldn't find the words. In any case, Saul had already focused his attention on Sergeant Cope, who was waving his arms around as he stressed the need for defensive measures. Prosper English was known to be in the vicinity of the airstrip, Sergeant Cope explained. The suspect was armed and dangerous, but was apparently proceeding on foot. For that reason, he might try to hijack a car.

"Or a plane," Saul interjected. "We can't leave this airport unsecured or he might come back." Before anyone could comment, he addressed the youngest uniformed policeman. "You're Cam, aren't you? I'm told you have my gun."

Startled, Cam threw a questioning glance at Sergeant Cope. But the sergeant shook his head.

"I dunno, mate. That gun was in the possession of a fugitive," he demurred, gesturing at Vadi—who sat staring straight ahead, his face utterly impassive. "I dunno if we should let it go. Not right now. Not until it's processed."

"For Chris'sake, Ian, give him his gun," another policeman objected.

"It's evidence," said the sergeant.

"It's *protection,*" said one of the plainclothes officers.

"It's all right." Saul raised a hand. "I just thought I'd ask."

"Aren't you taking those kids?" Sergeant Cope inquired, making a halfhearted attempt to reassure his unarmed colleague. "You won't need a gun if you're getting them outta here. I mean—I wouldn't advise that you *slow down* for anyone, but other than that—"

"Yeah, I know. You're right." Saul spoke abruptly, as if the whole subject was distasteful to him. "Where are the others? On their way?"

"Yup."

"Then wait for them. Just to be on the safe side. Don't split up, for god's sake—because you're gonna need all the help you can get, if you're taking on Prosper English."

And Saul turned on his heel, walking away with his arm draped around Cadel's shoulders. One of the plainclothes officers called after them, not unsympathetically, "If he tries to shoot you, Saul, just drive straight over the bastard!" But Saul didn't acknowledge this jocular advice.

"What's wrong?" Cadel asked, with some apprehension. He eyed the detective's rigid profile. "Are you mad about something?"

"They think I screwed up," Saul rejoined. His tone was flat. "Which I did, of course. Letting that asshole jump me. No wonder they won't give my gun back. I already lost it once."

"That wasn't your fault!" Cadel hated to see Saul's dejected look, because he felt responsible for it. "Alias is a master of disguise—he'd fool *anyone*! And he didn't fool you the second time!"

"No," Saul conceded, relinquishing his grip on Cadel in order to drag out his car keys. "But Prosper's no expert, and he fooled me, too."

"Only because you weren't expecting him! You didn't think he knew where I lived!"

"That's right. I didn't." Saul stopped beside the four-wheel drive. "I guess I wasn't fully informed."

Saul's words were carefully chosen. They hit Cadel with as powerful an impact as the detective's heavy, reproachful gaze. Cadel blanched. The long-dreaded moment had finally arrived.

And he wasn't ready for it.

"You mean—are you talking about . . ." He took a deep breath. "Genius Squad?" he bleated.

There was a pause. Cadel was conscious of Sonja squeaking and twitching in the backseat of Saul's car, but couldn't drag his eyes away from the detective, whose expression he was trying to decipher.

"Is that what you call it? Genius Squad?" Saul finally said. "I have to admit, I'm still in the dark. There are people in Sydney who've been interviewing your Clearview House friends ever since Judith Bashford spilled the beans. But I don't really know what's going on. I've been too busy to find out." He heaved a sigh. "All I know is that I look like a goddamn fool."

"I'm sorry! I'm so sorry!" Cadel was frantic. He couldn't bear the thought of Saul's disapproval. "I'll tell you everything! I've been wanting to all along, I swear! I *hated* lying to you!"

"Why did you, then?"

"Because . . . because . . ." Hesitating, Cadel glanced through the open car window beside him. Sonja seemed to be in a highly emotional state; she was whimpering and grunting, her fingers splayed, her back arched. "Because there was nowhere else for us to go," he said at last, hopelessly.

During the silence that followed, Saul studied him with the shrewd, dispassionate, hard-bitten appraisal of an experienced policeman. It was a long and uncomfortable moment. Then the detective placed a hand on Cadel's head, leaning forward to drive home the point that he wanted to make.

"Don't lie to me again, Cadel."

"I won't."

"If you lie to me, I can't protect you."

"I promise I'll never lie to you again! Not *ever*!"

Cadel meant it. He meant it with all his heart. And this must have shown in his strained and desperate air, because Saul's own demeanor softened, suddenly.

"I don't want to believe you," Saul muttered, "but I can't help it. There's something about your face." He pulled open a car door. "Now get in. We can talk on our way out of here."

FORTY-FOUR

Sonja was very stressed. When Cadel climbed into the car beside her and tried to lift her head into his lap, her lunging hand connected with his jaw.

Her cheeks were tearstained, and there was blood in the saliva smeared across her chin.

"She's bitten her tongue," Cadel groaned, trying to smooth the sweaty black hair away from her eyes. "She's hurt herself!"

"She's had a tough time," Saul observed grimly, from the driver's seat. "Our first priority is to get her somewhere safe."

"It's all right. I'm all right." Cadel attempted to soothe her, without much success. As Saul completed a three-point turn, she became so agitated that she nearly rolled off the backseat onto the floor. "You don't have to worry. It's over now," Cadel declared, then was struck by a sudden thought. He raised his head. "*You* didn't get hurt, did you?" he asked Saul. "Prosper said you didn't, but . . . well, Prosper lies. Ow!" Sonja had jabbed him in the neck.

"I wasn't hurt," Saul assured him, swerving to avoid the bronze sedan. "No need. They just came over and asked me to open the cupboard. Next thing I woke up in it." His tone became pensive. "I don't really remember the chloroform."

"They told me they tied Trader up. So he could pretend he wasn't involved." Cadel was probing for information, even as he struggled with Sonja's uncooperative limbs. He saw the detective nod.

"Yeah." Saul spoke dryly. "It didn't work, though. I knew that guy was dirty the minute I met him." He clicked his tongue. "I should have figured out he was working for Prosper English."

"He wasn't," said Cadel. "Dot was, but he wasn't. Trader worked for Rex Austin. He was just helping Prosper, in exchange for leverage against GenoME." Sonja's shrill piping interrupted him at this point, causing him to abandon his conversation with Saul. "Sonja, it's *all right*!" he exclaimed. "What's the matter? Are you in pain?"

"What's wrong?"

"I don't know. I can't tell." Cadel was ashamed at having to make this admission. "She needs her DynaVox."

"We'll get it. We'll sort it out, just as soon as we can." Plunging into a stand of scrubby forest, Saul left the airfield behind. He never once took his eyes off the road ahead. "Why the hell did Prosper want her, anyway?"

"To stop me from trying to escape," Cadel replied. After a moment's hesitation, he added, "You do realize that Trader was after GenoME, don't you? We all were. Did Judith tell you that?"

At first Saul didn't answer. His car bumped over a pothole, and slowed when it reached a shallow dip. On both sides of the road, paper-barked eucalyptus trees with bowed, misshapen trunks looked as if they were bending down to peer through the windows.

But they couldn't have seen much, because Saul was driving too quickly.

"It was chaos at first," he finally confessed. "I figured Trader must know something, so I didn't let him leave. And I rounded up the rest of his crew, just in case. Brought them back from Maroubra to Clearview House."

"The squad, you mean?"

"The kids. The staff. Everyone. At first they acted like butter wouldn't melt in their mouths. But then Fiona gave me your message, and I asked Judith Bashford about it. That's when Judith opened up." Saul braked for a lizard, which crawled across the dirt track at a glacial speed. "She was mad," he continued, with obvious satisfaction. "Really mad. She realized Trader was to blame straight off, because he'd talked her into letting him use her cabin. She said she never would have if she'd known he was helping Prosper English."

"Judith's a good person," Cadel insisted. "She cares about Sonja."

"I guess she must." With the lizard safely out of his path, Saul accelerated again. "Because she really laid into him. Boy! She let him have it."

The detective explained that Judith had accused Trader of putting his own pocket ahead of a child's life. She'd demanded that he tell her *instantly* where Prosper would be taking her plane. And when Trader had claimed to know nothing about Prosper English, she'd proceeded to expose all his secrets.

"He went crazy," Saul reminisced, "because she spelled everything out. How he'd probably made a deal with Prosper because Prosper must have given him stuff on GenoME. And when Trader tried to claim that she was deluded, telling me he wasn't remotely interested in GenoME, she mentioned that room downstairs. Which is when he blew his stack." Saul sounded rather pleased. "I thought they were gonna kill each other."

"Really?" said Cadel, fascinated despite himself. "What about the rest of the squad? Did *they* tell the truth?"

"I wouldn't know. I didn't hang around long enough to find out."

"Oh. Right."

"I had to get over here before it was too late," Saul continued. "And I don't have a phone right now, so I haven't been getting regular updates." For the first time, he glanced into the rearview mirror. "I guess you don't have your mobile on you?"

"No." Cadel flinched away from Sonja's flying fist. "Prosper took it."

"Yeah. He must have taken mine, as well." Saul's voice was stern as he swung off the dirt track onto paved road. "Unfortunately."

This last observation had such an ominous ring to it that Cadel was alarmed. "Did you have a lot of personal stuff on that phone?" he queried, raising his voice over Sonja's guttural cawing.

"You could say that," Saul replied.

"Not *Fiona's* number?" Cadel said anxiously.

Then Sonja hit him in the mouth.

It was the last straw. "For god's *sake*!" he cried, in sheer exasperation. "What is it? What's the matter? We're *safe* now, I told you—ow!" Her fingernails had grazed his upper lip. "Please, Sonja, will you calm down? Listen. Look at me. *Calm down.*"

He placed a hand on each side of her head, to steady it—and as he did so, he saw the look in her eyes.

It made him catch his breath.

"Something's wrong," he gasped. "Saul? She's trying to tell me something."

"What?"

"I don't know." Desperately, he racked his brain for a series of questions that would narrow the possibilities. "Listen, Sonja, blink twice for yes, once for no. Can you do that?" Promptly, she blinked. Twice. "Okay. Now. Is something wrong?" Two blinks. "Are you hurt?" One blink. "Are you angry at me?" One blink. "Are you scared?" Two blinks. "She's scared," Cadel announced.

"Why?" The car slowed. "Am I driving too fast?"

"Maybe." Cadel once more addressed Sonja. "Is Saul driving too fast?"

Sonja whimpered. She blinked, her feet churning.

"No. It's not that," said Cadel.

"Nobody's gonna arrest you, sweetheart, if that's what you're worried about." Saul spoke loudly, as if concerned that she wouldn't hear him. "There's no way on earth anyone would put you in jail."

"Is that it?" Cadel asked her. "Are you scared of what will happen to us in the future?"

One blink. By now she was distraught. Tears were trickling into her hair.

"Gnn-nn," she moaned.

Her fear was beginning to infect Cadel, who turned to scan the road behind them. But no one was in pursuit.

"Did you see something scary, back at the airfield?" was his next question, to which Sonja's reply was two blinks. "Before the police came?" One blink. "After?" Two blinks.

"Did you see Prosper English?" Saul interposed, and Sonja blinked twice, exploding into a flurry of movement.

"She did," Cadel croaked. "She saw him."

"Where?" Saul demanded. "In the hangar?"

One blink.

"Did you see him running away from the police?" asked Cadel. One blink. "Did you see him hiding?"

Two blinks.

"She saw him hiding," Cadel gasped, and Saul barked, "Where? Not in the other plane?" But Sonja only blinked once.

"He wasn't in the other plane," said Cadel. "Was he near the office, Sonja?"

One blink.

"Was he in the bush?"

One blink.

"What about the second hangar?"

"Oh, for heaven's sake," a familiar voice drawled, from behind Cadel. "I'm in this *car,* you fools."

Cadel was paralyzed. Time seemed to stand still; there was too much to process all at once—the hand on his neck, the rustle of canvas, Sonja's wail, Saul's shocked eyes in the rearview mirror. Then the car screeched to a halt.

"Oh no, you don't," said Prosper. "Keep driving. Or I'll shoot somebody."

And they started to move again.

He had been hiding under a tarpaulin in the load space at the back of the vehicle. Cadel realized this even as he struggled to understand how it could have happened. And when. While the police were concentrating on Vadi and Alias? While Saul and Sergeant Cope were in the hangar?

By concentrating on these questions, Cadel hoped to control his own mounting sense of panic and disbelief.

"Pick up the pace, Mr. Greeniaus," Prosper instructed. "I'm aiming straight at the girl, in case you don't have a clear view." And a hard, chilly weight settled onto Cadel's right shoulder.

It was the base of the handgrip on Prosper's gun. Cadel could see it out of the corner of his eye.

He didn't dare move his head, though.

"I told you I'd be back," said Prosper into Cadel's ear. "You shouldn't have got so impatient."

"Please put the safety on," Saul requested, almost eerily calm. He was staring straight ahead, his knuckles white on the steering wheel. "If you don't, there'll be an accident. The road's too rough."

"Why, Mr. Greeniaus," Prosper sneered, "are you attempting to *advise* me, by any chance? That's rather amusing, all things considered."

"I'm worried about the kids," Saul replied.

"Then you shouldn't have left your car unsecured." Prosper spoke in a light, conversational tone, which contained just the faintest hint of contempt. "At the very least, you should have double-checked your luggage. Speaking of which, were you intending to take a camping trip while you were out here? Indulge in a spot of trout-fishing, perhaps?"

It was a moment before Saul answered.

"This isn't my car," he said at last, without expression. "I borrowed it."

"Oh, yes. That's right. *I* took your car, didn't I? And your phone. And your gun. And your cheap Kmart tie." Prosper's dislike of Saul was beginning to mar his placid demeanor. Black malevolence dripped from his tongue like poison. "You really are a joke. I've never seen such incompetence. No wonder my son's been fretting about you. You're incapable. You need looking after, like a pet."

"That's not true," Cadel faltered. But it was Saul, not Prosper, who cut him off.

"Don't worry, Cadel. I'm fine. Don't worry about me."

"He's right, dear boy. Don't worry about him." Prosper gestured with his gun. "You should be worrying about Sonja. I think she's about to have a stroke."

Looking down, Cadel realized that Sonja was almost drowning in her own tears. Gasping and gurgling, she had rolled about until her head was dangling off the end of his knee, unsupported. Her face was red; her eyes were bulging.

Quickly he adjusted her position, racked by guilt at the thought of how terrified she must have been, while she was trying so desperately to deliver her urgent message.

The message he'd been too stupid to understand.

"I'm sorry," he whispered. Then he raised his voice—and his chin—until he was staring at the back of Saul's head. "I'm so sorry."

"Stop apologizing!" Prosper snapped. "I've told you before, it's an abominable habit!"

"You've nothing to be sorry for," Saul agreed. "This isn't your fault, Cadel."

"Quite right," said Prosper. "But I can do without your support, Mr. Greeniaus. Just concentrate on your driving, please."

There was a short silence. Surveying the roadside bush as it slid past, Cadel saw nothing that offered any hope or protection: just endless stretches of shaggy eucalyptus trees and dry, spiny undergrowth, broken up by the occasional creek bed, dirt track, or rearing boulder.

"I guess you know that Carolina took out a contract on you," Saul remarked suddenly. Reflected in the mirror, his gaze flicked toward Prosper before returning to the windshield. "I guess you know you're lucky to be alive."

"Luck had nothing to do with it," Prosper retorted. "What you saw at that courthouse wasn't luck, Mr. Greeniaus. It was good management."

"Yeah, but there's a price on your head. That's what I mean." Though Prosper sighed impatiently, Saul added, "I'm guessing Earl Toffany is the one who's willing to pay that price, and we've got nothing on him. Not yet. So right now you're living on borrowed time."

Prosper pulled a face and shook his head. "You see, Cadel, this is what I've been talking about—this complete inability to think through a situation with any sort of logic," he complained, in long-suffering accents. "Isn't it obvious that Earl Toffany has nothing to fear from me as long as I'm out of jail? *His* great fear was that I'd cut a deal at his expense. Which I'll hardly be tempted to do if I'm not in custody."

"But that's no guarantee," Saul pointed out, his voice colorless and even. "What makes you think he won't kill you, anyway? Just to be on the safe side?"

"What makes you think he'll be able to?" Prosper sounded almost roguish, as if he was toying with the detective. "You really mustn't worry about me, Mr. Greeniaus. Assuming that Earl Toffany *does* want me dead—which I'm not confirming or denying, by the way—he'll never get to me before I get to him. I'm rather well-informed, you see. On certain subjects." All at once he stiffened, and his voice changed. "Just turn left up here. Beyond that sign."

"Where are we going?" asked Saul, eliciting a snort of amusement from Prosper.

"You don't honestly expect an answer to that, do you? If so, you're even dumber than I thought."

Without another word, Saul spun the wheel, and they jolted off the paved road onto an unpaved one. Clouds of dust billowed up behind them as they rattled over its corrugated surface, which was lined on each side by posts bearing red reflector patches. Bits of gravel occasionally bounced off the doors and the undercarriage.

"Good thing you chose a four-wheel drive," said Prosper, addressing Saul in a companionable kind of way. "This looks as if it's going to get rough."

"Did you see that we caught your two friends?" Saul replied, working hard to control the shuddering wheel. "They'll end up talking, you know. They might even feel let down because of the way you ran off and left them."

Prosper chuckled. "My dear fellow," he said airily, "if I'd done anything else, I think they would have died of pure shock. Isn't that right, Cadel?"

Cadel said nothing. He kept stroking Sonja's hair, his head bowed, his lips pressed tightly together.

He wasn't about to agree with Prosper on any subject.

"My son can tell you that I loathe violence," Prosper continued. "It's the last resort of the idiot—and it's inherently risky. If I'd started a shooting match, what good would have come of it? The odds weren't exactly in my favor, after you'd handcuffed Vadi. Whereas now, of course, I'm in a position to campaign more efficiently on his behalf."

"No, you're not." Saul displayed a momentary flash of feeling. "Not by a long shot. I wouldn't call this free and clear, would you?"

"No," Prosper allowed. "You're right. I still have a way to go yet. But *you* don't, Mr. Greeniaus." He leaned forward suddenly, his rib cage pressing against Cadel's scalp, and leveled his gun at the detective. "Stop the car," he ordered. "*Now.*"

FORTY-FIVE

Saul braked. Looking around, Cadel saw that they had stopped halfway up a hill, near a bend in the road. On all sides lay half-cleared land studded with fallen logs, lichen-encrusted boulders, and outcrops of eucalyptus trees that seemed to be huddling together for protection. Glimpses of a distant valley were visible through the leaves.

A collapsing wire fence and a faraway scattering of sheep on golden pasture suggested that somebody, somewhere, must have been interested in this obscure corner of the world. But the complete absence of roadside litter told Cadel that the route wasn't a popular one.

No doubt Prosper had chosen it for that very reason.

"Please," Cadel implored, "don't hurt anybody. I won't make trouble, I promise."

"Turn off the engine," Prosper said, ignoring Cadel's plea. And when Saul obeyed, Prosper added, "Now pass the keys back here. Slowly. Don't do anything stupid."

The keys were delivered into Prosper's custody, after which he ordered Cadel to get out of the car.

Cadel hesitated.

"What about Sonja?" he asked.

"Just get out."

"Get out, Cadel, please!" Saul said sharply. "Do as you're told!"

So Cadel pushed open the door next to him and climbed awkwardly onto the road, leaving Sonja sprawled across the backseat. She didn't, however, remain there for long.

"Right," said Prosper. "*Now* you can take her. And don't get smart, or I'll shoot Mr. Greeniaus."

"You-you mean . . . pull her out?" Cadel stammered, causing Prosper to roll his eyes.

"Can you think of any other options?"

"No."

"Then do it."

Hastily Cadel slid his hands beneath Sonja's armpits. With a single heave, he jerked her halfway out of the car, staggering slightly as she bucked against his grasp.

Though his retreat was as careful as he could make it, he couldn't prevent her feet from flopping heavily onto the ground once she was clear of the vehicle.

"Sorry," he whispered, and dragged her to the side of the road.

"Okay, stop. Stop there. Where I can see you," said Prosper. He was climbing into the backseat, his gun still aimed at Saul. "And don't even *think* about stuffing your socks into the exhaust pipe."

Such a thought had never crossed Cadel's mind; he was much too concerned about the gun to attempt anything so rash. Instead he remained where he was, crouching in a shallow ditch full of dead leaves and bull-ants. Sonja's head was lolling against his rib cage. Her pajamas were rucked up around her knees.

Please don't, Cadel prayed, his pulse hammering high in his throat. *Please don't, please don't, please don't kill him.*

"All right," Prosper said to the detective. "Keep your hands on the wheel. Where I can see them. That's it." He was now directly behind Saul; his chin was almost resting on Saul's shoulder, while the barrel of his gun was rammed against the detective's skull. "As you've probably realized, Mr. Greeniaus, I don't like you very much. I don't like the way you've wormed your way into my son's life. Into his *affections,* one might almost say—like some flea-bitten stray cat. You've taken advantage of his unfortunate predilection for losers and cripples and social rejects."

Prosper's glance slipped sideways at this point, suggesting that his last remark had been designed more for Cadel's benefit than for Saul's. Cadel, however, didn't comment. So Prosper went on.

"Nevertheless," he acknowledged, "the fact that you've been so hard to shake off indicates that you have at least one redeeming feature: namely, a personal interest in my son's welfare." Prosper inclined his head, as if trying to scrutinize Saul's expression. "Am I right, Mr. Greeniaus?"

"I wouldn't lock him in a baggage compartment or threaten him with a gun, if that's what you mean," Saul retorted. Then he moved his own head slightly, until his gaze met Prosper's. "I wouldn't have to."

It was hard to see if Prosper had colored. The car's interior was too dark. But he drew back and was silent for a few seconds.

When he finally spoke, his voice had lost its smooth finish.

"My point, Mr. Greeniaus, is this," he growled. "Owing to your really woeful performance, there's every chance you'll be taken off this case. And if you are, I want to know whether you would promptly abandon my son, or continue to exert yourself on his behalf." Before the detective could do more than inhale quickly, Prosper continued. "Not that you've done a very good job of looking after him so far, but my real concern is that Cadel should be properly housed and cared for until I can do it myself. I didn't like that Donkin arrangement. And I gather that you didn't like it, either—that you were, in fact, trying to remedy the situation. Is that correct?"

Saul didn't reply immediately. He seemed to be thinking. At last he cleared his throat and said, "Cadel is a very special kid. He deserves more than you can offer." A pause. "If you really cared about him, you'd realize that."

"If I didn't care about him, I wouldn't be here," Prosper pointed out. But he failed to convince the detective.

"You're only here because you think he's your son," Saul declared, with unusual vehemence. "And I have my doubts about that. He doesn't look like you. He doesn't act like you—"

"Wishful thinking, Mr. Greeniaus."

"Then why not agree to a DNA test? Give me your authorization. That way we'll know for sure."

"I already know for sure."

"Not necessarily."

Cadel frowned. He couldn't understand what Saul was up to; why raise such a thorny subject? Prosper must have wondered the same thing, because his whole demeanor changed. It became more focused. Less sportive.

"What are you implying?" he asked Saul, his eyes narrowed. "I thought you and your colleagues were determined to *prove* my paternity, not disprove it."

"That was before I met you," Saul admitted. "Now I can't help thinking you're mistaken."

Prosper smiled. "Well, I'm sorry to disappoint you," he said (sounding not in the least bit sorry), "but if you want to establish that Cadel isn't my son, you're wasting your time. A DNA test was carried out the day he was born. It proved conclusively that I'm his father."

"You can't be certain of that," Saul stubbornly insisted. "You're not a scientist. What if there was a mistake?"

"There was no mistake. I used a very highly qualified geneticist—"

"Who might have lied."

Prosper made a disdainful noise. "Why on earth would he have lied?"

The detective shrugged.

"It would have given him a lot of leverage. You would have been ripe for blackmail, if he managed to convince you that Cadel was your son."

"Mr. Greeniaus, the gentleman whose services I engaged didn't *need* leverage." To Cadel's surprise, Prosper obviously felt compelled to argue the point. "He already had a great deal of power and influence—and he certainly never attempted to acquire any more at my expense. In fact, he never mentioned the subject to me again."

"Because you killed him?" Saul queried.

"Of course not!" Prosper's tone was impatient—even waspish. "For your information, he's alive and well."

"Then you must have paid him off. So he'd keep your secret from Phineas Darkkon."

Opening his mouth, Prosper was about to answer, when he was suddenly struck dumb—as if paralyzed by doubt, or by a flash of understanding. He stiffened and swallowed. Then, very slowly and cautiously, he said, "You're assuming that the geneticist in question was acquainted with Dr. Darkkon. Which wasn't the case. He worked for an independent laboratory."

"Really? The way you were talking, I figured he must have been one of Darkkon's crew. I figured you would have gone to someone at NanTex, to keep the whole thing in-house." The detective waited for a moment before adding, rather delicately, "Someone like Chester Cramp, say."

All at once, Cadel understood what was happening. By needling Prosper on the controversial subject of Cadel's parentage, Saul had been trying to collect information that would implicate Chester Cramp. What Saul wanted was a slip of the tongue, directly linking Chester with Dr. Darkkon's evil empire.

Prosper must have realized this, because he abruptly ended the conversation.

"Mr. Greeniaus," he said, with an alarming degree of menace, "let me make one thing clear. I'd shoot you right now if I wasn't worried about leaving Cadel all alone." He then ground the end of his gun barrel into Saul's head, as if wielding an electric drill. "Now get out of the car."

"There's water in the glove box." Saul spoke breathlessly, wincing at the pressure on his scalp. His jaw was almost pushed against the steering wheel. "Can I take that with me?"

"No."

"But—"

"Get out. I won't ask again. And shut the door behind you."

Saul obeyed. It was only after he had retreated ten steps, as ordered, that Prosper finally scrambled into the driver's seat. This maneuver was accomplished so quickly and efficiently that Saul didn't have time to take advantage of it.

He couldn't have reached the car, let alone wrestled Prosper out of it, before receiving a bullet in some portion of his body.

"Good," said Prosper, starting the engine. After a rapid juggling act with his keys and gun, he was once again holding the weapon in his right hand—and aiming it out the window at Saul. "If I were you, I'd sit tight," was Prosper's recommendation. "There's bound to be passing traffic some time in the next couple of hours, and if you try to carry that girl, you'll injure yourself. Or she'll injure you." He released the hand brake and adjusted the gearshift without once taking his eyes off Saul. "Needless to say, I'd rather you didn't go away and leave these kids. It wouldn't be safe."

"I don't make a habit of endangering children," the detective replied, unable to suppress his anger.

Prosper ignored this remark. Instead he addressed Cadel, his gaze still fixed firmly on the detective.

"I'm sorry I can't take you with me, dear boy. But it's going to be hard enough without a problematic teenager tagging along. If only you were a little more cooperative, it would make things *so* much easier. Never mind. The next time I come for you, things will be different, I'm sure. After you've had to endure another long spell with another set of foster parents." At last he risked cutting a quick glance at Cadel. "In the meantime," he finished, "I want you to have a serious think about your current situation. Because I'm the only one who can improve it, remember. Without me, you'll be back in limbo, floating around. And that's no way to be. Not for someone like you."

Suddenly the car surged forward. Gravel flew and dust rose as Prosper executed a hasty U-turn, hauling at the wheel with fierce concentration. But before he could roar off down the road, Cadel waved at him, shouting, "Dad! *Dad!*"

The car screeched to a halt.

"What is it?" Prosper sounded wary—even anxious. He looked back at Saul, who hadn't moved. "I can't take you with me, Cadel. I can't trust you to behave yourself."

"Cadel," the detective warned, "please don't do anything you'll regret. He's still armed. Just let him go."

But Cadel had something to say. Though he was unutterably tired, and hungry, and frightened, he'd nevertheless been alert enough to identify a hint of genuine sympathy in Prosper's final directive. And it had unlocked a great tide of memories, dating back many, many years: memories of Prosper's generous birthday gifts; of Prosper's lavish praise; of Prosper's crooked smile, as he'd lowered his silver gun and allowed Cadel to walk out of his life into the arms of the police.

These recollections had forced Cadel to reconsider Prosper's motives. All at once, he'd realized that things might not be as simple as they looked. Perhaps Prosper wasn't *entirely* influenced by warped notions of entitlement, ownership, and personal gratification.

Perhaps he was also moved by a vague desire to shoulder his paternal responsibilities.

"I can't hate you," Cadel reluctantly confessed. "Not even after the way you've treated Sonja. I guess you've worked that out."

Prosper waited, his eyes bright and black and hyperalert. They kept flitting from Cadel to Saul, and back again.

Cadel wanted to stand up. He would have, if Sonja hadn't been such an awkward burden. But he was afraid that Prosper might grow impatient and drive away before Sonja could be lifted to her feet.

So Cadel delivered his speech from the bottom of a roadside ditch.

"What you don't understand is that things have changed," he said. "Even if I do end up in limbo, it won't be for long. Because I'm growing up now. I'm old enough to get a job. Soon I'll be sixteen—and sixteen-year-olds aren't children anymore. You can get married when you're sixteen." Peering into the car at Prosper's unreadable face, Cadel forced himself to forget all the lying and manipulation and downright cruelty in their shared past, so that he could concentrate on the man who had once described Cadel as his "crowning achievement." By doing this, it was easier to speak with a certain degree of warmth. It was easier to formulate an argument that might just make an impression. "The thing is, you really don't have to worry about me," Cadel quietly insisted. "I'm all right. I can look after myself. What I want is independence. I want to make my own choices, because that's what growing up is about." Taking a deep breath, he put everything he had into his concluding remarks—all the maturity and intelligence and fervor and insight that he could summon up. He used his tongue and his brain and his huge, limpid eyes; with every natural endowment at his disposal, he tried desperately to breach Prosper's armor-plated defenses. "You can't go on making my choices for me—not for the rest of my life. No father should do that," he pointed out. "Sometime, you'll have to accept that I can make my own mistakes. You'll have to just . . . let me go."

There was a long silence. No one moved for several seconds. Cadel waited, but Prosper's reaction was disappointing. He didn't speak. He didn't even smile.

Instead the car leaped forward, whipping up clouds of dust.

As Cadel watched it depart, he felt as if his heart had turned to liquid, and was draining slowly through his ribs. But then he saw a bottle of water fly out of the driver's window, bouncing onto the road and rolling into a pothole.

It was a concession, of sorts. And it lightened his mood a little.

"Cadel," Saul gasped, from somewhere close by. "Christ, I'm so sorry. I'm *so sorry* . . ."

Cadel looked up. The detective was standing over him, having dashed to his side as soon as they were both beyond the range of Prosper's gun.

"He threw out the water," Cadel said faintly. "Did you see?"

"Yeah." Saul squatted down. He laid a hand against Cadel's cheek. "Are you okay?"

"Yes." If numb was okay. "Are you?"

"Sure. I'm fine." The detective's hand shifted to Sonja's sweaty forehead. "What about Sonja? How's she doing?"

"I-I don't know," Cadel said feebly. "I can't tell."

Sonja's answering squeak was barely audible. It made Saul frown.

"Tell you what," he proposed. "You go get that water, and I'll take care of her. We'll have a drink before we move."

Cadel stared at him in bewilderment. "We're moving? You mean, we're going to walk?"

"Are you up to it? Can you manage?"

"Well, yes, but . . ." Cadel glanced down at Sonja.

"Don't worry. I can carry her. If I do, we'll get picked up more quickly. We just have to reach the paved road." Saul hesitated when he received no immediate reply. Studying Cadel, he seemed to have a change of heart. "Unless we'd be better off staying?" he said. "It's your call. I figure that Prosper was trying to slow us down and give himself more time, but you understand the way he thinks. What should we do?"

It was a serious question, which Cadel couldn't answer. He regarded Saul with growing distress as he saw how earnestly—how respectfully—the detective was awaiting his response.

Cadel realized that his impassioned speech had fooled the wrong person.

"I was lying, you know," he confessed.

"Huh?"

"It was all a big lie. About being grown-up. I only said it because I wanted him to stop interfering." Cadel's voice began to shake. "I'm good at lying. I've always been good at lying. Thanks to him."

"Hey," Saul murmured. Though obviously taken aback, he tried to offer what comfort he could. "Hey, don't fret. It's all right. We'll be all right."

"I can't really look after myself. I can't even look after Sonja," Cadel said brokenly. "It's no good asking me what we should do. I don't *know* what to do. I don't know anything. I'm hopeless."

"Hopeless?" Saul echoed, in disbelief. "What are you talking about? For Chris'sake, you're an incredible kid!"

"No. I'm not. If I was, I'd know what to do." Cadel felt as if he had been cast adrift—and not just because he happened to be sitting in the middle of nowhere. When he tried to envisage his immediate future, it contained one big nothing: no Prosper, no school, no Donkins, no Clearview House, no official status. And no Sonja, perhaps, if there was no Genius Squad. "What am I going to do?" he cried. "I don't know what to *do*!"

"Shh. It's okay." Saul kneaded Cadel's shoulder. "I know what we have to do. We have to take things one step at a time. That's all we *can* do, right now. One step at a time. All right?"

"All right." Cadel sniffed.

"Let's go, then," urged Saul. And he stood up. "Let's get started."

FORTY-SIX

Cadel lay on his bed, staring out the window at a gray, wintry sky.

He didn't have much else to look at. His room was a plain white box with a beige carpet. It contained a single bed, a desk, a chair, and a built-in wardrobe; there were no pictures on the walls or colorful patterns on any of the furnishings. Even the blind and the lamp shade were white.

The only personal touch in the room was Cadel's name, scribbled in pencil under the window ledge. He had written it there during his previous occupation of this particular safe house, immediately after Prosper's arrest. Upon returning, he'd found that same piece of graffiti right where he'd left it nearly twelve months before.

The discovery had depressed him because it seemed to underline the fact that nothing had really changed.

Nor was this the only cause for depression in Cadel's life. After three weeks, Prosper English was still at large. Alias and Vadi wouldn't cooperate with the police. Dot had managed to evade capture. Sonja had been put in a temporary home, pending a departmental decision on her placement. And Genius Squad had been disbanded.

As far as Cadel knew, none of its members had remained at Clearview House. Trader was in custody, having been denied bail on charges of abetting a forcible abduction. Though the other staff had managed to stay out of jail, all were engaged in legal disputes of one kind or another. Cliff (who had fled to Brazil at the first sign of trouble) was fighting extradition from that country. Judith was negotiating a deal with the police, to avoid various charges of embezzlement. Even Zac Stillman was living under a cloud. Like Cadel, and Hamish, and the twins, he'd been involved in an illegal hacking operation. So it was felt that he had some explaining to do.

Cadel's own legal predicament was now so complex that not even he had a firm grip on it anymore. In fact, he'd given up. Rather than worrying himself into a frenzy about his uncertain future, he had decided to take things one step at a time—just as Saul Greeniaus had counseled. The detective's advice had been good. Why look too far ahead, when there was nothing to see but dark clouds? Life was miserable enough already without the added burden of nagging fears and disappointed hopes.

Cadel sighed and turned over. Part of the problem was that he had been placed in a secure facility. No one knew what else to do with him. A foster home was considered inappropriate because Prosper had identified the last one. For the same reason, Cadel's new address was a closely guarded secret. It was feared that Prosper might be keeping tabs on Cadel's old haunts and acquaintances—so Cadel's friends weren't allowed to visit him, and he wasn't allowed to visit them. He wasn't even allowed to use a computer, in case Dr. Vee tracked him down.

Whenever Cadel asked how long these restrictions were likely to apply, he received a vague and unsatisfactory answer. Only Saul Greeniaus seemed willing to commit himself. "It can't go on forever," Saul had said on one occasion. "Even if Prosper English isn't found, you can't be kept like this indefinitely. There has to be a better way."

But Saul still hadn't found one—and meanwhile, Cadel did practically nothing all day except read, play games, and watch television. He played cards with the plainclothes police who watched over him around the clock. Sometimes he played chess with them. Every afternoon, he went to a park or beach with Saul, who made him take a walk or throw a ball around. Occasionally they met with Fiona, at a specified time in some carefully considered location: a picnic hut, perhaps, or a parked car. Cadel had also met twice with his lawyer, high in a Sydney office block.

And never, during any of these activities, had he escaped the constant attendance of his interchangeable bodyguards. They followed him into public restrooms. They flanked him at meetings. They pursued him on walks, and even formed an opposing team when he and Saul were engaged in their lackadaisical softball games. (Not that Cadel liked softball much; he wasn't exactly a sportsman. But Saul was determined that they should both get some exercise.) No matter where Cadel went, his surveillance team had to be right there with him, cluttering up the view. Intruding upon personal conversations.

Getting in his way.

He was only safe from prying eyes when shut in his bedroom—and even then he wasn't supposed to lock the door, just in case Prosper should climb through the window.

Gazing out the same window, Cadel reminded himself once again that Sonja's predicament was far worse than his. The restrictions that governed her life were crueller than anything he'd ever had to endure. And unlike Cadel, she could draw no comfort from the prospect of release, because her incarceration was permanent.

But he didn't want to think about Sonja. If he did, he would start to worry—and what was the point of that? He couldn't help her. He couldn't visit her. He couldn't phone her. All he could do was write letters and hope that she managed to read them.

It troubled him to think that she couldn't even open the envelopes by herself.

"Cadel?" A soft tapping interrupted his train of thought. "Can I come in?"

It was Saul's voice, and Saul's distinctive knock on the bedroom door. Cadel sat up. He checked his watch.

"Yeah, sure," he said. As his visitor crossed the threshold, he added, "You're early."

"I know." Saul was wearing a familiar dark suit and striped tie. He frowned to see Cadel sitting on the bed, empty-handed. "What are you doing?"

"Nothing," Cadel replied.

"What about those new books?"

"I finished them."

"Even the puzzle book?"

"Yes."

Saul bit his lip. Then he sighed. Then he said, "Well . . . I'm here now. So we can go. Are you ready?"

Cadel nodded. He thought that the detective looked unusually tense, and wondered what could have happened. Another disagreement with the top brass, perhaps? Another reported sighting of Prosper English? Cadel knew that Saul was having a tough time all around. There was a general feeling that Prosper's escape could be blamed, to some degree, on the detective. And the possibility that Prosper might be lurking somewhere close by couldn't have improved Saul's spirits.

Cadel noticed how alert the detective was as they emerged from the anonymous-looking, two-storied house in which Cadel had been installed. Tucked away behind a gloomy screen of camellias and rhododendrons, this bland-faced, mustard-colored building was located at the end of a very long driveway. All around it, bankers and lawyers and advertising executives lived on huge, sprawling, leafy blocks of land; they could afford to keep themselves to themselves, and only intruded upon Cadel's strictly enforced privacy when their car or burglar alarms went off.

Saul's own car had been returned to him. Having been found, identified, and thoroughly processed, it was now parked near the front door.

Cadel climbed into the backseat, as usual. He had to sit between his two bodyguards.

"Where are we going today?" he asked Saul, who was driving.

"Glebe Point," the detective answered, and Cadel raised his eyebrows.

"That's a long way. I guess we must be meeting Fiona."

"Good guess," Saul answered. He gave the impression of being a little keyed up.

"Does she have any news?" Cadel inquired, without much curiosity. He had stopped expecting good news, because most of it lately had been bad. And when Saul hesitated, his fears were confirmed. "Something's gone wrong, hasn't it?"

"No!" Saul's denial was vehement. "No, not at all. I just—I'd rather discuss it when we get there. If that's okay."

Cadel shrugged. "Okay."

"It's complicated. And . . . well, we need more space."

Saul didn't so much as glance at the bodyguards when he said this, but he didn't need to. Cadel knew exactly what was meant by the code words "more space." So he settled back and let his three companions discuss various uninteresting subjects (football, duty rosters, and superannuation) until they finally rolled down the gentle incline leading to Glebe Point park. Only then did it occur to Cadel—for the very first time—that Fiona might actually live in the area. She was just the sort of person who would feel at home in a neighborhood of pretty, elderly little houses crammed together on narrow streets.

"She said she'd be waiting on that bench we used before," Saul declared, as he pulled into the curb. Sure enough, Cadel spotted a tousled mop of reddish hair over near the water. He instantly recognized Fiona's narrow shoulders and pale green floral jacket.

She was watching seagulls wheel overhead, her attitude uncharacteristically tranquil.

Saul turned to the surveillance team. "We need a little privacy today," he announced. "That's why I chose this location. I figured you'd have a good, clear view of every approach, with no obstructions and no through traffic. Can you keep your distance for half an hour?"

On receiving an affirmative response, the detective climbed out of his car just as Fiona looked back and saw them. Immediately she jumped to her feet. And while the bodyguards were busy deploying themselves, she began to cross the wide expanse of lawn that lay between the road and the harbor.

Saul and Cadel reached her in the middle of this lawn, where a patch of bare earth marked the site of many informal soccer games.

"Hello!" she chirruped, wrapping her arms around Cadel. "How *are* you, sweetie? Are you all right?"

"I'm fine." Cadel still wasn't used to being hugged, and found it hard to respond gracefully. Instead he flushed, and ducked his head.

At which point, with a start, he noticed that Fiona was wearing a brand-new diamond on her left hand.

He caught his breath and looked up.

"Are you engaged?" he said. "Is *that* what you wanted to tell me?"

Fiona colored. Then she released him. Then she threw a telltale glance at Saul, who placed his hand gently on the small of her back.

"It's one of the things we had to tell you," he affirmed. "The fact that we're getting married."

"When?" Cadel demanded, so abruptly that Saul leveled a solemn and searching stare at him. Fiona's brow puckered.

"You mustn't worry about it," she implored. "It doesn't mean we're going to run off and abandon you. On the contrary!"

"I'm not worried. I'm pleased. It's great." Forcing a smile, Cadel tried not to sound as confused as he felt. On the one hand, he knew that he ought to be delighted. Two of his favorite people were forming a unit; that was cause for celebration, surely? It would mean that neither of them would now be tempted to hook up with anyone Cadel didn't like.

On the other hand, when he saw them standing together—linked by such a warm and delicate regard—he felt as he had once felt at school, watching all the other kids playing in the sun, while he lurked alone in the shadows.

"Let's not talk about this here," Saul suggested. He took Cadel's arm and scanned the array of benches surrounding them. "Come and sit down. There's something else you need to know, and it's important. We have to get comfortable."

Cadel didn't want to ask why. He had a horrible feeling that Saul was afraid of what his reaction might be. And that could only mean one thing.

Bad news.

"It's all very complex," Fiona was saying. "And everything's connected, so we have to give you the whole story from the beginning." She sat down beside Cadel on a bench under a tree; Saul seated himself on Cadel's other side.

Then the detective took his hand.

"It's about Prosper," was all that Cadel heard before he interrupted Saul, his voice cracking on a high note.

"He's dead, isn't he? Prosper's dead!"

"No!" Saul's grip tightened. "No, it's nothing like that!"

"As far as we can tell, he's still alive," said Fiona. And Saul added, "If he was dead, we'd find out about it somehow. He's not dead, Cadel. It's just . . ."

He paused.

"What?" Cadel was starting to feel sick. "What is it?"

"You might find this hard to accept—"

"What is it?"

But Saul couldn't seem to locate the right words. He sat there with a frown on his face and a muscle twitching in his jaw until at last Fiona spoke for him. She pushed a dangling curl out of Cadel's eyes and said, "He's not your father, sweetie. Prosper English isn't your father."

Cadel's mouth opened.

"Remember that DNA sample the police took off him? After the prison guard died?" Fiona continued. "Well, because of what Prosper told Saul about you, and because Prosper's lawyers haven't been paid lately, the police were able to use that sample for a paternity test. Which showed that you aren't Prosper's son."

"But-but I have to be." Cadel couldn't believe it. "He has to be my father!"

"He can't be, sweetie. It's impossible."

"But . . . but . . ."

Cadel didn't know what to think. He didn't know what to say. Then he realized that Saul was crushing his fingers.

"Ow," he complained. "You're hurting me."

"Sorry." The detective released him. "Cadel, there's an upside to this."

"I know." Not wanting to look like a fool, Cadel said defiantly, "I'm *glad* I'm not Prosper's son. It doesn't matter to me. He's an asshole."

"Well . . . yeah. Sure. I'm glad you feel that way." Saul seemed unconvinced, however. "The thing is, if Prosper isn't your father—"

"My father must have been Phineas Darkkon," Cadel spoke with a kind of brittle indifference. He could feel himself trembling on the edge of hysterical laughter, and he battled to suppress the urge. "Another asshole. Oh, well. At least he's dead, I suppose."

"No, listen. I'm not finished." Saul proceeded to explain what he himself had done after discovering the truth. "It got me thinking," he said. "About that paternity test Prosper ordered fifteen years ago. Do you remember?"

"Of course I remember." Cadel began to rub at his forehead. "You were trying to make Prosper admit that Chester Cramp did it."

"That's right."

"Only he wouldn't give you Chester's name."

"No. He wouldn't." Saul grimaced. "All the same, he was about to. I'm sure of it. So I did a bit of research into Chester Cramp and discovered something interesting. Seventeen years ago, Carolina Whitehead filed for divorce. She divorced him, and then she remarried him about a year later."

"Oh," said Cadel blankly, wishing that he could concentrate. "Why?"

"Well, that's what I decided to ask, when I talked to her on the weekend." Seeing Cadel blink, the detective once more clasped his hand. "You see, she was picked up in Brisbane last week. She's been hiding out there all this time."

Cadel said nothing. Following so closely on the first big shock, this second one had rendered him speechless. But he tried hard to collect his thoughts as Saul described how an apartment, a bank account, and a false identity had been awaiting Carolina in Brisbane ever since her move to Australia. "They were part of a contingency plan, in case anything happened," Saul revealed. "She was supposed to keep her head down for a couple of months, and leave when all the fuss was over, using a forged passport. But she didn't. Because she was caught." After a momentary silence—during which he appeared to be savoring a particularly gratifying recollection—Saul continued. "She wasn't very cooperative at first. In fact, she wouldn't give us a thing until I mentioned that paternity test. I was wondering if it had anything to do with her remarriage, since the two events were so close together."

"And did it?" asked Cadel.

"It sure did. I came straight out and asked why her husband would have lied to Prosper English about the results of that test. Because I assumed she must have known about it. But she didn't. In fact, she hit the roof."

Cadel waited. And waited. Finally he abandoned his dazed contemplation of the harbor's choppy surface to look at Saul, who once again was lost for words. Clearly, he would rather have hit Cadel with a blunt instrument than with another piece of unwelcome information.

So Fiona had to break the news that Carolina Whitehead had divorced her husband because he'd been having an affair with Cadel's mother, Elspeth. According to Fiona (who related the story in a calm and soothing manner, as if to imply that such things happened all the time), Chester had then ditched Elspeth in a successful bid to win back Carolina. And after Elspeth moved in with Phineas Darkkon, Chester had remarried his ex-wife.

"But Elspeth and Chester must have kept seeing each other," Fiona said. "That's what Carolina thought, anyway, when she heard about the paternity test. Which was why she got so mad, I suppose. You can't blame her."

"She felt betrayed, and blew her top before she could stop herself," Saul interposed. "I guess she figured that Chester must have lied because . . . well, because . . ."

He looked to Fiona for assistance. And Fiona shouldered his burden.

"Because Chester Cramp is your real father, Cadel," she said.

There was a long silence. Then Cadel started to laugh. He couldn't help himself. His laughter was thin and shrill, and it made Fiona recoil.

"Dad number three!" he exclaimed. "This is crazy!"

"I know."

"Who's next? The Dalai Lama?"

"I'm sorry, sweetie."

"But are you sure?"

"Fairly sure." This time it was Fiona who appealed to Saul for help. And Saul obliged.

"We're not a hundred percent sure," he said. "There haven't been any tests run on Cramp's DNA. But he's confessed to being your father."

"*Cramp* has?"

"We got him on tape."

The detective went on to recount how the police, in cutting a deal with Carolina, had persuaded her to entrap her husband. The ploy had been quite simple. It had involved a call made to Chester by his wife, during which she had claimed (falsely) that she was still on the run. She'd said that she and Prosper had decided to cooperate while they were both in hiding—an unlikely scenario, but not impossible. ("We pretended that Prosper didn't know she'd tried to have him killed," Saul explained. "And Chester accepted that.") Under Saul's guidance, Carolina had announced that Prosper was very angry. Why? Because by some mysterious means, he had discovered that Cadel wasn't really his son. Meaning that Chester had lied to him, all those years ago.

And Carolina had demanded an explanation from her husband.

"He gave her one," Saul disclosed. "He said that you were really his, but he'd been afraid to tell her because he loved her so much despite everything." Saul's tone took on a sarcastic edge. "Personally, I'm inclined to think he was more afraid of Phineas Darkkon, not to mention Prosper English. But I'm just a cynical old cop."

He paused to examine Cadel's face, as if expecting some kind of comment. When none was forthcoming, he plowed on.

"Cramp also said that during the various tests he'd carried out, it became clear that Phineas Darkkon was infertile. Some sort of genetic abnormality. That's why Cramp decided to point the finger at Prosper instead of Phineas—just in case Darkkon became aware of his condition at a later date. In which case Prosper would take the blame for lying, not Chester Cramp."

The detective broke off again. Perhaps he was anticipating an inquiry, or a request. But still Cadel remained silent, staring at the broken, shifting reflections on the water.

Saul and Fiona exchanged an uneasy look.

"Anyway, that wasn't all we got on tape," Saul concluded. "There was other stuff, too. We're using it to go after Chester Cramp. And GenoME, of course."

He related how police on both sides of the Pacific were currently working to have GenoME shut down; how Earl Toffany had disappeared, taking a great deal of his money with him; how Rex Austin was now under close scrutiny, thanks to his flagrantly illegal dealings with Prosper English—not to mention his funding of Genius Squad. At last, however, the detective could restrain himself no longer. "Are you all right, Cadel?" he asked.

"Oh, yeah. I'm fine." Cadel's harsh tone made both his companions turn pale. "I was just thinking: How on earth did my mother fit Prosper in, when she was already having it off with Chester Cramp *and* Phineas Darkkon? I mean, she must have been pretty busy!"

Saul shut his eyes for an instant. Fiona put an arm around Cadel's shoulders.

"We don't really know what happened to your mother," she pointed out. "She was very young, don't forget. And these were unpleasant, overbearing men. We're not in a position to judge her, Cadel. You mustn't think the worst of her."

"Besides, no matter what she did, she didn't deserve to be killed," the detective declared firmly. When Cadel clenched his fists, Saul added, "At least you know now that your father didn't kill your mother."

"Oh, yeah," Cadel spat. He could hardly contain his fury and dismay. He wanted to punch someone, or overturn the bench on which they were sitting. "Terrific. That's a real bonus, that is."

"Cadel. Look at me." Saul's firm grasp moved to Cadel's wrist. "It doesn't matter who your parents are. It matters who *you* are."

"Tell that to Prosper English!" Cadel snarled, finally erupting. "If he finds out about this—god, he'll be *furious*! He'll kill me!"

"No—"

"He will! He'll kill Chester Cramp, and then he'll kill me!" Cadel threw off Saul's hand and Fiona's arm. He sprang up and spun around to confront them both. "I know too much! He can't afford to let me survive! Not now that I've turned out to be Chester Cramp's!"

Saul reached for him. "Listen—"

"And what does *that* mean, anyway?" Cadel cried, stumbling backward as the detective rose. "Does it mean I'm American? Does it mean I'll be deported? Am I going to have to live with *Chester Cramp*?"

"Be quiet." Saul spoke sharply. He caught hold of Cadel with fingers like steel rods, and shook him. "Calm down. Look at me. Cadel? *Look at me.* Chester Cramp was born in Australia. He had an Australian father. Which means that you're part Australian. And that's *good* news. Are you listening?"

Cadel nodded. All his red-hot energy had suddenly evaporated like steam. He was close to tears.

Saul must have seen this, because his grip relaxed.

"Chester Cramp is not your problem," he said quietly. "I haven't finished with Chester. You don't have to worry about him—he won't be in a position to make any demands on you." Saul took a deep breath. "As for Prosper English—well, that's something else we have to talk about. Because I agree: He's still a risk. It's my belief he won't want you anymore when he finds out you're not his son, but you're right, that doesn't mean he won't try to get rid of you. As a potential witness." The sound of these words, spoken aloud, seemed to pain Saul. He flinched, as if he himself were the one threatened with physical harm. "I'm sorry, Cadel. This can't be something you want to hear. It's just the situation as I see it."

Cadel swallowed. "I know," he whispered. "Me, too."

"So unless we catch him, you're always gonna be looking over your shoulder. And we don't want that." Saul's clear, brown, sober gaze contained not only an immense amount of sympathetic resolve, but also the faintest, most fleeting glint of excitement. "Which is why I have a proposal to make," he said. "A proposal about Genius Squad.

"Because I happen to think Genius Squad might be the solution to our problem."

FORTY-SEVEN

The meeting was held at Sydney University.

It was a Sunday evening, so everything was very quiet. The grounds were largely unoccupied, save for the occasional lone pedestrian. The library was shut, and the quadrangle deserted. The long, dingy corridors were empty, and most of the doors that lined them were locked.

But one small corner of the History Department was filling up slowly. As the shorter hand on the tower clock crept toward five, a few people began to arrive at a top-floor seminar room. Some used the ancient, creaky lift; others slowly ascended the stairs, their voices and footsteps echoing off shiny linoleum. All of them converged on the numbered door behind which Saul Greeniaus was standing, next to a silent, gray-haired, flinty-faced man in a three-piece suit.

This man was introduced to Cadel as Garth Renmark. "Mr. Renmark will be signing off on our project," Saul muttered vaguely, leaving Cadel none the wiser as to Garth's actual job. But it was apparent, from Saul's edgy and watchful demeanor, that Garth was either a very senior police officer or a government official.

Cadel decided that the Audi parked near the downstairs entrance probably belonged to Garth.

Cadel himself had come in his lawyer's car, along with Fiona Currey and the surveillance team. Mel Hofmeier, Cadel's lawyer, was a fat, untidy, middle-aged troll of a man, with the face of a wise old frog. His clothes were all custom-made; he wore platinum cuff links and a gold signet ring, and the look in his pouchy eyes suggested that nothing on earth would ever surprise him. When Cadel saw Garth Renmark, he was very glad that Mel had decided to attend the meeting. Because even someone as formidable as Garth couldn't intimidate Mel Hofmeier.

After exchanging names and handshakes, Mel and Saul and Garth made a few desultory comments about the large, shabby seminar room in which they were gathered. This room was painted a dispiriting shade of buff. It contained a battered collection of furniture made of steel and plastic and melamine, together with an empty bulletin board and an oil heater. The room had been Saul's choice, selected because it was central and private.

"Hotels these days are like sieves," he remarked, in reply to a question from Garth. "And people might notice a bunch of kids heading into an office block."

Garth sniffed. He didn't give the impression of being someone who spent much of his precious time sitting on plastic chairs under flickering fluorescent lights. Perhaps he was offended that no one had thought to serve him drinks or canapés.

The next arrivals were Hamish Primrose and his parents. His mother was plump and flustered, while his father was skinny and severe; they sidled in apologetically, looking confused. Standing between them, dressed in a blue blazer and tie, Hamish had the appearance of a prisoner under escort. He was almost unrecognizable without his leather jacket and biker's boots.

When he spotted Cadel, his mouth fell open—exposing a wad of gray chewing gum.

"Hello, Hamish," said Cadel. To which Hamish replied, "Wow. You are here."

"Yeah. I'm here."

"I heard you were locked up in the hospital or something. I heard they wouldn't let you out."

"Who said that?"

"I dunno." Hamish shrugged. "Lawyers. Lexi."

"Have you seen Lexi?"

"I saw her the other day. She told me Prosper English tried to kill you. That's why you were locked up."

"No." Cadel shifted uncomfortably, glancing over to where Fiona and Mrs. Primrose were deep in conversation. "No one's tried to kill anyone."

"She said Prosper threw acid in your face," Hamish scoffed. "She's so full of it."

As if on cue, Lexi herself appeared at the door, closely followed by Devin and a pair of total strangers. Cadel never discovered the names of these two female attendants, because he was instantly swept up in a noisy reunion with Lexi Wieneke. She bounded across the room toward him, threw her arms around his neck, and planted a series of smacking kisses all over his forehead.

"Thank god you're all right!" she exclaimed shrilly, pressing her cheek against his. "I thought he was going to kill you!"

"What was all that crap about an acid attack?" Hamish demanded, as Cadel tried to extricate himself from Lexi's embrace. "I don't see any scars on him, do you?"

"I never mentioned an acid attack," she said, rubbing purple lipstick off Cadel's temple. Hamish scowled.

"You did, too!" he insisted, and appealed to Devin. "*You* were there! She told us Prosper English threw acid in his face!"

"Oh, I never bloody listen to her," Devin said. He was skulking uneasily against one wall, as if all the suits in the room were making him nervous. Unlike Hamish, he had retained his Clearview House clothes: namely his beanie, sweatshirt, anorak, and camouflage pants.

Lexi's outfit was also familiar to Cadel, who had once rejected the black net tank top that she was wearing, when it was offered to him as a disguise.

"You weren't listening," Lexi informed Hamish. "What I *said* was that I'd kill anyone who *did* throw acid at him." She was enormously difficult to repel; Cadel had no sooner peeled one of her sweaty hands off his chin than she had clamped the other over his ear. "It would be a *crime against humanity* to ruin this face. Like blowing up the *Mona Lisa*, or something."

Then Fiona approached them, and the conversation became more stilted. It was difficult to forget that during her previous encounters with the inhabitants of Clearview House, Fiona had been thoroughly hoodwinked. Hamish seemed very conscious of this fact; he stared at the floor and mumbled. Devin glowered. Lexi took one look at Fiona's left hand and said, in tones of unflattering surprise, "Are you getting *married*, or something?"

Fiona blushed. Cadel said crossly, "She's getting married to Mr. Greeniaus," and slipped out of Lexi's clinging headlock just as Judith Bashford wheeled Sonja into the room.

Judith was accompanied by Sonja's social worker, and by a bald man in pinstripes who must have been a lawyer, to judge from the way Mel Hofmeier hailed him. But Cadel wasn't interested in lawyers or social workers. He headed straight for the wheelchair, wearing a tremulous smile.

As far as he could see, Sonja looked well enough. She was dressed in a new velvet skirt, and her hair was neatly braided. Someone had been keeping her nails trimmed.

Her feet were encased in the slippers that she had received from Cadel.

"Hi," he said. "I've been waiting for you. Did you get my letters?"

Sonja jabbed at her DynaVox. Unfortunately, however, she was too excited to spell out a coherent reply: She kept missing the keys, partly because her neck muscles were going into spasm. She couldn't even direct her eyes toward the screen in front of her.

Seeing this, Cadel dropped to one knee beside the wheelchair and took her clawed hand in his.

"It's okay," he muttered. "I heard the news from Saul. He told me you'll be living with Judith."

"Providing that I *have* anywhere to live after the dust settles!" Judith blared. She was draped in layer upon layer of embroidered cheesecloth, and had thrust her wide feet into a pair of sequinned sandals. "What with all the bloody lawyer's fees I'm having to shell out, and the way the tax office has been poking its nose in, I'll be lucky if I'm left with the price of a cappuccino!" She leaned forward to pat Sonja's shoulder. "But if Sonja's around, they'll think twice about turfing me onto the street. In fact, I'm hoping this scheme goes ahead, so she'll be able to support me in my old age."

Cadel smiled uncertainly. He knew something about the complicated agreement that Judith had thrashed out with the police, in an effort to avoid paying too high a price for her activities at Clearview House. He also knew that her offer to look after Sonja was regarded with suspicion by everyone who'd heard about it—except Sonja herself. A lot of people had tried to dissuade Sonja from even considering the placement, which was considered "highly irregular" by various health and welfare offices. But since Sonja was about to turn eighteen, and Judith could easily afford round-the-clock nursing care, it was hard to find any solid grounds for refusing the application. Not unless Judith was actually convicted of a crime.

Cadel himself was cautiously optimistic. He had long ago decided that Judith was genuinely attached to Sonja; in fact, he believed that Judith had blown the whistle on Genius Squad purely out of concern for his best friend's safety. And after interrogating Judith for several hours, Saul now shared this opinion. "I suppose DoCS would have to keep an eye on them both," he'd mused at one point, "but I think Judith Bashford is Sonja's best option right now."

Cadel agreed. Judith Bashford was undoubtedly Sonja's best option, because her overpowering personality and skewed sense of humor didn't seem to faze Sonja at all. Certainly Sonja didn't flinch when Judith loudly demanded, "So what are we waiting for? I thought this thing was supposed to start at five!"

"We're waiting for Gazo Kovacs," Saul explained. The words were barely out of his mouth, however, when someone coughed over near the doorway and a small voice said, "I'm here."

Turning, Cadel saw that Gazo had, in fact, already joined them. He had somehow managed to enter the room without attracting notice—perhaps because he was clad in such dull, unassuming clothes. Catching Cadel's eye, he gave a little half smile. But before either of them could say anything, Saul began to address the assembled company.

"If you could all just find a seat," he announced, in a slightly strained fashion, "we can kick off the proceedings." Over the subsequent clatter of steel chair legs, he added, "As you know, we're here to decide how the so-called Genius Squad concept can be used to facilitate the capture of Prosper English. And I realize you must have discussed this idea at length, in private meetings with various—ah—advisors and interested parties. But my intention today is that we should clarify exactly what we want to do here, and exactly what we're all expecting to get out of the proposed scenario." As everyone sat down, Saul unexpectedly walked around the circular arrangement of graffiti-covered desks until he reached Cadel. "I'm hoping," the detective said, laying a hand on Cadel's shoulder, "that most of you who know Cadel, and realize what a special kid he is, are partly motivated by a desire to make sure he's not gonna be living in fear of Prosper English for the rest of his life."

"Hear, hear!" cried Lexi, causing Judith to roll her eyes, and Hamish to snort. Almost everyone else looked startled, including Saul Greeniaus—who was thrown off his stride, and had to think for a moment before continuing.

"Basically," he said, "we have some ground rules to lay down, some terms to negotiate, and also, I presume, some questions to answer. Once that's done, then maybe we can tackle the important issue of locating Ulysses Vee. Because Vee's still at large, and we know that Prosper's been using his services. If we can find Vee, we might find Prosper English." Then Devin put his hand up, and Saul blinked. "Uh . . . yes, Devin?"

"What about Cadel?" Devin asked, to which the detective's answer was: "What about him?"

"Well, we can't do this without Cadel. He knows more than any of us, especially when it comes to Prosper English." Though Devin spoke as if it pained him to make such an admission, Cadel was touched. "How can he help us, if you've locked him up somewhere and won't let him out?"

"Good point," drawled Mel Hofmeier, with a sideways glance at Saul, who dragged his fingers through his hair in a clear sign of agitation.

"Um . . . Cadel isn't locked up, exactly," Saul replied. "But I agree, his situation could be better. Which is why it's important that Genius Squad starts work pretty soon. If we can locate Prosper English, then we'll hopefully be able to anticipate and prevent any attack on Cadel. And if we can do *that,* then we can take him out of the high-security environment in which he's currently placed."

"And put him where?" Judith wanted to know. Before the detective could respond, however, Lexi interrupted.

"He'll be earning money, too, won't he? Like the rest of us?" she said. "You'll be paying him to be on Genius Squad?"

"Well, yes. That's the theory," Saul confirmed. "If we can get the budget approved under a special provision—"

But Lexi wouldn't let him finish.

"Then Cadel could move in with us! With me and my brother!" she cried. "We're going to share a house with Gazo Kovacs and pay part of the rent out of what we earn! Why can't Cadel live there, too?"

"Because he's only fifteen." Fiona torpedoed Lexi's proposal with a kind of sympathetic regret. "He's just a bit too young. You're sixteen, Lexi, you're old enough to live without much supervision."

"Yeah, but—"

"Anyway," Saul broke in, "we're working out somewhere for Cadel. We just haven't finalized the details yet. When we have, you'll be the first to know."

Cadel stared at him in surprise. If plans were afoot to change the current arrangements, Cadel hadn't been apprised of them. He would have liked to hear more. He even raised his hand, to request further details.

Saul, however, wasn't ready to indulge him. "I'll talk to you later," he said, without waiting to hear Cadel's question. Then he launched into a long speech about Genius Squad's proposed operational parameters and how it would be a highly confidential experiment, with built-in safeguards and a strict probationary period for all concerned. He explained that much of the equipment from Clearview House would be requisitioned for the squad's use, although some of it was being held as evidence; he stressed that rules had been bent slightly to acquire it, and that everyone had to be very careful about following various codes of conduct relating to its custody and treatment or it would be taken away.

Cadel already knew most of this; it had been explained to him several times. So he let his attention drift around the table, studying one face after another, as he wondered where he was going to end up. Obviously he wouldn't be staying with Gazo—Fiona had made that quite clear. And it was just as well, too, because Cadel didn't want to live with Lexi again. His heart went out to Gazo, who probably didn't know what he was letting himself in for. Lexi was an awful lot of work, and Gazo didn't respond well to sudden shocks. He might get jumpy if the twins were always fighting. He might lose control of his stench and knock them both out by accident.

Gazo and Cadel exchanged another fleeting, embarrassed smile. *It would be nice to have a chat at some stage,* Cadel thought. Then his wandering gaze alighted on Sonja, who was having an especially bad bout of painful muscular contractions. Normally Cadel would have leaped to her aid. He would have tried to stop her from hurting herself, by supporting some of her limbs and intercepting others. But Judith seemed to have mastered that knack. She did it almost instinctively.

Watching her, Cadel decided that she was the right person to care for Sonja. The question was: Had Judith volunteered to take him in, as well? Was that the option being "finalized" by Saul? Or had someone else made an offer? Mr. and Mrs. Primrose, perhaps?

Surely Cadel wouldn't have to live with the Donkins. Or, even worse, with *Chester Cramp*!

After Saul had finished his speech, there was a lot of discussion among the lawyers and social workers about evening shifts, supervision, reporting lines, and legal accountability. Meanwhile Lexi yawned, Devin added more graffiti to his desk, and Hamish played with his chewing gum. The three of them only perked up when the talk turned to specifics—to pay scales, for instance, or to their assigned duties as members of Genius Squad.

But according to Saul, it was too early for specifics. And the meeting ended soon afterward, when it became clear that nothing could be settled until Garth Renmark had secured a "final go-ahead" for the project. Cadel, who had observed Garth's folded arms and sour expression, wasn't hopeful. Especially disappointing was the fact that Garth slipped out early, having mumbled something to Saul and not bothered to thank anyone else. In Cadel's view, Genius Squad was dead in the water.

Apparently, however, he was wrong.

"That was great," Saul declared, as he shook hands with Mel. "I think we're in with a good chance. Garth's a hundred percent behind us now. He'll push it through, I'm certain."

"But he looked like he hated us all," Cadel protested. "What makes you think he's going to help?"

"Because he told me he'd have an answer by tomorrow," Saul replied. "Which means he understands how important it is to get this thing kicked off."

Mel nodded. He explained to Cadel that Mr. Renmark always looked as if he hated everyone. "It's a technique," Mel said. "To stop people pestering you. When you're in a hush-hush kind of job like Garth Renmark, you don't want to be answering too many questions."

Then Mel offered Fiona a lift, which she politely declined. By this time everyone was leaving; the Primroses, in fact, had already gone, shepherding Hamish out of the room before he could do more than aim a quick thumbs-up at Cadel. Gazo slipped out as quietly as he'd arrived, with only a wave at Cadel to signal his departure, while Lexi had to be dragged away by her attendants, loudly objecting that she hadn't had a chance to "talk to people." "It isn't fair!" she complained. "I haven't seen Cadel for ages! I want to ask him about what happened! Why does Sonja get to stay and I don't?"

"Sonja's not staying, stupid—where'd you get that idea?" growled Devin, from inside the lift. And it was true. Judith wouldn't linger, not even to oblige Cadel. She was afraid of overtiring Sonja, who hadn't been sleeping. ("Nightmares," Judith said succinctly, by way of explanation. "She still hasn't got over that business with Prosper English.") So Cadel had to kiss Sonja good-bye without exchanging more than a few words. He couldn't even accompany her to Judith's car, because Saul wanted him to wait behind.

"There's something we need to discuss," the detective informed him. "I know it's hard, but you'll be seeing Sonja again very soon, I promise. It's just that we have one last decision to make."

"Is it about where I'm going to live?" asked Cadel. "Is it about Chester Cramp?"

Saul frowned. Suddenly he turned to the surveillance team and ordered them outside. To Cadel's astonishment, they promptly obeyed, closing the door behind them.

Their withdrawal meant that only Saul, Fiona, and Cadel were left in the seminar room.

"I think that went quite well," Saul opined. He returned to where Cadel was slumped in a chair, and sat down opposite him. "I think Genius Squad will be operational in a couple of weeks. And if it is, we might have some solid leads on Prosper by the end of the month." He regarded Cadel intently. "What's your view?"

Cadel shrugged. "Like I said," he replied, "I've got a few ideas. But Vee's very good. And Prosper's not stupid. It's going to be hard."

"That's why we need Genius Squad," the detective asserted, and began to argue his case in a well-reasoned, quietly impassioned way, while Fiona stood over him nervously. "You once told me that you could protect yourself online way better than anyone else. I didn't believe you, back then, because I didn't know you. Now I do. And I can see that you're the best hope we have when it comes to locating Prosper English. When it comes to ensuring your own future *safety,* in fact."

Cadel was bemused. "Yes, I know. You already told me this," he said.

"We're just trying to explain why we haven't mentioned our idea before," Fiona chimed in. "The idea we're about to run past you, I mean. And we didn't want to get your hopes up. Not until we'd done a bit of research—"

"There are security issues," Saul interjected. "This whole arrangement won't be possible until we're feeling a bit more confident about Prosper's movements."

"What whole arrangement?" Cadel looked from Saul to Fiona and back again. He was utterly lost. "What are you talking about?"

"Cadel . . ." Saul took a deep breath, both hands resting tensely on his knees. "Chester Cramp isn't particularly interested in you. I guess you realize that."

"Yeah," Cadel said flatly. "I'm supposed to be a genius, remember? I managed to work *that* out."

"Of course." The detective licked his lips. He was choosing his words with enormous precision. "What you probably don't realize is that Cramp's currently being investigated, and he's *terrified* of Prosper English. The last thing he's worried about at present is making any sort of parental claim."

"Which he'd be *completely unjustified* in doing, anyway!" Fiona added, before she was silenced by a warning look from her fiancé.

"The thing is, Cadel," Saul continued, "now that we know Cramp's your father, and that you can claim Australian citizenship . . . well . . ."

A pause.

"Well what?" said Cadel.

"Saul's trying to say that it's up to you," Fiona stressed. "We don't want to pressure you into anything."

"Pressure me about *what*?" Cadel was fast losing patience. He didn't need all this ambiguity and circumspection. He was anxious enough already.

Sensing this, the detective finally made his announcement, in a hoarse and hesitant voice.

"As you know, Ms. Currey and I are getting married next month," he said. "And once that happens, we'd like to adopt you."

Cadel stared at him.

"If you're agreeable," Saul amended, rather nervously.

"You can think about it as long as you like," Fiona was quick to point out. Whereupon Saul backed her up, with clumsy haste.

"Oh-uh-yeah, sure," he stammered. "That's right. Don't rush your decision."

"You can talk to someone about it," said Fiona, obviously flustered by Cadel's speechless regard. "There are special counselors. You can even talk to Mel, if you're worried."

"We wouldn't want you to change the way you act, or . . . I mean, I wouldn't expect you to think of me as your father. Or Fiona as your mother." Saul was almost squirming with discomfort. "We just want to give you a home, and make sure there's always someone to look after you. Once it's safe enough for you to leave police custody."

"Oh." Cadel swallowed. Suddenly he felt as if his thawing heart had been snap-frozen. "So you're doing this . . . just to keep me out of the Donkins' house?" he mumbled, and saw the detective start.

"Hell, no!" Saul exclaimed, almost with horror, and his fiancée enveloped Cadel in a fierce hug.

"Sweetie," she said, "I can't *tell* you how much we want this. This is so important to us."

"You see, Fiona and I . . . we're looking forward to a great life together," Saul carefully explained. "But you can't start that sort of life while you're missing someone, and worrying about them, and always feeling that things aren't right because—well, because someone's not there who should be."

"You were in this from the beginning," Fiona remarked, her breath warm on Cadel's ear. "Without you, Saul and I would never have met. We'd never have ended up on the same side. You're part of this family already. We just have to make it formal."

"If that's what *you* want, of course," Saul finished, so awkwardly that Cadel had to smile. It was a joke, really. How could there be any doubt? How could such a clever man be so foolish?

But Cadel wasn't foolish. He knew what he wanted.

"Oh, yes. Yes, please," he gasped, his eyes shining.

Then he returned Fiona's embrace. And though he did it clumsily, without the skill that comes from long years of practice, he displayed the sort of enthusiasm that makes up for everything else.

Coming next . . .

THE GENIUS WARS

It takes a genius to fight a genius.